The G Awakens

Magic VS Tech

Volume One

David Witt

David Witt

Fat Chance Publishing

This is a work of fiction. Names, characters, places, and incidents either are the product of the author's imagination or are used fictitiously. Any resemblance to actual persons, living or dead, events, or locales is entirely coincidental.

The Goddess Awakens

Copyright © 2024 TX 9-435-768 by David Witt.

All rights reserved. No part of this book may be reproduced or transmitted in any form by any means, electronic or mechanical, including photocopying, recording, or by any information storage and retrieval system without the prior written permission of the publisher, except for the inclusion of brief quotations in critical reviews and certain other non-commercial uses permitted by copyright law. For permission requests, please contact the publisher by email at: fatchancepublishing@gmail.com

ISBN 979-8-9867945-2-5

FIRST EDITION

Cover Design by Matt Witt

Printed in the United States of America

To Karen, my awesome and lovely wife. Without her unending support this novel would not have been possible. She always listens to my ideas with support and never judgment. Her ceaseless encouragement is an important reason this book is coming to market. Karen is my travel and life partner and I can't wait for our next adventure!

David Witt

Special thanks to the Paris Bourbon County Public Library who provide the meeting space for our writers group. Phil Gladden, Morgan Williams, Denise Craycraft, Paul Simpson, Mary Heffner, Mike Rawlings, Barry Cook, Nicholas Helton and Pat Holland always provide honest feedback in a safe environment. You all offered me an education and a sense of community for which I am grateful.

I thank Morgan Williams for his perspective and editing. I admire his ability to take a good scene and point out ways that I can make it better.

I also thank Denise Craycraft for her perspective and editing. She has an incredible eye for detail and an understanding of characters that makes my work shine.

Sincere thanks go to Matt Witt, my multitalented son, who created the cover for this book. Even as a child, he had an eye for color and design, and it was a special pleasure to see him take my input and create something far beyond what I imagined.

The Goddess Awakens

Chapter One

Geeja, the Goddess of Uwan, clutched her side as she gutted out a desperate cry. "Faster, Vozzu! Fly faster!" Shot by some kind of unknown weapon she fled in full retreat, her free hand gripping the nape of her bonded dragon's neck. Vozzu beat his wings mightily in a bid to ferry her to safety. Dazed by the speed and ferocity of her attackers, she shouted in desperation. "Go!"

Never-before-seen, or even imagined machines dogged them in the air, firing blasts of red light as they closed the distance. Vozzu bellowed as a bolt hit his side, just as had hit his master minutes before, resulting in an uncontrollable dive. The massive beast swung his long, spiked tail to guide their rapid fall.

Geeja's eyes watered as searing pain pushed her to the edge of her physical limits. She struggled to send a telepathic order to her five Sworn Warrior guards. *"We are going down! Cover us!"* Even in the chaos of this unforeseen battle, one thought haunted her. *This is the danger of which the Ancients warned.*

Her remaining warriors spun around, aiming their own beast's fiery breath at these alien crafts. One scored a direct hit, sending a bumble bee-shaped contraption spinning to the ground, but the opposite happened for the other four. Beams of lethal light from a swarm of flying vessels blasted the exposed chests of their dragons, sending them and their riders spiraling to certain deaths.

Vozzu crashed on the smooth path of a country lane where Geeja spilled from his back. For a moment the goddess lost her breath. The jolt, combined with the pain from her burning injury, blurred her vision as she struggled to maintain consciousness. In the haze, she hoped this attack might only be a horrible dream, but the searing agony radiating through her body told her otherwise. Still, between gasps, she mumbled. "This *can't* be real."

Vozzu struggled to stand. The defiant dragon staggered, using every ounce of energy to turn toward those who hunted them in order to send another burst of fire their way. They struck first, hitting him with more beams from their strange flying crafts. He released one final yelp before collapsing in a crumpled heap.

The bonded dragon's demise stung like a barbed Sharzer blade being shoved into her heart, then twisted. Her ripped-soul scream pierced the stench of smoke-filled air.

Her pursuers landed behind them, all now stalking Geeja on foot. A bolt of their straight-line lightening ripped through a fold of her forest green gown as others sent up clods of earth in near misses. Struggling to remain conscious, she reached out to the planet with her mind. **"Help me, Uwan… rain down our own lightning. We must fight back!"**

The planet's plaintive reply terrified her. **"Something is wrong…I do not understand…what is happening to me?"**

Susomi, her lone surviving Sworn Warrior, landed just as multiple zaps of energy hit the warrior's own dragon. She raced toward the stumbling Geeja, sweeping her up in stride. "I've got you, my Goddess!"

Geeja's sweat dampened hands gripped Susomi's neck, grateful for the warrior's gift of strength. She again pleaded with her world. **"Please, Uwan! Anything…"** Her thoughts trailed off as she fought to keep her eyes open, using all the magic she could draw from her planet to avoid succumbing to her injuries.

Trees bent and branches lowered behind them, swatting at their trailing attackers, momentarily slowing them. Uwan's eternal voice filled Geeja's mind, sounding confused. *"At least I can still communicate with our plant life! All is not lost!"* Uwan's momentary optimism turned dark. *"Geeja! It feels as if I've been stabbed! What are they doing?"*

Another volley of this new weaponized light came at them as their attackers cleared the trees' attempt at a roadblock. More vegetation lashed out in a desperate bid to slow the assailants, helping Geeja and Susomi put some distance between them and their enemies, at least for the moment.

Geeja strained to maintain consciousness as they reached a fork in the bucolic road, not much wider than a farm wagon pathway. With her life hanging by a thread, she couldn't fully process the moment. *This can't be happening.* But it was. Wincing, she whispered direction to Susomi. "Go left."

With the gentle downward slope of their route, they gathered speed until Geeja spotted their best hope to evade their assailants. She spoke in a low reedy voice as a barely visible footpath diverged away from the road. "This way." Huge plork tree limbs, supporting hundreds of leaves cupping giant gobs of sap, moved out of their way. They snapped back in place as soon as the duo passed, ready to unload on any who would follow.

Moving as quietly as possible, they soon arrived at a small cave entrance. Dense foliage obscuring the opening spread for the desperate pair. Her heart swelled at the gesture. "Thanks be to the Holy Twelve and our worlds."

The Goddess Awakens

Sustained blasts erupted nearby as the assailants tried to fight their way forward. Curses and rants rang out behind them in the humid forest. "Yuck! That blurfing goo is nasty!"

For the first time, Susomi looked into her goddess' honey-colored eyes, her voice quivering. "My Goddess, you must live." Even with her own ability to draw small amounts of magic from the planet for extra strength, Susomi breathed hard, trying to catch her breath after the long run carrying Geeja. "Take my body! Save us! Save our world!"

They both knew that a Sworn Warrior in the personal detail of the goddess should make this exact suggestion. Though an honor, it also symbolized an immense sacrifice. "My child…" Geeja's heart ached for the soldier who joined her service barely a year ago. *If only I had recognized the true severity of the threat earlier, we would not be in these dire straits!*

Geeja knew she must act, not second guess past mistakes…but she wished another alternative would present itself. It didn't, and if Uwan could be saved from the tyranny of this attack, it would be Geeja that would lead the response. With that as a certainty, she narrowed her eyes, addressing the brave woman who raced her to temporary safety. "Your parents would be so proud of the warrior you have become. Your name will be revered for all ages."

"Our sensors have a lock on those two!" The shouted declaration from the attackers ended any possibility of delay, or consideration of other solutions.

Geeja stared forcefully into her guard's eyes. "Take us deeper!" As Susomi moved, Geeja reached out to Uwan again. ***"If you are able, please show us the way in this darkness."*** No answer registered, but a glowing blue line appeared to her eyes only, marking the path into the farthest hidden recesses. She whispered directions as her guardian carried her deeper into the pitch-black cave. When they finally reached the place that Uwan indicated to be a vaulted-roof cavern, she squeezed the woman's neck gently. "Please, lower me here."

The cool firmness of the cave floor welcomed her after the jostled emergency ride. Unfamiliar weapons sounded behind them, making muted blinging noises. Geeja touched her side, expecting to feel the sticky wetness of blood, but didn't. She gasped, tracing the outline of a perfectly round hole in her torso. *What kind of weapons do they possess?* The large diameter of the circular wound warned her of the seriousness of her injury, even if blood no longer spilled. Her voice quivered, contrasting with the calm attitude she hoped to project. "The process will all seem like a dream. Relax."

Despite performing this ritual countless times, Geeja had rarely been stress-free, even in normal circumstances. Now, weird weapon fire echoed as the assassin's shadows and the first signs of flashes appeared on the walls of the cavern. Apparently, the pursuers used these strange armaments to light their way in the gloom of the twisting natural rock tubes. Time ran low, so Geeja sent wordless direction to Susomi as she struggled to get into position for the ceremony. ***"On our knees we face each other."***

After almost blacking out from the effort, Geeja kept her elbows tight to her sides while extending her arms, palms up. Panting, she continued. ***"Your hands to mine."*** In the total blackness of the bowels of the planet, Susomi responded as directed.

Hearing the cursing aggressors approaching Geeja took two deep breaths, quieting her anxiety for a few seconds. That moment of calm faded as she reached out to the planet. ***"Uwan, can you do this?"***

"I will do my best." He sounded apprehensive.

With no other options, Geeja took that as a yes and continued by sheer force of will. Focusing, she communed in silence with her young protégé and the ancient planet. ***"Our collective soul to yours, joining as one. Our shared knowledge to yours, as we expand our mind."*** The tingling began as it had the hundreds of times Geeja had performed this ritual, over the thousands of years of her existence.

Usually, a host had months to prepare for the event, and even then, it could be an overwhelming process. This would be traumatic for Susomi. The psychic current that would send Geeja's mind into Susomi's body, aided by Uwan's magical power, intensified as the seconds ticked by. A thought intruded on what should be a solemn ceremony. *I will need to leave a sliver of my being in my vacated body to serve as a decoy.*

Geeja's new host's form shook under the stress of the accelerated transference. She hated rushing what should be a holy affair. She remembered when she inherited her current vessel forty years earlier, and how proud the other woman's family had been to have their daughter selected to receive the goddess' being. Every memory or experience of their child's life joined those of the goddess, for the betterment of their world. On this occasion, however, only blind spiders and nut bats hanging from the ceiling witnessed the event. The opposition soldiers' clanging progress grew closer, so Geeja surged her remaining consciousness, causing Susomi's stunned corporeal being to spasm. Whispering, she tried to reassure the younger woman. "You are doing wonderful and your sacrifice will never be forgotten."

The gravelly bass voice of the apparent leader of the attackers echoed in the black depths. "Sensors indicate they're close! Hurry!"

As Geeja prepared to ram her remaining life spirit through the willing donor's skin, an immense shockwave shook the entire planet. Gripping the Sworn Warrior's hands tightly, Geeja crammed their entire being into Susomi, then their connection broke. Both bodies let out muffled groans as the rushed process unceremoniously ended. The two fell limp to the damp dirt floor.

Geeja regained consciousness seconds later in Susomi's body, shivering, unsure of what just transpired. *No other transference has been like this, ever. By the Twelve Holy Gods, what happened?*

The assassins' voices grew louder as they neared their prey. "They are less than a hundred feet ahead. We're close!"

Geeja shook her former shell, trying to wake the other form to pull off the deception. A wisp of her essence now resided in the injured, discarded body. This receptacle, in any other transference would be dead and empty. It would then be cremated in an elaborate ritual. The entire ceremony symbolized the perpetual renewal of Geeja as an eternal goddess in harmony with Uwan. She whispered urgently as her old body stirred. "Can you do what you must?"

Geeja's former shell nodded. "They will believe I am you." Looking disoriented from the process, both women struggled to their knees. The sliver of personality left behind spoke. "Run! Save our world!"

Knowing the cruciality of the action didn't ease the sting of knowing that a fragment of lifeforce, which should have been in this host with their newly combined essences, would soon be snuffed out. Geeja steadied herself, regaining her senses in this new receptacle. At the same time, she seamlessly melded Susomi's memories with hers, and all the others who had preceded her. Flashes of sparring drills, childhood swim lessons given by Susomi's loving father and all other experiences of the Sworn Warrior's life became part of the new whole. All were one now. Geeja knew this as she reconnected with her planet, as she had after every transference. But even this familiar process seemed out of sync.

Uwan's thoughts reached her. *"**Something terrible has happened to me! My injury has worsened…you must hurry!**"*

In the cave system devoid of external light, Uwan lit her escape path once again as the fine glowing blue line reappeared. She spoke her final words to this bit of a being in her former body. "Your sacrifice will be revered forever."

The full light of the approaching assassins shone around the corner as Geeja slipped into a crevasse that led to another set of tunnels. These moved downward, deeper toward the core of the ancient planet, the source of Geeja's powers. While she had weathered the trauma of the hasty transference better than the unprepared Susomi, Geeja's knees wobbled, as if she had run all day in the sun with no water. *This is not right…* Her head spun, triggering her new host's body to heave up its last meal. Retching, one thought rose above all others. *I must reach a healing station…* Before Geeja could finish her thought, she heard the encounter between the aggressors and the sliver of essence left behind.

"You will never take Uwan!"

The enemy responded with a hail of blasts, followed by shouts of victory. "We already have! Nothing can stop the Impercium! Not even the famous Goddess of Uwan!"

Silent tears streamed down Geeja's face as she stumbled deeper into her world in this new body, following the pathways lit by her planetary partner. She whispered as exhaustion slowed her progress. "I have to succeed…" Falling to her knees, she trudged forward in the beige, dirt covered one-piece uniform of a member of her personal detail. With great effort, she mustered every ounce of energy, as well as any she could collect from the planet. In this compromised state, she whispered a desperate plea. "Help me, Uwan…before it is too late."

Alone in the silence of the unmapped warren of underground chambers that riddled this world, Geeja sensed her salvation. *A healing station!* With each labored inch onward, it became obvious something else besides the rushed transfer of essences happened. *This is bad.* One saving thought drove her. *In time, Uwan will heal me…if I can reach that life-giving rock.*

Dropping to her stomach, her new body crawled forward, one elbow pull at a time. She rounded a final corner, spying her destination. The raised flat stone glowed a soft, pale shade of green, symbolizing life-giving aid…if she could cover the final fifteen feet. Fear gripped her as she realized the radiance appeared diminished from its normal illumination. *What is happening to my world?* With no time for worry or distraction, she doggedly pushed forward toward her only chance at survival. It took an hour, but at last, Geeja reached the hard, but welcoming bed. With trembling gasps, she dragged her new form atop it, then collapsed. Panting, she whispered. "I don't know what's going on, but five days of rest and I should be rejuvenated." She paused, then spoke through gritted teeth, calling out the suspected perpetrator of the attack by name. "Then the battle to cast out Djurga and his cursed troopers begins."

Chapter Two

Coughing, Geeja awoke. Her head throbbed. No two transferences were alike, but this one didn't even register in the same universe of experiences as any of the thousands before. She moaned, sitting up stiffly in the inky darkness of the cavern, then rubbed her neck at the base of her skull. "I am starving and feel like I have been run over by a centipede ungulate in the desert." Forcing her legs over the edge of the stone bed, she wondered aloud. "How long have I been out?"

Geeja blinked, her eyelids grinding like sandpaper. As she tried to shake the cobwebs from her mind, she noted a change in her surroundings from when she drifted into sleep. "I am covered in dust and the healing bed is barely glowing." Her brow furrowed. "I have never seen that before."

Things weren't adding up. Brushing silt from the soldier's uniform she now wore, she struggled to process the scene. Finally, a thin film of moisture coated her dry eyes and mouth. In a connection reflex she had exercised for thousands of years, Geeja reached out to the planet …and she truly startled, sensing nothing. Her thoughts searched the unaccustomed vacuum. *"Uwan! Where are you? What is wrong?"*

When the planet finally responded the reply sounded both alarming and muted, barely audible above the background hum of the universe. *"I am dying…"*

Jumping to her feet, Geeja nearly fell on her face. Regaining her balance, she pressed for answers. *"What do you mean, you are dying?"* This didn't make sense. Just a few days ago the planet thrummed with vitality. She swallowed hard, remembering in clear detail everything leading to her collapse. *"Then the invasion happened."* Her mind focused. *"Tell me, my friend. What happened to you…to me?"*

"Your recovery took a long time, a very long time. I had no guarantee you would survive."

The whispered answer sent a spear through her heart as her mind scrambled to process. She swallowed hard. *"How long?"* Chill bumps raised in the lengthy pause before the planet's response.

"Two thousand years."

Geeja staggered, landing on her backside on the bed. *"What?"* As if being hit by a tsunami, her collective being reeled, trying to comprehend. She gasped. *"That is impossible…is it not?"*

Uwan sighed. *"The healing stone sustained your body's physical needs while repairing the corrupted transference process. In my debilitated condition, it required monumental effort."*

The reality of the situation punctured her spirit, and a flood of tears burst like a dam failing on the mighty Abhainen River. *"No!"* Sobs racked her to the core as she fell onto the dirt floor. Moans sprang from her soul as the dire state of Uwan became real, mixing with the messy waterworks pouring from her eyes, mouth and nose. *"This cannot be true!"* Her mourning and torment went on as if tapping an inexhaustible supply of grief.

When the crying and gnashing of teeth abated, she begged. *"What happened? Why are you dying?"*

A beleaguered feeling transmitted with Uwan's thoughts. *"Without you as my eyes and ears, I can only tell you what I know. They shoved a spike through my crust, then everything changed. They took my magic and left pain in its place. I became nearly paralyzed, unable to resist. Now, our atmosphere is severely degraded and much of our natural resources have been stolen."* The planet paused once again. *"The shouts of protest against my violation have long since gone silent."*

"Djurga did this, right? He is behind this." Geeja's mind filled with righteous rage. *"He did this!"*

"I cannot say with certainty…but it is a fair assumption."

"I will right this wrong!" Geeja stood, wearing the beige one-piece uniform of her guardian soldier in this new body. The dirt she had crawled through two thousand years ago stained the garment, and her waterworks in the dust added new dark patches. "We have not yet begun to fight!" Her spirit soared, but her body flagged. She staggered toward a wall she could barely see in the dying glow of the healing bed. "But first, I need a meal and a gallon of water."

"I will guide and help you to the best of my ability, but our powers are greatly diminished."

Geeja had been in this glorious symbiotic relationship with Uwan for eons, and now everything she knew stood threatened. She occasionally wondered what it would feel like to be fully human again, and vulnerable. To know that she could die. *"Thank you for all you have done, Uwan, and for whatever help you can yet provide."* She raised her chin, setting it firm as she spoke aloud. "And as you are my witness, I shall do all I can to return you to your former glory."

Stepping forward, Geeja stumbled. Falling to the floor, she scraped her knee as a rock tore her uniform. Her next words were far humbler. "But I will need some time and all the help I can find."

Rising, her defiance modestly returned. "The restoration of Uwan begins now."

Chapter Three

In the planet's weakened condition, only the thinnest thread of blue light projected in her mind to lead Geeja from the depths of the cave to the surface. She breathed easier, thankful for the assistance, but saddened by the state of Uwan. She sent a determined message to her world. ***"Your health WILL be restored."*** Instead of a telepathic reply, Geeja received a warm planetary hug. Though it seemed like a few days ago, she smiled for the first time in two thousand years.

Nearing the entrance to the cave, noxious chemical laden smells assaulted her senses. "What the..." A few more steps revealed the first rays of light as well as the threshold between the cool air inside and outside heat. Both light and air seemed off. The sun shown as if through a hazy filter. She mumbled, confused. "How can it be this hot here?"

Stepping across the threshold it seemed as if she were transported to another universe. Expecting the dense forest she left behind upon entry, she saw nothing but ashen rocky outcroppings. Fine brown powder filled the spaces in between. Geeja gasped for breath, placing a hand to her mouth. Her words choked. "What have they done to you?"

For the briefest of moments, she wondered if she might still be sleeping, that she would wake soon and this would be nothing more than a horrible nightmare. Glancing upward, the sight of blue sky had been replaced by a grimy brown film, rendering everything in sandy tones. Taking in another breath that burned her throat, Geeja knew this was real…so real it hurt both her lungs and ancient soul.

A single tear rolled down the smooth skin of this younger form's right cheek. Her lips tightened against both the odor and uncertainty of deciding what to do next in these unfamiliar surroundings. In addition to the nasty environment, her need for water and food added to her discomfort. Pulling up the decorative green neck scarf from the soldier's uniform, Geeja covered her nose in the blowing wind, mumbling to herself, then stepping forward. "When I entered the cave, a road wandered just ahead. Perhaps it is still there."

Each step drained Geeja, though a grin eased onto her face seeing the country lane still where it lay so long ago. Reaching it she realized it too, had changed. *By the Holy Twelve, what is that weird black stuff?* Instead of smoothed stones, she found a perfectly flat unbroken surface. Strong wind blew wispy swirls over the roadway as she squinted.

With no answer from Uwan, she glanced in both directions. To the right, the road traveled uphill, while to the left, it trailed down. She shook her head. "I have no idea, in this time, what may lay either way. However, I am in no shape to climb that grade." With a shoulder shrug and smirk, she turned left. "I have found my first helper–gravity."

Even walking downhill, every step sapped her strength. Her thoughts ran unfocused and untamed, like a herd of wild shimras running across the plains of Gurunden, the western-most province on Uwan. "I sleep two thousand years in a snap of finger and thumb, yet walking less than a mile feels like an eternity."

Tapping into the scant energy of Uwan revealed memories of the trees that were here before, and just ahead flashed a remembrance of a small hamlet. *Please still be there!* Sweat ran down her face, into her eyes. Stumbling, she came upon the remains of the village. The few hand-quarried stones still stacked atop one another stood like defeated sentinels. Exhausted, Geeja sat, then leaned against the dusty rocks.

Thoughts she previously had about human vulnerability turned to fear, as her breathing became labored in the harsh environment. Geeja's vision blurred even when she wiped the sweat away. Her heart hammered as her lungs struggled to take in air. *Is this what dying feels like?* Try as she might, Geeja couldn't stop her eyes from closing, as massive exhaustion pressed from all directions. *This is bad…really bad.*

**

Smiling, Raflo flew over the recently paved road in his new skimmer. By bribing the sector administrator to move this highway up in the maintenance order, he secured a smoother ride for land bound cargo vehicles traveling this route to his compound. However, the kickback he received from the asphalt company pleased him most. It more than covered both the cost of the bribe and purchase of his new ride. *Win, win!* Testing his skill, he accelerated faster as a satisfied grin slashed across his face. *Life is good!*

Riding in the passenger seat, Huanoc grunted. "Did you see that?"

"See what?" Most days his business partner and unofficial bodyguard spoke less than a hundred words in total, so he perked up at this limited burst. "What did I miss?"

"Turn around."

"Two more words." Raflo teased the Nafportonian man who stood over eight feet tall and weighed at least five-hundred pounds. "It must be important." Slowing, he did a U-turn on the lightly traveled thoroughfare, then retraced their path. "This better be good. You know we have that call with Zernon at three."

Huanoc ignored Raflo until they reached the wide place in the road, then pointed. "Grhrmp."

"Okay. That wasn't a real word, so I won't add it to your total for the day." Raflo caught the tiny grin on Huanoc's huge face. Though his best friend, the large man had a weird code. He would speak freely and unleash his enormous laugh for almost anyone else, but he refused to do so for him. The weird dynamic made Raflo try even harder to get a reaction whenever he could.

Scanning, Raflo spotted what Huanoc had already spied. "Is that a person? Out here without any protection in this storm?" He reached for his breather before raising the clear shell, then exited the hovering craft. "This air is bad enough on a good day, but everybody knows you need gear when the wind picks up."

He stepped down to the road and curiosity colored his words. "Let's take a look." Both cautiously approached the crumpled form. Raflo poked the uniformed body and it fell to the side, exposing a female face. He glanced at Huanoc. "Think she's alive?"

The big man shrugged, then knelt, placing two fingers on the side of her neck. After a few seconds, he proclaimed the one-word verdict. "Alive."

"Quick, get her in the skimmer. She needs air!"

Like lifting a feather, Huanoc scooped the woman up, then gently placed her in the back seat. In moments they again flew fast towards their compound.

Switching the craft to autopilot, Raflo turned his attention to their new passenger. Two questions came to mind. "Who is she, and what's she wearing?"

Blinking rapidly twice, his modified right eye shifted to scan mode. His gaze traced her entire body, lingering longest at her head to get a good capture of her face. He uploaded the image and in seconds, had half of his answer. "Where in the name of the Holy Eleven did she get a genuine two-thousand-year-old Sworn Warrior uniform?" His thoughts automatically went to money. "Computer, what is the value of that item of clothin'?"

The integrated processor replied in a monotone voice. "In its current condition, six point five million units. If you can authenticate this as a uniform of Captain Susomi of the Goddess Geeja's final personal detail, as the name tag indicates, then the value is incalculable."

Raflo gave a long whistle. "Jackpot, Huanoc! We're goin' to be rich!"

Huanoc twisted his head to the left and the bones in his muscular neck cracked like fireworks. A cautious, "Hmm," his only reply.

The vehicle slowed as the force field gate at the entrance to their compound lowered. Raflo took back manual control and maneuvered into the garage. "We've got to help her if we can. She looks to be in rough shape."

The big man nodded.

Chapter Four

Awakening, relief washed over Geeja, thankful to have survived the windstorm. Smelling fried food, her stomach growled. It only took the one whiff to identify it as one of her favorite breakfast meats. *Crispy kaston. Yum.* Instead of opening her eyes, she turned to her other senses, trying to figure out where she might be, and under what circumstances. Hearing voices in conversation, she remained still, listening.

"Who do you think she is? I mean, how many people do you know that can't be identified by facial recognition or genetic testin?'" After a breath, the man, young by the sound of his timbre, continued. "And that uniform? It's two thousand years old. It makes no sense."

"Hmm." By the reverberation of the single syllable, she identified an additional male in the room…and he sounded huge.

The voices comforted and confused her. *I am glad I can understand them, but that accent? I have never heard it anywhere on Uwan.*

A whirring sound moved close as the first man spoke again. "She's been under the care of our robomedic for five days."

He sounded concerned, which reassured her, but she had no idea what he was talking about. *What is a robomedic?*

The young male continued. "I hope she wakes up soon, or we'll have to take her to the regional care center." He paused for a moment, then continued in the odd dialect. "It would be mighty hard to explain how we found her, then waited days to bring her in."

Another, "Hmm," echoed in the room full of clean, breathable air.

Pieces were coming together. *Okay, they found me and rendered care. That is a good sign.* She subtly moved her fingers, touching a smooth sheet covering her prone body. *They have shelter, food and clean bedding. More good signs.* Slowly, and with as little movement as possible, Geeja flexed her wrists and met no resistance. *And I am not restrained.*

With those basic facts, she made the decision. *I cannot stay like this forever, so time to take a risk. I will try to open my eyes.* Struggling, her lids cracked apart like lazentern eggs, giving her the first look at her surroundings. Through a light haze, she indeed saw two figures. As suspected, one of the voices belonged to a young adult male who wore pants that clung tight, in a shade of bright green she had never seen before. His shirt glowed sunshine yellow, made from a foreign cloth that shimmered like stars. The other man happened to be a light-blue-skinned massive beast who wore no shirt, only a sleeveless black leather vest over pants of the same color and material. He noticed the slits of her eyes.

"Look!" An index finger almost as big as a plork tree branch pointed toward her.

The other man smiled and his tan cheeks dimpled. "She's awake! You had us worried, Darlin.'"

Having lived thousands of lifetimes, Geeja quickly picked up on the vibes of most rooms. Reading subtle body cues and verbal intonations had become second nature. Unless human interactions had changed significantly, just the way the man said 'darlin,' told her all she needed to know. Having seen this playbook many times before, Geeja made an educated guess about the men. *A rake and his muscle.* She blinked to rid the blurriness from her vision. *It could be a lot worse.* She weighed her next move. *Play for sympathy and get as much information as I can...without lying...unless necessary.* She had sworn vows and intended to abide by them even in these new and uncharted circumstances. With no need to exaggerate about her parched condition, she spoke in a hoarse whisper. "Water...please?"

The probable womanizer rushed to her side while directing the big man. "You heard the lady, Huanoc. Get her somethin' to drink!" His warm hand gently wrapped around hers. "Thank the gods of the Eleven Holy Worlds. You're alive!"

Eleven Holy Worlds? Geeja masked her shock. For millennia, the phrase had always been, 'Thank the gods of the TWELVE Holy Worlds.' The realization that this phrase changed had dark implications. *Is it Uwan who is no longer considered holy?* Sadly, that made sense from what she had seen. She drew a second inference. *Everyone must think I am dead...and I need to keep it that way, at least for now.*

The large man banged around in the adjoining room, so the young guy yelled. "Hurry up, Huanoc, you big lunk!"

Huanoc? Sounds vaguely familiar. She silently tried to figure out which planet the giant might hail from. *Nafporton maybe?* She said his name in her head again and noted the particular shade of his blueness. *Huanoc.* It fit. *Definitely Nafporton.* She mulled that conclusion and it spurred a new mystery. *How is a Nafportonian who is not a God here on Uwan, halfway across the universe?*

"Here." The scant speaking giant, who had thick muscular arms, handed the glass to the man who stood beside her. In the classic

Uwanian style, the man sported soft black curls that accentuated mischievous almond shaped eyes. This local fellow with the strange accent touched a round button and the head of the bed rose.

The mechanical sensation startled her. *How?* She then noticed the lighting that held a steady glow, without flames. *What...*

The young guy showed a tender bedside manner as he angled the glass to Geeja's lips. "Drink."

While surprised by the automated action of the bed, her thirst trumped everything, so she ignored the technology, gulping water greedily. "Ahh."

"Easy does it, Darlin.' There's plenty where that came from."

He winked one of those endearing eyes and Geeja noticed the right and left didn't exactly match. She smiled in return, then realized how chapped her lips were. It didn't matter in the moment as both her eyes and raspy voice begged. "More?"

In seconds, the two men had another glass filled and back to her lips. The handsome one continued his banter. "Looks like we found you just in time, Sweetie. You've been out for days."

With the second glass of the most precious liquid in the universe downed, she answered in a whisper. "Thank you." Her voice sounded as rough as the bark of the jargonzo tree.

"Good. Good. Looks like you're goin' to be okay." The Uwanian man put a hand to his chest. "I'm Raflo, and this is my friend and business partner, Huanoc." He pointed to her. "What's your name?" His dimples deepened, going from cute to adorable as his smile widened. His tight fitting, brightly colored clothing, however, shocked her. All citizens of Uwan wore natural shades of greens, blues and yellows, usually in flowing styles.

So many things have changed.

In his sugary but accented language, he continued. "Speak up, unless you want me to keep callin' you 'sweetie' and 'darlin.'"

My name. Hmm. I cannot introduce myself as a goddess who has not been seen or heard from in two thousand years, now can I? I will go with my nickname...that is a version of the truth. "I think my name is Gigi, but I am not sure." Her rasp cleared a bit as she smiled innocently.

"Gigi. That's pretty." His grin remained as his head tilted. "And where in the name of Hasprin are you from? That's some twang you've got there."

Her eyes widened, realizing she sounded as strange to them as he did to her. *Over two millennia, language evolves.* Her eyes shot around the room noticing walls painted bright shades of blue and orange not found in nature. *Like everything else.* She muttered the truth in a way that might put the issue to bed. "I was born this way." Glancing up, she blinked as harmlessly as she could. "I hope it does not offend you."

"What?" Raflo blushed, just as she hoped. "Forgive me. I didn't mean to insult you. We've all got our issues." He paused and looked up, seeming in thought on how to change the subject. "So, Gigi. What were you doin' out in the middle of nowhere without any atmospheric protection from the windstorm?"

Stall. I need more information before I have that conversation. "Thank you for the water, Raflo." She made an exaggerated sniff. "Is that crispy fried kaston I smell? I'm as hungry as I was thirsty."

It worked, as Raflo turned to his protégé. "You heard Gigi. Get the woman some food."

As soon as the plate arrived, Geeja snatched a crunchy strip of her favorite breakfast meat. Some of her prior vessels preferred the common food to be prepared tender and flexible. But once, long ago, she took the form of a chef. With that woman's exceptional sense of taste and culinary expertise, a consensus formed. *Crunchy is best.*

It wouldn't have mattered though. Famished, she ate everything on her dish, like a Sunsasole cat devouring its prey. Then it hit her. *I am in Sunsasole and it now looks like a desert instead of a jungle…I wonder if that species still exists?*

Raflo sat with a bemused expression, as if watching an animal greedily consuming a carcass from the safety of a safari palanquin. "How long has it been since you last ate?" He snickered. "Glad I got my fingers out of the way."

She needed to give them some kind of answers to gain their trust, and perhaps help her in some way, but the situation remained uncertain. There were too many variables to come clean just yet. She rubbed the back of her neck and focused her eyes on the most distant point in the room to help sell the performance. She sighed. "It feels like centuries. I am having a problem remembering anything…even when I last had food." She turned toward Raflo, then batted her lashes while adding a slight tremor to her words. "It is scary not to be able to remember what happened. Think you could help me fill in some blanks?"

His eyes sparkled, as if he saw himself as a gallant hero coming to the aid of a fair lady. "We'll do our best, won't we, Huanoc?"

"Hrmph."

"That's his way of agreein.'" Raflo shook his head as he spoke with a lightness to his words while glancing at his friend. "In fact, that's his way of sayin' a lot of things." Turning back toward her, he quizzed. "Even if it's only fragments, what do you remember? Let's start with that."

That would be a reasonable beginning place for a normal situation, so she tweaked the idea, staying as truthful as possible. "It is odd. I can remember all kinds of things about the ancient days of Uwan, but nothing else. Seems I know all things about the goddess and those times, but that is all I can access right now. I have a vague memory of being somewhere safe and reading about the attack on our world." She rubbed her chin, then spoke in uncertain tones, hoping to prod them into coming up with a theory she could make her own. "What do you think that means?"

Raflo's eyebrows lifted for a moment. "Not sure about that, but there's not much more to fill in. Emperor Djurga's forces overran our defenses in like a day or so with their overwhelmin' tech advantage. Then they commenced makin' an example of Uwan. Seeing what happened here, planet after planet fell rather than have this be done to them." His hands went up in apparent contempt. "And our world hasn't been the same since."

Emperor? He didn't stop with Uwan? With blood boiling at what must have happened, she barely masked her true feelings. *That son of a wastling! I knew Djurga had to be behind this!* Taking in a calming breath, she continued, speaking as naively as possible. "And the other holy planets? What of them?"

A shrug and sigh forecast his reply. "After seeing the devastation here, one by one, they fell in line." His words dripped sarcasm. "We're a big happy empire under the thumb of the one and only, Emperor Djurga."

"Oh..." Geeja's eyes widened upon hearing how history unfolded. *Djurga was not a god. How could he still be alive all these millennia later?*

Raflo almost jumped from his chair when an idea seemed to come in a flash. "Hey, Huanoc. Think she could be a runaway from one of those denier cults? There's one about a days walk from here."

Nodding, Huanoc answered. "That would fit."

Laughing, Raflo jabbed at his partner. "Three words! We got three words in a sentence. That must mean we're onto something."

Geeja's face twisted. "Denier cult?"

"Yeah," continued Raflo, "They're groups who deny that the Goddess of Uwan died in that shootout with the Impercium. They claim she's been layin' dormant, waitin' to arise in…" He snapped his fingers. "What's that phrase they use…they put it in all their recruitin' pamphlets?"

The big man grunted, then supplied the answer. "In the fullness of time."

Raflo seemed so excited to perhaps solve the mystery, he didn't even give his partner a hard time about stringing five words together. "That's it! The Goddess of Uwan will rise in the fullness of time!" He shook his head. "Can you believe that?"

She spoke the truth. "*Sounds* impossible."

"I know. Yet these nut jobs segregate themselves from society, livin' off the land without technology. They believe she will show up one day, then toss out the Impercium and heal this world." He seemed on a roll. "They still pray to her and claim they can feel her spirit." He spread his arms. "I guess it takes all kinds."

Despite the excitement of learning key snippets of the history she missed, the body Geeja now inhabited made its own demands. She yawned loudly while feeling a crushing tiredness. "Gentlemen, as hard as it might seem to believe, I am sleepy again. Could we continue this discussion later?"

Their eyes went to each other and each gave a microscopic head nod. As usual, Raflo spoke for the pair. "We have a business meetin' tomorrow. How about we continue when me and Huanoc return?"

An undercurrent flowed between them that she couldn't decipher, but this receptacle demanded rest. She yawned again. "Think I could tag along?"

Raflo answered, uncommittedly. "We'll see what the mornin' brings, huh?"

Against her will, Geeja's head fell back toward the pillow. Her eyes pulled down as if they were window shades being drawn by someone as large as Huanoc. "Fair enough." She added heartfelt words. "And thank you both for saving my life. May the gods and goddesses of the Tw… ELEVEN Holy Worlds bless you." *I almost screwed that up.* That turned out to be her last waking thought as in seconds sleep snatched her, as though her will had been abducted by a benevolent slumber witch.

**

The two men retired to the comfort of the living room where Raflo poured them each a glass of desert berry wine. "What do you think of her story?"

"Humph." Huanoc shrugged.

As if the gesture contained several distinct ideas, Raflo responded in a serious tone. "I agree. She does seem like a nice person." He lifted his eyebrows. "And, you're right, she is cute…but I'm not buyin' that memory loss thing either." He paused, weighing the pros and cons of bringing her along on the trip. "Who knows what revelations tomorrow might bring? Let's put off the decision until then. You good with that?"

A single sharp nod said it all.

**

Harstra, a low-level Impercium data mining official, manually reviewed a flagged image from a database search made on Uwan. One of her eyebrows twitched as everyone knew what happened to that planet halfway across the universe. It neared the end of her shift, and she nearly left it until morning. But glancing at the time, she decided to complete one last task. *I'd better finish, my boss has been on me about my quota.*

In less than a second, the eight fingers on each of her hands simultaneously pulled up the image and enlarged it on the screen. She mumbled in the privacy of her cubicle located near an outer wall of this one-hundred-thousand-person outpost. "What do we have here?" All three eyes stared. "A vintage Goddess of Uwan Sworn Warrior uniform…and the name tag indicates it once belonged to one Captain Susomi."

It rang no bells from recent bulletins. Switching tabs, she looked to see which branch of the Impercium had standing orders to flag any system searches matching this item of clothing. It had been a long day and her shoulders sagged under the weight of working ten hours. When the screen filled, she startled, suddenly as alert as after the first morning cup of calefine juice. "Whoa!" Her hands shook. "I've never identified anything for the Impercium Directorate." She swallowed hard as she thought of their reputation. *People in their custody tend to disappear.*

Her fingers trembled over the implications of her decision to pull up one more case file. *I would have gotten fired, or worse, if I had put this off.* Now, new possibilities danced before Harstra's eyes as she scrolled, gathering more information on the flag order. *But since I did my job well, I might get a raise!* Her coiled tongue flew out for a tiny snack from the tray on her desk, then snapped back into her mouth in a flash. She savored the salty tidbit, dreaming bigger. *I might even get a promotion!*

All of her eyes widened as she saw the initiation date for this particular alert. As if seeing the triple moonrises on Voltriste for the first time, she spoke in awe. "They posted this notice centuries ago!" She clicked the appropriate cover document form as fast as she could, then forwarded both to her boss. "This is the most exciting thing that's ever happened here!" She jumped from her seat and ran down the half-mile hallway, trying to get to her supervisor's office before she opened the report. "Crijj! We're going to be famous!"

Chapter Five

Emperor Djurga sat in his rejuvenation chamber facing east awaiting Speglow, today the first of the two suns to rise on Emblaka, his home world. The suns precise twenty-year dance of rotating positions cast either red or yellow first rays, depending on their order of ascension, against the blue sky. With the thousands of variables, when including local weather factors, it provided one of the few genuine unique experiences each daybreak in his more than two millennia long life.

He rarely slept these days, so when home he cherished mornings not attending to duties far and wide across the universe he ruled. Inside a transparent bubble the emperor breathed in an exotic cocktail of gases. Their inky blue, dense black and slimy green hues swirled around him, keeping him youthful. The hum of the pumps circulating this daily life-extending elixir between his once in a decade Revival Day process, served as an irritating but necessary accompaniment to his final uninterrupted moments each morning.

In the shifting light he caught his reflection on the glass and smiled, proud of his taut white skin, chiseled chin and thick head of hair, which these days he kept in the fashionable 'high and tight' style. Exactly on time red beams of first light penetrated heavy, deep-blue rain-bearing clouds, creating a rich glow across the horizon. He spoke in awe of the gorgeous sunrise. "Ah, royal purple! An exact match to my eyes!"

The sound of boots running toward him across the granite floors of the control center interrupted his moment of peaceful contemplation. His irritation exploded like an over-pressurized calefine pot. "Axayzor!! Interrupting my morning meditation has a cost. For your hide's sake, this better be worth it!"

Axayzor, the plump Majordomo of House Chryselta, bowed deeply, displaying his brilliant white hair pulled back and worn in a bun in the customary style among people of high nobility on his home planet. "Your Excellency, your time in contemplation is sacred. I would only disturb your moments of reflection for the most important of reasons." He remained bent at the waist, head inches from the floor, until addressed by the ruler.

"Out with it." From inside his clear egg-shaped chamber, Djurga spat his words. "It's a purple start to the day, a portentous omen. Don't dare disappoint."

Rising to face the youthful looking monarch, Axayzor maintained his formality. "It is with great pleasure that I announce a find of tremendous importance."

Djurga released an annoyed sigh. "Your dawdling has ruined daybreak. First light has passed." An aggravated growl preceded his next words. "Spit out this supposed big news."

Clearing his throat, the plump head of the household dressed in the black and white colors of the empire, resumed. "Your Excellency, one of your data mining centers has identified an image search of a long-ago flagged item." His shoulders pulled back even further than usual for this announcement. "Someone on the planet Uwan uploaded an image of what appears to be a Goddess of Uwan Sworn Warrior uniform. The name tag identifies it as belonging to the one named Susomi."

Jumping to his feet, Djurga banged his head on the top of the rejuvenation chamber. He yelled as he pressed the emergency release button, venting gasses toxic to most beings. "Susomi! Is that what you said?"

Tight lipped as he held his breath, Axayzor nodded vigorously. His face turned as red as the first rays of today's dawn.

"Get General Scanda, now!"

The majordomo spun crisply, then sprinted to the door. A loud exhale could be heard from the hallway on the other side of the heavy wooden doors hewn from plork trees, harvested millennia ago on Uwan.

Emergency filtering units kicked on to deal with the poisonous gasses floating in the room. Djurga again turned east and addressed the first rising sun through ancient leaded glass. "Speglow, you have indeed been a good sign today." He paced between colossal stone pillars which supported a massive domed roof as his floor length purple robe fluttered behind. His movement and the first sunrise of the new day warmed his old bones. "I've waited so long that even I began to believe the Goddess of Uwan was dead, that my theory of her doing one of those transference rituals might be wrong." He didn't smile often these days, but this news crept across his face, pulling both tips of his lips upward as he bellowed in the empty hall. "You arrogant femitch. You will bend to my will like the others. If not, I will drain the oceans of Uwan, burn every square inch of land, then use it as target practice for new weapons."

At a full run, General Scanda, head of the Impercium Directorate, rushed in, his shined boots sliding across the enormous polished black and white marble slabs laid on the diagonal. He stopped just in front of his master. Saluting, he bowed as had Axayzor, but instead of remaining in that position, he bolted upright as straight as a Zni stalagmite. He spoke breathlessly. "Your servant awaits your orders."

"Send your best battalion to Uwan." The words were clipped and sharp as a Duralian razor. "Find the woman who goes with the uniform Axayzor showed me. Kill anyone with her. No one else is to know of this mission until the Goddess of Uwan is brought before me…bound, gagged and on her knees!"

Scanda gave another smart salute. "Your will be done, Your Excellency!"

"I remind you, Scanda. Failure has consequences."

Gulping, Scanda replied as his hand snapped back to his side. "Understood, my Lord. I will not fail." With that he spun, as Axayzor had earlier, sprinting toward the huge double doors.

Once again turning to the east, the second sun, Seaglince, peeked over the horizon. It added yellow rays to the building purple thunderhead. This combination of colors resulted in a dirt brown monster that now bore down on the castle. Torrents of fat, driving droplets assaulted the slate roof of the observatory section of the control room in a roaring cacophony. Djurga couldn't help dark thoughts from souring his smile. *Surely her luck will run out, won't it?* His gaze returned to the muddy cloud. "More omens."

Chapter Six

Hearing wails, Jacastra and three other Sworn Warriors rushed into the Holy Mother's bed chamber. She called out in the dimly lit room. "Holy Mother! We are here!"

The Holy Mother sat upright in bed, her simple white gown drenched in sweat…again. The ancient leader's wide eyes searched the room in the seeming ethereal dimension between the spirit and waking worlds. A wild scream sprang, sounding as if coming from her soul, echoing against the stone walls of her monastic home. "War is nigh!"

"Holy Mother!" All three young women wrapped the frail leader in their embrace while Jacastra smoothed her damp gray hair. "You are free from the vision realm. You are safe in our arms."

In the younger women's embrace, tension slithered from creaky bones like an arthritic serpent, finally dissipating through thin, wrinkled skin. Gathering her bearings, the old woman spoke in a wispy, far away voice. "I saw it once more…the battle that is to come."

The normally sedate Goddess of Uwan Training Academy, had been abuzz for the past ten days with similar pronouncements from the Holy Mother. The last two had been the most buzzworthy yet. Reports from Jacastra informed the Holy Mother of a clear split between those who believed her statements, versus others thinking she had gone mad.

In the first moments of waking from the visions, their ancient leader sometimes seemed to doubt herself. Yet, as the images from these night travels settled, her voice carried the clarion ring of certainty. "Somehow, as fantastical as it might sound, Emperor Djurga and The Goddess of Uwan will clash once again."

This morning, gnarled fingers reached toward her personal guards, taking time to tenderly touch each of the three smooth-skinned faces. Drawing strength, she spoke plainly, and without reservation. "On this night I saw the Goddess, not in the robes of yore, but in modern dress…she is restored."

"You must be exhausted, Holy Mother." Jacastra held the woman's frail hands. "A breakfast of desert berry jam and freshly baked bread awaits."

With surprising strength, the wise woman replied. "Yes. A meal to fuel my body, such as it is, is in order. We have much to do today."

Jacastra nodded, as Luculencia and Esbatique rose from the bed to make the meal arrangements. "Come, Holy Mother. I will wipe your brow and dress you for the day." Jacastra gingerly helped the elderly woman from the bed to the dressing area. She removed the drenched gown, then took a sponge from the basin of warm water to purify their leader as gently as a mother stone-tooth tiger licks her cub.

After the cleansing, Jacastra swathed the Holy Mother in a forest-green silk gown modeled after the one worn by the goddess on the last day she had been seen on Uwan. The loose-fitting outerwear shimmered, even in the dim lighting of her private chambers.

As the Holy Mother walked toward the communal dining hall, each warrior they met went down on their left knee, offering their right hand. The benevolent woman obliged each supplicant with a kiss and blessing. "May the goddess show her favor on you today."

While the daily walk had recently proved increasingly exhausting, this morning it seemed the opposite. With each step she drew power from her sister warriors and from the charged air itself. Even her sagging cheeks looked tighter, rejuvenated by the visions.

Reaching the dining hall, five lengthy dark wooden tables, worn by centuries of use, ran parallel in east to west cardinal directions. The usually chatty din of gossip silenced this morning as word of her latest vision must have surely spread. Standing more erect with each stately stride, the Holy Mother reached the head of the center table. She turned, facing her three hundred soldiers.

Jacastra and Esbatique stood a step behind the esteemed leader, one on each side, their form-fitting khaki honor guard uniforms smartly starched.

Taking in a deep breath, the Holy Mother lifted her arms slowly toward the heavens. Taking her time, she locked eyes with what seemed at least half of the consecrated women. Now staring toward an unseen eastward point, she addressed the soldiers dressed in desert camo. "Over thousands of generations, millions of daughters of the goddess have sat where you sit today, awaiting the news that you are about to hear."

Expectant mumbling filled the great hall all the way to the ancient plork tree timbers supporting the vaulted roof. The leader let the side chatter continue for almost a full minute, then nodded.

At the signal, Jacastra and Esbatique raised their ceremonial spears, then slammed their shafts down in unison. The sudden contact of hardened wood against solid hand-mined granite echoed throughout the hall, silencing the hopeful crowd.

With arms still raised, the Holy Mother continued. "I have received visions." She paused, her eyes scanning feminine faces scrubbed clean of makeup, unlike the style worn by women in the mainstream civilization.

All seemed to hang on her words in hope.

"The visions have been wonderful…and terrible. My soul soared to never before visited heights, and to the depths of despair." She took in a great breath. "While our fight is just, and holy power will be on our side, this will be a real battle." Her voice darkened. "Many of us will give the greatest sacrifice to achieve victory."

A dropped Impercium coin could have been heard clanging to the ground from any spot in the vast space as a deafening hush flooded the room. Her arms lifted higher and a gentle breeze ruffled her silky gown, adding shimmering brilliance to her proclamation. "The Goddess of Uwan is here! In the flesh!" She refilled her lungs, then shared her vision. "The fullness of time is NOW! We must prepare for the final battle to save Uwan!"

An earsplitting roar echoed against the stone walls as soldiers hugged, leapt onto tables with war cries, or simply sat in firm-faced resolve. The fierce woman's arms were now aimed toward the heavens with hands balled into fists over her head as the planet's meager energy graced her. With only a sliver of the goddess' power available to a mere human such as she, her voice still carried loud above the celebratory shouts. "The long wait is over! With our goddess leading us, we WILL reclaim Uwan as our own! We will take the fight to our oppressor!"

Jacastra stood firm, eyes narrowing as she joined in the response. "The fullness of time is now!"

Chapter Seven

On a quiet morning, Geeja opened her eyes in a still room, feeling surprisingly refreshed. Even the robomedic, now parked on what the men called its charging station, no longer startled her. Dim first light bled into the room, so she pushed back the blanket, again noting the uniform she wore had been removed. Her clothing had been replaced by a light-blue gown with ties in the back. Since she had seen no one else, she assumed the two men had undressed her in their rendering of care. Having just inhabited this vessel, a quirky thought formed. *They have had a better look at my new body than have I.*

Having lived as long as she, and taking so many forms, Geeja had no modesty concerning nakedness. *My body is not me.* Hopping off the bed, she noticed a full-length mirror that seemed to float in place without wires. She crept over while pulling the ties that held the delicate covering in place, letting it fall to the floor. Geeja grinned, as she had so many times before when gazing on a new vessel for the first time. The physique of this form pleased her.

Geeja tensed her arms and clearly defined musculature bulged in her reflection. Raising on her toes, her calf muscles swelled and her tush firmed. Her smile appeared friendly, flashing gleaming white teeth between full lips. Turning slowly, perky breasts stood over scars on her rib cage. There were more healed combat injuries on both her arms and legs. *Susomi is a beautiful vessel with a fighter's badges of courage...good. She has lived a warrior's life, and we are appreciative.* Because all her donor's essences, including Susomi's were now a part of her being, she often spoke of herself in the plural.

Susomi's body was not Geeja's first soldier form. She had inhabited many, and they were among her favorites because of their strength and conditioning. Of course, her blended being also included artists, philosophers, mathematicians and almost every other Uwanian calling. *Harmony and balance make us one with our world. Considering everything, this physical manifestation makes a marvelous first impression.*

With her first body inspection complete, she took time to center herself mentally. Still nude, she pulled a pillow from a chair in the room, then placed it in front of a low window. Upon wakening in the cave days ago, she had hastily reached with her mind to connect with the planet. Now, she could commune properly. Sitting cross-legged, she closed her eyes. Softly, Geeja rolled her mantra in a non-stop loop. ***"We exist to serve Uwan...we are one with Uwan...we exist to serve Uwan...we are one with Uwan..."***

Time ceased to exist as she connected with the weakened planet. While once again shocked at the deteriorated condition of her world, she at least knew what to expect. Unhurried, Geeja surveyed the five continents, starting with the one where she sat now, and it saddened her. ***"Sunsasole...you once provided fruits and vegetables to all, and now you are a desert. I give praise for the spindly succar trees that now thrive in your harsh environment and nourish those animals who survive."*** She inhaled deeply. ***"I will give my all to restore your jungles."***

Her drift next went to the northernmost point of this globe, sensing its current condition. ***"Jostecal, my favorite frozen place no more. I see that the heat has baked you as well, and the woolly land*** *birds no longer sing their winter songs. I will keep their memory and whistle their melodies forever. Praise be to the grain that now grows where ice growlers once roamed. I will give my all to restore your frozen fjords."*

Geeja's tortured tour of the planet next went to Rezalig, and she saw yet another revolting scene. Rolling grass-covered hills were gone, replaced by massive pits dug into the ground. They seemed long ago abandoned. Nonetheless, the stench on the breeze and abrasive touch of leftover chemicals transmitted to her being. Only the good balance and strength of this body kept her from falling backwards. *"Rezalig! You have suffered the most! What has been done to you?"*

Uwan's voice sounded as sorrowful as the call of a sorrow crow. *"Machines rumbled across my surface, stopping every few feet to burrow deep, narrow holes. They were filled with strange substances that sizzled against my rocks. Once the burrowing stopped, the metal treads of the mechanical beasts crawled away. All would go silent, then massive explosions erupted from each filled hole, shattering my layers."*

"Why? Why would Djurga want to crush the rocks of Uwan?"

She sensed a planetary shrug. *"When the rumbling stopped, heavier rolling devices rambled onto the devastation, then sharp, finger-like claws scooped up the rubble, taking it away."*

Geeja struggled to make sense of Uwan's explanations. They matched nothing she had ever seen. *"Why would anyone want to make big rocks little, then carry them away?"* Uwan stayed silent as she tried to reason an answer to the question. *"What good are little rocks?"*

The answer came fully formed from the depths of her memories. She could picture the ceremonial crown she donned on special occasions. Made of gold, craftsmen then inlaid diamonds, sapphires and other gemstones. It was beautiful; with every part formed by mining the planet. But the new method differed. Men digging in tunnels with picks didn't leave giant swaths of useless land. Scars were sometimes made, but they were always back filled, keeping the soil productive. Uwan described machines that defiled the planet instead of protecting it. Geeja recalled her first connection with her world upon awakening and now understood the gravity of his sentiment. *'The shouts of protest against my violation have long since gone silent.'*

Conflicting emotions surged as she silently babbled. *"I am so sorry…I had no idea…I feel a fool for underestimating Djurga…"* Her body shook as sloppy tears mingled with the drool dripping from the corners of her mouth. Geeja's head dropped forward like a boulder rolling off a cliff's edge.

A cough from behind, followed by sincere sounding words, broke her concentration. "Hey, Gigi. You okay?"

Geeja breathed deeply, temporarily breaking her connection with the planet as she centered her feelings. *First things first, I need help from these gentlemen. I can mourn later. Who wants to be around a sad, strange woman?* In her time, she would plant a telepathic suggestion in his head, but with Uwan's waning power that might no longer work. *Think, Geeja! Think!* The answer came like lightning. *Change the subject – fast.*

She cleared her throat. "Just having a little cry over my memory loss, but I am done indulging in self-pity." *Lighten things up.* "How should we start this glorious day?"

A teasing invitation came from Raflo. "I've prepared some breakfast if you would like to join…clothin' optional, of course."

Right…I am naked. With her back to him, she smiled. *Then let us see if you are as comfortable in your skin as I am in mine. This should make him forget all about my tears.* She stood, then turned to face Raflo. "That is fine with me…but only if you shed your garments as well."

Raflo's strange right eye blinked twice in a gesture she didn't understand, then those cute dimples reappeared with his smile matching hers. "I'd like nothin' better, but see, Huanoc is kind of a prude about seein' men naked. He would enjoy *your* company, of course, but find mine offensive." He shrugged. "I'm nothin,' if not polite, so I guess we'd better find you somethin' to wear besides that patient gown you dropped over there." His grin widened. "Guess you won't need it anymore." Raflo's eyes seemed to drink in her image. "You look pretty healthy to me."

Geeja followed as he walked into an adjoining room. Seeing several large crates with lids removed, she watched as he rifled through clothing in colors she had never seen. In short order he selected a few outfits.

"Let's see." He glanced at some sort of label on each brilliant blue, dazzling red or vivid yellow garment; some even studded with gems. He presented the selection. "See if these fit. If they do, they're yours."

She casually walked toward him, noticing his eyes moving to capture her every angle. *Go ahead, let these views be permanently etched in your brain. It will make it so much easier for you to agree when I ask to join your trip today.* Purposefully brushing his hand with hers, she accepted the pants and shirts. "These should do nicely." Taking a closer look at the strange styles, she noticed the blouse fastened in the back, giving her the opportunity to flirt more. "Do you mind staying here to secure the top?"

Raflo performed an exaggerated bow. "Anything for a lady."

Moving a few steps away, she put on one of the outlandish outfits. Geeja wore gowns on most days. In fact, most women on the planet wore loose fitting clothing or utilitarian uniforms. Not even the women in her personal detail, like Susomi, wore pants that fit this tight. Surprisingly, they didn't squeeze like a voca constriction snake, instead feeling natural, almost like a second layer of skin. *I guess I should expect some fashion changes after two thousand years.* The blouse fit almost as snug. Glancing in the mirror she smiled, pleased by the way it highlighted the curves in this body. *I guess not everything got worse during my absence.*

Stepping toward Raflo, she turned so that he could fasten the top button on the back. Once secured, Geeja faced him, batting her eyes. "How do I loo…" Her stomach clinched, and as if gut-punched, she bent at the waist. "Oof!"

Uwan signaled, urgently. *"Evil comes your way…fast! Run!"*

Raflo reached for the doubled over woman. "Gigi! What's wrong? Are you sick again?"

In a frozen moment, she saw her eyes in the mirror, and they were wide, with flashes of wildness. "Something bad heads towards us! We must flee!"

His forehead wrinkled as he questioned, seeming not sure if they were still messing with each other, or if something had truly changed. His neck twisted slightly. "What are you talkin' about?"

With her heart pounding in her ears, she forced a calm sentence. "You must simply trust me." She grabbed both his arms, begging. "I have a sixth sense when trouble is near." Now her panic burst through again. "Please! We must leave now!" She could read the confusion on his face as he kept his gaze fixed on her.

Raflo yelled. "Huanoc. Check out our remote cameras. You know, the long-range ones we installed after that disagreement with Roge Galak."

Geeja had no idea who Roge Galak might be, but Huanoc must have. She couldn't see him on the other side of the wall, but his heavy footsteps sounded as if running. After a few seconds, the quiet giant bellowed. "Impercium speeders! At least ten!"

Raflo gulped. "Impercium speeders? You sure?"

"Yes!"

Grabbing Geeja's hand, he pulled, leading the way to the back of the building, while at the same time calling to Huanoc. "Escape plan B!"

I do not know why these men have coded escape plans, and I do not care. I just hope this one works…and if not, maybe they have an escape plan C?

Running straight toward a wall, it miraculously slid open. As soon as they dashed through, it closed behind them with a heavy thud.

Ahead the ground opened and she knew where they were headed. *The tunnels. Refuge of goddesses…and criminals it seems.*

Behind them she heard a loud explosion, then shouts. A female voice stood out above the rest. "There they are!"

Now, the same sound as the strange weapons used in the attack on her all those years ago rang out. Bright light bit into the tunnel wall beside them sending chunks of stone flying. Raflo gave the weapon a name. "Lighters!"

Running at full speed, Geeja could barely keep pace with the heavy Nafportonian. He inched ahead in the tunnel, lit in the same fashion as the men's home. *Can they illuminate every corner of our world?*

Huanoc shouted. "Must run faster!"

Raflo yelled to his fleet partner. "Are we goin' to make it?"

The big man turned his head for a moment, his thick black eyebrows drawn together. "Maybe?"

I must do something…if I can. Geeja faked a fall, stumbling to the ground in a controlled roll.

Raflo stopped, turning immediately with an outstretched hand. "Get up! We've got to run!"

She waved him off. "Go on without me. I am slowing you down." She flicked her hand again. "I will catch up if I can." She could see the struggle play across his face.

Raflo swallowed hard. "I can't leave you!"

"Yes." She used the authoritative tone she honed over the centuries for occasions like this, where delay could mean death. "You must, and you will."

He took a half-step back. "Okay. We'll go on ahead. Get the ship fired up. Hurry! We'll wait until we see either you or Impercium troopers rounding the last corner." He raced after Huanoc, then looked back one last time. "It better be you that comes out first! Understand?"

Nodding, Geeja closed her eyes. *In the time before, with Uwan's help, I had the power to conjure an earthquake on the other side of the planet.* Sitting under this strange and unforgiving light, in the equally bizarre outfit, she patted the packed ground of this tunnel's floor, unsure what power she would be able to summon now. *Is even a simple roof fall out of the question?*

In the distance, she heard dozens of boots thundering toward her. *I will get my answer soon, or meet the end I first avoided millennia ago.* Calming her mind, she estimated she had less than fifteen seconds to find out the extent of the weakened planet's power. Staying on the ground, she crossed her legs, then placed a hand on each knee. Taking in a cleansing breath, she released it slowly. **"From my mind to the core of Uwan."** Pausing, she raised an arm and pointed toward the approaching troops. **"In service to your**

well-being and rejuvenation, I respectfully ask for a rockfall thirty feet from my location."

Nothing happened, not even a quiver. ***"Oh, Uwan! Your injuries tear my heart! I am so sorry…"*** She patted the hard soil gently, repeating her mournful words. ***"I am so sorry…"*** Burning tears ran down her cheeks, then spilled onto the packed dirt floor.

Armed troops closed rapidly, and in the otherwise silent tunnel, she could hear one of their voices shouting commands. "Take the woman alive. The emperor has plans for her." After a beat, the female leader of the attackers continued. "Kill everyone else. The Impercium can't have any rumors of hope spreading on this butt-smudge of a planet."

Geeja's blood boiled. Capturing, or even killing her was one thing, but the murder of innocents always triggered holy rage. Standing, she rubbed her hands in preparation. One unarmed woman couldn't do much to stop them, but she would try, perhaps giving Raflo and Huanoc enough time to escape. She picked up a rounded rock, hefting it. She snarled as she awaited her fate, cocking her arm to sling the stone. *If only one of these scum leaves with a headache, I will consider my death worthy.*

The company of troopers rounded the bend, stopping in apparent surprise upon seeing her. The leader called out, her voice low and threatening. "Surrender. You won't be harmed!"

Her mind spun to the future. *At least not until I meet the emperor. I shudder to think of* his *plans for me.* Heaving the chunk, Geeja made her intentions clear. "This is our world, and we will protect it with our last breath!"

The soldier closest to the commander easily deflected it with a clear shield attached to his forearm. The rocked thumped on impact, then skittered away harmlessly.

Clear? And so strong? This new tech amazed her yet again.

The head trooper, dressed in an armored but form-fitting black uniform, answered Geeja's threat. "It may be your world, but it's the emperor's universe. His will triumphs over all." Her high-pitched laughter echoed in the well-lit space, then she gave orders. "Alpha team, secure the prisoner. Delta team, find and terminate the others."

As the troops responded, the ground shook. The mild tremor lasted only ten seconds, then stopped. Geeja's eyes popped wide. *"Uwan, you still have power!"*

Stepping forward, the commander growled. "Move! Let's complete this mission and get off this cesspool of a world."

As if the planetary insult sparked a response, the ground trembled harder, knocking Geeja down. The troopers staggered as small pebbles dropped from the ceiling. Pointing forward, the senior officer yelled. "Run!" The shaking turned violent as a slab fell, smashing the entire company of black-clad Impercium soldiers.

Covered in dust, Geeja stood, mere inches from the huge hunk of rock now blocking the passage. She touched its surface as blood oozed from beneath, then communed with her world reverentially. *"Your power may be diminished, Uwan, but it is not gone. Thank you for saving our lives."*

Geeja heard hope in his response. *"WE are Uwan."*

"Yes, we are, my friend. I do not yet know how, but together we will fix the damage they have done." More immediate actions pushed forward in her mind. *"And as much as I would like to stay and plan with you, our mission starts with me hitching a ride away from this place before more trouble shows up. Thank you again."* Pausing for an extra second, Geeja patted the huge fallen stone. Her jaw set firm, repeating their affirmation aloud with the finality of an executioner. "WE ARE UWAN!"

Chapter Eight

Raflo primed and initiated the pulse engines on the *Phantom Star*, their unregistered Gravarian class cruiser. Custom-formulated black sensor-deflecting paint covered the spaceship's angular shape. Combining these avoidance techniques with Huanoc's electronic wizardry made her super stealthy, and these were only some of the many special features they integrated into her systems since acquiring her. He reflected on their motto: *If you can't outrun them, you better be invisible.* His thoughts turned. *Too bad she belongs to a 'friend' we met in prison.*

On the ground, Huanoc touched the screen that triggered the removal of the camouflaged bubble top that hid their secret ship in this open-roofed cavern. It took an extra minute to exit, but it also kept them safe from snooping eyes above.

Moving from the cockpit to the entry ramp, Raflo stared with narrow eyes, hyper focused on the tunnel opening into this nature-formed rock cavity. He whispered to himself as whiffs of the noxious outside atmosphere drifted down once the bulbous blast-resistant glass retracted above. "Come on, Gigi. Come on!"

Feeling the ground shake, Huanoc yelled as he ascended the ramp into the belly of the craft. "Go time!"

Standing at the top of the incline, Raflo pointed. "I told her we would wait until either her or Impercium troops exited that tube."

"Hrmph." Huanoc bumped him as he boarded.

"Hey, man." Raflo's arms splayed out as he regained his balance. "I gave her my word...besides, the ship is ready. We can be out of here in seconds, if need be."

The large man mumbled, but didn't waste any more words.

"Hurry up." Raflo spoke anxiously under his breath toward the tunnel exit, not wanting to anger his partner. "Get your pretty little self out here." A belch of dust, looking like a nasty planetary burp, spewed from the opening. His muscles tensed as his voice pitched higher and louder. "Huanoc...be ready!" Fearing the worst, he pulled a small Lighter from a holster mounted inside the door for just such emergencies. *I hate these things.* He recalled his reluctant basic training. *Point at the bad guys, then pull the trigger.*

As the dust settled, a single figure burst through the brown powdery haze. "Wait for me!"

"Gigi!" He waved to her. "You made it!"

From the cockpit, Huanoc grunted. "Good."

When Geeja's foot hit the bottom of the ramp, Raflo mashed the button to start the process of raising and locking it in place. He hugged her as soon as she reached the top. "I knew you were faster than a bunch of Impercium troopers!" His cheeks warmed. "I want all the details, but first we get out of here." He directed her to a seat with shoulder harnesses. "Buckle up!" Before their last belts were fully snapped, Raflo watched G-forces push Gigi down as the ship rocketed straight up from its hidden lair.

Seconds later, the force shifted as the craft zoomed forward, sending crushing pressure against their chests. More twists and turns pushed and pulled their bodies as Huanoc apparently took evasive actions in case they were being tracked. Ten minutes seemed a long time until he piloted the vessel in a straight line which soon took them past the atmosphere and into the darkness of space. Huanoc could be heard flipping switches, then he exited the semi-open cockpit, arms crossed. "Autopilot."

A surge of relief washed over Raflo as he took his time unbuckling his harness. "Wow." He stretched as he stood. "Impercium troopers..." He locked eyes with Huanoc. "What did we do to warrant those guys crashing our pad? We did our time, paid our debt to society...well *some* of it. Right?"

The big man met his question with a silent nod.

Raflo continued his stream of consciousness reasoning. "I mean, we're just a couple of small time smugg..." He cast a glance at Gigi as his lips tipped upward at the edges. "Like I said, we're just a couple of *businessmen*. We don't deal in arms...anymore. We're simply entrepreneurs in the import and export trade."

He noticed Gigi's grin as he paced in the middle of the cargo hold that doubled as a passenger bay, where ten jump seats lined the hull. *Kind of slipped up there...but, whatever. She seems smart. Would have figured us out soon enough.*

**

Geeja kept up a plastered smile, hoping to hide her shock at both their mode of travel and checkered pasts. *Ordinary smugglers have their own space ships? Even those who have been incarcerated? In my day, there were only twelve spaceships – one for each holy planet given to us by the Ancients.* Wide, curious eyes wandered around the craft, taking in the massive advances in technology. *I had to wear a space suit for launch in my time.*

A quick self-help talk ran in her head. *I need to act as if all this is normal, because apparently it is. I cannot blow my cover yet.* Her mind calmed, focusing on what she had just learned. *They are smugglers…totally fits. It also explains why he had crates full of women's clothing. He probably has more boxes of stolen lady's wear ready to be delivered to some middleman.*

She almost began another round of teasing them to hide her surprise at the ease of space travel, when her eyes sprang wide. Her jaw dropped as her gaze locked on a portside window. "What in the unholy name of Kelzedur is *that*?"

Raflo's easygoing vibe shifted in a breath. "What do you see? An Impercium star cruiser?"

Geeja and he both rushed to the side-by-side windows, her voice quivering. "No, no star cruiser." Though not completely sure what a star cruiser looked like, she knew it wasn't *this*. Her hand momentarily covered her mouth until she spoke again. "What is…*that*?"

"What are you talking about, Darlin?' I don't see anything."

Geeja's whole body trembled as she pressed her forehead against the clear window. Sobs shook her strong soldier's body. Between gasps, she forced out words. "What…is…that…giant…*thing*?"

"What?" Raflo's eyes narrowed and his brow scrunched. "Are you talking about the Terminus Stake?"

"That is what the thing is called, the Terminus Stake?" Saying the name of the awful object resembled sandpaper scraping the roof of her mouth. Geeja recalled Uwan's proclamation that a spike had been driven into his core the day of the invasion two thousand years ago, but she had no idea he spoke so literally. A gigantic metal cylinder extended from the planet's surface to the edge of space. With heart racing, she tried making sense of seeing something so horrible. Her vision blurred as she reached for Raflo, realizing she might pass out. She squeezed out a whisper. "I do not feel well."

Raflo eased her into a seat. "What's wrong, Sweetie?"

Taking deep breaths, Geeja grasped the meaning of Raflo's lack of discomfort with seeing that terrible nail piercing Uwan. *It has been here for so long that no one considers it out of the ordinary. That makes sense, but it is also the saddest thing I have learned since awakening.* Her lips tightened as she knew her acting skills would be put to the test. *I must pretend that disgusting thing is totally normal. Here goes.* "I…I have just never seen it from space, that is all." She wiped her damp cheeks. "I mean…it looks big from ground level, but seeing it like this?" Geeja sniffed. "Up here one really gets the full scope. Right?" *I hope I pulled that off, because I need to get a better handle on things before I reveal who I am.*

**

Raflo shot a suspicious look toward Huanoc and seeing thick raised eyebrows, he gave a small head bob. *Good, we're on the same page. She's hidin' somethin.'* Turning toward their female guest, he beamed his most comforting smile. "It's big alright." He gently touched her shoulder. "Hey, Gigi. Seems whatever you've been through still has a hold on you." Pointing, he tried to reassure her. "There's a bunk in the back. How about restin' for a few minutes while Huanoc and I figure out our next move?"

The young woman's eyes were wide, as if disoriented. "Yes. I think you are correct. I am not feeling like myself."

Showing her the way, he spread a blanket over her as she settled. "Get some rest."

Geeja gave a nod as she pulled the covering under her chin.

Walking to the front of the *Phantom Star*, he stood beside Huanoc with their backs to their passenger. Raflo stated the obvious. "Seems our muscular kitty is a hot commodity, on multiple levels."

"Hmm."

"You're absolutely right. We haven't smuggled anything that would warrant even a glance from Impercium troops in ages. And even the way we got out of prison wouldn't merit *those* kinds of troops. They weren't after us, they were after her."

With arms still crossed, Huanoc grunted a syllable. "Umph."

"I agree. There's money to be made here." Raflo glanced to the nearest window, seeing the Terminus Stake still in view. Its reflective silver skin topped by a transmission cone mounted just above the atmosphere's upper limit was as unchanging as the planet's sun. "That thing totally freaked her out. But why?"

He pondered what had transpired since they picked up Gigi on the side of the road, trying to divine the truth. He shrugged. "We need answers I don't have." Turning toward his partner, he stated a cold hard fact. "Most importantly, however, we need to figure the easiest way to collect without becoming squished like bleebles under Impercium boots…and do it without being sent back to prison."

Huanoc splurged with four words. "Still heading to Kaliega?"

Raflo nudged his giant sidekick. "That's right. Set course for the one place where businessmen like us can find answers."

Chapter Nine
Six Thousand Years Earlier

Sunlight pushed through the slats of Geeja's palace bedroom in the same way her insistent sleagle wouldn't stop until it made its way into her lap. Like the young pet, sunrise kept up its annoyance until it got its way. Waking with a smile, she saw the silhouette of Charl. Her heart warmed watching his chest rise and fall in a steady rhythm. After a few minutes she moved closer, then gently placed her hand on her consort's broad shoulder, speaking whispers meant only for the morning stillness. "These are the best days, the ones where you are strong and healthy. I will cherish them forever."

Leaving him asleep, she slid out of bed, her bare feet gliding over royal granite mined specifically for this room. Hundreds of years earlier the architect said its pink veining set against the stark white base color represented her feminine purity. Reaching the lavatory, she paused in front of the mirror. She liked all her vessels and the experiences each added to their whole, but she also found things unique that pleased her about each body. In addition to this singer's lilting song-bird voice, her dark-skinned form had the thickest, most luxurious long black hair she had ever experienced. She enjoyed it equally whether being brushed by an attendant, or when using it in foreplay with Charl. She finished her morning dressing rituals, as always, by connecting in silence with Uwan. ***"We are one with Uwan, and Uwan is one with us."*** A wave of warmth filled her as she continued. ***"Together, we live in peace and harmony."***

Before Uwan could respond, the morning serenity broke. A firm knock on the twelve-foot-tall doors echoed against the granite bedchamber walls. Geeja rolled her eyes. "Enter."

Lieutenant Vondretta strode in wearing her verdant green field uniform. The wide pant legs fluttered with her quick pace. The Sworn Warrior's apology didn't match the determined steps. "Sorry to intrude, Goddess, but there is an incident at the Archdale and West Vale border. Blood has been shed."

Geeja snapped her head toward the soldier. "Ready your guard. We leave in five minutes!"

Charl sprung out of bed as both women gave pleased grins. The well-built naked man fumbled for his tan trousers. "I'm going with you."

"That won't be necessary, sir." Vondretta always preferred keeping civilians to a minimum in the company of their leader. She claimed their presence complicated her main priority, the goddess' safety. "We have it covered."

"He's going with us." Of Geeja's many consorts over the prior thousand years, Charl had risen to the top of the list. All of them had been devoted to her, that being the key requirement of the honor, but Charl stood out. He was an easy conversationalist with impressive knowledge on subjects as diverse as horticulture and philosophy. It also didn't hurt that his touch sent shivers to all the right womanly places.

"Fine." Vondretta gave a clipped reply as her eyes moved from him toward Geeja. "Your will is my command."

Dressing quickly, Geeja and Charl arrived in short order at the stables, finding her dragon, Justice, and a mount for Charl at the ready. Geeja spoke as she gave a kick, signaling Justice to launch into the air. "We will be there in two hours."

Vondretta zipped beside her queen on her own magical beast, opening her mouth to speak, but evidently deciding to stay quiet.

Geeja knew they needed to get there as fast as possible if her subjects were killing each other. Every second mattered, and citizen's lives came first. Vondretta understood any objections would be swiftly dismissed. Once on the move an orion named Stottia was launched. Geeja sent the fastest bird on the planet telepathic instructions. *"Fly to the Archdale and West Vale border, then show me your eye."*

As they flew to the location an image from the orion flashed in Geeja's mind. She saw two medium sized forces backing away from each other with a few souls on the ground between them, either wounded or dead. She connected with her eye in the sky. *"Thank you for your service, Stottia. Please alert me if the two sides clash again."*

Seeing the forces no longer in active battle, Geeja's tense shoulders lowered. After a solid hour of flying, they came to the eastern branch of the Lo'Orion river, stopping for a few minutes to water the dragons. Geeja addressed Vondretta. "What do we know of the conflict?"

Holding the reins of Cleo loosely, the commander answered. "We have learned that Aurnode the Decent is commander of the Archdale forces and DeSandra Spoondrift leads West Vale."

"Hmm. Two capable leaders." Justice finished drinking and rubbed his muzzle against his master's arm as Geeja thought back through hundreds of years of memories of the two city-states. One source of tension surfaced regularly. "Are they feuding over water rights again?"

"That's what's reported."

Sighing, Geeja readied to remount Justice. "Makes sense. They signed the last treaty seventy-five years ago. They are due for a scuffle. Let us settle this quickly and keep the casualty count low." She pointed. "And that means getting there fast. All lives matter." With that, Geeja reined Justice toward the clear blue sky. In short order, she spied a red angular bird circling, and knew they were getting close.

Reaching the large plateau where the skirmish played out, Vondretta moved her dragon to the protective position in front of Geeja. "This way, Goddess."

Two armed groups of soldiers, at least five hundred on each side in either red or green uniforms, remained separated since their initial clash. They shouted warnings at each other. Medics on the red side tended a female soldier bleeding from a wound just under her knee.

A man from the green army bellowed. "Yield, or we attack again!"

A sword raised aloft accompanied the red's response. "We will kill you all! Stay off our land."

Geeja's party touched down a safe distance away, then dismounted. She strode into the gap between the angry troops flanked by her personal guard, plus Charl. Her traditional forest-green silk gown shimmered in the light breeze as she seized the initiative with this vessel's alto lilt floating above the bravado. "Honorable warriors! Let us find harmony and peace amongst fellow Uwanians!"

The Goddess Awakens

As she moved to the center of the conflict, she casually wiggled her fingers. Dormant lillion flowers bloomed to each side, creating a sweet-scented violet pathway. The level of grumbling on opposing sides lowered. "Commanders." Her eyes went to each force's leaders. "Join me in parley." Her voice carried more than a thousand years of authority, so despite any misgivings, a man moved from the red side as a woman came forward to represent the greens. Standing between them she questioned. "What is the reason that fellow citizens quarrel on such a beautiful day?"

Aurnode, the Archdale man wearing a red coat with white cape, snarled. "Those West Vale dogs are thieves!"

"We are not stealing." DeSandra, who sported a green commander's uniform with double-breasted bronze buttons on her wool jacket, snapped back. "We're simply utilizing a natural resource for the good of our people."

"Goddess!" Spittle flew from the mouth of the light-skinned Archdale officer, his face now nearly matching the red shade of his tunic. "They have dammed the Lo'Orion river! That is theft under the law, and a sin against Uwan!"

Geeja gasped. She had expected a diversion of the precious resource, not an act so much bolder. Damming the flow of any river marked a major escalation. The Lo'Orion being *the* most sacred made this astounding. Everyone considered it so holy because the spring at the source of its main branch is where the Ancients first brought human life to this world. On top of that, the goddess' home town hugged its banks, making it doubly revered. She spoke wide-eyed. "Is this true?"

DeSandra stood tall, chin held high. "Our people desire peace and prosperity. This is but a temporary situation as near normal flows will continue downstream once our reservoir is full."

"See!" The red of Aurnode's face deepened to crimson, matching the shade of a ripened rind of a lush melon. "Archdale speaks truth to the greed and sin of West Vale."

Geeja's wide eyes bulged further. "Why? Why would West Vale do such a thing?"

DeSandra leaned forward. "We have been experimenting and think we've found a way to generate lightning, as you can, Goddess. However, it requires the power of falling water. We seek to control our destiny, just as you do."

Aurnode pulled his sword from its scabbard. "Add blasphemy to the charges! She is not a goddess like you! The judgment must surely be death!"

With lips pressed tight, Geeja turned back toward DeSandra, withholding her final decision until she got to the root of this rebellion against neighbor and nature. Her gaze narrowed. "I wish happiness and prosperity for all citizens, but what you are doing takes life-giving water from fellow Uwanians, and it disrupts the river's natural course."

The sergeant-at-arms for DeSandra stepped beside her holding some kind of brass horn with a wooden handle. He kept the bell pointed at Aurnode as his commander responded. "Times are changing, Goddess. The people of West Vale want better lives for their children and their children's children. We are taking control of our own destiny."

With that declaration tension seemed to grow from all corners. Lieutenant Vondretta made a sharp downward movement with her right arm, signaling the goddess' personal detail to close ranks around her. They then put their hands on the hilts of their swords.

Aurnode's outrage seemed to overtake his control. Sunlight reflected from his blade as he raised it overhead, then ran toward DeSandra. A war cry launched from his depths. "Blasphemer!"

With the goddess's guards focused on her protection, Charl stepped between the two leaders trying to prevent bloodshed. "Halt, man, before you do something you will regret!"

A sound like compressed thunder roared in the clearing, louder than any Geeja had ever heard. The wooden-handled metal horn had been the source of the explosion, and now pungent smoke hung in the wake of the blast.

Charl screamed like a wounded plexur beast, reaching for his back as he fell to the ground. For a moment, everyone stood in stunned silence trying to understand what happened. Geeja ran to Charl's side, seeing his shirt shredded with his flesh blackened and flayed. It seemed as if hundreds of tiny hot coals had somehow been shoved through his clothing, then continued deep under his skin. Confused, she called out. "He needs the healer. Now!"

Charl breathed in ragged gasps as he lay face down on soft grass, his voice raspy. "Please! Do not let me die!"

Blood oozed from every prick in her consort's injured body. Righteous rage rose from Geeja's core like the magma of Mt. Mendesan. Her angry stare found its target. "DeSandra! What did your man do?"

The West Vale leader's eyes had gone from narrow determination to round distress. "I did not order this, Goddess. I swear on the Twelve Holy Worlds. He will be dealt with firmly. You have my word." She and her entire army scrambled backwards, away from the scene of the confrontation. All the haughtiness of moments ago bled away, replaced by anxious words. "We meant no harm to you or any of your entourage."

The healer, Nocasia, delivered grave news. "I am so sorry, Goddess."

Geeja turned toward Charl's fallen body. "No!" She dropped to her knees then placed her hands on him, sending soft energy through his corpse. "This cannot be happening! I can save him!"

Nocasia rested a hand on Geeja's. "I have never seen wounds such as these, Holiness. This vessel cannot be saved, even by you."

"Then we take him to a healing bed. Uwan can save him!"

Lowering her shaking head, Nocasia spoke just above a mournful whisper. "There are limits to even that power, but we can rest in the knowledge that Charl's journey is just beginning. His soul rejoins Uwan this day."

Geeja's head fell back. Her personal war cry filled the air, causing even those in her own guard to take a step away. Rising, she saw the entire West Vale contingent in full retreat. Tensing, she connected with Uwan, demanding raw energy. *"Fill me!"* It would take several seconds for her to gather the force from Uwan that she would need to pronounce her verdict, giving everyone around her more time to step back further.

Uwan pleaded. *"Please! Do not do this in anger."*

Rage swelled within. *"Do not withhold your power."* She could feel Uwan's conflict, but in the end, he gave her what she asked.

Now aglow with more blue energy than she ever held at one time, Geeja raised her arms toward the troops running for their lives. With all ten digits splayed like the claws of a gleeger, she pronounced judgment. "You have been accused of blasphemy, greed and murder!" As if attempting to inhale all the oxygen on the plateau, she filled her lungs. "I find you *all* guilty, on *every* count!" Directed energy sprang from her fingertips like jagged lightning, racing across the verdant plain. The bolts of erratic light ran between the soldiers in the West Vale regiment.

In a flash, five hundred Uwanian citizen soldiers lay dead with eyes burned out, many with arms and legs severed and blasted yards away. The charred bodies smoldered as the smell of burned flesh rode the breeze, mixing in a putrid combination with the scent from the flowers that bloomed moments earlier.

Aurnode's red cheeks of seconds ago faded to chalky white. He knelt as words of reverence, or fear…maybe both, were spoken just above a whisper. "Justice has been served."

Geeja surveyed the desolation she wrought as her arms gradually lowered. Her countenance darkened as she spoke in a deep growl. "Technology, like that strange weapon that killed Charl, invites a disproportionate response."

The harnessing of large amounts of power, as Geeja had just unleashed, always took a toll. In a controlled descent, the goddess fell scissor style, landing with legs crossed, her hands on her knees. After a few deep breaths, she reached again to Uwan, beginning with her standard greeting. *"We are one with Uwan, and Uwan is one with us."* In place of the normal warmth of connection, she experienced a void. She didn't mean her next words in this moment, but she continued. *"Together, we live in peace and harmony."*

Not a single person dared to speak, leaving her in silent, gruesome reflection. Charl's lifeless corpse filled her mind. *This one was special…I loved him.* Loss and anger swirled in a toxic brew named vengeance…yet that emotion quickly faded when the realization of what she had wrought upon so many of her own people sunk in.

Waiting in silence for a response from Uwan, she replayed her actions. Closing her eyes, Geeja saw everything in excruciating clarity, as if experiencing the event in a slow-motion rerun. She saw every combatant's face as her rage smashed into their defenseless bodies. She flinched at her merciless judgment. Like an over-carbonated bottle of grum, the contents of her stomach spewed, leaving splatters on her gown.

Between the residual effect of channeling such massive power and the clashes of her conflicting feelings, her head throbbed as if being used in place of a hammer drum in a parade. Bowing, drool dripped from her mouth as she babbled. "I will rip every bit of banned technology from the entire planet."

Uwan remained silent.

The stench of burning bodies thickened as exhaustion pressed into every fiber of her being. While no one uttered a single syllable, she could hear several around her also retching from the sight and odor of hundreds of soldiers burned to a crisp. A vortex of emotions churned between the anger over Charl's murder, and her killing of so many in response. Geeja wailed, giving voice to her agony. She sobbed, tearing her clothing as a sign of her shredded heart, then beat her breast with her fist before falling face forward, landing in her own vomit.

With her head against the ground, Geeja banged both fists into the moist, fertile soil. When totally exhausted, she raised her head, filling the air with a ragged scream. "Why?"

Either no one had an answer or they lacked the courage to speak up…probably both. Not even the birds dared chirp. All left Geeja alone in her heartache.

When her tears finally subsided, Uwan ended his silence. *"Let us talk."*

She sat with sagging shoulders, slobber dripping from the corners of her mouth. **"What is left to say? They murdered Charl, then I pushed you into giving me power, which I turned against our people."**

"Hmm." A long pause stretched until the last of the fires that consumed the soldiers winked out. ***"Then we both fell short of the holy vows you spoke so many years ago."***

"Vows?" Her words were flat, smashed by her grief. ***"I broke more than half of them in a fit of rage. What sort of holy being does that make me?"***

Uwan did not hesitate. ***"One who is flawed, but aims to always improve. One who feels joy as well as agony. One who will surely learn from this incident for the betterment of future generations of our people."***

Geeja's gaze went to the smoldering corpses, again scanning the carnage she wrought. Tears welled again from a seemingly endless source. In her pain, she mumbled the seven pledges she spoke on the day of her ascension. "A planet is holy, and as goddess, you are its voice. A goddess will always do what is best for her planet, not herself. A goddess shall not murder. A goddess shall not lie except to protect the life of her planet. A goddess shall not enslave any humanoid beings. All who live under a goddess' rein shall have the right of free expression. No technology may be allowed that harms the planet, regardless of the help it may be to the people."

When Geeja finished, her heart ached, completely broken. ***"I am sorry, Uwan. My failure today was catastrophic."*** She sniffed. ***"From this moment forward, I must be better."***

"Remember Geeja, you are neither perfect, nor alone. We are one and we will strive together."

Chapter Ten

Raflo spent the past hour staring at the ceiling of the *Phantom Star*, thinking in silence. During that time, he reviewed the puzzle pieces of their guest, turning each one in his mind as he tried to discern the bigger picture. He faced a conundrum of how to reconcile finding a sick woman on the side of the road, claiming amnesia, with a raid by Impercium soldiers. Then, throw in the fact that when they found her, she wore an ancient Uwan uniform of extraordinary value. Nothing made sense. *Very interestin' indeed.*

Three theories gradually formed, each with reasons to believe, but also with their own set of doubts. The first he articulated yesterday. 'She's a runaway from a denier colony.' The pros began with proximity; they came upon her just a few miles from the Truth in Geeja Retreat. *Gigi's a thief who discovered the group had a secret ancient relic from olden times. She puts it on, then someone sees her. Escapin' without a breathin' apparatus, she succumbs to the toxic air just before we fly by.*

The simplicity made this hypothesis appealing, but certain things didn't fit. *Secrets like that can't be kept for centuries, especially with an emperor who's rumored to have spies in those places. On top of that, her shock at seein' the Terminus Stake appeared real, regardless of her attempt to cover it up. But I do like thinkin' of* her as a thief. She could bring a new set of skills to our little operation. "Hmm."

He rolled his shoulders, then considered a second idea. This version also featured Gigi as a thief, but this time as a master burglar. *Djurga has been stuck on all things Uwan since the beginnin.' He even comes here personally once a decade to rub our face in our disgraceful state of existence. His henchmen must have discovered that uniform forever ago and he's kept it a part of his private museum. Our girl boosts it and brings it back here where it belongs, except she's barely one step ahead of the long arm of the empire and comes unprepared. She ends up desperate on the side of the road.*

His smile spread thinking of Gigi as robber supreme. *I could be in the presence of an empresario of criminality, but...* He glanced toward the resting woman. *I don't buy that amnesia thing for a minute, and besides, she hasn't asked for that uniform back. If she stole it for the money, both she and it would be long gone by now.*

Raflo sighed before considering a third hypothesis. It seemed the most bizarre of all. *What if she really is the awakened Goddess of Uwan?* Without thought, his head shook. *The goddess died, if she was ever real. Everyone, except those deniers, knows that.* But try as he might, he couldn't discard the idea out of hand; it answered too many questions. *If she had been in hibernation or somethin,' that would explain the amnesia thing.* He rubbed his chin. *And it would also explain where she got the uniform. Some say even Djurga thinks she did one of those transference things at the last minute. And if she just woke up, it also explains why she was out in the open without a breather.* He ran his fingers through his curls. *The only problem with that explanation is that it's impossible. I don't believe a goddess could stay hidden all that time, then show up two thousand years later layin' on the side of the road waitin' to be picked up by a couple of guys like us.*

Huanoc called from the cockpit. "Listen."

Raflo shuffled to the front. "What's up?"

Touching one of the screens, Huanoc repeated. "Listen."

An audio transmission played over the speakers. 'Smugglers Raflo Duo and Huanoc D'Nafp are wanted for questioning in the ambush and murder of Impercium troopers this morning. If seen, do not approach. Consider them armed and dangerous. Contact local authorities, or the Impercium directly via our app for reward information.'

Raflo shot a quick glance toward the rear of the craft, seeing Gigi resting, then turned his attention back to his partner. He voiced wonder. "Our cute guest took out a bunch of Impercium troopers? Single handed? Without a weapon?"

Huanoc stared at the blanket-covered woman. "Hmm."

"Hmm, indeed." Raflo tapped his chin. "Think this twist will change our meetin' with Shuggilar? I mean he did contact us with a new job that will pay more than enough to cover that crystal recharge bill we skipped out on. What are the odds he just takes us captive, then turns us over for the reward?"

Huanoc remained quiet, his forehead wrinkled in concentration.

Raflo broke the silence. "Can you think of any other places where we won't *automatically* be handed to the Impercium for that price on our heads?"

Huanoc blurted an instant reply. "No."

"Yeah, and at least Shuggy has a job he wants done that might be worth more than the reward." Another thread spooled from Raflo's thinking. "It's interestin' that we're wanted, but there's no mention of our little lady back there. What do you think that's about?"

"Hmm."

"You're right. Definitely suspicious." Raflo patted his friend's shoulder. "Let's hope we can find some answers in Odallisdad."

**

Emperor Djurga waved, giving permission for General Scanda to enter his presence. "This better be good news after that debacle in the tunnels of Uwan earlier today."

The senior officer bowed, then stood with shoulders straight. The medals on the left side of his chest reflecting the bright light directed toward the interrogation circle a few feet in front of the emperor's throne atop the three-tiered dais. "Yes, Your Excellency. A ship matching the description of the scum believed to be sheltering that woman has been spotted. They're headed to the pirate city of Odallisdad, in the forested area of Kaliega."

"Gooood." The emperor drew out the word with a crooked smile. "What do we know of these so-called scum, and how soon until the goddess is in our custody?"

"The two aiding her are small time criminals who have previously been in our prison system." Scanda's voice trembled. "In fact, they should still be there, but somehow they gained early release." His face pinched as he snatched a quick breath through his nose. "I have an investigation started on the circumstances of their unusual…luck. I can assure you they won't be so fortunate next time."

"And the goddess?"

Scanda's neck craned straight up to directly address the emperor, his eyes bouncing between the red rubies and yellow spheres. They were embedded in the massive throne on which the leader sat, representing the twin suns around which Emblaka orbited. "A squadron is almost in position. We should have the goddess ready for transport here within the hour."

"I want her brought to me immediately upon capture. Have I made myself clear?"

"Yes! Yes, Your Excellency! As you say, so it shall be done."

The ancient ruler waved his unnaturally smooth-skinned hand again. "Be gone from my sight."

Scanda bowed deeply once more, then spun one hundred and eighty degrees, scurrying away like a kackering bug suddenly exposed to light.

Djurga leaned back in the elaborately bedecked chair, then folded his hands over his waist. *The bad blood between the goddess and myself didn't have to end this way. But, because of her arrogance, it must.*

**

Jacastra raced into the domed desert prayer garden finding their ancient leader on her knees, deep in meditation. "Holy Mother!"

Startling, the elderly woman broke her spiritual deliberation. Wide eyes reset to normal, as if returning from a mental journey to some distant place. She spoke in measured tones. "You have news, my child?"

Catching her breath, Jacastra replied. "I do, Holy Mother." Her mind raced, but she tried, only slightly successfully, to match her leader's calm demeanor. "Impercium troops executed a raid this morning, here, on Uwan. A roof collapse in a tunnel killed them all!"

"Help me up, Warrior!" Urgency replaced her contemplative tone. "The fullness of time is at hand! The Goddess of Uwan is alive and with us!"

"Your visions are true? You are certain?"

The old woman vibrated with excitement. "Yes! I'm certain!"

Jacastra's strong hands helped the Holy Mother to her feet with resolve overcoming her exhilaration. "There's more, Your Holiness. Our spies tell us that a ship blasted off just a few miles away, and is now being tracked by the Impercium to Odallisdad, on Kaliega."

The Holy Mother stood taller. "That means the goddess must be on that vessel. She is alive, but hunted! We must render help."

"But how. We have no ships to travel to other worlds. We're forbidden to use advanced technology." Jacastra understood the strict interpretation of the goddess' precepts, but challenges like these made her sometimes question the ancient ways.

Grabbing her staff, the Holy Mother headed back to the temple. "There are exceptions. Contact Talla Ignestilsen."

Jacastra stammered. "But you banished her from our order. Would she help us? Could we trust her?"

"We have units to spend and she has a spacecraft. Her greed is what got her excommunicated in the first place. It's our best chance to beat the Impercium to Odallisdad, unless you know of another way." Aged eyes flashed as hard as granite. "Do you?"

"No, Your Holiness."

"Then assemble your brigade and get there ahead of the emperor's forces." The old woman radiated certainty. "With righteousness guiding us, we cannot be defeated!"

Chapter Eleven

Galloping hard on her horse at the head of the battalion, Jacastra mulled her situation. Despite her occasional wish that their Order would loosen the rules around technology, she understood the reason they were in place. After all, Emperor Djurga's tech turned the universe upside down…and brought about Uwan's devastation. However, all these years later, different interpretations were held by similar groups as to where to draw the line. The most liberal among them even allowed adherents to carry personal communication devices, while their sect remained among the strictest in limiting the use of machines. Her mind dwelled on that as they galloped toward their destination. *Talla's going to flip out when she sees me. If I had a PCD, I could have called ahead.*

Secretly, Jacastra's stomach fluttered, excited by what would happen if she could prove successful in this negotiation. She would have the chance to see Uwan from space, then travel to another world. *Is it a sin to be thrilled by this opportunity?*

Before that question could become relevant, Jacastra would need to gain the cooperation of Talla Ignestilsen. Riding hard, she spied the compound of a woman with whom she had once been friends. She muttered a prayer as she leaped from her mount. "May the goddess bless our efforts."

While not utilizing machines within their own retreat, Jacastra had a basic understanding of how the world worked. After all, she had taken over as the main liaison with the outside world when Talla had been kicked out. The position exposed her to things like the automated system mounted on the gate. She shook the tension from her arms, then pushed the red button as she stood in front of the camera. *This better work.* She cleared her throat as if being a nervous plebe about to start oral exams at the academy. "Hello Talla, bet I'm the last person you would expect to show up on your doorstep."

There was no reply, so after half-a-minute or so, a mild curse slipped from Jacastra's lips. "By the hairy balls of a fat man, she's not even here."

A giggled response bounced through the speaker. "Sister, sister. What would the Holy Mother say if she could hear you now?"

Jacastra's cheeks warmed. "I would probably be on floor scrubbing duty for a week." A cheery grin formed. "But it would be worth it just to have heard your voice again."

"That's so sweet." Talla must have surveyed the entire squadron. "But, by the looks of your crew I know this isn't a social call."

"No, this is business. Important business."

A buzzing sound accompanied the opening of the gate as Talla gave directions. "Intriguing! I'll have my old man take care of the horses while you and the girls get out of that polluted soup we call air."

"Old man?" *I don't know why I'm shocked she's in a relationship. I mean, she left the Order eight years ago.* The celibacy requirement for goddess warriors had always been another of the rules that Jacastra would like to see loosened. "Then both of us have news to share."

A thick-chested, dark-skinned man with tight curly hair met them as they entered her old friend's apparent combination business location and home. His easy manner around the animals and friendly greeting triggered admiring smiles from all the women in her retinue. He gave a right-sided head toss as both hands were filled with the reins of their steeds. "Ladies, you'll find Talla through that door."

Jacastra's second, Esbatique, gave a breezy assessment as the group walked toward the house. "He's sure easy on the eyes."

Snickers mingled with muffled, "Praise be to the goddess," from the other women.

When the door opened, something else unexpected bounded toward them. A young child with deep-brown bouncing curls rushed out, squealing in obvious happiness. "You're mommy's friends!" When the girl reached Jacastra, she wrapped her arms around the stunned woman's legs.

Dumbfounded, Jacastra patted the top of the youth's head awkwardly as Talla trailed behind the energetic toddler. Jacastra's voice wavered as she stood still in the leg embrace. "Yes. Yes we are. Seems your mother is full of surprises."

Reaching the group, Talla beamed as she made introductions. "Everyone, this is Matly, our pride and joy."

With years of sparse exposure to children, Jacastra repeated the flat-handed head pat as if touching a prickly spongo melon for the first time. "Nice to meet you, Matly."

Talla scooped her cute offspring up and onto her hip as she greeted her former battalion mates. "Come inside." Her green eyes, the ones that always stood out when wearing matching silk formal attire at the academy, danced around the team. "Even though you didn't need breathers today, from the dust you've sucked in, I would say a glass of cold water might be welcome."

"Yes." Jacastra's nerves sizzled under the surface, excited about reconnecting with her old friend. With these new twists her emotions were even more off balance, but in a good way. Throwing decorum to the wind, she stepped forward, hugging Talla and Matly. "I'm so glad to see you again, and to witness your happiness."

A few joyful tears spilled down Talla's cheeks as she responded to the embrace. "We're on different paths now, but you will always be my sister." Matly wiggled as Talla lowered the active young girl to the ground, then waved. "This way to the kitchen."

During the short walk, Jacastra's eyes darted between one modern device to the next. Screens with moving images were everywhere; some very small and others massive. She watched with fascination as Matly picked up a controller and switched views on one of the large displays, then danced along with moving cartoon images. It occurred to her that in many ways, this pre-school child knew more about functioning in the modern world than she did.

Opening a kitchen cabinet, Talla easily reached the top shelve glasses without even going up on her toes. With thirteen matching elegant pieces of stemware retrieved, the tall woman set to filling them with chilled water for her parched guests, then crossed her arms. "I know you didn't ride all the way here for a social visit, although you surely must realize I would love that. What brings you to my humble abode?"

Setting the translucent blue water glass on the counter, Jacastra got right to the point. "We need to get to the city of Odallisdad, on the planet Kaliega, as fast as possible. Like leave within the hour."

Jaw dropping shock registered on Talla's face. "Academy girls wanting to travel off-world? I know things are tough on Uwan these days, but I didn't know these were the end times." Her brow creased. "Seriously, why are you really here?"

Esbatique leaned close, speaking to Jacastra in a loud whisper. "This is a waste of time. She turned her back on us once. She'll not help us now."

Talla glared. "This is a messed-up world, but last time I checked, women still have the choice to live how they wish!"

"Whoa, Talla." Jacastra shot a sharp glance toward Esbatique, her hard charging, but less experienced junior officer, then turned back to Talla. "Emotions are running high for women of the Order." She moved closer to her former friend and reached for her hand. "You see, it's not end times." A smile that began in her burning heart now graced Jacastra's face. "It the fullness of time."

Talla's spine stiffened, and the tall woman loomed over them all, responding with a shadow cloaking her words. "What do you mean, 'It's the fullness of time?'"

"It's her." Jacastra squeezed the hand she still held, noticing moisture. "The goddess has returned…and you are here to witness it."

Talla looked down with a tight-eyed stare. "That's a bold statement. There have been hoaxes before. What evidence do you have, and what does it have to do with traveling to Odallisdad?"

"Impercium troops were sent here today, and now they're dead. This is real, Talla." Jacastra needed to move things along, so she went to her best argument. "We have units and you have a ship. We're not asking for charity, we can pay." Jacastra saw her friend's tight eyes loosen at the mention of payment. "Get us out of here within the hour and I'll tell you everything on the way."

"There and back, that's it?"

"We'll need some time on the ground of course, but yes. There and back…but only if we hurry."

"Is the trip worth two thousand units?"

Jacastra feigned shock. The sum proved to be lower than she expected, but she expressed the opposite view. She might not be technologically experienced, but she knew human nature. Talla needed to feel like she won this negotiation by getting paid handsomely. "Two thousand units? You've got to be kidding!"

"Look. You're the one waltzing in asking me to leave my family at a moment's notice." Talla glanced toward Matly. "It needs to be worth my time, and besides, who else will understand the needs of academy women traveling into space better than me?"

Jacastra paused as she looked away for a moment, selling the drama, then turned back. She held her gaze, pretending to waver on whether to accept the deal. Eyes locked, she knew that money had always been important to Talla, but the pilot also made a good point about working for technologically greenhorn women. It would be a fair deal to both sides. It was time to do business. She answered in a whisper. "Fine. There will be a spiritual reward as well…but yes, we can pay two thousand units."

The thrill of bargaining seemed to sweep over Talla's smiling face. "Glad to be getting paid…and to be working with my old friends again."

Chapter Twelve

As the *Phantom Star* approached Kaliega, Raflo and Huanoc were on edge. Memories of the beatings he suffered during Impercium incarceration put Raflo in a foul mood. His technologically advanced eye twitched, just thinking of the pain he endured during its forced implementation. "Let's land in that clearin' beside the park we used on the Eltzen job. We'll activate cloakin', so no one will even know we're here. Then we'll walk into the city, keepin' a low profile until we see if everything is cool."

"Hmm." Huanoc grunted agreement.

Geeja approached, just waking from her nap. "Almost there?"

"Slight change of plan, Cupcake." Raflo spoke in clipped words. "Seems your escape at our compound put me and Huanoc back on the Impercium's radar."

"What?" Geeja's quick reply seemed to leap from her soul.

"Well, Darlin', when a battalion of Impercium soldiers is killed it doesn't go unnoticed." Uncertain of her true identity, Raflo kept his cards close. He thought about just coming out and asking who she was, but knew that would likely involve a long conversation, no matter what answer she gave. He itched to have that discussion, just not now. Time not being on their side, he snapped.

"Somethin's goin' on, somethin' big. Until we figure it out, we'll make the decisions. Got it?"

She backed away with hands raised. "Oookay. I guess I will just stay out of the way and let you gentlemen do your thing…whatever that is."

Huanoc spoke from the cockpit as the *Phantom Star* made a soft touchdown. "Cloaking on."

Raflo looked out a porthole window seeing a wall of trees between the ship and a grassy park on the other side. Green leaves fluttered, and not for the first time, he silently questioned why he continued living on Uwan when a beautiful planet like this existed not so far away. The answer was simple. *There's less chance of Impercium involvement on our pitiful world.* He turned to Geeja, pointing his finger. "The ship is hidden from view and we're on the outskirts of the city. If you stay onboard and out of sight, you should be safe. Am I clear?"

Both hands raised again. "Whatever you say."

Raflo touched the red button at the top of the ramp, lowering it to the grass below. Mostly fresh air swept upward, filling the entire ship. He breathed deeply, not needing to filter it through a mask. He glanced toward Geeja once more. "We should be back in an hour, so don't get any ideas about goin' out."

"Do not worry about me. I will be right here."

Huanoc followed Raflo, then touched the button at the bottom to raise the ramp to the closed position.

**

When the ship resealed, Geeja went to a window where she watched the two men walk away. They headed for the line of pashel trees, a species that once grew on Uwan. In the light breeze, tapered leaves showed their silvery bottoms. Soon Raflo and

Huanoc were completely out of sight, and seeing so much greenery made her heart both mourn and sing.

She grieved the stark contrast between this view and what she saw on her home world. It made the level of damage done to Uwan that much clearer. However, the beauty she saw cheered her, stoking her desire to restore her planet back to its once pristine condition.

Another thing seemed clear. No way would she stay locked up on this spacecraft when a world of green awaited on the other side of this glass. Raflo's warning to stay inside came to mind. "I have not let anyone, man or woman, boss me around like that since…" She thought hard, then shrugged. "I cannot even remember how long." Strolling over, she pressed the same red button they had, lowering the ramp.

Clean air, or at least cleaner than on Uwan, rushed in. Geeja inhaled greedily. "This is what a planet is supposed to smell like." Reaching the bottom, she stepped on soft green grass, then fell to her knees. Her hands ran through the supple blades and her heart pounded as if it would explode in joy. "Wonderful nature still exists."

Bowing until her forehead touched the ground, her mood turned wistful. "This is my wish for Uwan…to be returned to his natural state."

Rising, she walked from under the shadow of the ship, then into bright sunlight. Turning back, Geeja saw nothing except the trees on the other side of the clearing. She gasped. "Where did the ship go!" Her hand went to her mouth while recalling Raflo's words about cloaking. "Oh…wow. So much technology."

Geeja shook her head, then walked toward the clearing. Along the way she caught unfamiliar floral scents, and purple flowers a few feet away seemed the likely source. A leisurely stroll brought her to them quickly. Bending, she inhaled a pleasing, complex aroma. "I will introduce these to Uwan when he is restored."

During her rein, Kaliega ranked among the least important planets near Uwan. It certainly wasn't a Holy Planet, and as far as she knew, it hadn't become sentient. As Geeja thought more, she realized this visit represented her first time on the small world. *A good first impression.* Looking around, she saw children of all ages playing in the adjacent park under the watchful eye of adults. Looking closely, she saw that Kaliegans were a tall, wiry type of humanoid. Studying them, she saw that their legs appeared longer than hers, relative to their body size. For a first-time visitor, it seemed their most distinguishing feature. Seeing several of them running, they looked very fast. They also had hair as orange as the rind of a flame melon, which most wore in a long, straight style. When they ran it flowed behind them as if ablaze, making them appear even swifter.

Geeja sat to observe, as well as bathe in the pale-yellow glow of their single sun. Her very core rejoiced. Without conscious thought, her mind did what it had done for thousands of years; it reached out to commune with the planet. **"We exist to serve Uwan…we are one with Uwan…we exist to serve Uwan…we are one with Uwan…"**

"Who is Uwan?" A soprano female voice rang urgently in Geeja's head. **"Who is 'We?'"**

Moments before, Geeja relaxed in a meditative mood. Now her eyes blasted open as if roughly wakened from a dream, frantically searching for the source of the voice. She spoke low in response as she shot quick stares around her surroundings. **"Uh, Uwan is the place where I come from."** The only movements she could detect were from the people she had been observing. **"And we are called Geeja."** Remaining as still as possible, she asked a question. **"Who are you?"**

A torrent of rapid-fire words sounded in her mind. *"I am, well I don't know who I am. You're the first...I don't know what you are...that I've been able to connect with. I've heard other voices but they don't seem to hear me. What's a planet? Are you still there? Talk to me, please!"*

In a flash, Geeja understood she connected with *this* planet. In a rush of memory, she recalled her first connection with Uwan. It had been in a green field like this on a similar sunny day, but one huge difference stood out. Young people all around Uwan had been tested for sensitivity to receiving planetary signals by a team of Ancients. Up until that day, there seemed nothing special about Geeja. As the daughter of a farming couple, she lived in a small agricultural village. Though smart, her intelligence had never been measured. That would have been difficult, since at the time her parents hadn't bothered to send her to school. She couldn't read or write. No, she became a goddess because she was born with the natural ability to easily connect with a living planet. Nothing more, nothing less.

Sure, over time, through thousands of lives, she learned the importance of her role and became a leader for her people. But on Anointing Day, she stood as an unassuming backwoods sixteen-year-old simpleton. Then, in a grassy field, surrounded by family and the entire population of the village, one of the Ancients touched a hand to the ground before using her other to hold one of Geeja's.

A surge of energy entered her body that day, like nothing she had ever experienced. It didn't hurt. It simply overwhelmed her in its intensity, like standing under a narrow waterfall and trying to drink every drop. Then, as if by magic she could suddenly commune with Uwan.

"Who are you?" Uwan's first words were almost the same as Kaliega just spoke.

That realization broke her mental trip to so long ago. This was evidently the first conversation for this young planet. Chill bumps raised on Geeja's arms, due to the unexpectedness of the event, and because it had been tens of thousands of years since she had that first conversation with Uwan. *Wow. I never dreamed I would be doing this again.* She inhaled deeply and centered herself. *Here goes.* She took another breath. **"Like I said, I am Geeja. I am so glad to meet you!"**

"Yes! I'm not alone!" Like an unrelenting wind, the planet continued. **"I'm glad to meet you, Geeja! Who am I? Where have you been? Are you and I the only two? I have so many questions!"**

In the time before the Anointing, the Ancients taught her meditation skills in preparation for the big day. Those lessons were swamped by the moment, but both Uwan and Geeja survived and thrived. Although not having done this in a long time, she had so much more life experience now. Though excited to be part of this seminal moment, her mind calmed. **"You are called Kaliega."** She paused. **"That is your name."**

Silence reigned for a moment, then came a shaky response. **"Kaliega?"** A stillness settled between them as this world seemed to process the information. **"My name is Kaliega. Did I say it right?"**

"Yes. Your pronunciation was perfect."

A declaration followed an excited squeal. **"I am Kaliega!"**

Somehow the formal name didn't jibe with the youthful planet, so Geeja improvised. **"Would you like to have two names? One for special occasions and one just between friends? That is what I do, and it works great."**

"Yes, yes! I want to be like you! Give me another name, too!"

Geeja mused aloud. "So eager...just like Uwan and I." The biggest grin she could remember stretched across her face. *"Okay! Now this should be a name you choose, so if you do not like it, we can pick another."*

"I can't wait! Tell me!"

"How about Kalli? It is a shortened version of your full name, and I think it sounds more fun, like you seem. What do you think?"

"Kalli." The planet spoke slowly, as if rolling the syllables through a mouth it didn't possess. This time, she said it more forcefully. *"Kalli."* Then came the third test. *"Kalli!"* She delivered the verdict with verve. *"I love it! Geeja, you are so smart."*

Geeja blushed, thinking of all the mistakes she had made, the biggest being how she misjudged Djurga. *"I know a lot, Kalli, but I am not perfect. Just like you, my education continues."*

"Mine has just begun! Can we talk forever?"

Things with Kalli had moved fast, and Geeja hadn't stopped to think that she would be leaving soon. Her heart broke knowing she had given this living world first contact, only to fly away on a spaceship. It seemed cruel, but she couldn't stay here; she had to save Uwan. "Another mistake. I'm definitely not perfect." Her shoulders sagged, knowing she needed to come clean. *"So, Kalli. Uh, I wish I could, but like I mentioned earlier, I am not from here. I am from Uwan, and my home planet is sick and needs my help. I will have to leave very soon."*

If planets could cry, this one sounded like it. *"But...but I'll be all alone again! It was one thing when I didn't know I could have more, but now? Now I know what I'm missing."* The pitiful voice turned sour. *"I wish you had never come to me!"*

"Yes. You are right." Geeja sniffed, knowing the pain she inadvertently caused. *"You deserve better than what I did. You deserve a permanent partner, like I am for Uwan."*

"Is that possible? Could there be someone here for me?"

Geeja thought back to her introduction to Uwan. There had been a limited connection before, but the Ancients helped her with the first true contact, and from there it seemed predestined. *"I do not want to get your expectations up, Kalli, but the answer is yes. It may be possible."*

"Good! Good! Could it be the one who comes here every day and tries so hard?"

"What is she talking about? Hmm." *"Tell me more about this person."*

Kalli sounded excited. *"So, they come to the park every day and I can actually feel them reaching out!"* Her energy dipped. *"But there is no clear connection like there is with you. I can sense their frustration. I liked feeling something, but never knew there could be more, until now."*

Going back in time, Geeja remembered she had experienced something similar with Uwan before the Ancients arrived. Like a lot of kids who could channel an unknown force to do tricks, she could think very hard and make a coin laying on the ground flip over. No one on the planet really paid those kinds of things any attention because they were relatively common.

But Geeja was an odd child and liked to spend time alone outdoors, simply being one with nature. Sitting quietly in the randa orchard of her father's farm, she often snacked on the tree's blue fruit, while sensing something more just beyond her reach. But the harder she tried to connect, the fainter the feeling became. *Could it be the same here?* *"When does this person visit, and how would I recognize them?"*

"Oh. I can always feel their presence. They're in the park now."

Geeja's eyes had closed in concentration, but now she opened them, scanning like an orion searching for its next meal from a thousand feet above the surface of Uwan. *"What can you tell me about them?"*

"Uh, I don't know." Kalli's voice shook. *"I've never really considered that; they're just 'the one who tries.'"*

"Okay." Geeja changed tactics to make it easier for an inexperienced being. *"How do they compare to me?"*

"That's easy. Your words sound light and high, while theirs are deeper. Does that make sense?"

Geeja mumbled. "We sound different to Kalli? What does that mean?" Geeja recalled the first lesson the Ancients taught; instead of trying harder, let your mind flow. After a deep breath, she connected at a new level with Kalli and could hear the difference between her sound and that of this local. The answer was obvious. *"He is a man! Male voices are often lower than those of females."*

"Male, female? What do these words mean?"

"Basics. Remember, this is Kalli's first connection. Keep it simple." *"Well, Kalli, here is the root answer. You are a planet and live a long time. Most humanoids do not. We live a fraction of your lifespan, so we have to reproduce to perpetuate our species. To do that it takes a special connection between a male and female of our own kind. There is a lot more to it, but that is the short answer."*

"I want to learn more, but for now, does it help you to locate this man?"

"Yes." Being able to train her search on only the men in the park, she had it narrowed down to two in a very short time. *"Kalli, can you judge distance?"*

"What do you mean?"

"If I move closer to the man, could you tell me when we are in the same place?"

A slight hesitation hung in the air before the planet replied. *"I...I think so, but I have never tried."*

Smiling, Geeja stood. *"Here is a lesson for you, Kalli. When you do not know the answer, then try your best option. It might or might not work, but you will learn something either way."*

The two likely suspects were in opposite directions, so she walked toward a sitting man leaning against a tree. *"Am I getting closer?"*

The reply came quickly. *"No. You're not closer."*

Now near enough to see the man, Geeja noticed a wine bottle in his right hand. "Good." She turned, heading for a lanky, younger Kaliegan sitting in a meditation pose with lips moving, appearing to mumble. "That seems to fit."

Drawing closer, she studied him. His long legs appeared twisted like fancy breetels in this contemplation pose. He had a smooth-skinned face dappled with wisps of reds and yellows, which complimented his orange hair. While most wore their long locks flowing, he braided his and it reached most of the way down his spine.

Kalli spoke brightly. *"You are very close!"*

Geeja nodded, then whispered to herself. "The question becomes, how do I ask a man I have never met if he would like to change his life forever, literally forever, by communing with a planet?"

Chapter Thirteen

Jacastra craned her neck to look out the window beside her seat, then blushed. *I'm acting like a little girl on my first pony ride.* But seeing stars and planets fly by at quantum speed for the first time fascinated her, so she gave herself permission to loosen the always tight grip she held on her emotions. *I'll probably never have this experience again.* After a few more minutes staring out the port hole, her face hurt from smiling so broadly.

With the *Curious Lady* on autopilot, Talla joined the women in the passenger compartment that doubled as cargo space, finding all of them glued to a lookout. "It's beautiful, isn't it?"

Jacastra turned toward Talla, her smile dimming a few degrees, not wanting to appear too overwhelmed by the experience. "It's more fantastic than I dreamed." While true, this was a mission, not a sight-seeing tour. Jacastra nodded toward a table near the back. "Let's talk."

A circular seating area surrounded a polished chrome metallic table in the middle, bolted securely in place. It made an intimate setting for their discussion. Talla took the initiative, getting straight to the point. "What is so important that a brigade of Goddess Sworn Warriors bend at least a dozen of their holy rules to get to another planet?"

A shy grin accompanied warming cheeks, surely turning as pink as a Tolairian rose. "Only a dozen?" Jacastra rubbed her forehead. "Really Talla, I'm still not sure all of this isn't a dream."

"Oh, it's real. It's two thousand units deposited into my account, real." She leaned back, then chuckled. "I bet the Holy Mother had a conniption fit parting with that much money to send you and your women into space." A crooked smile formed. "After everything she said about me on the way out, it must have been a bitter pill for her to swallow to need me now."

"No." Jacastra answered plainly, without malice. "While disappointed in how things ended, she still loves you. She made this decision without hesitation."

Talla leaned forward, elbows on the table. "Alright, you've piqued my interest. Why *are* we headed to Kaliega in such a hurry?"

Matching her counterpart, Jacastra moved closer. "Don't think me crazy." She hesitated, still unsettled by her broken trust with this woman whom she once considered her best friend. "You said the vows once, remember?"

"We said a lot of vows, sister. Plus, it's been a few years since I left. You're going to have to narrow it down a bit."

Jacastra pressed her hands together, nervous to say aloud that which, only hours ago, she had doubts about herself. "In the past few days, the Holy Mother has been taken to the vision realm during her sleep."

"She's getting old. Is mental fatigue setting in?"

"Some think so. But many more believe her, as I do now."

"Well, obviously. You're on a ship using advance technology, which the Order forbids." Talla sighed. "Something's up, and you're shook." She reached across the stand, cradling her old friend's hand. "I won't judge, I promise. Just tell me what's going on."

A day full of nerves quavered in her voice as if she looked over the precipice of a high cliff. "The Holy Mother's visions have shown her the final battle is upon us, that the Goddess of Uwan is returning…has returned."

"What?" Talla released her grip as she sat back, then crossed her arms. "I love her heart, but the old lady has clearly lost her jaggles."

Leaning farther across the table, Jacastra objected. "If that were all, then it would be easy to believe age had claimed her mind. But there is more." Her lips tightened. "This morning, Impercium troops executed a raid on Uwan. A roof collapse in a tunnel killed them all!"

"So what?" Talla waved her hand. "They're always busting people for breaking the law. In fact, I heard they crashed the compound of a couple of friends of mine." She rolled her eyes. "I know those guys regularly cross the line. There's even a reward for info about them. That proves nothing."

"How often are the emperor's personal guard sent to Uwan on a mission like that? Huh?" Talla's eyes darted as Jacastra continued. "You know we have sympathizers in the Impercium, especially on our home planet. They confirm that an elite team was wiped out. Could your friends do something that amazing?"

"Still, you have no hard proof of anything." Talla said the words, sounding less sure of herself.

Jacastra locked eyes with her. "That's why we're headed to Kaliega. We are to verify that the fullness of time is not *at hand*, it's here!"

Talla laughed breezily. "And if it is, how are you going to fight against soldiers armed with Lighters?"

Back stiffening, Jacastra spoke proudly. "Even if I simply slow those forces down, as the goddess' final guards did, I will die a blessed woman."

Talla shook her head. "Sister, I've learned a lot since I left the Order. One of those is that you fight fire with fire…or in this case, Lighter against Lighter." Leaning back, she pulled one from a hidden compartment. "I'm not walking off this ship without one of these babies in my hands."

Chapter Fourteen

Raflo and Huanoc made their way from their ship to the Bontana district of Odallisdad. The walk didn't take long, but it looked so different from their landing site that it might as well have been on another planet. The green space of the park and surrounding grassland were an anomaly. By Impercium law, cities of more than half a million humanoids were required to have one of these green spaces every five square miles…except on Uwan. Emperor Djurga always singled out that world for harsher treatment.

But, on the Impercium spectrum of polluted cities, Odallisdad scored better than average. The air carried smokestack pollutants of all sorts, but didn't require the use of breathers. Many, such as the elderly or infirmed, used them anyway. Raflo and Huanoc, reveled in not to have to don them; in fact, even this quality of air put them in a good mood. Raflo summed it up as they approached their destination. "Can you imagine a day when we don't need breathers on Uwan?"

Huanoc simply shook his head, as if the comment were so far-fetched it didn't even merit a single-word response.

Raflo nudged him with an elbow as they strolled past concrete walls smeared with shades of gray grime overlaid with colorful graffiti that either cursed the empire or extolled the local spike ball team. "Guess we're about to find out how much of a grudge Shuggilar carries."

"Hmm."

"Yeah. How much interest do you think accrued on that recharge debt?"

The big Nafportonian was far better at all things technical or mathematical. A slow head tilt foreshadowed his stiff estimate. "At least twelve hundred units."

Raflo's high whistle echoed from the gray, smoke-stained concrete walls lining the narrow street. "That much? Think we can talk him down?"

"Hmm."

"Right. His other two options are to use us on some really big job that nets more, or turn us in for the Impercium reward." In the next few steps Raflo lowered his gaze as his mood turned dark. "I'm bettin' his payment would be more just by makin' a call to the local garrison."

Huanoc sighed.

"You're right, of course." Raflo looked back up, trying to shake bad vibes as they continued toward Steeds, Shuggilar's bar that fronted for his smuggling business. "But because of that woman, we're here. Without any other options, we're stuck, and sooner or later the Impercium will get wind of us. I can't do another stint in the system, can you?"

A head shake signaled Huanoc's only reply.

"And I'm not sellin' her out to Djurga, so unless you can think of another way, this is our best bad choice." They walked the rest of the way in silence. Painful memories from their incarceration ran through Raflo's brain. He wondered again whether the medical experimentation, the beatings or the electro sessions were worse. A single thick cloud blocked the sunlight as it drifted over them while he mulled the different methods of torture he endured at the hands of the Impercium. By the time they reached the door, he still hadn't decided which of them seemed most awful.

Steeds sat in a rough neighborhood, like most working-class bars around the universe. It featured dim lighting, worn furniture, and a cloud of smoke from both legal and illegal products hanging near the low ceiling. A good crowd gathered even before noon because several nearby factories worked around the clock, and one always had a shift change happening. Thin Kaliegan men and women moved out of the way as Huanoc plowed toward the bar.

Raflo followed in his wake, stepping beside his partner when they reached the heavily stained wooden top. He spoke to the closest barkeep, who sported a long scar of recent vintage. It ran from just below his left eye all the way through his upper lip. "Ales for me and my friend."

The tender took their measure, then nodded.

Raflo glanced around, seeing a tavern lined with tired workers. Many had smudges of soot on their cheeks from furnaces while others wore glove enhancers on their hands to increase their speed on production lines. The men and women quietly sipped, chatting in low tones. *These are the workers of this world, doin' their best to make ends meet.*

Another set of customers gathered in a faintly lit back corner, clustered around four or five tables. Not dressed flashy, their clothes looked clean and laughter erupted from them occasionally. *And those are the smugglers of this world, doin' their best to make ends meet.*

When the barkeep returned with two mugs capped by foam edging over the rim, he stared harder. "That'll be two units."

Raflo fished a fiver from his pocket. "Keep the change."

Slender fingers reached for the gray metallic coin as the man gave an appreciative smile. "Thanks. We don't have the best tipping clientele around here."

"Oh." Raflo grinned. "By the way, is Shuggilar in his office today?"

The smile of moments ago dissolved faster than a sweet basalva wafer on one's tongue. "Who?"

Tapping the bar, Raflo's grin increased in direct proportion to the decrease of their server's. "You must be new here, right? It's okay." His words rang calm and confident. "We've done business with him before. He'll be glad to see us." He paused, pulling a ten-unit coin from his pocket, laying it in the center of a circular stain which made it appear as a bulls-eye. "Just tell him Raflo and Huanoc are here for our meetin.'"

The tall man licked his lips with a long, thin tongue as he gazed at the coin. His hand swiped quickly, snagging the tip. "This better not get me in trouble or I'll turn the house on you. I swear by the Holy Eleven."

Raflo's grin remained steady. "No worries. He'll be glad to see us. I promise."

Maintaining eye contact, the man backed away, speaking warily as he pocketed his reward. "I'll let him know." When he reached the other end of the bar, he picked up a PCD and spoke in a volume too low for Raflo to hear.

"Guess we're about to find out where we stand."

Huanoc grunted.

As they stood sipping their drinks, two muscular men wearing black vests with no sleeves approached. The only difference between them and Huanoc was skin color. His was blue while theirs was white, and their cheeks sported distinctive splotches of orange and red. While most Kaliegans were lanky, these two grew thick. Each had a black tattoo of a skull behind bars on their foreheads. Men like these did it to advertise their toughness for having served time in an Impercium prison. Raflo gave a crooked smile as he greeted them, then pulled his sleeve up to show the same ink in a less conspicuous location. "I see we've vacationed at the same resort."

The shorter of the two bulked-up men snorted as his lips tipped up ever so slightly. "Come with us."

Leaving their drinks, they followed the guys who probably served as both guards for the owner as well as bouncers. Passing the end of the bar they went down a dimly illuminated back stairwell. Between the heft of Shuggilar's men and Huanoc, the steps groaned and creaked like planks on an old smeglup trawler in rough water.

Reaching the bottom, they traversed a long stone-carved hallway lit only by a faint blue bulb that flickered erratically. It seemed to decide between each blink whether it would continue to live in this dank purgatory, or just give up. Fortunately, it chose life until they reached the end, where a heavy steel door blocked further passage. The bouncer's coded raps announced their arrival. *Knock…knock, knock…knock.*

The door swung open and light streamed from the room, nearly blinding them as their eyes had adjusted to the dimness. Raflo's arm went up reflexively, and he called out as they entered. "Love what you've done with the place, Shugg."

Shuggilar sat behind a large wooden desk with arms crossed over a big belly. This was Shuggilar's home world, but he looked different than most locals. He had lived hard, and sampled life's riches to excess. Because of that lifestyle, he seemed older than his years. Now, all his flowing orange hair had faded into a gray mop that he wore in a short topknot. The wisps of red and yellow that decorated most people's face on this planet had washed-out to the point they were almost invisible, even in this bright light. He spoke in a low, gravelly timbre. "You came back. I guess you're either braver or stupider than I gave you credit for. Which is it?"

Raflo chuckled. "Probably a little of both, but we're here and ready to settle our debt, and talk about that new job. That's what counts, right?"

The businessman's expression didn't change as he picked up a ledger from his desk. "Seems you two were in a hurry to leave on your last visit." His eyes moved from the page to Raflo. "Care to explain the crystal recharge bill you neglected to pay?"

"Yeah. About that. It was truly a mistake on our part." Raflo gave his biggest grin. "You are a respected man; we'll do whatever you want to get back in your good graces." He paused, hoping for some kind of reaction, but nothing changed on the man's weathered face. "What do ya say?"

Shuggilar stared at Raflo without blinking. After several seconds he made his demand. "Ten thousand units and I'll consider us even."

"What?" The word leaped from Raflo. "That's almost ten times more than we owe!"

Shuggilar fired back. "Perhaps you would prefer I contact the Impercium? Simply collect the bounty on your heads?"

Those words hit Raflo as forcefully as one of the electro torture sessions he endured in prison. "Now.... let's just...wait...hold on a second." His hands shook as he held them high. "No reason to make threats like that, Shugg."

Raflo's heart raced as his eyes darted toward the door where they entered, now guarded by two henchmen. The chances of escape seemed slim. *I'm not goin' back in. I can't. Just keep talkin.'* "I didn't say we wouldn't pay. I am just surprised by the high interest rate. That's all."

Shuggilar shifted his weight. "Let's talk about a job that could set everyone right."

Raflo's shoulders dropped. He shot a quick glance toward his partner, seeing the stoic blue frown on Huanoc's face ease. "I prefer discussin' anything other than the Impercium."

"Good. I have cargo that needs to be transported from point A to point B." His flat line lips lifted into a cunning smile. "*Special* cargo."

Raflo's voice rose, but didn't crack. "Special?" Shuggilar only moved illegal items, so if he deemed the shipment 'special' how much riskier could it be? When dealing with this man the answer was simple: a lot. He swallowed hard, getting his voice and nerves a bit more under control. "I'm sure we can work somethin' out. I mean, movin' stuff is what we do." He glanced back. "Right Huanoc?"

"Hrmph."

Turning, Raflo translated his partner's grunt, leaving out the growl of a curse word or two. He plastered on a smile. "Great! Huanoc says we're all in." Keeping the inflated grin in place, he probed. "So, what are we movin?'"

Shuggilar's eyes twitched. "Your part will be to transport stolen Impercium tech."

"Are you insane!" He could feel his eyes bulging like a hooked smeglup fish.

Laughter rolled from the grizzled man. "Seems you're destined to challenge the emperor's power, either as a prisoner or a smuggler." He leaned back, seeming pleased with the negotiation. "You should be thanking me, Raflo. I am at least giving you a choice."

Huanoc growled, low and deep.

Head over his shoulder, Raflo whispered as he tried to calm his partner. "Hey, buddy. Let's think about this…I mean it could be worse." No sooner had the words left his mouth than muffled sounds of a commotion echoed from the upstairs bar.

Sounds of blood-curdling screams and the screech of Lighter fire wormed their way down the stairs like a sonic snake. Shuggilar shouted what everyone knew. "Impercium raid!"

Raflo's eyes darted around the room again. "We're trapped!"

Shuggilar jumped to his feet, reaching for a sconce on the wall behind him. He twisted it and a section swung open. "This way, everyone!" In a stampede, they all rushed toward the secret passage into a receiving area. When all were through, the door slammed shut. They stood in darkness for a moment until a jury-rigged lighting system illuminated a hand carved tunnel that narrowed to just over shoulder width, ten steps in. "This will buy us a few seconds, but not much more."

Huanoc brushed aside Shuggilar's guards with a swat as he stuck close behind the aged smuggler, with Raflo tight on his heels. The passageway proved a snug fit for Huanoc, and he raised his voice. "Get us out, fast!"

While not as large as Huanoc, the walls were also close-fitting for old Shuggilar, and it wasn't exactly the sprint to the exit Raflo wanted. The single file of men squirmed between the rough stone walls at what seemed a smikler's pace, past one bare bulb strung on exposed wire to the next. Raflo wondered what part of Impercium raid Shuggilar didn't understand. He whispered his frustration ahead as loudly as he deemed safe. "How about a little sense of urgency up there!"

The encouragement did little to speed their escape. Lighters firing behind them, however, did. The old man suddenly showed himself capable of a sprint. Raflo mumbled. "Thank the Holy Eleven."

Their head start gave them a cushion, but it quickly disappeared as a blast from behind triggered a dying man's desperate scream. The orderly retreat turned into pandemonium as those in the back pushed forward, just as they came to a fork in the tunnel.

The lighting continued down the path to the left, but Shuggilar stepped into the total darkness to the right. Turning, he called to Huanoc. "This way. Trust me." Another blast signaled more dead guards.

Huanoc followed Shuggilar into the pitch-black branch, with Raflo just behind them, as close as a shadow. Shuggilar's men, in full panic mode, chose to run away into the sparsely lit left side of the divergence.

Shuggilar whispered. "Follow me."

Raflo gave Huanoc a gentle push as he kept his pressing voice low. "You heard the man! Go!"

Even their slow gait from earlier seemed like a flat out run as they crept ahead. Raflo moved his hand in front of his face, seeing nothing, reminding him of his days as a kid exploring caves on Uwan. Reaching forward his hand touched Huanoc's back, finding his partner's leather vest damp with sweat.

He now remembered the terror Huanoc experienced the first time he took him in the tunnels back at their compound. He patted his friend's clammy shoulder. "Don't worry big guy; we're goin' to make it."

They stopped after what seemed like an hour, but couldn't have been more than a few minutes. In the darkness the screeching sound of metal against metal filled their little corridor. When the sound ceased, Shuggilar whispered. "I need help pushing this door open."

Raflo sensed Huanoc step forward, then heard his friend's hand slap against something.

The big blue man grunted. "Grrr."

Light rushed in as a rectangular door with rounded corners opened on squeaky hinges. Raflo's eyes quickly adjusted, seeing a single lamp lighting a bedroom containing a four-poster bed. The incongruous room's wallpaper featured pink heart-shaped designs.

A woman pulling sheets up around her naked body greeted them, seeming not scared by their abrupt entry. "Shuggy baby, what's with the dramatic entrance?" Pointing, she continued. "And who are these two?"

Shuggilar answered as he pushed the door closed, spinning a wheel that locked it securely. "No time to explain, snookums. We just all need to get out of here, pronto."

Seeing her jump out of bed nude, Raflo lowered his gaze, but snuck a quick peek at the woman. *Shugg's wife or mistress?* Her orange hair looked a mess, but brilliant in color, indicating she must surely be much younger than her man. She quickly threw on a neon green tee-shirt that served as a short dress, making her long Kaliegan legs seem to go on forever. He watched as she zipped up stylish knee-high black boots, then stood, running her fingers through her bedhead. Taking a good look at the woman, his eyes widened. *She's gorgeous. I guess I have underestimated Shugg.*

Shuggilar's voice took on a business-like air. "Everyone to the speeder."

The woman led the way as the three men followed.

Just as Raflo exited the bedroom, the sound of Lighter fire filled the air. Two more shots followed as they all ran from the basement bedroom, upstairs to the main floor. A loud thud echoed behind them, then Raflo yelled. "I think they're through the door!"

Rushing through the elegantly appointed living room filled with furniture featuring hand-carved wooden details, Raflo modified his earlier thought. *I've definitely underestimated Shugg.* They raced from the house into the attached garage where a four-seat personal vehicle sat on the concrete floor with the bubble cover open. They self-sorted with Shuggilar and his lady in the front and Raflo and Huanoc in the rear.

The glass roof settled in place over them as Shuggilar called out. "Hold on!" The garage door raised, then the speeder lifted off the ground. As soon as it reached high enough to exit, Shuggilar engaged the thrusters, sending them down a short driveway onto a quiet neighborhood street. He glanced at the rear camera monitor. "I think we've lost them…for now."

Raflo sat back, taking a relieved breath. "That was close." No one disagreed as all four turned their heads in different directions, scanning for potential pursuers.

Shuggilar called back to the guys. "I know there's a warrant out for your arrest, but what in the name of Sigel's scrotum did you two do to bring this much Impercium heat?"

They looked at each other and shrugged. As usual, Raflo spoke for them. "We're not a hundred percent sure, but I think it's safe to say we've accidentally pissed off the emperor himself."

Head shifting side to side, Shuggilar pressed. "You owe me more than that. The Impercium just raided my headquarters and probably killed my accountant and lawyer, in addition to those guards."

"It's a long story, Shugg. Get us someplace safe and I'll tell you everything. Deal?"

Turning a corner, a local police cruiser hovered ahead at the next intersection. Shuggilar slammed his hand on the center console between the front seats. "Looks like you boys got the entire planet hunting for you. And by extension, me!" He slowed the vehicle, then pulled into a curbside parking space. "Let's wait here for a minute in hopes they haven't seen us yet."

In a very short second, red and blue lights flashed ahead. "Son of a drunken spinter rustler." Shuggilar spun into a quick U-turn, accelerating to maximum speed. "Seems they're already on the lookout for this speeder, so they're probably watching all of my means of escape." He took a right turn at an extremely high speed, barely nicking a signpost. "We might all hate the Impercium, but they're not stupid."

Raflo held the door brace in a death grip as Shuggilar demonstrated superb driving skills. *Definitely underestimated the man.*

Once again at full speed, Lighter bolts burst from the trailing cruiser. "You two still flying that illegal black bucket?"

"Modified." Even in this distressing situation, Raflo insisted on his description of what they had done to their ship. "The word is modified."

"Whatever…but if it's not close, we're all going to an Impercium prison, or worse."

Raflo snarled. "They'll take me back over my dead body."

Shuggilar veered left this time, just as fast as the prior turn. "You're going to get your wish if you don't tell me where you've parked that cloaked beauty."

While he didn't want Shuggilar anywhere near their ship, Raflo knew of no other choice. About to answer, an idea came to mind. A profitable one. "If Huanoc and I get us out of here our debt is canceled, right?"

The old contractor glanced toward his lady. His voice sounded soft, not gruff as usual. "Yes. I want to get out of here, but whatever happens, promise me you'll keep Chella safe."

The sincere gesture warmed Raflo's heart. He shot a confirming look to Huanoc, who nodded. "Deal. We landed her in the vacant field on the other side of that park a few blocks from your bar."

"Great, we're already headed in that general direction." Shuggilar looked at the monitor again. "It's a good thing because they're gaining on us." His voice rose. "And more are joining the chase by the minute."

Looking back, Raflo tensed, seeing the cruisers close the gap on this personal vehicle. He mumbled. "We have to make it. I can't go back into Djurga's torture chamber." Turning his gaze forward, the park loomed straight ahead. "Thank the Holy Eleven."

Lighter fire connected, causing the speeder to swerve. Raflo screamed in searing pain as more beams cut through the shell of their vehicle. "I'm hit!"

The hovercraft slowed, then dropped, skidding to a stop at the grassy edge of the park. Shuggilar gave orders. "Everyone out. I've got one more card to play!"

The bubble popped off as Shuggilar and Chella scampered out, followed by Huanoc picking up Raflo.

The big guy threw his injured partner over his shoulder, calling to the others. "This way!" Even with the extra weight of Raflo, Huanoc ran fast, followed by Chella, as Shuggilar held back.

When the police arrived, their crafts parked by Shuggilar's damaged speeder. When close enough, Shuggilar pointed a remote device toward his vehicle, then pressed a button. An explosion lit the area, accompanied by a tremendous boom. He smiled, then turned to catch up with the group.

Huanoc questioned when he got close. "What was that?"

"Just a little something for our friends." He laughed. "You don't live as long as me without picking up a few tricks along the way." The laughter disappeared as more Lighter shots sprang at them. "Spreg's pearls. Huanoc. What did you two *do*?"

Saying nothing, he simply kept running until seeing Gigi near the park, instead of safely onboard the *Phantom Star*. "Grrr."

Chapter Fifteen

"How am I going to do this?" Geeja thought aloud as she slowed her approach to the Kaliegan man that appeared deep in meditation. "There is the direct approach. 'Hey, want to do something mind blowing today?'" *No.* She closed her eyes and exhaled. *I get one shot. I cannot have him think I am insane.*

Maybe I flirt? She considered the pros and cons. *This body is clearly attractive, so I will get his attention. But then how do I get him thinking about something besides me? Too many ways that could go sideways.* Standing only a few feet from the young man, she could hear his repeating mumbled chant.

"I am open to the universe and to my world. I am open to the universe and to my world. I am open to the universe and to my world…"

Kalli squealed. **"I can see through your eyes and hear through your ears!"** After a moment, she spoke again, still excited, but also sounding unsure. **"What exactly AM I seeing?"**

Geeja answered. **"This is your surface and the man in front of me could be your permanent connection to it."**

"Wow! So much…everything! I have so many questions."

Dread draped her shoulders like a lead cape as she spoke to herself in a low voice. "I do not know how to do this. What if I fail?" She shook tension from her arms. "Only positive thoughts. I *can* do this. I *will* do this."

Her words apparently broke the man's concentration. "Are you talking to me?" He opened confused eyes.

Geeja smiled reflexively. "Sorry. I did not intend to interrupt your meditation." *Not a total lie, right? I did not* intend *to disturb it. Okay, evidently, I am just going to wing it.*

His smile matched hers. "I like your mantra. What did you say? 'Only positive thoughts. I can do this. I will do this.' Mind if I use it sometime?"

The sun lit his face and she could see that he wasn't as young as she initially thought. *Not a teen like me. That is good. A little maturity is helpful.* "Sure." She pushed blowing strands of blond hair behind her ear. "I meditate often, too. Mind if I join you?"

The man shaded his eyes from the bright sunlight. "You are welcome to share this beautiful day." His gaze lingered. "We don't have many off-world visitors in this part of the city. Where are you from?"

"Uwan." She awaited his reaction to get an outsiders take on her world's state of existence.

"Ooh." The man took a sharp breath as he blushed a bright shade of orange. "Sorry, I didn't mean to imply... It just sounds like a tough place to live, you know, after everything that's happened."

"Do not worry. You are right, it is a rough place to call home, but my meditation makes it a little easier." She kept her smile pasted on. His assessment didn't offend her; it simply hurt, because that was truly the current state of affairs. "By the way, my friends call me Gigi. What is your name?"

"People call me Zimo."

"Zimo. That is a fun sounding name."

He laughed easily. "The shortened version is better than the full family surname. It's Zimoniorio, which happens to be the scientific name of a stink plant here. I got teased mercilessly in school."

He seemed like a very normal person…like her before the Ancients arrived in her world. She kept her thoughts from Kalli. *Normal. Is it fair to make the attempt to connect he and Kalli? His life will change forever.* She thought of the second vow: 'You will always do what is best for your planet, not yourself.' *I guess that applies here as well, even though Kalli is not my planet.* A spark of memory from her first full encounter with Uwan flashed in her mind. *The Ancients had not asked me what I thought of the idea; they just connected me to Uwan.* It had been the best thing that ever happened to her, and she would do it again in a heartbeat, one thousand times over.

She took in a breath and centered. *I need to stay in the here and now, I do not have much more time here.* "You heard me chanting. Did I hear you saying something?" She did know what he said, but this approach made the conversation flow easier. *Is that really a lie?* Vow four came to mind: 'A goddess shall not lie except to protect life or your planet.' *I am doing this for the good of this world.*

Zimo's smile broadened. "I am open to the universe and to my world." His eyes sparkled as he glanced toward her. "You probably think I'm some kind of flake."

"No!" She responded forcefully. "I happen to feel the same way. There is so much to this universe that cannot be explained or accessed by most people."

"Exactly!" Zimo's reply matched hers. "I sometimes get in a zone and swear I can hear whispers just outside my mind's reach." His smile froze. "I bet that sounds crazy coming from someone you just met."

Geeja turned toward him; their eyes meeting. *I am not sure I am doing the right thing, but let us see where this goes.* "I believe you, Zimo."

He laughed lightly. "Then that makes you the first. Not even my mother understands."

She needed to know his motivations before going further. *Does he want to rule this world? Is he mentally ill?* "Why is this important to you? What would you do if you could communicate with the planet?"

Zimo laughed a little louder. "That's the thing. I don't have some grand agenda." His eyes stared unfocused across the green grass of the park. "My parents are environmentally aware, so maybe it's in my DNA, but for as long as I can remember, I've always cared about our world." His hands squeezed his knees. "Then on a nature hike I started hearing…it's kind of hard to describe what I heard that day. It's kind of like standing beside a river rushing so loud it drowns out the voice of someone right beside you. Perhaps you catch a syllable here, or the fragment of a word there, but it's never anything I can really grasp."

"What do you hope the voice is saying?"

"I don't know." He gave a tiny shoulder shrug. "Maybe it's something as simple as, 'I'm here.'"

He sounded so thoughtful and sincere, certainly far wiser and more mature than when she first connected with Uwan. Besides, it would tear her heart to leave Kalli alone after finding out she could possibly commune with another being. *It is worth the risk.* She moved a hand and placed it gently on his. "You mentioned crazy a moment ago. Would you think me crazy if I said I heard the whispers as well, and that I can understand them."

"Really?" He held her gaze with a wavering smile.

"Really." She paused.

Hearing the words she hoped to hear, he sounded as much relieved as curious. "I knew I wasn't nuts, though I've been called that more than a few times." His eyes moistened. "Can you teach me?"

"Maybe." To be fair to him and Kalli, she had to lay out the risks. "But first I need to ask a few questions."

His eyes widened, like someone who knew they held a winning lottery ticket if the last number matched. "Ask away."

"First, how do you feel about the Impercium?"

"I hate them." His response carried a bite. "They conscript young people into their military from nowhere worlds like ours. I've lost three friends to their stupid heavy-handed rule."

Geeja nodded. "Believe me, I understand how you feel. Just know that if I help you and the Impercium discovers it, they may try to kill you. This is important, Zimo. Are you willing to take that risk?"

"I have to. I feel like I've been on the edge for so long. For my sanity alone, I'll take any risk to see what's on the other side."

"Okay." Zimo seemed to understand that risk, at least at a surface level. Geeja continued, making sure to maintain eye contact, feeling certain she would know if he were lying. "This will be a massively life changing experience. Can you keep it a secret? If one wrong person were to find out and tell the Impercium…well, we covered that."

"I can. I'm a bit of a nerdy introvert, so there aren't a lot of people I would want to tell anyway."

"Not even your parents?"

"Not even them. They're in academia and while they're committed to sustainability, they reject anything even smelling of mysticism." Zimo nodded. "That's what we're talking about, right?"

Hmm, it was not always thought of in that manner, but maybe that is the way it seems now. I will have to somehow communicate with the other holy worlds to figure that out. Tell the truth. "I view it differently, but I am guessing that is what your parents would think."

"Like I said, I won't tell anyone, especially my folks."

She thought about asking more questions, but the clock in her head signaled that Raflo and Huanoc would return soon. "Would you like to give it a try?"

His face brightened. "Yes! Please!"

She cast a quick glance around. More people had come to the park on this fine day. She pointed to a spot closer to the cloaked spaceship. "How about we move to the other side of those trees for a little privacy."

He sprang to his feet, then offered a hand. "Perfect."

Zimo's long legs and obvious excitement made it a challenge for Geeja to keep up. When they reached a secluded space, she spoke. "This looks ideal. Let us sit."

The excited young man dropped to the ground in an instant. "Is this right?" His voice quivered as he confessed. "I haven't been this nervous since I asked Dezilia to the Moonbow Dance."

As Geeja joined him on the ground, she realized she forgot to tell Zimo something important, and it might change his decision. "There is one other thing you need to know, Zimo. If this connection works, there is a good chance you will not be able to father children."

Zimo stared intensely and she could almost see the gears in his brain turning. He spoke tentatively. "But I would still be able to have…relations…right? You know, the physical kind."

"Yes. Definitely."

Relief washed over him as most of the tension left his voice. "Kids sound like a lot of work, but missing out on the fun part would have made me think twice about this deal."

Geeja laughed, but only on the inside. *Men.* She caught the sexism in her thought. *Who am I to judge? I feel the same way.*

Relaxed eyes tightened again. "Is what we're about to do dangerous?"

"No." *I will keep this simple…for both of us.* "I do not know why, or how, but those who connect with worlds are blessed with an eternal link that changes us physically." She touched his hand. "This is a choice. No one would blame you if you decide this life is not what you want. But once made, it cannot be undone."

Zimo's mouth twitched. "Any regrets? If you could go back in time, would you do it again?"

The words leaped from her soul. "I would do it a thousand times over."

A thoughtful grin emerged. "That's what I would have guessed." Taking a deep breath, he gave his final reply. "Then I'm in."

With that settled, she squeezed his hand, then gave direction. "For this first time, I will hold one hand as you place the other on the ground." He did as instructed, then she placed her free hand on the soft grass, completing the circuit. She spoke in hushed tones, wanting Zimo to hear the proper way to address his planet, but not drawing unwanted attention. "We exist to serve Kalli…we are one with Kalli… We exist to serve Kalli…we are one with Kalli…"

The planet responded immediately. *"Geeja! You did it!"*

Glancing, she saw the blood drain from Zimo's face and she knew he heard it, too. She smiled as if being the only witness to a grand eternal wedding. *"It seems I did. Would you like to say hello?"*

In her style, Kalli's words came fast, nearly running together. *"Zimo. Such a nice name. My name is Kalli. Nice to meet you. I've been trying to talk to you for so long. Can you really hear me?"*

The young man's mouth hung open until his mind answered enthusiastically. *"Yes!"* Consciously or not, Zimo matched her style. *"It's so nice to finally be able to hear you! I've tried so long, and today it's happened! I can't believe it!"*

Geeja held her breath as she lifted her hand from the ground to see if that would break the connection for Zimo. It didn't. She gave a sigh of relief, thrilled at being able to help Kalli and Zimo connect. This happened the same way she first connected with Uwan all those years ago, and now she had performed the same task as an Ancient. This was something she would think about later, but first things first. She stepped back into the conversation. *"Good news, you two. Now that you have connected, looks like you will not need me as an intermediary."*

"Really?" Zimo's brows raised. "It's that easy?"

Freeing Zimo's hand, Geeja stood, then verified the result. "It is not so much the difference between easy and hard, it is more like all the pieces just needed to come together. That is what happened today."

Kalli and Zimo answered in unison. *"Thank you."*

The pale sun seemed to bless the day as warm feelings filled Geeja. "I will step away and give you two some time to get to know each other."

While not completely disconnecting from the planet, Geeja tuned out their conversation as she strolled toward the cloaked ship. A sense of contentment and peace filled her. *It certainly was not on my agenda when I woke this morning, but I did something good today.* She took in a deep breath of mostly clean air. *Now, if I can do the same for my world, all will be as it should.*

Sitting, she ran her fingers through tender blades of wonderfully green grass. The sensation tickled, boosting her mood higher. *I cannot remember the last time I experienced this level of joy.* The feeling didn't last even a second as she spied Huanoc running at full speed toward her. "What is he carrying?" Her eyes locked on two other people. "And who is that with him?"

Huanoc must have seen her as well as he yelled. "Run! Ship!"

Jumping to her feet as the huge Nafportonian got closer, she realized what he had slung over his broad shoulder. "That is Raflo!" The man's limp body bounced with each of Huanoc's long strides. "He is hurt!" Then she saw a mass of people chasing the four, firing weapons shooting bolts of light, the same as had injured her all those years ago.

"Impercium soldiers…"

She shot a quick glance behind her, seeing Zimo in rapt conversation. She pushed back into their inaugural talk. ***"Sorry guys! We have trouble! Impercium trouble!"***

Zimo jumped as if pinched. "Where? What do we do?"

"You need to get to safety. Run far away as fast as you can. Kalli and I will handle this."

"We will?" The planet sounded confused.

"Yes." Geeja clenched and unclenched her hands. ***"I just need permission to tap a tiny bit of your power."***

"If it's safe for you, then it's safe for me." Zimo rushed to Geeja's side. "We're in this together now."

With no time to argue, she gave him one order. "Fine. Just stay out of my way."

Kalli sounded terrified and Geeja knew why. Her solitary existence had ended minutes ago and she rightly feared it might be snatched away, plunging her back to a lonely eternal life. ***"Yes! Take what you need to protect yourselves."***

As Geeja prepared to arm herself with planetary energy, a loud noise from above broke her concentration. With a hand over her eyes, she saw another ship coming in fast for an apparent landing. "Who is that? More trouble?"

Huanoc yelled again, his voice as loud as an angry trumpeter warbird. "RUN!"

Closing her eyes and calming herself in this suddenly out of control situation, she opened her mind, preparing to commune silently. She stopped, seeing this as a teaching moment she glanced toward Zimo. "Watch what I do, but promise me you will not try this on real people without practice. There is a fine line between stun and kill. Believe me, I know. I have made that mistake." Her response to Charl's death centuries ago still haunted her.

Zimo nodded.

After another deep breath, she spoke to Kalli. ***"From your might, for the protection of those who serve you, I thank you for this gift."*** Geeja opened her mind and power flowed in. She sensed her body glowing a light green tint. *That is interesting. All worlds are different, but on Uwan the energy always surges blue. I wish I knew why, but there is no time to figure it out. I must save my friends.*

Her vessel filled with energy as the shouts of women came from behind as the new ship on the scene landed. Containing the power she had drawn in, she turned and saw uniformed women running toward her, most armed with spears. *Who are they?*

The fastest woman belted out a war cry. "Our lives for the Goddess of Uwan!"

More bolts of light were fired by the Impercium troops toward Huanoc and his group. The charging women shrieked, sprinting headlong into a fight against a superior armed foe.

Geeja barked toward the women. "Stay where you are! It is time for action, not introductions." She turned back toward the soldiers chasing Huanoc and Raflo. As had happened so many years ago, directed energy sprang from her fingertips, but this was unlike the lightning on Uwan. Here, the energy that ran from her hands looked like green liquid flames. "What the…"

Screams of pain filled the charged air as the wave of energy hit the Impercium soldiers. Their cries were horrendous as they seemed to be burning alive in a wildfire that raced through and around them. One by one they fell, twisting and screaming. Many rolled on the ground, trying to extinguish the flame that licked their skin, while leaving the grass unsinged.

The smell of burning flesh mixed with new screams from families in the adjoining park. The awful sight worsened as the soldier's uniforms caught fire, adding orange swirls to the green liquid flames. The eerie fire seemed to have a will of its own, searching out bodies that still moved, targeting them until every soldier lay dead. Geeja stood horrified. *No! What have I done…again?*

Zimo raised a hand to his mouth, then spoke as if in shock. "What happened?" His tone sounded accusatory. "You said you wanted to stun them!"

To her left, the women who rushed forward in her name, stopped. Their mouths hung open, then they fell to their knees in what looked like worship. With heads bowed they chanted in unison. "The fullness of time is here…the fullness of time is here…the fullness of time is here…" The chant looped continuously.

Confusion reigned on the grass field around Geeja. *First things first. Center my emotions, then console Zimo.*

A few centuries ago, Geeja wept when something similar happened. This encounter registered differently because her friend's lives were threatened, and since then she had seen death millions of times in thousands of forms. Sometimes the end came quietly, as while holding the hand of a good friend who had grown old. They passed peacefully, entering their next stage as part of Uwan's spirit.

She had also witnessed accidents, as when a horse fell on its rider. An unexpected tragedy. Geeja had even watched helplessly as her own people turned on each other in battle when her mediation failed.

She no longer shed tears because all deaths were final, none could be reversed, even with planetary magic. The loss of so many lives at once, like now, ripped her insides to shreds, but salty drops on her cheeks no longer made her feel better. Her voice shook as she answered Zimo, with self-loathing regret gnawing at her guts. "I made a mistake, and those Impercium soldiers paid the price. The energy from Kalli is different than from my home planet."

Turning away from the smoldering corpses, she stared hard into Zimo's eyes. "Trust me, I did *not* intend this outcome. I only wanted to stun them to save the lives of my friends." She took in a trembling breath. "That is why you must take your time as you learn what is possible in *your* eternal connection with Kalli." Her hands went to his shoulders, squeezing hard. "Do you understand!"

Nearby, the chanting from the bowed women rolled endlessly. "The fullness of time is here…the fullness of time is here…"

Zimo met her hard stare. "Who are you? What are you…really? Are you some kind of monster?"

Huanoc yelled again. "Hurry!"

Zimo is asking the correct questions. Geeja looked up into the cloudless sky, then toward the group of chanters, and finally back into the young man's eyes. She spoke softly. "You deserve a far more complete answer than I can give you today." Her brows gathered as she looked back toward the carnage she had just caused. "Unfortunately, there is no time for that now. Both of us must leave before more Impercium troops arrive."

"But who are you?" He pointed to Huanoc, then the gathered women. "I must know."

Geeja closed her eyes for a few seconds, then revealed her secret. "I am Geeja…Goddess of Uwan."

Zimo's pupils flared. "But that's impossible! I know the stories. You're dead, killed by the Impercium."

Glancing over her shoulder again, she saw the strange green flames take final, dying leaps. "Then how do you explain that, or the fact that you can now commune with Kalli?"

His jaw hung as he processed everything. "But…but, how?"

"That is a long story. I promise I will come back to explain everything. You deserve that, and so much more."

Huanoc called again, sounding desperate. "Raflo hurt bad!"

Geeja pulled the young man into an awkward hug. "Look, I must leave. I might be able to save my friend's life. Keep your head down and mouth shut. You and Kalli get to know each other. The

Impercium will be after anyone involved in this incident. Understand?"

Zimo nodded. "It's a lot, but I understand what I must do…for now." He pulled back, staring with his thin-lined eyebrows squished together. "So, if you are the Goddess of Uwan, what does that make me?"

A proud smile graced Geeja's face. "I think you know the answer, Zimo. We owe you an official ceremony, but as of today, you are the God of Kaliega."

Chapter Sixteen

To reach the ship, Geeja had to run past the women who just arrived. The cloaking fell away from the *Phantom Star* and she knew she had to move fast. "Look, my friend is injured and we must leave. I am sorry we do not have time to introduce ourselves."

One of the women sprang to her feet. "We have witnessed your power, Goddess, and we are here to serve you!"

Genuine warmth touched her heart as she pointed toward the entry ramp. "That sounds wonderful, but really, I have to leave."

Huanoc called impatiently. "Must go. Now!"

The apparent leader of the group of women spoke determinedly. "Then we go with you. We swore an oath."

Time ran low, so she made them an offer. "Look, this is a small craft. Four of you can come with me, and the rest follow in your own." She pointed a finger and stared. "Either that or I leave you all."

Sharp nods answered, and in seconds the chosen four raced behind her.

Once inside Geeja saw Huanoc place Raflo on the bunk in the back of the ship. After strapping him in hastily, Huanoc hustled to the cockpit, launching them back into space.

Prepared this time, Geeja took the G-forces of the fast exit in stride. The women who joined her seemed surprised as muffled screams filled the combo passenger - cargo compartment. She smiled. *Evidently, I am no longer the least experienced space traveler onboard.*

Repeating the evasive maneuvers as from their quick exit out of Uwan they were soon zipping through the darkness of space.

Huanoc left the cockpit, coming back to the suddenly crowded area. "Introductions later. Raflo now."

Geeja unhooked her harness and moved toward the bunk where the injured man lay. Surprisingly, the Kaliegan woman who raced onboard with Huanoc already knelt beside Raflo. Pushing hair behind her ear, Geeja greeted her. "I am Gigi." Her brow's arched. "Who are you?"

The beautiful, but slightly disheveled woman replied with a sweetness in her high-pitched voice. "I'm Chella." She glanced over her shoulder at a heavy-set man with a scowl that seemed to have taken permanent residence on his face. "I'm with Shuggilar."

"Oh." Their names were the only thing Geeja got out of the exchange. *Like Huanoc said, introductions later.* "Okay, Chella. Do you have medical training?"

"Yes." The red and yellow dapples on her face darkened to a deeper hue. "I was a nurse until I met Shuggy."

Geeja's tight shoulders relaxed. *At least she has modern training.* "Good. Let us look at my friend. This man saved my life a few days ago, so I hope we can figure out how to help him. I want to return the favor."

Beside them, Raflo lay unconscious as low groans slipped through his lips.

Chella took the lead, unbuttoning his shirt, revealing an oozing scorched section of skin on his left side, just below the rib cage. Spying a first aid kit, Chella opened it, then donned thin black gloves.

Geeja scrunched her face. "Why use those?"

"To prevent infection, of course."

"Right." Once again, her two-thousand-year absence showed. *How do those prevent infection? I have missed so much.* She watched over Chella's shoulder as the woman examined a wound, the likes of which Geeja had never seen.

A soldier from the late arriving group joined them, falling on her knees as she approached. "Goddess, I've dreamed of meeting you for my entire life."

Geeja smirked, trying to lighten the mood as Chella flinched, but said nothing. "Bet you never pictured it this way, did you?"

The wide-eyed supplicant stuttered. "Uh…not really."

Putting a hand on the woman's back, Geeja invited her into the conversation. "What is your name, and do you have medical training?"

"Jacastra. My name is Jacastra. As a soldier, I have field medical training." Her voice steadied, adding her assessment of Raflo's condition. "Looks like they used ribelsome enhanced Lighters."

Geeja's expression went blank, barely knowing what a Lighter did, much less an enhanced one. So, she listened to the medical exchange.

"That's bad," Chella said, "though it looks like a grazing wound. It isn't the worst I've seen, but the latent toxins will kill him even if the burn doesn't." She shook her head, sounding disgusted. "I hate the Impercium. They're the only ones who use this tech. It should be outlawed."

Geeja shot them a curious look. "Why do they use it?"

"It's Djurga." Jacastra's angry glare went to Geeja. "When you were injured all those years ago, you escaped and survived. He developed a weapon that would kill, even if only initially wounding someone." She paused, then stated the obvious in an almost growl. "He doesn't want a repeat if his troops ever got another shot at you."

Chella's hands went up. "I have so many questions." She pointed toward Geeja. "Starting with, like, who are you?"

Geeja directed her attention back to the wounded patient. "Can we save him?"

"If we can get him to a hospital, maybe." Chella seemed placated for the moment, now dabbing some sort of gel on the wound she had just cleaned.

Jacastra offered another alternative. "There is a plant native to Uwan that inhibits ribelsome spread. If we could get there in time, it might be possible."

Huanoc must have been listening to their discussion. "No." Stepping close, the man of few words now used a full day's worth. "The Impercium must be crawling like a bledron snake herd over Uwan by now, and the same for Kaliega. Neither of those places are safe." He sounded pained as he ran thick fingers through Raflo's sweat-drenched black hair. "If it's between dying or going back to an Impercium prison, he's made his feelings on that quite clear, many times." He squatted beside the women, still towering over them. "I need new options. A place that's close, where we can get help outside the Impercium health system."

Neither of the other women offered a suggestion. Then Geeja spoke, her voice carried on a nervous quiver. "How far is Politar?"

Huanoc looked up, as if doing calculations in his head. "Uh, roughly two hours at maximum speed."

"Is that enough time?" Geeja shot quick looks toward the more experienced healers.

Chella responded first. "No guarantees, but I think so."

Huanoc stood, questioning Geeja. "Can we get help there?"

She shrugged. "I have a powerful friend who used to live there, but I have not seen him in quite some time."

Huanoc spun on his heel, heading to the cockpit. "Good enough."

Chapter Seventeen
Three-Years Earlier

Waking on the stone-cold cell floor, Raflo's body shook uncontrollably. "No! No more!"

Huanoc knelt beside him with his large hand resting on Raflo's chest. "They've gone. You are safe…for now."

Raflo's entire body stiffened as a do over of the forced surgery without anesthetics he had just endured, played in his mind. It triggered a blood curdling scream.

The big hand patted. "Shh. You're going to be all right. Don't give them the satisfaction."

Raflo's formerly board-straight figure relaxed, then curled into the fetal position as he sobbed. He squeezed out a few anguished words. "They're winning, Huanoc. I can't take much more of this."

"Hmm." Neither said anything for some time as the Nafportonian kept a hand resting on his new friend. The after-effects of the torture Raflo endured eased in the next hour, then Huanoc helped him to a seated position leaning against the wall. He squeezed the smaller man's shoulder, returning to his habit of using as few words as possible. "Better?"

Raflo forced a weak smile. "Yeah." He rubbed his pounding head. "Thanks, man. You've been a life saver." He pressed his fingers into his temples, then lightly touched the bandages covering his eye. "I'm serious man, I don't think I can hold out much longer."

Huanoc whispered, now using plenty of words. Important words. "Are you desperate enough to attempt an escape? Knowing that if caught, we would be executed?"

Head snapping as if hearing a shockel's call in the dark, Raflo didn't pause. "Yes! I'll be dead in a month anyway if I don't get out of here."

"Shh!" Huanoc put a finger to his lips. "Ears always listening."

"Sorry." He matched his friend's low volume. "It's just that this is the first good thing that's happened since I got nabbed. What's the plan?"

Shifting, Huanoc looked Raflo in his one good eye. "You need to steal a guard's PCD."

"Me? Why me?"

Huanoc held out his huge hand with fingers as thick as the steel bars of their cell door.

"Gotcha, not exactly those of a pickpocket." Raflo cocked his head. "What then? Are you goin' to call some buddies and have them break us out?" His uncovered eye darted, accompanied by a crazed laugh. "Even if that's your stupid plan, I'm in. Seriously, I'll try anythin.'"

The big man sighed. "No vision."

Raflo's hand went to his injury. "Hey dude, that's a sick joke. Besides, I'm just messin' around. I didn't mean to offend you; I just didn't realize you had some grand scheme." Raflo's brows lifted. "*Do* you have some master plan?"

He nodded. "Step one, steal a PCD. Then I tell you step two."

"Alright. I'll need a diversion in the exercise yard this afternoon. Can you do that?"

Huanoc smiled.

**

Five hours later all the inmates of cell block Q milled around under the watchful eye of armed guards, all protected by an impenetrable clear dome. The facility had many incongruities, but none as jaw-dropping as this one. You were removed from society and stranded on a large asteroid, but as a prisoner you also had spectacular daily views of deep space.

Raflo leaned against a wall, smothering the throbbing pain of his forced surgery, while keeping his good eye on Huanoc across the crowded space. He picked this spot because three guards came together here most days to discuss the results of the previous evening's professional spike ball matches. *Sports. Mind numbing diversions for the masses.*

Today, the shorter of the three argued with the heaviest one about a foul not called. "Just because no blood spilled, doesn't make it a legal play! Without that penalty, the Blades didn't cover the spread. Cost me forty units!"

Raflo gave a slight nod as a signal to his collaborator.

Responding, Huanoc moved closer to an inmate named Wraigreth. Huanoc shoved him hard, knocking him to the ground, then yelled. "Pay up!"

The ghostly white, muscular man regained his footing.

The action caught the attention of the guards near Raflo as they all pulled their J-sticks from their black leather belts.

Now, Wraigreth charged Huanoc, lowering his shoulder as he struck the Nafportonian, landing them both on the ground. A no-rules grappling match seemed underway as the guards arrived, joining all the others of the cell block in cheering on one or the other wrestlers.

The Nafportonian guard named Jooloc yelled above the noise, but not to stop the brawl. "I'm betting on Huanoc, any takers?"

Huanoc and Wraigreth wrestled to the ground again, taking turns walloping one another in the head. Raflo winced as Huanoc took a blow square in the ear. *Got to give it to my cellmate. He's sellin' the show.*

Jooloc holstered his J-stick and whipped out a pad to record bets as the other guards formed a perimeter around the action. He shouted encouragement toward his champion. "Come on, Huanoc. You can't let a Blongarian thug beat you!"

In the chaos Raflo moved close behind the energetic guard. He thrust a hand past Jooloc's ear, toward the action while simultaneously yelling. "Punch him in the face!"

The guard startled, spinning toward Raflo. "Back off, scum!"

The combined distractions worked perfectly. Grinning through a stabbing jolt from his injured eye socket, Raflo complied, palming the officer's PCD. With the mission complete, he stepped away. "Hey don't mind me." He pointed again. "What a move!"

Jooloc spun back to the fight, needing to see if he was recouping his losses from the previous night, or if he would be falling deeper into debt. "Woohoo!" His fist raised in the domed atmosphere. "Never bet against a blue skin!"

Wraigreth tapped out, then Huanoc released him from a headlock. Jooloc collected his bets as the other guards dispersed the crowd.

Once on his feet, Huanoc limped to the wall where Raflo leaned once more. "Get it?"

A sharp nod and wry smile told the story. "You put on quite the display out there. I had no idea you were such a good fighter."

Huanoc grinned. "That?" He glanced over his shoulder at his defeated foe, then turned back to Raflo. "Staged."

"What? I couldn't tell! How?"

The blue grin widened. "Step two. New partner."

Raflo's good mood sank as he looked around his friend, toward Wraigreth. "I don't like this. It's hard enough to keep a secret with two people, much less three."

"You knew this would be dangerous."

"Yeah." Raflo shook his head. "But a Blongarian? Seriously? Aren't they all mobbed up?"

"Uh-huh."

"Then why him? We get him out of here and he might turn around and kill us."

"I have a plan."

"Really? What role does a dangerous criminal play?"

"He stars as 'man with spaceship.'"

Raflo's lips formed an exaggerated circle. "Ohhh. That role." He winced, then laughed. "The more I learn, the better I like this plan of yours."

Chapter Eighteen (Present Day)

Distracted, Emperor Djurga stood in the grand hall facing a massive 3-D representation of the universe. He called the wide room, with marble columns running the entire length, his control center but it functioned as much more. He designed the space so that at every hour, either one of the two suns, sometimes both, or the moon were visible through the huge windows placed between the tall pillars. The continuous connection to the celestial objects of his world reminded him of his own immortality. Therefore, he took all meals and meetings here when not traveling his realm.

The only time they weren't visible, like now, happened during one of the storms that rejuvenated this section of coastline during Jestona, the monsoon season. The weather control system on the planet worked well…mostly. But every time he tinkered with the algorithms to shorten the duration, or lower the number of rainy days this time of year, it always triggered an unwelcome drought. So, he learned to accept it, but not like it. "Blasted weather."

The door opened behind him. He called out to whoever now silently awaited his command. "Come."

The Goddess Awakens

General Scanda joined the emperor. "We have reports from Kaliega, Your Excellency."

The emperor's eyes went toward the map as his hand spread, magnifying the holigraphic representation of the small, insignificant world in the Tan Cretus system. "Good news?"

Scanda's lips tightened. "Mixed news, I'm afraid."

He raised an eyebrow. "Mixed news? You are right to be afraid."

The general stiffened. "Yes." He swallowed, then continued. "The ship we were tracking disappeared, but we were able to pick up the two former Impercium prisoners on surveillance cameras. They went into the hideout of a known smuggling contractor."

Djurga interrupted. "What do you mean, the ship disappeared?"

A bead of sweat appeared on General Scanda's forehead. "Seems they've developed some sort of cloaking device of unknown technology."

A low growl escaped the emperor's lips. "More on that later." His eyes left the map, then turned a deathly glare toward Scanda. "You said mixed news. It would be best for your health if you mention the good part next."

"Yes, Your Excellency." He swallowed again. "We raided the lair of one Shuggilar D'Hovrat and the scum fled through escape tunnels. Our troops spotted them and gave pursuit."

"Scanda!" Djurga bellowed. "Did you not hear me? Tell me the good news!"

The chastened general bowed sharply, causing sweat to splatter on the polished marble floor. "Yes, Your Excellency!" Straightening, his voice cracked. "As our forces caught the runaways, they spotted a woman in the grassy area where the fugitives fled."

"A woman?" Djurga pressed. "Tell me it's her."

"Witnesses report that the woman stood apart from the others, and directed, I'll quote here, 'green fire' toward our troopers. She incinerated an entire brigade of over two hundred soldiers by some sort of unexplained chemical flames." He inhaled shakily. "I believe that counts as confirmation…right…Your Excellency?"

Like the rise of Speglow, a smile eased onto Djurga's face, brightening his mood. "Yes, Scanda. That counts." His eyes went back to the huge map. "Where are they now? In custody?"

Scanda's brief smile dropped into a frown. "We did injure one of her companions, but after killing every trooper, they escaped."

"Find them!"

"Yes. Yes, Your Excellency! We will. They must get medical attention for their wounded man and his biomedical records are flagged. As soon as a drop of blood is drawn or his face scanned, we'll have the closest brigade on the way."

Ignoring his general, Emperor Djurga stared at the map, wondering to which system they would flee. He stomped his right foot. "Send an entire division of the fleet next time!"

"Yes, Your Excellency. Your will be done."

"Leave me!" As the general scampered away, Djurga mumbled. "I caught you once, you so-called goddess. I'll catch you again. You can't hide from me forever."

Chapter Nineteen

Geeja saw Huanoc leaving the cockpit, knowing the time had come to officially reveal her true identity. Casting an eye around at her travel companions, she caught them all staring at her. *I am sure they have already put the pieces together.*

Huanoc took one more look at Raflo, who rested in the bunk, then sat in an open seat. "We should arrive at Politar soon." He crossed his arms. "I want to know who is on our ship." His eyes darted to Geeja. "The truth."

With her long lifespan, she had been in embarrassing spots before, and didn't even hint at blushing as she recalled her ruse of losing her memory. She tried to keep the session light. "So, I will start, unless someone else wants to go first? Anyone?"

No one uttered a peep.

"Alright." Standing, she walked to the center of the small space, holding her chin high. "I will get right to the point. As some of you have already surmised, I am Geeja, Goddess of Uwan."

Jacastra and her fellow warriors gasped, hearing their longing confirmed. The warrior leader spoke as tears flowed. "The fullness of time is here!"

Shuggilar shifted closer to Chella. "Look, we're not from Uwan, so all we really know about you is that Djurga became emperor by defeating you long ago. What's your deal?"

Geeja chuckled. "You do not mess around, do you? You have asked the most important question."

The faded orange and red patches on Shuggilar's cheeks darkened slightly in a soft blush.

"Here is the short version. You have heard of the other eleven holy worlds and their gods or goddesses?"

All heads bobbed.

"Well, approximately twenty thousand years ago, the Ancients visited. Through a testing procedure they selected one being on each world to serve as partner and mouthpiece for their planet. I am the chosen one for Uwan."

Huanoc responded in a low growl. "Cleaudra was our goddess."

"Was?" Geeja whipped around to face Huanoc upon hearing him use the past tense to describe an immortal being. "What happened?"

"She stood up to Djurga and he sent a hit team. They killed her."

Geeja's hand went to her mouth. "I am so sorry. We were friends."

"You knew her?" Huanoc's voice rose.

"Yes." She sighed. "The twelve of us met every two years. Cleaudra had a kind heart and an iron will." After a brief pause, she asked the next obvious question for someone who had missed the most recent two millennia. "What happened after her death?"

Huanoc tilted his head as behind him, starlight seen through the porthole, blurred at Quantum speed. "It is said our world connected with a new person, as foretold. When the woman revealed herself,

Djurga put her under house arrest until she swore allegiance to him, as all others have done."

"And now? What is her role?"

He gave a half-shrug. "All I know is her name is Dorsta. She lives like a hermit in her palace and is rarely heard from or seen."

Hearing Huanoc's rendering of Nafportonian history, Geeja wrapped her arms around herself. *That could have been me. Who am I kidding? If not for Susomi's sacrifice, that would have been me. I would have died.*

Feeling unsettled, Geeja sat, knowing all eyes remained on her. "Twenty centuries ago, Djurga's troops severely injured me, but my loyal guard, Susomi, offered her body for transference. Because they drilled that Terminus Stake into Uwan and soldiers were closing in, it resulted in a rushed process. The procedure was flawed."

Chella piped in above the low drone of rapid space travel. "Like Shugg said, we're not from a holy planet, so that whole transference thing has always sounded mysterious."

Geeja glanced toward Jacastra. "Seems you have studied me and my life. How about you explain transference for everyone?"

Jacastra's lower lip quivered as she spoke. "In those days thousands volunteered to be considered as the new host for the goddess. It was the highest honor to be selected." Her eyes shot to Geeja, appraisingly. Seeing a nod, she continued. "As it is written in sacred texts, Geeja doesn't replace the consciousness of new vessels, they simply add them to the thousands who have served before." She squinted as she looked toward Geeja. "Right?"

Geeja stood again. "You are absolutely correct. I, or more accurately *we*, contain all the knowledge and experiences of every form we have ever inhabited." She paused for effect. "We come from all backgrounds. We are artists, scientists, farmers, and soldiers."

"Wow." Chella's brows arched. "You must be really smart."

"Back then, most considered me one of the most intelligent beings in the universe." She clasped her hands together. "Now I am utterly lost. I have missed two thousand years of advancements in every field." She smiled. "But I can tell you everything you wish to know about ancient history."

Huanoc had been quiet. "Yeah. Everyone thought you were dead, then Raflo and I find you unconscious on the side of the road."

Jacastra pointed toward Huanoc. "Not all of us thought she died! Some believed…and we were right."

He shrugged. "Fair enough." His gaze turned back to Geeja. "Then you simply awoke?"

Taking in a deep breath, she wrapped up her story. "Under normal circumstances, it should have taken five days to revive my body. But, with Djurga's constant draining of Uwan's power, it took a lot longer…two thousand years longer." She shook her head. "Imagine my surprise when I finally opened my eyes again, not understanding the profound changes that had taken place during my long years of hibernation."

Huanoc seemed to put the pieces together. "That's why you were in the open during a storm, without a breather."

"Yes. Fortunately for me, you and Raflo were in the right place at the right time."

He looked back at his wounded friend. "Perhaps it is more accurate to say we were in the wrong place at the wrong time."

That response hit hard, but her expression didn't change. In her years she'd had many tough conversations. "He's right." The weight of all their lives crashed down on her shoulders. "I am Djurga's enemy and by proxy that makes anyone who associates with me the same. Regardless of whether you are here on purpose or by accident, you are now on the Impercium's most wanted list."

All were quiet as she glanced at each of them, seeing excitement in some eyes and terror in others. She pulled in a deep breath of resolve. "One way or another, I am going to fight Djurga for the good of Uwan, and perhaps the universe. This may not be a battle you want to join, but the truth is the Impercium knows who you are. You have until we reach Politar to decide if you are with me or wish to go into hiding on your own." Her words were firm. "I urge you to do what is best for yourself." Spine stiffening, she offered her final piece of advice. "We all know what Djurga is capable of, so choose wisely."

Chapter Twenty

Geeja moved between small clusters of passengers aboard the *Phantom Star* for the remainder of the trip. The Sworn Warriors seemed giddy at seeing her as the realization of a prophecy, and at their first time traveling into space. They would steal a glance at her, then dive back into a huddle, talking excitedly. No doubt, all would join her in the fight, and while she didn't need the adulation, it provided a nice counterbalance to the attempts on her life by Djurga. *Not everyone wants me dead.*

Moving next to check on Raflo's condition, Geeja chatted with Chella, now joined by Shuggilar. The injured man's fever had risen, but otherwise he remained in stable condition. She rubbed the nurse's back. "He would be dead without your healing hand."

"Maybe." The woman answered in a matter-of-fact manner. "But he needs more help than I can give, and very soon."

Nodding, Geeja weighed the chances that Chella and Shuggilar would join her. They hadn't tipped their hand as to whether they would side with her or go into hiding, but she considered herself a realist. *I literally dropped into their lives a couple hours ago and now they are faced with joining a longshot revolution or hiding from an emperor who has spies everywhere. There is much to sort and weigh.* She would not push them either way, but simply offer support, whether that be with Raflo's care, or their decision. She spoke soothingly. "Let me know if there is anything I can do."

After taking a moment to stare through one of the port holes, Geeja spied Huanoc approaching. "It still takes my breath." She smiled. After all, space travel this easy was a new experience for her. "I am amazed at how much has changed during my absence."

Huanoc glanced back at his friend, his large forehead creased with worry. "We'll reach Politar soon, and I'm sure the emperor has eyes everywhere. What's your plan?"

"Politar." An old memory triggered a contemplative inkling of a smile. "The first foreign planet I ever visited."

He shook his head, remaining silent, seeming as if his recent binge of talking had used up his vocabulary allotment for the day, perhaps the week.

"After the Ancients anointed me as Goddess of Uwan, they left, instructing me to bond with the planet and explore my gifts."

"Like shooting green fire?" Huanoc's well of words hadn't run completely dry.

Geeja shifted her gaze back to the window, hoping to see the star her home planet orbited. She spoke in hushed tones as she searched. "It is blue lightning on Uwan, but yes, things like that." She paused, thinking she might have spotted her sun. "When the Ancients returned, they brought a space ship for my use. They gave us only two tech items, and that was one. They said if we tried to take it apart and reverse engineer it, the craft would self-destruct."

"Hmm."

"I believed them, but Gilbrar, the God of Plawan did not. The darned thing started beeping and the technicians fled just before it blew up, as we had been advised."

He spilled three more words. "They spoke truth."

She turned again to face him. "Yes, they did. The Ancients were not fans of technology. In fact, they expressly told us to ban it except for limited use. They even told us they had seen worlds destroyed by dangerous machines that initially offered the hope of better lives."

"Really?" Huanoc raised his brows.

Geeja swallowed hard. "They told us they quashed the threat, but that we must be vigilant and stamp out any sign of its return."

Huanoc continued saying a lot while using few words. "Djurga?"

She released a silent curse hidden in a sigh. "Apparently, though I am sure he had help from somewhere."

"Hmm."

"Hmm indeed." Geeja pushed a strand of blonde hair behind her ear. "Enough talk of that evil man. It is time to focus on the here and now." Her eyes danced around the interior of the craft, remembering her first times traveling to other planets. "If the *Phantom Star* ranks as a level ten, then the ship they gave me would be a three, at best. While primitive, it eventually took me to the eleven other holy worlds, Politar being the first."

"Hmm."

"That is when I met Bregent, God of Politar. We had our inaugural Twelve Holy Worlds conclave on his planet, and he and I hit it off right from the start. Finally, I could talk to someone who understood the responsibilities and pressures I faced."

"Friends, or more?"

The warmth of a rare blush spread as Geeja thought of one of her vows: *'A goddess shall not lie except to protect life or your planet.'* She shook her head. *Why am I embarrassed?* "Very perceptive, Huanoc." She raised her shoulders. "It started as friendship, but blossomed into something more…for a while."

Her lips tightened in a reticent smile. "But long-distance relationships are hard, especially with the literal worlds of responsibility that we both carried." She paused and he did not fill the space. Huanoc seemed a good listener. Finally, she spoke again. "We ended things on good terms, but then I disappeared for twenty centuries. Who knows what he has been through during that time?"

"Hmm." He shot a quick glance to the cockpit. "Where should I land?"

"Find the most deserted place close to the capital, then set us down."

"Doesn't matter where?"

"I just need to connect with Bregent. I can do that anywhere." She reached up and placed her hand on his black leather vest. "Trust me."

Nodding, he called out. "Take your seats for landing."

Politar belonged to the class of planets where water covered the majority of the world's surface. Here, three major continents appeared to float in the vastness of the oceans. From space, the lush green flora and desert browns looked as if they were jewelry settings on a fancy Citizen's Day ornamental decoration.

Huanoc set the *Phantom Star* down in a blustery blast of fine sand launched into the air by their thrusters. "We're here."

Unstrapping, Geeja stood. "If memory serves, the temperature in this desert is unusually high. I will head out by myself and make contact."

Jacastra and three Sworn Warriors wrestled with their harnesses. "We're coming with you."

Geeja considered arguing the point, then thought better. "Why not? You have trained your whole life for this."

Huanoc lowered the ramp. "Be careful."

Walking past him, she gave him a reassuring pat on the shoulder. "Just another day in the life of a goddess." As the small group descended to the powdery hot surface, she looked back into the ship, seeing Huanoc holding a Lighter. It served as a security measure for those onboard, but also a small gesture of support for her. *He is a good man.*

Geeja met a wall of heat and the blistering breeze blew grains of sand against exposed skin like tiny searing coals. She elected to stay under the shade of the *Phantom Star*, lowering to her knees as she prepared to connect. Bowing, Geeja extended her arms forward, then placed her hands on the silty surface. Though not essential to touch the surface of a magical world to connect, the habit began in her youth. She thought it also a sign of respect, as well as a literal grounding of the relationship. The sand burned, but she ignored the pain as her guards encircled her, taking outward-facing positions.

The second ship landed, sending more sand swirling. As soon as the engines shut down, the Sworn Warriors who traveled on the other vessel rushed out, joining their comrades. They too, took up defensive positions to protect their goddess.

Slowly, she breathed in scorching air, reaching out to this once friendly world. Mind centered, she searched for connection. ***"Politar, an old friend returns. Greetings from Uwan… Politar, an old friend returns. Greetings from Uwan…Politar, an old friend returns. Greetings from Uwan."***

A familiar soprano voice filled Geeja's head, as unexpected tears fell on the dry surface. *"Geeja? Can it be?"* The planet paused. *"Is it really you?"*

"How I have missed hearing your voice, my friend!" She sniffed. *"It has been far too long."*

"It is you! But how? Bregent said you were gone forever."

She laughed aloud, then responded. *"Then I guess forever is only two thousand years."*

Politar giggled. *"I've missed that humor! Welcome, my friend from Uwan."*

Spiritually renewed by her reception, Geeja turned the conversation. *"Thank you for your welcome. So much has happened since we last communed, dear one, it will take some time for us to catch up. But I come to you now in a profound moment of need. Can you connect me with Bregent?"*

"There have been changes here as well." Politar's previous enthusiastic mood melted away. *"We shall speak of those after rendering what help we can. I'll beckon Bregent."*

As Geeja waited in silence, the wind repeatedly lashed, spraying her with sand, then calming in no set pattern. Her new reality filled her brain. *Everything has changed, and it is I who must adjust.*

A surprised male voice interrupted that train of thought. *"Geeja? I had given up hope. Where have you been?"*

Geeja smiled. *"Bregent!"* Her spirit soared, like the orion birds of Uwan. *"Wow! Do I have a strange story to tell you!"*

"I can't believe you're here!" Like his planet moments ago, Bregent's disposition quickly turned from excited to dark. *"And I have a story to tell you as well. Until we swap tales, Politar tells me you are in need. How can I help?"*

"It is a medical emergency. One of my traveling companions has suffered an Impercium Lighter wound and needs immediate assistance."

A long silence ensued before Bregent answered. *"Impercium wounds?"* He sounded wary, but as if trying to cover that emotion with his own humor. *"Geeja, you always knew how to make an entrance."*

She waited through an uncomfortably long pause, hoping they hadn't traveled here in vain.

"Listen, Geeja. Things are different now…very different."

She could hear tension in his voice.

"IF I help, you must promise to leave immediately afterwards."

"I swear on the Holy Twelve! I promise we will leave at your command." While Bregent sounded anxious, desperation coursed through Geeja's veins, willing to pledge almost anything.

"Alright. Stay where you are and I'll be there after nightfall. This must be kept secret. You can't be seen here under any circumstances. Understand?"

"Yes! Yes!" She breathed a sigh of relief. *"Thank you, I know it is a risk."*

His reply chilled her, even in this blazing heat. *"You have no idea. Djurga has his thumb on a button that can do to every holy planet what he's already done to Uwan."*

Chapter Twenty-One

Once back inside, Geeja stood by a porthole, staring. *Hurry up, sun! Set already! I have already lost too much to lose anyone else.*

Chella joined her with an update on Raflo's condition. "His temperature is climbing and he's shivering as his body fights the toxin."

Casting a worried glance toward the patient, Geeja asked the most important question. "Will he survive until sundown?"

"I don't know." Chella wrung her hands. "We've done all we can with what we have." Her eyes went to Raflo. "We'll see if his body is strong enough."

For a moment, Geeja considered simply taking Raflo to the planet's surface, asking Politar directly for the magic to heal her friend. She lowered her head, recalling what just happened when she tapped the power of an unfamiliar planet. *It has been a very long time since I communed with Politar. As tricky as healing is, I could accidentally kill him as easily as heal him. I must wait.*

Munching emergency rations Huanoc retrieved from an escape pod, everyone onboard sat subdued.

Geeja's eyes met Chella's as she motioned to a couple of open seats. "Care to join me for a hot cup of calefine juice?"

Chella nodded as they each picked up a mug and moved to a quiet corner not far from Raflo, keeping a watchful eye on her patient. Once settled, Chella brought up the decision that Geeja asked them all to make. "Shuggy and I have been mulling our options." Her shoulders sank. "He's pissed that everything he's worked for all these years has been destroyed."

Geeja almost said that she understood. That this is what happened when Djurga attacked Uwan…but that wasn't true. There were warning signs she missed, or ignored. Instead, she reached for the woman's hand in sympathy, saying nothing, simply trying to share her pain of a life tossed by a tempest.

After a couple of minutes, Chella continued. "Shuggy hates the Impercium, like many people in the universe, but no one has even come close to challenging his rule…ever. Plus, Shugg had a big job lined up, one large enough that we could retire with no money worries. Now, that's probably blown." She glanced toward her partner. "But today he saw you kill a battalion of their troops with some kind of liquid fire, then you tell us you're a goddess." Tired eyes went to Geeja. "He doesn't know what we should do next."

Geeja squeezed Chella's hand. "If it makes you feel any better, I do not either. In return for Bregent helping Raflo, I had to promise to leave immediately afterwards." Leaning toward the other woman, Geeja bumped shoulders. "I have always found that the night is darkest right before the morning birds sing. How about we save Raflo, then go from there? Okay?"

"Sounds good."

Huanoc stepped toward them. "Dark now. Instruments indicate an unidentified flying…something approaches. Its image on the sensors matches nothing I've seen."

The chat with Chella took Geeja's mind off the imminent sunset. Thankful for the conversation and diversion, her shoulders squared. "It is time."

Chella moved to Raflo's side, her voice shaking. "He's still alive…barely."

Huanoc again lowered the ramp as Geeja prepared to exit, bodyguards in tow. He whispered a single word. "Hurry!"

Nodding, Geeja and crew rushed to the bottom. She expected some sort of craft with a medical team, but instead a single man riding a giant desert hawk swooped in, landing near the ship. The huge bird squawked as the rider slid down a wing. The man wore a form-fitting white suit that hugged close around his wrists and ankles, obviously designed to keep the sand out. Once on the ground, he ran a hand through long, thick white hair.

Lillie snaps flapped their wings in her stomach. Bregent had changed bodies many times since they had last seen each other, but he usually favored the form of the classic Politarian male. His pattern held true as a gorgeous white mane flowed over his shoulders, complimenting his porcelain skin that seemed to glow in the rising moonlight.

He reached out telepathically and the tips of his blue lips smiled as he caught his first glimpse of Geeja. *"It really is you!"*

She ran toward him, emotions surging. Embracing, he gripped her as tightly as she held him. Stepping back, her guard completely fell. She initiated a deep, long kiss. Finally pulling apart, she locked eyes, returning his greeting that only he could hear. *"By the Fires of Horia, we meet again!"*

Seeming assured he embraced the real Geeja, he spoke aloud. "You have no idea how happy I am to see you!" His sparkling Politarian green eyes glowed in the ethereal desert moonlight. "I thought you were dead."

Chella walked down the ramp followed by Huanoc carrying Raflo. "Sorry to break up the reunion, but if we don't do something soon Raflo's going to die."

"Right." Geeja spread her arms. "We could really use your help."

Bregent fell to his knees, digging in the fine sand. "Help me dig a trench long enough and deep enough to bury him."

Geeja and her warriors joined, sending grains of the brown, almost powdery surface flying as if in a tornado. In just a few seconds a trough roughly Raflo's size emerged.

"Put him in, then cover his face with a cloth." Bregent directed as he remained beside the newly dug ditch. "Be quick about it."

Jacastra ripped the sleeve from her uniform and handed it to Bregent. "Will this do?"

He examined it. "Perfect."

Huanoc lowered his friend into the ground, them mumbled what might have been a prayer in his native tongue before stepping back.

Chella jumped to Raflo's side as a muffled groan escaped Raflo's mouth. "He's stopped breathing!"

Bregent placed the ragged cloth over Raflo's face, then yelled. "Help me cover him! We might save him yet." A man-made sandstorm completely entombed the injured man as Bregent issued a warning. "All except Geeja must get back on your ship, or risk death."

A near stampede occurred as they complied with the dire notice.

"Alright, here we go." Bregent placed his hands on the surface of the new grave and motioned for Geeja to do the same. "I want you to feel the energy, should you ever need to do this process again."

She did as requested. "Let us hope that never happens."

Nodding, he chanted, with Geeja joining on the second round. "A poison removed, replaced by a debt to be repaid… A poison removed, replaced by a debt to be repaid… A poison removed, replaced by a debt to be repaid…"

After a minute where nothing happened, Geeja worried they might be too late. *Did my momentary embrace of Bregent cost Raflo his life?* Her fingers dug into the sand. **"Please, Politar. Save him if you can."** Her chants became more fervent. "A poison removed, replaced by a debt to be repaid… A poison removed replaced by a debt to be repaid… A poison removed, replaced by a debt to be repaid…"

Nothing changed as their chanting looped. Geeja could feel drops of sweat rolling down her face, so she cracked open her eyelids. It did not surprise her to see Bregent's hair also drenched. **"Please, Politar. If you can save him, I too, will owe a debt to you."**

The ground now shook low and steady, not violent like an earthquake. The tremor continued as the area surrounding Raflo began glowing a soft white, crackling with a magical charge, contrasting with the shades of brown sand surrounding them. Bregent opened his eyes, then lifted his hands from the surface. He motioned with his head toward the right. "Your friend was half-dead, so Politar needed time to calibrate the remedy. We have done our part, now we step back and wait." Standing a short distance away, Bregent put an arm around Geeja as they stood together in the silence, lit only by the silvery moon.

Nightfall triggered the quick release of the day's hot, dry air, causing Geeja to shiver. He pulled her closer, like so many other times. The warmth of his embrace stirred intense emotions. *I cannot think of those long-ago days. I must focus on the here and now.* A very old habit raised its head as she chewed a fingernail while mumbling. "Come on Raflo. You must pull through."

The glow of Raflo's shallow grave faded until finally blinking out. Bregent stepped away from Geeja, rapping a knuckle on the bottom of the *Phantom Star*. "Come out."

As the ramp lowered once more, everyone emerged.

Bregent and Geeja moved to the spot where Raflo lay buried as he directed again. "Let's uncover him and see if our efforts were successful."

Geeja expected a miracle cure, that her new friend would jump up, just as lively as he had been earlier. They dug less frenetically than when they formed the pit as all seemed to not want to injure him in their exuberance. Geeja spotted signs of life first. "He's breathing!"

Chella whipped the cloth from Raflo's face, placing a hand on his forehead. "His fever has broken, at least for now."

On her knees, Geeja raised her arms in praise. "All thanks to Politar and her god, Bregent." She gazed skyward as she whispered. "A life has been saved and a debt is owed."

Raising Raflo's shirt, Chella shared more good news. "The discoloration around his wound is gone, and it's almost healed! I've never seen anything like this!" Her eyes shot to Huanoc. "Help me get him out of this hole and back on the ship."

Huanoc did as told, snatching his friend up, then rushing him back into the *Phantom Star*. Moments later, he returned, placing his large hands on Bregent's shoulders. His deep voice shook. "Thank you."

Bregent gave a tired smile. "I'm glad you got him here on time." He patted the large man's arm. "I'm sure we'll be seeing him again in the future. He owes a debt to this place."

Huanoc furrowed his brow. "Hmm." Releasing his grip on Bregent, he turned and went back inside.

Only Bregent and Geeja remained outside, not counting her determined entourage of Sworn Warriors. Bregent whispered. "We need to talk." He glanced at the women around them. "Alone."

She chuckled. "They are a single-minded bunch. Mind if I simply spread them out further? Trust me, it will be a much shorter discussion."

He shrugged. "As long as we can speak without being overheard, or perhaps limit the conversation to our minds only."

Her eyes locked with his. "I need to hear your voice, it has been far too long." Turning, Geeja gave orders. "Jacastra, widen the perimeter." With the women doing as instructed, she cocked her head as her attention went back to Bregent. "Why the secrecy?"

Bregent lowered his gaze, his white-booted foot tracing a circle in the sand. "Things have changed so much in your absence." That statement seemed to trigger a question. "Speaking of that, where in the universe *have* you been?"

Leaning against the front landing strut of the *Phantom Star*, she crossed her arms. "I wish I had some fascinating tale, but the truth is I was in a form of hibernation. A rushed transference occurred as Djurga's troops closed in, then that Terminus Stake hit Uwan. I managed to find a healing bed in the tunnels and lay down." She spread her arms wide. "I woke thinking a few days had passed, but no...I can still scarcely believe two thousand years went by."

He bobbed his head. "That explains why a new goddess didn't emerge." Bregent rubbed his chin. "Then Djurga got it right. He had lots of theories about what had happened, and whether you survived, but he always thought you were alive...somewhere."

"Djurga." She spat on the ground. "I am furious at what he did, but I am just as mad at myself. He said he had amassed great power and wanted to be treated as an equal, but I did not believe him."

She kicked the sand. "It stared me in the face and I could not see it. I let this happen."

Bregent leaned toward Geeja, then draped an arm over her shoulders. "*We* didn't believe him. You were just the most vocal in denial of his petition to join the Holy Twelve. None of us could fathom that technology could ever rival the power of a magical planet and their god."

They remained silent for a few moments under a space ship swathed in a velvety night sky where blinking stars seemed close enough to touch. Geeja turned to him. "I am really glad to see you."

"Same here." Bregent's lips tightened. "Seeing you again floods my mind with thoughts of what could have been if we had simply dealt with him when we had the chance. But we can't go back in time. What's done is done."

"What is done is done…" Eyes still locked, she questioned. "You know my story. What happened to you and the others?"

Once again, his gaze lowered. "What the emperor did to Uwan stunned us all. It sickened us–scared us." His free hand rubbed his bowed forehead. "Initially we assumed you were dead. Meanwhile, Djurga made a spectacle of his butchery of your world, broadcasting pictures of gaping open-faced mining and image after image of that damned Terminus Stake."

Bregent kicked sand into the air. "He summoned us to Emblaka…and we stalled, trying to come up with a plan…except for Cleaudra." Bregent faced Geeja with glistening eyes. "Cleaudra openly defied him, so Djurga labeled her a war criminal to be executed."

Geeja beheld a man with bulging veins and flared nostrils. "I heard things did not go well."

"No." Bregent's words cut as sharp as Hesba's famed ax. "He executed her with a Lighter in front of all the remaining gods." His voice trembled. "A new goddess emerged a short time later and he put her under house arrest until she swore allegiance to the Impercium."

She glanced up at the *Phantom Star*. "The pilot of this ship is from that planet. No wonder he hates the emperor so much."

"We all do." Bregent sighed. "But when Djurga summoned us again a few years later, we all complied." He removed his arm from her shoulder, then crossed both tight. "He offered us a truce…and we accepted. After all, we witnessed his killing of one goddess, and you were presumed dead."

Geeja stared straight ahead, not knowing what to say or think.

As if ashamed, Bregent continued, almost choking on his words. "Every Holy Planet now has a Terminus Stake, same as Uwan, except smaller amounts of energy are extracted. In return, we were allowed to live, but with restrictions."

"Let me guess. You've sworn your allegiance to the Impercium."

Bregent inhaled deeply, tilted his head back and released the breath into the night air. "Not just the Impercium, but to Djurga personally. In exchange, we keep our titles, but we no longer rule our planets. The emperor appoints an administrator who rules in his stead. I can still commune with Politar and conduct transferences as needed, but that's about it." His head shook as he lowered it once more. "I'm a figure head who makes proclamations at major events but holds no real power. I can't even leave the planet without his approval."

Head cocked, Geeja pushed. "I do not understand. Why keep you and the others around instead of killing everyone, repeating what he did to Cleaudra?"

"Simple. Having ancient, defeated gods bend their knee is a powerful reminder to all that his rule is total. If he can dominate and humiliate us, who would be fool enough to fight back?"

Geeja raised her hand. "I guess I am the one who is foolish enough."

"What?" He stood straight as an auditor's rod. "Are you insane? You wake up after a centuries long nap and think you can take on the emperor who bested you already? The one who's millions of times stronger now?"

"What *is* my other choice?" She stepped away to face him head on. "Hide like a common thief, always looking over my shoulder?"

He flung his arms out. "Contact him. Beg for mercy. I'm sure that's what he wants."

"Beg for mercy? From an evil man who has done the things he has done?"

"Yes." Bregent's voice cracked. "At least you would be alive. Then you could perhaps begin the process of healing your planet."

She pointed a finger. "You call this living?"

Even in the moonlight she could see his green-tinted blush.

"You're just like Cleaudra." Bregent shook his head. "And like her, you're going to get yourself killed...for nothing."

She lifted her chin. "At least I will die with dignity."

His words carried an edge. "You know *nothing* about this time. You misjudged him then, and you're repeating the same mistake."

Geeja's eyes bore into him like the beak of an ironweed bird cracking a nearly impermeable gossard seed, but she remained silent in her anger.

Bregent blinked, breaking the stare down. "I risked my neck helping you tonight, Geeja. I'll not risk the health of Politar to do it again." He glanced toward the other spaceship. "You all must leave before sunrise."

Geeja watched as he again ran a hand through that gorgeous hair, then took a step toward his magnificent giant bird. She grabbed his hand. "Thank you for healing my friend."

He nodded, his shoulders rigid. "Good luck, Geeja."

Backing away from the hawk, she smiled. "And to you as well." Her gaze lingered as he settled into flying position. "I did love you, Bregent. I have never regretted that."

Tears rolled down his smooth-skinned cheek. "I never stopped loving you." With a kick, his magical beast launched effortlessly into the black sky.

Open jawed, she stared as the pair faded into the darkness.

David Witt

Chapter Twenty-Two
Two Thousand Years Earlier

Djurga rubbed sweaty palms on his tailored black pants as he stood in an empty field on a sunny Emblakan day. His thoughts went to the hand written note, which he had memorized, delivered by a farmer from this district. One key passage fired his imagination. *If you are amenable to a new trading partner, we can help you develop technologies beyond your imagination. Devices that can defeat even the most advanced enemies.*

His thoughts were a nervous mixture, starting with the fact that there might not be a meeting at all. The farmer reported that a ship of some sort had silently floated down from the sky. His own labs had produced models of a vehicle that could spin blades and lift itself into the air, but they were noisy. Surely this simple tiller of the soil exaggerated.

Glancing at his watch, another invention from his lifestyle technology division, he saw the appointed time had come, yet no vehicle of any kind appeared. *It has all been an elaborate prank.*

The Goddess Awakens

That old man will pay dearly for wasting my valuable time! Perhaps I will torture him with one of our new devices.

The idea turned up his drawn lips as he spun to walk away. As he did, he caught sight of a white dot zipping across the sky. He kept his gaze on the speck as it traveled at incredible speed before turning, then sinking as it headed directly toward him. He shaded his eyes from the twin suns, then mumbled. "What is that thing?"

The closer it got, the better he judged its size. It wasn't a small vessel, but a huge white egg-shaped one that slowed, then hovered in front of him. He whispered in amazement. "It's bigger than a deep-water levitone!"

Three feet-like struts extended from the bottom of the craft, with two in front and one toward the rear, as it softly touched down. Even with no one else to hear, words continued to force their way from his mouth. "In all the Twelve Holy Worlds, no one has ever witnessed anything like this."

A sound, like pressure releasing from a carbonated bottle of grum, broke the silence, then a ramp lowered from the belly of the vehicle. When it reached the tender green grass of early spring, a figure with square shoulders walked down the slope. He saw a man's face sporting a confident smile that would look right at home on an Emblakan street. The traveler wore an impeccably tailored white suit paired with a black shirt. He had the same high cheek bones and light purple eyes as Djurga and other highborn of their society. Overwhelmed, Djurga muttered a single word. "How?"

The figure extended a hand. "I am Ambassador Ka Sherka, of the Truise Dimension. You may address me as Ambassador, or simply as Ka."

With jittery words, Djurga shook a cold hand. "It is my pleasure to meet you, Mr. Ambassador Ka Sherka." *Pull it together, man! Use one name or the other, not both!* With a bit more control, he continued. "I'm Governor Djurga and I welcome you to Emblaka."

An enigmatic smile graced the ambassador's face. "Would you like to see your two suns up close?"

Djurga's jaw dropped as his moment of keeping his emotions in check evaporated. "Uhm." His eyes darted to the ship. "You would do that…for me?"

Ka delivered a flat laugh. "That and more, governor." He half-turned, then waved. "Come aboard. See your place in the universe from a different perspective."

Like a kid invited to a dranzel cake tasting, Djurga hustled up the ramp, then sat beside Ka as the foreigner operated the controls. In seconds they cleared the atmosphere, zipping into the darkness of space. Ka maneuvered the vessel to spin and face the world they just left, floating in a vast black void. Dumbstruck by the offer, Djurga had to remind himself to blink. He knew his words would be inadequate, but a few spilled anyway. "It's all so beautiful…"

Ka said nothing, seeming content to watch his passenger call the names of continents and oceans from this vantage point. After a few minutes, he redirected the craft, then accelerated. In a few seconds they swung around the massive red sun, Speglow, then toward the yellow Seaglince.

"Amazing…" Djurga sat paralyzed by the experience, so overpowering that he could only stare through the clear glass. Even simple words failed him. "It's…"

A controlled laugh from the ambassador finally broke the spell that captivated him. However, when the alien spoke again, it shocked Djurga even more.

"You belong out here with us, governor. Can you picture yourself captaining your own ship? Going wherever you wish?"

At the moment, he couldn't, but he believed it a good time to lie. "I can! My people deserve our rightful place in the universe."

"Good." Ka crossed his arms as he swiveled his chair to face his passenger. "Where would you go? What would you do if you had this ability?"

While he had been on unsettled ground to this point in the encounter, he knew with absolute certainty what he would do if he had this power. "I would go straight to the next meeting of the Holy Twelve and demand my place among them as equals."

"Hmm." Ka's face registered no emotion. "They don't welcome the advances you've already made?"

"No." Djurga's lips tightened into a thin line. "Just the opposite. They think we should abandon our achievements. They live in worlds with magic, insisting technology will ruin the universe."

"And what do you believe?"

"This is what I *know*." He jabbed the air for emphasis. "They have power and deny us the same right. Mark my words, someday they will see things my way."

"I see." Not an extra muscle on Ka's face moved. "And if you had the technology to build a ship similar to this? Would you be close to that day?"

Stunned, Djurga leaned forward. "What are you saying?"

Ka's flat demeanor persisted. "I'm offering you and your scientists a crash course in how to build a star cruiser, using the raw materials you already have on your world." He lowered his arms to the rests of the command chair, then stared with impassive eyes. "Are you interested in a partnership with that perk, and so many more?"

Djurga licked his suddenly dry lips, then spoke cautiously. "Partnership." He said the word slowly. "Your offer is *very* generous." His eyes danced around the cabin of the craft at glowing screens before landing again on the ambassador. "What *exactly* would you be expecting in return for such an extravagant gift?"

A smile smudged between fake and unnatural. "Nothing."

"Nothing? Seriously?" Djurga's senses screamed 'trap.' "In my experience, objects of value are never freely given away." He leaned back. "What's the catch?"

The enigmatic look lingered. "The catch? There is no catch for what I have outlined. You would be given advanced training to build different types of vessels, and instruction on how to fly them."

"But?" Djurga could almost smell the word waiting to be said.

Ka's expression never changed. "It is *my* world's experience that knowledge is addictive. You will be thrilled by what we give you, but a time will come when you want more."

The truth of that statement seemed self-evident. Djurga's scientists had done things, kept hidden from the Holy Twelve of course, he could have barely imagined a few years ago. But those gains only whetted his thirst. "And when that day comes? What will you ask of us then?"

"We propose a partnership, governor, and partners make business deals. They trade goods and services that benefit both. Only when you reach a point when *you* ask for assistance will we discuss a trade. It will then be up to *you* to decide if the benefit to *you* is worth the exchange."

With hands pressed to the sides of his legs, Djurga pondered the offer, which sounded almost too good to be true.

"Besides, who knows what you might request?" The ambassador turned his head towards Seaglince. "Until that moment, imagine all that you could achieve for your people. The mark you can make in the universe."

Like a starving man stumbling upon a buffet, every neuron in Djurga's brain screamed to take the offer. But there were so many unknowns. His thoughts spun as he moistened his lips again. "How exactly would this training and transfer of technology occur?"

Ka stood. "We could start right now, if you are interested. If we have a deal, you could take my seat and receive your first lesson in piloting a spaceship." Ka glanced at the open captain's chair, then back at Djurga. "Do we have an agreement?"

Djurga shot up before his mind even processed what happened, his hand reaching out.

Before shaking, Ka added an addendum. "One thing more. My visits to your world must be kept secret. I require that you kill the farmer through whom I sent the note. If so, we will seal our arrangement."

Djurga didn't hesitate. "I completely understand. I'm keeping secrets from some very powerful beings as we speak. Your request will be fulfilled as soon as we land." His hand met Ka's cold grip. Djurga's energy level surged as the thrill of commanding a ship such as this charged his very being. "I look forward to a long partnership between friends."

Ka's not-quite-natural smile came with reassuring words. "To a very fruitful relationship indeed."

Chapter Twenty-Three (Current Day)

Surrounded by Sworn Warriors but feeling alone in desert darkness, Geeja stared in the direction of her home planet. "Uwan, I am no closer to saving you now than the day I awakened." Her shoulders sagged for a moment. "I am sorry."

She took in a grounding breath. "First things first. We must leave by sunrise, so I need to know who is with me, and where we can go." She called to her guards. "Time for a meeting."

Once beside the *Phantom Star*, she sent word via her warriors for all to gather in the moonlit shadow of the ship. Seeing Huanoc and Chella standing side by side, her thoughts went to Raflo. "How is he?"

For the first time in a while, Chella's countenance lifted instead of falling when asked about her patient's condition. "His fever broke and his breathing is normal. He's going to make it."

Even Huanoc sounded upbeat. "He lives!"

Hearing the good news, Geeja gave a hopeful smile, then turned the conversation to the future. "So, everyone, here is the deal. As part of my agreement to get Bregent's help, I promised that we would not stay long. In fact, we must be off this world by sunrise."

Eyes darted between some of the collected group, however nothing but steady gazes came from the Sworn Warriors. Jacastra delivered their response. "We've pledged our life to this cause and won't shirk from our responsibility."

Geeja bobbed her head. "I am grateful for your service."

A not unexpected silence followed. Everyone, including Geeja, had been sucked into this predicament with little or no warning. Finally, Shuggilar stepped forward, his eyes narrow and words harsh. "Not only did your arrival put our lives in the crosshairs of the Impercium, but you ruined the best business opportunity of my lifetime." He glanced around. "I get why those women follow you, but why in the name of the Eleven would any of the rest of us? You've brought *me* nothing except trouble."

He has a fair point, but also ignores the mongladon in the room. "You are right, of course." Her eyebrows raised. "But there is no turning back time. What is done is done. At this moment the question before us is, what do we do now? Who goes where at sunrise?"

While Talla had introduced herself briefly earlier, she had kept quiet, until now. "Wherever we go, who's paying? My contract specified a round trip run for the Sworn Warriors, and I've already gone beyond that agreement. These ships don't run on prayers, and I *always* get paid…*always*."

Another fair point that Geeja hadn't considered. In her very long lifetime cost had almost never been a factor. She lived well, but not extravagantly. More importantly, however, she had the resources of an entire planet at her disposal if she ever needed to cover a large expense. The enormity of the situation fell on her shoulders. *Literally everything I knew has changed.*

Jacastra raised her spear. "This is a blessed cause. I am sure the Holy Mother of our Order will spend every unit of our treasury."

Talla smirked. "That's something, but even all her units won't last long. Face it, this is a fool's duty."

Geeja's mind churned trying to latch onto something, anything that would give them hope. *Revolutions feed on ideas, but they also need cold, hard resources.* She came up with nothing. Shifting on her feet, she realized the truth. *I survived the attack by Djurga so long ago…and it did not matter. I am on the run, with an eviction notice to heed in a few hours.*

Geeja could feel everyone's eyes bearing down as she stared at the ground. *What am I going to do? I cannot give up, ever. But they can.* Her mind returned to thoughts of revolution, of righteous causes…and funding. *Even if we had units, other than the Sworn Warriors, would the rest join?* It dawned on her she needed the answer to that most basic question first. "All right, humor me for a moment. If I had the ability to compensate everyone, would you join my crusade? Would you fight against the Impercium?"

Talla hesitated, but only for a few seconds. "That's a big ask, and it would take a LOT of units, but for the right price and a sound plan, I would fly the *Curious Lady* through the front gates of the Impercium headquarters itself."

Nodding, then biting her lower lip, Geeja turned to Shuggilar. "How about you and Chella? Would you join us if we could pay enough?"

Chella whispered in his ear so low Geeja couldn't hear.

Shuggilar's brows arched together, as he whispered back.

Geeja half-grinned. *They seem to be considering it.*

After a few back-and-forth exchanges, Shuggilar faced the goddess. "To be clear, what happened to Uwan is a shame, but it's not my fight." He glanced at Chella. "However, my place of business and our home have been raided, and we're surely on an Impercium most-wanted list." He rubbed a creased forehead. "Please understand, we wouldn't be signing on as true believers but simply as people who need a new source of income…who also *happen* to hate the emperor. We have no other options."

Geeja's half-grin widened. "That is a yes in my language."

That left Huanoc and Raflo. They were the most important to any plan that might be devised because they had the *Phantom Star*. Geeja turned her wide eyes toward the big man. "What do you think, Huanoc? Would you join if you could strike a blow against the Impercium as well as have a nice payday?"

Huanoc towered over everyone with his bulging blue arms crossed. Now hours after sunset, the temperature had fallen drastically and a cold breeze blew through their small group. "Hmm."

Without Raflo there to translate his grunts, Geeja hoped that grumble meant he might consider the offer.

He spoke again. "Hmm, indeed."

A groan and another word, I think that is a good sign…maybe.

The Nafportonian clenched his jaw. "My home is the only other that has experienced a similar punishment as Uwan. I hate Djurga." His nostrils flared as he breathed. "Raf and I are also the only ones present to have been in an Impercium prison. We do not wish to return."

She tilted her head, understanding his concerns, but just as aware of the risks. "I can assure you that whatever plan eventually evolves, it is going to be against Impercium law."

"Hmm." His arms remained crossed. "Plus, I can't speak for Raflo. Our decision must be made together."

From the belly of the *Phantom Star* a voice called out. "Did I hear my name?"

A surge of energy shot through Geeja. "Raflo! You are healed!"

He limped down the ramp with a hand pressed against the Lighter wound.

Huanoc charged toward him, wrapping Raflo in an embrace as he reached the sand. "You live!"

"Whoa, take it easy, big guy. I feel like I lost a fight against a Lighter."

Laughter roared from Huanoc. "You did, and lived to tell the tale!"

With feet on the ground, Raflo's eyes darted to the women. "Talla, right? I know you from Uwan." He pointed toward the others. "Who are you and why are you holdin' spears?"

"We are Sworn Warriors of the Goddess." Jacastra pointed at Geeja. "We are honored to serve her."

"What?" Raflo's voice rose. "I mean, I thought that might be a possibility, but it's preposterous. Right?" He turned his head, searching for someone who might agree.

Huanoc put a hand on his friend's shoulder. "She killed an entire troop of Impercium soldiers with green flames, then persuaded the God of Politar to heal you." He squeezed. "The woman we knew as Gigi *is* the Goddess of Uwan."

His eyes went as wide as a ten-unit token. Looking as if he might faint, he lowered himself to the ground. "You're not kiddin', are you?"

Huanoc dropped to one knee beside his friend. "It is all true. She saved your life…twice."

Raflo rubbed his head. "I mean, the clues were there, but…really?"

Huanoc raised his shoulders. "Really."

Geeja broke the jubilant mood. "We are overjoyed that you survived, but we still have a decision to make by sunrise. Do we fight together or burn separately?"

"Burn?" Raflo touched his side. "Who said anything about dyin'?"

With his hand still on Raflo's shoulder, Huanoc explained. "Because we've aided Geeja, we're definitely on an Impercium hit list." He turned toward the goddess. "She has proposed we work together and find a way to make some real money. Hopefully while staying a step ahead of Djurga's goons."

"And the alternative?"

"Go our own way, while trying to stay out of Djurga's clutches."

Raflo glanced at Geeja, then back toward Huanoc. "And the catch?"

Now Huanoc stared at Geeja. "She doesn't seem to have the money part...well any part of the plan worked out." He scanned the odd assembly. "Everyone else is in favor. I would not make the decision without you."

"Even Shugg?"

The Kaliegan answered. "Yes. Me and my wife."

"What do you think?" Raflo looked up at Huanoc.

The big guy snorted. "I think we should have left her to die on the side of the road."

Geeja poked him. "Hey! Come on now. I am the most exciting thing to happen to you two gentlemen in your lives."

Raflo gave a weak smile. "Seriously, Huanoc. What do you think about this idea and this..." He waved his hand in Geeja's direction. "Goddess?"

Huanoc turned his gaze toward her. "Djurga has ruined our planets and now he's personally coming for us." He sighed. "I say if we're on his most wanted list anyway, let's at least try to take a shot at him first. Maybe we'll even earn a few units." He leaned toward his friend. "What do you think?"

Raflo scoffed. "I think we're all dead degels anyway, but there's no way I'm ever goin' back to an Impercium prison." His weak smile strengthened. "So, if we're goin' out, let's do it in a blaze of glory."

The swift turn of events from worry about units to a willing team, filled Geeja's heart. "Join hands. Let us give thanks to Politar for providing healing and refuge for a few hours."

The Sworn Warriors snapped into place as the beginning of a group circle. Exchanging wary glances, the others fell in line, with Shuggilar being the final link.

With both feet squished down in the sand, Geeja released her thoughts as she spoke. "Gracious Politar. We came as desperate individuals seeking help." Her grateful smile stretched her cheeks, happy to find fellowship in her cause. "We thank you for blessing us with wounds bound and poisons removed."

Geeja sensed a buzzing energy rising from the planet which she redirected through her hands. "Most importantly, we thank you for your sanctuary which provided us time to find our unity."

The flow from the planet intensified and she gladly shared the positive vibrations. Opening her eyes, Geeja saw a physical manifestation of the magical energy flowing through her to the others. One by one, everyone in the prayer circle glowed a pure shade of white. It looked like a ring of individual stars radiating light into darkness.

Nodding, Geeja reconfirmed her promise. "We thank you as we leave your friendly world, secure in the knowledge that we will return to repay our debt of gratitude. May you and Bregent reside in peace until we meet again."

Geeja turned her attention first to Jacastra, then one by one to the others, locking eyes for a moment with each participant. Their faces shone bright, with disbelieving smiles. They looked at one another with mouths ajar.

As Geeja expected, Politar replied in her lilting soprano. ***"Blessings of peace and success to you, my friends."*** Geeja wasn't sure the others would hear the planet's words.

Obviously, they had, as many gasped at hearing the world's words. Gathering their emotions Geeja heard calls of, "thank you" mingled with "peace to you as well."

Raflo kept his grip on Huanoc with one hand, and Jacastra with the other. Tears ran down his face, splattering on the sand. "I thank you most of all."

Morning jays sang in a chirping choir as the group's harmonious glow faded and the first hints of light snuck over the horizon. Now, all the Sworn Warriors wept openly. Shuggilar and Chella weren't immune either, each tearing up with broad grins. However, Talla's reaction surprised her the most as Geeja saw the pilot's mouth hanging agape.

As their glow winked out, they released their hands, clustering in small groups babbling about the experience. Talla made a bee-line to Geeja, dropping to her knees before the goddess. "For the first time, I truly understand the vows I spoke all those years ago, then walked away from."

Talla looked up with pleading eyes. "I finally understand what it means to be one with a world, even if this one isn't ours." Her voice went from shaky to determined. "Know that I'll give every fiber in my being to help you save Uwan."

Geeja held her hands out, then pulled Talla to her feet. "We each have our own journey and I am pleased our paths have crossed. *Together*, we will save Uwan."

Releasing Talla's hands, Geeja headed to the *Phantom Star* to honor her pledge that they would be gone by sunrise. Looking back, she saw an unlikely band committed to helping her. It gave her hope. *Now I must come up with a plan...and I have no idea where to begin.*

Chapter Twenty-Four
Three-Years Earlier

Once lights out had been ordered, Raflo choked back pain, then spoke from the top bunk of their spartan two-person cell carved inside their asteroid prison. "All right, big man. Can't wait to hear step three."

Huanoc tapped the bottom of Raflo's bed. "Hand me the PCD."

Gingerly hopping out of bed, Raflo turned over the pilfered device. "Who you gonna contact?"

"No one."

Raflo gave a one-eyed squint in the dim light. "No one? Then why steal it in the first place?"

Huanoc sat up in his bed examining the device, then popped off the back. "Time to hack this place's network."

"What? You can do that?"

Huanoc snorted irreverently. "I have advanced degrees in computer science as well as structural and electrical engineering. I also worked for the Wojceeka crime syndicate. How do you think I ended up here?"

"Huh." Raflo crooked his head to the side. "Guess I should have asked more questions when we met." Raflo watched in silence as his cellmate wiggled a metal clip into the back of the device, then tapped surprisingly quickly on the small screen for someone with such large fingers. His curiosity finally got the best of him. "Are you going to trigger the locks and open our door?"

Snorting, Huanoc continued pecking. "That would be silly. How would we get past the twelve guard stations between here and the outside?"

"Okay…then what are you doin?'"

"Got it!" Huanoc sat the device on the bed. "It's done."

"Come on, now. Don't keep secrets. What's step three?"

Shutting down the device, then hiding it, Huanoc yawned. "Better get a good night's sleep because we'll have a busy day tomorrow. I got us assigned to the janitorial detail."

Jaw dropping, Raflo stammered. "W–What? Janitorial detail? Why?"

Huanoc settled in bed, yawning. "Because it gets us to the places we need to go. Trust me."

Laying down, Raflo reviewed his day. It started with a torture session that left him a cyclops. By mid-day, he questioned if he had the strength to continue living. He shivered, then pulled the paper-thin blanket under his chin. *That is as close to lettin' go of the rope as I've ever been.*

As his muscles relaxed, Raflo's thoughts skipped forward to Huanoc's invitation to join a dangerous escape attempt. *Even if we fail and I die, it will be better than endurin' more torture.*

Now, he reflected on the conversation he just had with his cellmate and smiled as he closed his unbandaged eye. *The big man has put a lot of thought into this scheme. Who knows? It just might work.* He sighed before drifting off. *What a difference a day can make.*

**

To start the new day, harsh lighting blinked on simultaneously all over prison 6831, known throughout the universe as 'Djurga's Budget Hotel.' Other facilities held more dangerous criminals, like serial killers, and they surely had worse conditions, but this one held a special place compared to all other detention centers. Everyone knew its reputation. The warden had won Djurga's favor as an Impercium officer by smashing a minor civil war on Uerlon Prime. It had disrupted the delivery of vital metallurgic raw materials, and as his reward he asked for this assignment. It turned out he's a sadist with a thirst for human experimentation. The emperor gave him authority to run the place as his own personal house of horrors. Therefore, as soon as the lights flipped on each day, a recorded scream of a different torture victim blared from the sound system, announcing another day of randomized violence.

Hearing the guttural shriek this morning, Raflo's stomach churned. *That's my voice…from yesterday.* He swallowed hard. *I've got to get out of here.*

Huanoc called out with brightness instead of his usual gruff tone. "Big day! Janitorial detail!"

Raflo still had no idea how cleaning up nasty messes would help him get out. But even the possibility of escape, no matter how much of a longshot, seemed better than giving in to depression…or worse. He voiced a determined response through his post-surgical agony. "Whatever it takes." Then he added fake enthusiasm. "Here's to dirty jobs."

Huanoc laughed. "No. I do most of the dirty work. You stay clean."

"This is a strange plan…but, hey, it works for me." He shook his head as he hopped from the top bunk, landing lightly. "At least it's a plan. Let's get some breakfast before we start this strange day."

They marched into the common area, them dined on sorgusmeal, served prison cold instead of toasty. As they ate a guard approached, then shoved a work order in Huanoc's face. "Follow me. You're to report to Section D, node four, for instructions."

Smiling, Huanoc nudged Raflo. "Let's go. We have a schedule to keep."

"If you say so." Raflo rolled his good eye. "Food disposal backflow problem?"

Huanoc bit off a chuckle. "Better. Sewer clog."

Raflo spit out his last bite. "Gross."

With their work orders in hand, and a guard leading the way, they were escorted through three security stations. They then traveled down four sets of stairs in route to a grate in a sparsely lit corridor. The vile stench of humanoid waste wafted in the air as they arrived. The armed man covered his nose and mouth with a bent arm as his eyes watered. Stuttering, he stepped back, speaking between gags. "You two handle this…I'll wait back here."

Reaching down, Huanoc easily lifted the heavy metal grill.

Raflo glanced at the tight opening and offered to change their deal. "Look, I'm not even sure you can squeeze down there. I'll do it."

Huanoc stuck out his large hand. "No. I do this. You stay clean."

Stifling the urge to barf, Raflo acceded. "Whatever." He placed his nose in the crook of his arm, then whispered. "It's your plan."

Angling his shoulders to diagonal corners of the square opening, Huanoc managed to lower his big body down, using the chipped orange-painted rings of the attached access ladder.

Raflo heard a splash as his friend reached the bottom. That sent a fresh wave of nauseating odor through the opening. Holding his breath, Raflo leaned closer. "You okay down there?"

He could see Huanoc's smiling face below. "Fine." He put his big blue index finger to his darker blue lips. "Shh. It's only a tripped switch that's draining sewer water, but it's too soon to come out." He banged randomly on a pipe with a wrench. "That's for the guard. He needs to leave us here for an hour. We have a schedule to keep."

"What about me? What do I do while you're rollin' in piss and poop?"

"You are good at talking. Hang with him, make friends."

"Oookay." Raflo shrugged. "I'll see you in an hour." Standing, Raflo pasted on a fake grin like a space pirate about to board an out-of-fuel freighter. He started a conversation about a project he hoped to never see to fruition. "I admire your undercover gambling operation. Ever think about opening a secret hooly bar? I bet you could make a fortune from guys like me."

The square shoulder guard glanced both ways down the hallway, seeing no others around. Still, he whispered. "Funny you should ask. A couple of us have been talking about that very subject." He winked. "We might need some labor in exchange for reduced priced product. You in?"

Like the guard, Raflo shot a quick peek around, answering in a matching low voice. "Does a forggie want the keys to a lazentern house?"

Sixty minutes later, Huanoc emerged from the stinking pit, smiling. "Repairs complete."

The communication device on the guard's belt beeped. Pulling it eye level, an ugly laugh erupted from him. "It's your lucky day.

Garbage compactor malfunction on lower level eight." He snorted, then covered his nose again. "Seriously, with the good fortune you guys are having today, you should find a way to play the Galactic Lottery."

Raflo wanted to say, 'Seriously?' But instead returned a blank stare, not wanting to start any trouble.

Walking down five more levels and through an equal number of security stations, they soon reached their next putrid destination. A rotten smell greeted them, almost as rank as the sewer, but distinct. The acrid aroma of spoiled food provided a zesty top note to this particular garbage perfume milieu.

With the prior hour to get to know their escort, Raflo comfortably called the guard by name. "Hardle. What's the problem?"

He pointed. "The order says that unit fifteen has locked up. They've tried everything from the outside, and nothing worked." He moved closer to the door, then rapped on it with his knuckles. "There's a transformer inside on the opposite wall that needs to be switched out."

A civilian sanitation worker approached, handing Hardle a black cube-shaped electronic part. "All you have to do is dig through the waste, pull out the old unit, then replace it with this one."

Raflo chimed in. "If you know what the problem is, why don't you guys handle it?"

Hardle pulled his arm to his face, taking in a shallow breath. "Why do you think?"

Huanoc sighed. "I get it." He cast an eye to Raflo. "I'll handle this alone. No need for both of us to smell like this."

Raflo put up a hand and protested, but just a little, sensing the outlines of a plan. *Ah. He wants me to become friends with the guard for some reason…and I'll be glad to stay clean by playin' along.*

Huanoc opened the hatch. A more intense invisible wave overwhelmed the strong initial whiff of putrid rotting refuse that washed down the hallway.

The white-uniformed sanitation worker turned a light shade of green, then threw up.

"Gross!" Hardle stepped away. "Let's get out of here and let Huanoc do his job. He can't go anywhere down here."

Raflo, Hardle and the worker all fell back behind a sealed door, keeping out most of the stench. Finally breathing normally, Raflo made small talk, starting with providing a partially distorted view of Huanoc. "He may not be the smartest lunk in here, but he's stepped up as a friend today. Why should both of us have to smell like the wrong end of a bratha hauler?"

For the next hour Raflo pushed away his pain and chatted with the other two men about their favorite spike ball players on the circuit, the top stripper bars on Emblaka and the odds being given for the final three contestant pairs on the reality show, *Till Death Do Us Part*. "I'm glad they let us watch it in here. I think that couple from Plawan has the best chance to take the title…and the wife is smokin' hot."

Hardle had his own spin. "She's certainly the best-looking woman left, but she's dumb as a rock. There's a maze coming in the next episode, and you know it. There's always a maze in the finale. Do you really think she can beat the chickee from Mekneece? Huh?"

Raflo's dimples formed when he smiled. "I think she can, and even if she can't we'll get to see her drenched in that tight tee-shirt!"

Laughing, Hardle nodded. "We all want to see that, but I don't think she's got the smarts to make her way out of a one-way tunnel." He cocked his head. "Want to place a little wager on it?"

Raflo shook his head. "As much as I want to, I'm low on units in here. I best pass."

Hardle opened his mouth to reply when the door opened.

Huanoc and his accompanying odor stepped through, carrying the faulty transformer. "Compactor working."

The clean members of the crew reacted to Huanoc's smell in unison, taking a few steps backwards. Raflo's good eye watered. "Hey man, we have to get you a bath before you kill everyone."

Huanoc shrugged. "Just doing my job. I'm trying to do my time with as little drama as possible."

The device on Hardle's belt beeped again. Taking a glance, he shook his head. "If it weren't for bad luck, you two would have no luck at all."

Raflo shot a look at Huanoc, then back to Hardle. "What's that mean?"

"Means you're going to the depths of Djurga's Budget Hotel."

Raflo stiffened. "That doesn't sound good."

Hardle and the civilian worker burst out laughing. "I'm busting your balls. We're just heading to the bottom level of this place."

One thought jumped to the forefront of Raflo's mind as he glanced to his friend. "Does it stink?"

"Nah." Hardle shook his head. "At least not nearly like this place does, but it is frosty. There's just one layer of insulation from the cold of deep space."

They waved to the sanitation worker, then headed back to the central stairwell to travel down six more floors, with six more security checks. The air temperature dropped a few more degrees with each set of stairs.

An office worker bundled in a heavy jacket and mittens awaited them. The woman spoke in a high-pitched voice, and the air formed fog as she delivered a chilly greeting. "About darned time."

Rubbing his hands, Hardle shivered. "What's the problem?"

She stood beside an open frost-covered gray door. "The conveyor belt that spits our recycled material into bins to be loaded onto trash freighters is jammed." She pointed toward three large square compacted bundles of plastics. "My shift is over as soon as these get processed, so hurry up. I'm freezing down here." She took a breath as if to continue, then stopped, her face contorting. "What is that smell?"

Huanoc grinned. "Me." Then he stepped toward the stuck apparatus, kneeling to take a closer look.

Raflo joined him with hands on knees, whispering. "Are we goin' to escape on one of those freighters?"

A furrowed brow met his gaze as Huanoc matched Raflo's low voice. "No. You want to freeze to death?"

"Then what?"

"I'll take care of business if you can get them out of here for a few minutes."

Raflo nodded, realizing this had been the end goal all day. He stood and didn't have to exaggerate. "My friend smells like fetid shimkee and it is freezin' down here. Why don't we wait where it's warm and let him and his stink bomb cologne take care of business?"

The woman gave him a side eye. "Prisoners aren't supposed to be alone down here."

Disguising the deception, Raflo winked at the young woman with his unbandaged eye. "Would you rather talk about who's goin' to win *Till Death Do Us Part* with a couple of interestin' guys, or hang out with a frozen man who smells like turd on a stick?"

She blushed. "Well, when you put it that way, I am due a break." She shot a serious gaze to Hardle. "You vouch for these guys?"

He smiled even bigger than Raflo, as if he found this woman working in the bowels of this evil place attractive. "They haven't given me any trouble all day."

"Okay. There's a calefine machine up one level." She grinned, especially at Hardle. "I think the couple from Plawan will win."

"What?" Hardle pointed to Raflo. "I can't believe both of you are picking them!"

Laughing, they headed out the door, leaving Huanoc alone.

An hour later, Huanoc came up the stairs, shivering. He nodded hard as his blue lips appeared almost purple. He barely spit out one shuttering word. "F-Fixed."

"Hey." Raflo filled a cup of hot liquid and rushed it to his friend. "Drink this big guy."

Hands shaking, Huanoc spilled as much on himself as he got down his throat. "More."

Raflo filled another cup. This time the big man chugged all the hot drink without dribbling a drop.

Hardle's device beeped and he took a quick glance. "That's it for today, fellas. Time to head to the showers before dinner and lockdown."

With an expectant wide eye, Raflo glanced to his partner. "We sure had a busy day. Glad we got everythin' done, right?"

Huanoc nodded. "Indeed."

David Witt

Chapter Twenty-Five
Present Day

Emperor Djurga sat in his rejuvenation chamber inhaling the exotic mixture of gasses that kept his body alive and looking like a young man for over twenty centuries. Speglow crested to a cloud free morning, sending red rays across Emblaka. Soon, Seaglince would follow with her yellow light creating a blend of hues unlike any other in the universe. While the sunrises were beautiful, his mood remained ugly. It had been a full day without any signs or sighting of Geeja.

This daily regimen usually provided a quiet respite from his full plate of duties, affording him solitude and time alone with his thoughts. Ideas and insights sometimes sprang forth as he sat with no distractions. Today, however, his mind wandered back two thousand years ago to his first and only meeting with the woman he now pursued. He remembered his excitement at being in her presence, and of the other eleven gods and goddesses.

**

Djurga paced outside the biennial Assembly of the Holy Worlds, this year being held on Uwan. In the long hallway of the goddess' palace, he strode back and forth in the marble-pillared antechamber, anxiously practicing the main points of his pitch. He whispered. "Quantum powered travel for the masses, not just for gods and goddesses. The ability to expand trade between worlds." He wore a self-satisfied smile as he quietly spoke, considering his next argument the most important of all. "A free flow of ideas between civilizations."

The door to the chamber opened and a female warrior carrying a steel tipped wooden spear called out. "Governor Djurga. The assembly will now hear your proposal."

With the vigor of youth, he walked in with head held high, standing tall. He wore his dark blue scholar's robe as a signal that while he might be young by their standards, he was learned. Proudly, he stepped into the speaker's well in the center of the seated holy beings.

Because Geeja hosted this year's conclave, she sat on the raised dais directly in front of him, wearing an emerald green gown. She addressed him formally. "Governor Djurga of Emblaka. You have been granted an audience to present your proposal for the embrace of new technology." She stared hard. "After which you will answer questions."

Even though confident, he rubbed his damp palms on the sides of his robe. "Yes, Your Holiness." His mind went into automatic mode spouting his ideas in an uninterrupted fashion. When he finished, he knew he hit all points, especially the ones having to do with raising the standard of living for all people on every planet, holy or not. Now, he barely remembered what he said that day, but he recalled his relief as he wrapped up his presentation so many years ago, sure that his arguments had won the day. While he didn't recollect his exact words, he clearly recalled the unexpected grilling that followed.

The Goddess of Uwan fired the first question, one he didn't anticipate. "Where did you get the idea, and who helped you design your first quantum-powered ship?"

They know! How? The stutter he overcame as a teen reappeared. "I…I c–came up w-with it m–myself." He swallowed hard at his response and lack of preparedness.

Bregent, God of Politar challenged him next. "I understand your spaceship uses new metallurgic alloys. Where did you get your training and expertise in this field?"

He stood in the circle among the most important beings in the universe, mouth agape. *I can't believe they found out! I took every precaution, just as Ka directed!* He bowed his head as shame burned in his chest.

Gilbrar, the God of Plawan, spoke in a nasal tone. "The Ancients warned this day might come and we have kept this information hidden. Since we are the only ones who know the prophecy, we can be certain that the evil ones foretold have appeared, spreading technology that will kill our worlds."

Djurga heard no emotion as Geeja again addressed him.

"We know you made small tech advances, but we purposely overlooked them, as Emblaka is not a holy world. However, this new technology cannot be allowed to flourish. The Ancients defeated the Darkness once before and warned of its possible return." She took in a commanding breath, then declared their collective verdict. "You are hereby directed to return to Emblaka and destroy or dismantle all equipment used in the design and manufacture of this banned technology. Do you understand this order?"

His hot humiliation turned to searing rage, but he knew better than show it in the presence of those who could kill him on a whim. *How dare you condemn me! I built things never before seen in this universe! Who do you think you are?* He wanted to say those words, but instead answered through gritted teeth. "I understand, Your Holiness."

With an air of superiority, Geeja threatened him. "An emissary will be dispatched to your planet in thirty days. Failure to comply with the council's decision will trigger an order for your execution. Do you understand?"

Sweat beaded on his forehead as he barely contained his fury. "I understand." He kept his head down, then made a silent vow. *Thirty days, huh? You don't know it yet, but you've just scheduled your execution date, not mine.*

She swung a gavel. "You are dismissed. We appreciate your compliance with our command."

Walking out, he balled his hands into fists. *I'll never let anyone treat me like this again…ever!*

**

Replaying the memory that led to his revenge on those Gods boosted his mood, as did the completing of his rejuvenation session. A hissing sound emanated in the room as the air-tight chamber automatically opened, signaling the true start to his day.

Majordomo Axayzor opened the doors to the control center, his posture stiff and regal. Walking at a royal pace, he bowed deeply to the emperor, now sitting on his raised throne. "Your Excellency. How may I serve you this morning?"

With Djurga's mind lingering on his remembrance, he smiled. "Send in General Scanda. Perhaps he will have word on our search that will further my good humor."

David Witt

Chapter Twenty-Six

Quiet filled the *Phantom Star* as most of the people onboard, who had been running for their lives for almost twenty-four hours, now rested. Geeja awoke in the center of the floor surrounded by four Sworn Warriors. She stretched, then stood, trying to make as little noise as possible. She hoped to let her traveling companions have as much shut-eye as possible. Huanoc and Talla agreed that a nearby nebula would be a good location to lay low until a destination and plan had been settled, so both ships sat idle, side by side. Twisting at the waist, her spine crackled like a string of miniature snap serpents.

Shuggilar called in a low voice. "Not exactly luxury accommodations, eh?" He held a mug up. "Hot calefine?"

Nodding, she stepped over one of her sleeping guards and headed to the open seat beside the smuggler. Accepting the newly poured cup, she sat. "Thanks. I do not know how I ever survived before we learned to brew those strange beans."

His eyes went round. "You were there for the discovery?"

"Not the very day, but my warriors introduced it to me soon afterwards." She took a small sip, not wanting to burn her tongue. "Those beans proved to be one of our biggest gifts to the universe."

"Hmm." His hum sounded mournful. "I'm sorry they no longer grow on your world. Too much pollution."

It proved another unexpected reminder of what happened in her absence. Geeja blew over the hot surface, then changed the subject. She wanted to get to know this member of her little team, and to put Uwan's suffering out of her mind, at least for a few minutes. "So, how did you get into the smuggling business?"

He kept his laugh low. "As a young punk I was smart, and good in a fight, but not educated. Smuggling fit naturally." He shrugged. "After quitting school, I got recruited into a crew. A year later I led it. It's been a good life and I have no regrets."

Seeing her reflection on the black surface of her beverage, Geeja could relate to much of his story. *I have made mistakes...like misjudging Djurga.*

As she considered her fate, her eyes landed on Shuggilar's sleeping wife. "You are a smuggler married to a nurse. There has got to be a story there."

The man's face softened as a loving glance went toward Chella. "It's not as long of a tale as you might think." His blue Kaliegan eyes twinkled in the low light. "One night my boys and I had an incident with a gang that tried to bully some customers in my club. We took care of them, but a few of us ended up at the hospital." The corners of his lips tipped slightly. "We met as she stitched this cut on my cheek." His hand moved to a faded wound of about a finger's length on the right side of his face. "Turns out she has a thing for bad boys that know how to treat a lady right."

Remembering an earlier conversation with the woman, Geeja posed a new question. "Chella said that you had a big job planned that would set you up with enough money to retire." She glanced around at the motley team sleeping wherever they could find room to stretch out. "Sorry our drama turned your life upside down."

Shuggilar leaned back, sounding philosophical. "You were the immediate cause, but the root of the problem is always the same. It's the Impercium."

Geeja nodded. "It is certainly the root of my problems."

A quiet voice beckoned from behind. "Is that calefine I smell?" Raflo whispered as he stepped over resting bodies until joining them.

"Have a seat. I'll pour." Shuggilar turned to the dispenser, quickly serving up hot goodness to their third awakened member. He questioned as he handed the injured man his drink. "That was a bloody ugly wound. How are you feeling?"

"Like I went ten rounds of bare-knuckle cage fightin' with a Talousian bouncer." He rubbed his side. "But I'm alive and that's all that counts."

Geeja joined Shuggilar with her back against the hull, then caught Raflo up on their conversation. "We were talking about the Impercium." Her head lowered as she confessed her role in its creation. "I do not know how history has told the story in my absence, but I had a chance to deal with Djurga all those years ago, and I muffed it. I will regret that for the rest of my life."

Shuggilar filled her in on the Impercium narrative. "You are portrayed as an obstructionist who got what you deserved for standing in the way of progress." He patted her knee. "But don't beat yourself up too much. That was a long time ago…a very long time ago. And since then, none of your god friends has done anything about it either." His voice brightened. "But I sense change in the universe. It feels like something new is in the air."

"Oh? What do you mean?"

The smuggler tilted his head toward her. "Well, there's your awakening, for one. Surely that means something."

A shoulder shrug was her body's automatic reply. "Maybe, but it does not seem to have helped much so far."

"But that's just the latest occurrence." The calefine juice must have kicked in as Shugg sounded more animated. "Look, I'm a small player but I do business all over the universe. There's a buzz out in the stars about new magic, and I'm not talking about the holy worlds."

At the mention of magic Geeja straightened. "What do you mean?"

"I know this might be hard to believe for the goddess of a holy world, but even some backwater places like Kaliega have things happening that can't be explained."

She feigned ignorance, trying to sound as clueless as possible, not ready to share everything she and Zimo had accomplished. "Like what?"

"There's this new fad going on with some of the young people where they can do tricks, like knocking the hats off of their friends heads without touching them." His head cocked. "A lot of people think it's simply some new kind of sleight of hand trickery, but I know better. I once had a magician on my crew and he schooled me on all their secrets. What's happening now is different, and it's not confined to my world, or even my star system. I've seen it with my own eyes."

Geeja's brows arched, genuinely interested, but also trying to hide what she already knew. "Really? Where?"

"On Torgose, for one. It's in the back corner of the Empty Quadrant. I mean it's so far off the beaten path that you can't even see the trail with a telescope." Shuggilar chuckled. "That's why I have a safe house there. See, I was moving some forbidden cloaking circuitry and things got a little hot, so I stashed it to let things cool for a while."

"Okay." She scooted to the edge of her seat. "What is the magic part?"

"I'm getting there, just hold on." Shuggilar took a sip. "So, as I walked to my favorite bar for refreshment, I saw young people showing off tricks far beyond anything I had seen on Kaliega. Instead of knocking hats off, they were making their school books float. That's what I saw just walking around. Who knows what else they can do?"

Geeja momentarily flashed back to her youth, before being selected as the goddess. *Several of my friends had those abilities...but none as good as me.* Snapping back, she sought confirmation. "You saw this with your own eyes?"

"Yes, and from everything I've heard, it seems to be happening in random places all over the universe."

That jibes with what Zimo was telling me. She kept her expression flat, not about to mention all she helped him achieve, including his unofficial status as a new god. That needed to stay under wraps. "Very interesting."

He nodded. "Yeah, it's even got Djurga's attention."

Geeja's hard stare locked on Shuggilar. "Why do you say that?"

Shuggilar chuckled. "Djurga placed a Terminus Stake in each Holy Planet and draws power from them. He takes a bigger share from Uwan, of course, but as you've learned, he takes some from them all. It is said he trades away all the magic he steals, that it's sent to another dimension. We don't know if that's true, but whatever the arrangement is, it has been in place all these years." He rubbed his chin. "Now it seems that the empire's requirements have grown. He claims he needs more."

Geeja's mind raced. *Could this help save Uwan?* Her voice rose. "Go on."

"I've learned that he plans to harvest power from these new magical places, though there seems to be a problem. Evidently it takes a lot of magic to drive a Terminus Stake, and these special new worlds don't produce enough to make them operate right. So, word is he's developed a new technology and now he's testing it."

Geeja's tone darkened. "That sounds top secret. How do you know about it?"

He guffawed. "Because I'm a smuggler…and a thief. This was to be my final job. My big payoff. I had a buyer for one of the new magic collectors and a plan to steal the unit that orbits the little planet I was talking about, Torgose."

Mind buzzing, Geeja sat silent, feeling conflicted. She stood steadfast in her resistance against new technology based on the warning from the Ancients. *But what if it could topple the Impercium?* Her thoughts splintered further.

Raflo grinned. "Could you still do it? Could you steal it?"

Shuggilar shot a glare at him. "Have you forgotten we're on the run from the Impercium?"

"Yes, I know." Raflo scooted up in his seat, looking his fellow smuggler in the eye. "But if we could figure that part out, would your plan still work?"

"That's a big if, even now that we have a goddess on our side." He glanced at Geeja. "I might have lost my shot at a jackpot, but that doesn't mean I want to die."

"Humor me." Raflo's dimple flashed as he continued questioning Shuggilar.

A flirty smile reflexively formed as Geeja listened to the conversation. *Raflo is very handsome.*

Raflo continued. "For the moment act as if we could figure a way to keep us safe. If we can make that happen, do you think we can get our hands on that thing?"

Shuggilar lifted his left eyebrow. "You believe that's possible?"

"Come on, Shugg. I said pretend." Raflo wrapped both hands around his cup. "All I'm askin' is for you to give me a straight answer."

"Okay, but just know I'm not signing up for a suicide mission." Shuggilar's lips pursed. "The *Phantom Star* was a key part of my plan, so that's good, but we'll need some help." He met Raflo's expectant gaze. "If we could get that, I guess it would be possible…theoretically."

"Yes." Raflo rubbed the location of his Lighter wound. "I owe the Impercium a little payback for this, and a lot more. Let's do it."

"Why steal it now?" His forehead wrinkled. "There's no way the buyer I had lined up would do business with someone as radioactive as I am. Stealing it might tick off the Impercium, but otherwise it would be a dangerous waste of time."

Raflo sighed. "Maybe we could repurpose it, turn it into a weapon or somethin.'"

Geeja's eyes tightened, knowing she had wondered almost the same thing seconds ago. Her conscious flashed more warnings. "Using technology as weapons is what launched the Impercium. I once murdered hundreds in a fit of rage and you just saw me kill those Impercium soldiers when I meant to stun them. Those errors stain my soul, so I certainly will *not* use technology to kill."

Huanoc now joined the conversation, his deep voice startling Geeja. "Gigi, what if we could use that technology as a force for good? What would you think then?"

Her voice quavered. "Is there such a thing?" Even a theoretical discussion about using advanced weapons upset her stomach. "Way back when, Djurga talked about all the advantages of tech and it looks like what he has really accomplished is damaging the environment of world after world. In the process it has made him a permanent dictator."

The big man countered. "What you say is true, but there have been positives as well. Like, education levels have increased everywhere. It's not the technology, it's how it's used."

The churn in her gut intensified as her lips pressed flat while she considered what to say next. *Could Huanoc be right?* She swallowed hard as thousands of years of commitment wavered in the light of this new era. *This is not black and white. Be smarter.* She wrung her hands. "Then…what *would* you do with it?"

Huanoc's broad shoulders pulled back as he smiled. "I want to use it to free Uwan, then Nafporton."

"What?" Geeja snapped around. "How?"

Beaming confidence, he glanced toward Raflo. "I'll need to get a closer look at the device, but if it does what I think it does, it can be used to destroy a Terminus Stake. Are you interested now?"

Her mind was split. Would endorsing this plan make her a hypocrite? Or, was it a greater good to destroy that terrible chunk of metal that crippled Uwan? *I did swear an oath to Uwan.* Making her choice, an uncertain smile spread across her face. "I say let us go steal the thing."

David Witt

Chapter Twenty-Seven
Two Thousand Years Earlier

The stinging humiliation of standing before the Holy Twelve and being treated as a child morphed into anger. Boarding the spaceship he helped build, Djurga's negative thoughts boiled as if in a pressurized furnace designed for the sole purpose of producing scalding rage. Settling into the captain's chair for the flight back to Emblaka, his mind molded black thoughts into a plan. "They will know my fury, but I will need help…and I know just who to call."

Barely a light year away from the gods and goddesses who had dismissed him, he connected on a call with Ambassador Ka. Having dealt with his contact from the Truise Dimension for several years, he got right to the point, respecting his benefactor's disdain for wasting time. "The day we met you told me that someday I would ask for your help." He could feel his anger churning, as if in a volcano's cauldron. "That day has come."

"Ah, just as I foretold." The envoy's voice sounded steady, as it always did. "What piece of technology would you want?"

Djurga squeezed the navigation handles. "I need a weapon that will kill a goddess."

"Hmm. Interesting request, Governor Djurga. Do you have a specific god in mind, or will any do?"

He spit words through gritted teeth. "Any would do, but to see one in particular dead would please me greatly." His pressed lips relaxed a fraction as saying these next words aloud was a physical release. "I want to kill Geeja, Goddess of Uwan, and I need to accomplish the deed in the next thirty days."

"You have grand ambitions, governor. Fortunately for you, I have experience in this matter. I assure you it can be done."

"Excellent!" The tightness in his chest eased. "How soon can you get me what I need?"

"I can deliver everything in ten days. How does that sound?"

"Fantastic!" Djurga lowered his shoulders. "You continue to amaze me with your kindness."

Ka paused. "Governor Djurga, do you remember the second half of our conversation that day?"

He did remember, but hoped it might have been forgotten by the ambassador. "Yes…I do." He sighed. "You will request a favor in return. Correct?"

"Your memory does not fail you."

Djurga braced for the worst as the vessel flew by stars at quantum speed. He spoke hesitantly. "And what might you want in return?"

The flat delivery matched the nonchalance of his reply. "It's a trifling thing and will cost you nothing personally. I'll inform you of our proposal when I deliver what you need. Until then, begin planning your revenge. You'll need three or four teams of your best soldiers for a coordinated attack. Select them and I'll see you in ten days."

Djurga stared into the darkness of space as he raced toward his home planet at a velocity he couldn't have imagined two years ago. The uncertainty of what he would be asked to do weighed on him as he replied, his voice as devoid of emotion as Ka's. "I'll be waiting."

**

Ten days flew by as Djurga readied not three or four teams, as suggested by Ambassador Ka, but twelve. He always preferred to over prepare rather than be caught lacking. Besides, twelve represented the most symbolic number in the universe. *A dozen just feels right.* He smiled as he watched them train.

The first time he met the ambassador had been in a remote field, away from prying eyes. Now, the ship from the Truise Dimension had its own secret landing pad at the new Emblaka Spaceport, because Ka insisted his trips here be kept under wraps. As always, Djurga personally met the emissary on his infrequent visits. He extended his hand when the diplomat stepped away from the ramp. "Ambassador Ka, it is with great pleasure that I welcome you to our world once again."

Ka dipped his head slightly in recognition, then clasped the governor's outstretched hand. "I can assure you the pleasure is all mine."

The representative's words were always precise, but never spoken with any feeling. Djurga noticed more as they shook. *It's like greeting an ice cube.* This time, he noted something different. *And he hasn't aged since we met.*

Djurga escorted his guest to an ornate drawing room inside his nearby palace. Luxurious draperies in yellow and red, symbolic of the twin suns of this world, framed massive windows. They overlooked a private garden that this time of year bloomed with orange dihors. He waved his arm toward a buffet of fruit and cheeses. "Would you like a snack or glass of wine after your journey?"

"Thank you for your hospitality, Governor, but I am fine. Shall we get down to business?"

The man always seemed focused. *Same old Ka. I know what to expect. Besides, he never takes a bite or drink. No refreshments next time.* He tilted his head, then motioned toward two velvet upholstered armchairs; one red, the other yellow. "As you wish."

Once seated, Ka inquired. "Are your forces prepared?"

Djurga shifted in his seat. "I think so. Your advice was a little vague. I have twelve elite teams pulled from my best units on standby. They represent my most skilled swordsmen, archers and riflemen." His fingers knitted together as he placed them on his lap to conceal their slight nervous tremor. "When I learn more about the armaments they will use, I will determine which troops to deploy."

Ka's tone and volume remained unchanged. "First, there are hand-held weapons that fire beams of light. They can be used in either close combat or at distance. We call them Lighters."

Djurga stiffened. "Lighters…" Thinking for a moment, it became clear which teams to use. "My riflemen seem the right choice. They are practiced in aiming and firing at their targets."

"Yes." Ka's flat expression didn't match the power of his words. "These weapons are deadly against most forms of life. Your assassins will have the element of surprise on their side as their opponents have never seen a weapon this terrifying before."

"Wonderful! Finally, the tables turn! That's exactly the kind of news I hoped to hear." Relief transitioned to satisfaction as he smiled. "I'll have my teams practicing by day's end."

Ka nodded. "That's not all. I want there to be no doubt of your success, so I offer more…in the spirit of our mutually beneficial agreement."

Djurga's heart raced. "More?" A huge smile splashed across his face. "Thank you for your generosity!"

Ka folded his hands over his waist. "You have experimented with craft that can lift and cruise in mid-air, correct?"

"Yes." He heard his heart pounding in his ears. "With all we have learned from you, we have made great strides in development of our hoverbugs."

"Hmm." The enigmatic man's lips uplifted a tiny bit at the corners, which passed as his full smile. "We have perfected the design and armed them with Lighters as well. With these flying machines you should achieve your goal of killing the goddess."

The governor released a huge breath. "Thank you, a thousand times, Ambassador!"

"Yes." Ka tapped his index finger on the velvety fabric of his chair's arm. "You shall have these arms today…if you agree to our wish."

Djurga swallowed. "Of course." His fingers tightened. "I look forward to fulfilling my end of our bargain. What do you ask of me?" He remained calm on the outside, but his stomach churned, sure that a great price would be demanded for such powerful gifts.

"It's very simple, really. In return for supplying these weapons, we require that a device be mounted on your ship. While your troops are roasting the Goddess of Uwan, you will push a launch button. Your end of the deal will then be complete."

He forced a smile. "And what will the launched device do…exactly?"

Like all facial expressions from the ambassador, his smile seemed a little off, lacking sincerity in a way that seemed hard to describe but easy to observe. "It will penetrate the planet's surface, then begin pulling energy out, which will be beamed back here, to Emblaka. When a sufficient amount has been stored, the system we install will deliver it to our world."

Djurga struggled in the past ten days to guess what an advanced species such as Ka's would want from his backwater universe. He thought it might be some sort of rare mineral or other physical resource. He realized his mouth hung ajar, snapping it shut before questioning. "Energy? You want energy?" He tilted his head. "Why? You seem to have all the energy one could ever desire."

Ka's bare smile disappeared. "We have an abundance of most types of energy, but we lack one."

"I don't understand."

The ambassador's hands flexed to his sides. "Broaden your imagination, Governor Djurga. We want their magic."

Djurga's eyes flared wide. "Their magic? What will you do with their magic?"

A different smile than the governor had ever seen etched Ka's face. Today, the right side of his thin lips lifted higher than the left. He interpreted it as signaling evil intent. For once it looked authentic.

"That is none of your concern, Governor Djurga…or shall I call you *Emperor* Djurga?"

Chapter Twenty-Eight

Geeja joined the Sworn Warriors in staring out portholes as Huanoc and Talla set their respective ships down in a clearing on a small moon orbiting the gas planet, Vaesona. While Geeja had some space travel under her belt, it remained an exciting, but relatively foreign experience. For the other women who had intentionally turned their back on technology, it was completely new. Once the purring engines quieted, a knowing smile emerged, watching the tough soldiers pledged to protect her giggling like schoolgirls. *It is easy to see the allure of this tech.*

When the ramp lowered from the belly of the *Phantom Star*, fresh air rushed in. Geeja's eyes widened. "A world with truly clean air still exists!"

A hush fell as they all shared the experience. Jacastra turned to Geeja. "Did Uwan smell like this in olden days?"

Geeja reached for Jacastra to steady herself. Tears rolled down her cheeks as if welling up from a deep spring. "Yes. This is what I have promised to restore."

Shuggilar grabbed the Lighter at the top of the ramp, breaking the reverential moment. "Well, this place may smell sweet, but it's no Impercium amusement park. Some of the most dangerous animals in the universe call this place home. That's why it's mostly unsettled."

Huanoc chimed in. "That's why we're here. We need to stay off the Impercium radar. Get our plan together." He pointed to Jacastra. "Secure perimeter until we can rig a force field around our ships."

Grabbing her spear, Jacastra nodded. "Finally, a job we're made for." The other women on the *Phantom Star* fell in behind her and were joined on the soft grass by their compatriots from the *Curious Lady*. She shouted orders to her squad that echoed off the stand of trees surrounding the opening.

Talla strode up the ramp of the *Phantom Star*, beaming. "Those women act like they've won the galactic lottery."

Raflo winced as he sat down at the small table, his wound still tender. "We're goin' to attempt somethin' with even bigger odds." He smiled mischievously. "And if we're successful the payout will be even greater."

Geeja refilled her cup, then sat beside Raflo. "I know we're going to steal some tech, but what *exactly* are we going to do?"

With everyone except the Sworn Warrior's around the table, Shuggilar gave a recap of what had been discussed earlier, presumably for Talla's benefit. "Things are changing with this new magic popping up in random places around the universe, and we're not the only ones to notice. Since Terminus Stakes apparently won't work on those small-scale magical planets, Djurga's testing a new technology."

Geeja raised her hand. "And we really do not know what he does with the magic he steals?"

Huanoc shifted. "Like I said, there are rumors, but even after all these years, no one knows for sure. It's certain he's not using it himself because while the Impercium's technological advances are remarkable, they all run on normal sources of energy." His eyes shot to Geeja. "Well, normal these days. An interstellar battleship is impressive, but it runs on the same crystals as the *Phantom Star*."

Raflo teased. "Where is the Huanoc who speaks only in short bursts, and what have you done with him?"

The large man's blue cheeks deepened in a Nafportonian blush. "Revenge against Djurga loosens my tongue."

Shuggilar stood. "What he does with the magic he steals doesn't matter at the moment. What does is how we're going to get our hands on some." His hands went out as he cocked his head impishly. "And maybe make some money while we're at it?"

Rubbing his side once more, Raflo chided his fellow smuggler. "I get it, Shugg, but does that come ahead or behind the priority of not getting shot by a Lighter?"

Both hands went up. "Just looking for a win, win here. After all, this was to be my big retirement score."

Geeja nodded. "If we survive the heist, we will do our best to figure out some way for you all to get paid." She crossed her arms while leaning back. "So, how do we steal it?"

Shuggilar clapped his hands, then bobbed his head. "Okay. In concept it's simple. This new system they're testing has hundreds of tiny spikes driven into the surface of a planet in a very remote location. According to my informant, these pull up small amounts of magical power that's drawn into a central collecting center on the surface."

He lifted a hand, pointing. "When enough is gathered, they shoot it up to a storage facility in stationary orbit. A large battery-like block concentrates the energy until there is enough to fire a focused beam back to Emblaka."

Geeja shook her head. "Uhm, I am confused." Her eyes narrowed. "What are we stealing?"

A bemused smile graced Shuggilar's weathered face. "They've done all the work, so all we need to do is snatch the battery."

Raflo grinned. "Just grab a large battery thing from an Impercium space station? Easy as stealing from a blind man, right?"

Geeja gave a quizzical stare. "Okay. How do we steal it, and what do we do with it?"

"Very direct." Shuggilar winked. "I like that." He took a deep breath. "First, we must take control of the collecting center on the ground and disable the force field it emits. That's what protects the orbiting station."

Raflo interjected. "Let me guess, the collectin' station is protected by a battalion of Impercium troopers."

"Actually, it's two battalions." Shuggilar shrugged. "So, breaking in and disabling that shield turns out to be the simple part."

"Shugg!" Raflo lurched halfway across the table. "I thought you had a plan?"

"Oh, I did. I had a band of mercenaries lined up to handle step one. They would turn me in for the bounty on my head before they would work with me now."

Huanoc placed his elbows on the table. "Let's assume we figure that part out. What's next?"

Shuggilar chuckled. "You surprise me, Huanoc. I never thought of you as an optimist."

"You're right." He clasped his hands. "I'm more of a determined realist. I'm reserving judgment until I hear the entire plan."

"A man after my own heart." Shuggilar gave a joking smile as he placed a hand over his chest. "Now, where was I? Oh, yes, after the force field is down, the next step is to either convince the troops on that space station to allow us to enter, or blast our way in."

Geeja bit her lower lip. "Is there *any* good news here?"

"Yes, as a matter of fact. There are only about ten soldiers up there. The rest are scientists." He wore a satisfied smirk.

"Shuggilar!" Geeja shook her head, blinking slowly before casting an uncertain gaze. "Alright, *supposing* we get in. What happens then?"

Shuggilar's eyes narrowed. "The final step is the tricky part."

She glared. "This part is harder than the other steps?"

"I didn't say hardest. I said it's tricky." His fingers went to his temples. "See, we'll have zero gravity on our side. But first, we'll need to detach that big battery from its moorings, then spacewalk it to this ship to make our getaway. One wrong move and it smashes into the *Phantom Star*. That would seriously impact our plan. I know for a fact that none of us want to be captured by Djurga's goons."

Raflo gave a mirthless grin. "So, we need to disable a protection beam guarded by troopers, which we don't have the manpower or weapons to do." His hands balled into fists on the table. "Then we somehow break into an Impercium space station?" His lips tightened. "And if everythin' goes well, all that's left to do is spacewalk a massive block of contained magic to our ship. That's your plan?"

Shuggilar's eyes went round and his furry eyelashes peaked. "Almost."

"Come on!" Raflo's head snapped back. "Let me guess. The next part is even harder, right?"

"Well, *harder* isn't the right word."

Raflo fired back. "What *is* the right word, Shugg?"

He sighed, then glanced at Geeja. "If we're going to destroy a Terminus Stake, we might need an artifact, an *ancient* one, if you know what I mean."

All eyes turned to the goddess as Geeja stared with mouth agape. "Do not look at me. I have no idea what he is talking about."

Rubbing his hands, Shuggilar continued. "Look, there's an old legend that the Ancients left a device that could magnify magic…to be used in emergency situations. We might need it to do this job."

Geeja's head tilted back as everyone again turned their attention to her. "Now it's coming back to me." She massaged her temples. "As I remember, it was shrouded in mystery, even from the Holy Twelve." Geeja closed her eyes as silence fell on the group. "The Ancients were very vague about it, never actually using the word 'artifact.' They told us about an ambiguous ability to focus massive power in the direst of times. None of us could deduce what they meant, so somewhere along the line, we decided it must be a device from their dimension, which we deemed an artifact. We guessed it to be entrusted to one of us, and only that god knew its true purpose."

Raflo put a hand on her shoulder. "Do you know who has it…or at least had it?"

"No." Geeja lowered her gaze. "I did not have it, so I forgot about it. I mean, I never needed it… Well, I did not know I needed it until it was too late." She clasped her hands. "One more thing I could have done differently."

With her troops deployed, Jacastra quietly rejoined the group, standing at attention just behind the goddess. She held a spear at the ready.

Rubbing Geeja's shoulder, Raflo offered consolation. "Everyone here has done things they regret. That just makes you —"

"Human? Normal?" Geeja pushed his hand away. "See, that is the thing. I had thousands of lifetimes of experience and I made a colossal mistake…one that almost killed an entire planet. I am not human or a goddess. I am a monster."

No one offered a rebuttal or a quip. Raflo stared at the small table. "Yet, you're here–alive." He paused. "None of us can change the past, but we will impact the future, one way or another. The question you must answer is, what are you goin' to do? Give in to despair, or fight?"

A single, sharp laugh escaped her lips. "You have known me for two days, so you already know the answer."

He gave a loopy smile and wink. "Guess you're in."

Her eyes tightened. "I am aggrieved, by everything that has happened, that is all." Taking a deep breath, she let it out loudly. "I am finished wallowing in my pity pit. It is behind me now." She gave Raflo's arm a soft jab. "Thank you for the pep talk."

Shuggilar chimed in. "Destroying a Terminus Stake with the stolen battery wasn't included in my original business venture. I simply planned to sell it to a well-funded, anonymous buyer. So, I don't have a plan in place to locate or secure the ancient item. I'm hoping you might have some ideas."

Geeja rubbed the back of her neck. "Since we have been talking, a memory has percolated. If my recollection is accurate, during a night of drinking a few of us speculated on who might have been charged with protecting the object. We narrowed it down to three planets: Bostor, Fontonce or Salostorce."

"Hmm." Huanoc nodded. "Much planning needed and we need to train your troops."

Jacastra jumped up from her guard position, spear in hand. "We've just found our lost goddess! By the *Twelve* Holy Worlds, there's no way she goes without us as protection."

Shuggilar lifted the Lighter from the table. "We're stretched thin, Jacastra. We will need your team trained on modern weapons to help us pull this off. We can't teach you if you're traipsing around the universe."

Geeja's eyes cut to her ramrod straight sworn protector. "We compromise. Three of you, plus Talla go with me while the rest stay with Shugg and Huanoc to train."

Jacastra rapped her spear against the floor. "But there's too much danger!"

Geeja stood, turning toward the soldier. "That was not a question, Commander."

With eyes bolting wide, Jacastra bowed on one knee. "Your wish is our command, my goddess. I'll make the selections and be ready to travel upon your word."

With that settled, Geeja turned toward Shuggilar. "I am asking again. If we manage to do all *this*." Her hand waved around in the tight space. "You are saying we can rid Uwan of that cursed spike?"

"Yeah." He shrugged. "With the device, we can blast that Terminus Stake into ten million bits."

His words thrilled her as Geeja recalled her promise to Uwan. *As you are my witness, I shall do all I can to return you to your former glory.* As she opened her mouth to speak, loud shouts from outside echoed up the ramp. She yelled. "Our people are in trouble!"

Huanoc sprang up, the first to reach the ramp leading to the surface. He grabbed the Lighter always kept there as he raced down. Geeja and Raflo followed on his heels.

At the bottom they stopped in their tracks, stunned by what they witnessed. In a coordinated attack by the women, spears slashed and stabbed a giant-sized animal that loosely resembled a fanged brancha species on Uwan. Their bad tempers on her world made it dangerous to simply cross paths in a forest.

Huanoc lowered the Lighter. "I might hit one of them from this distance." He sounded stunned. "Besides, I don't think they need help."

Two of the women stayed in front of the attacking animal. They thrust steel-tipped spears toward it in distraction, then leaped out of the path of claws that were easily as long as Geeja's forearm. Meanwhile, others jumped on top of the hairy beast, jabbing their primitive weapons into the base of the skull. Geeja's mouth hung open as the creature fell in a sudden heap. She spoke to no one in particular. "They are even better trained than the warriors of my day."

Talla broke her silence. "The Holy Mother may have faults, but her devotion to training could never be doubted. She believed the fullness of time to be at hand and pushed us hard. Turns out she was right."

Shuggilar stepped beside the two women. "We've definitely found the core of the forces we need to take on that collecting station."

He smiled broadly. "If the rest of our preparation goes this well, we'll be ready to attack by the end of the week!"

Chapter Twenty-Nine
Three-Years Ago

Raflo paced as he waited for lights-out in the prison. Huanoc refused to say anything about the escape plan, glancing toward nearby guards every time he nudged him for an update. After all his pleading stares failed to gain information, he climbed into bed with a grunt. Once darkness ruled the facility, he peeked with his good eye from the top bunk and could see the faint glow of a PCD under his cellmate's thin prison blanket.

Dropping to the ground, Raflo knelt beside the bottom bed, speaking in the lowest whisper of his life. "Hey. What's goin' on?"

For a big man with a deep voice, Huanoc also spoke in a voice that could hide on the smallest breeze. He kept the contraband device under his blanket. "Typing out release orders for you, me and Wraigreth."

"What?" Raflo sounded as excited as a kid getting his first remote control skimmer for their birthday. "You're doin' what?"

"I've hacked the Impercium's main system back on Emblaka and I'm getting us out of here."

Raflo buzzed with excitement, despite his aching injury. "Thanks, buddy!" Unable to contain his new found energy, he rubbed his friend's shoulder. "That's great, but how did you do it?"

While Raflo hummed with enthusiasm, Huanoc sounded as calm as someone taking a Paquant, the newest mellow party drug on the club scene. "First, I needed time alone with a local system router node."

"Ah! Let me guess, there's one in the sewer system."

"Mmm."

Raflo nodded. "Yep, that smell sure kept the guard away." He sniffed. "And it's *almost* gone." He shot a micro-glance at the door, then back to his partner. "And that got you into the main system?"

"No. Into the warden's private network."

"Look, I know you keep your word count at a minimum, but I'm dyin' to know what you did. Can you make an exception?"

A deep growl sounded under the gray blanket. "Fine." He shifted his weight on the bed and Raflo could hear his fingers tapping on the glowing screen. "Once in the warden's system, I got us sent to the jammed garbage compactor."

"Let me guess, another router or somethin' that let you get into the Impercium main system?"

"Almost." The steady rat-a-tat-tat of fingers continued. "It allowed me to bounce my signal to the final substation."

"I know where that had to be; the coldest place in the pits of this hell."

"Right."

Raflo sat beside the bed in silence, not yet truly believing Huanoc could really pull this off, when a thought bullied its way into his brain. "Thanks for doin' all the dirty work today…literally. You worked in some nasty stuff."

"Hmm."

"Right." He had started to pick up on the subtleties of Nafporton language usage, or at least this particular citizen. "It will be worth it if this works. What I'm wonderin' is why you wanted me to stay out of the muck? I mean I appreciate it and all…"

"Last stop."

Raflo thought back on the day. "I'm not sure what you mean. I just stayed in a warm place and chatted for a while."

"That location most exposed. More privacy needed."

"Okay…I'm still not followin.'"

He sighed. "Flirt. When you open your mouth near a woman, you are flirting."

Raflo's cheeks warmed in a deep blush. "*Maybe* you're right…" He shook his head. "Okay, you're right."

"You and Hardle did your job well."

"I get it. You know, she was kind of cute."

Huanoc smothered a laugh, then stuck his head out from under the blanket. "There. Now we sleep, knowing we escape tomorrow." He paused. "Or ruse discovered and we die."

"What?" The calm conversation took a decidedly dark turn. "I know it's a risk, but how much of one? I just want to be prepared."

Stowing the contraband PCD, Huanoc listed the obstacles. "Three signal relays, Wraigreth also involved, normal Impercium security." He put a hand on Raflo's shoulder. "However things go, we leave this place tomorrow— as free men, or in body bags."

**

Try as he might, sleep evaded Raflo. His bandaged eye throbbed and his mind raced, worrying about all the ways their elaborate plan could blow up. Not even the rhythmic snoring from the bunk below helped. When the lights turned on all over the Budget Hotel and the recorded sound of torture echoed against the concrete walls, he hopped down from the top. "How's this goin' to work? How soon until we get out?"

Huanoc rubbed his eyes, then stretched as bones cracked loudly along his long spine. Sitting up, he licked his lips. "Hard to say. Mid-morning?"

"That's kinda' vague."

Standing, then twisting at the waist, more large joints popped. "Take a breath. We escape or die. Either better than here."

He couldn't argue with the reasoning, so he didn't.

At breakfast, Wraigreth sat beside them. "We set?"

Huanoc nodded.

The rest of the morning passed unremarkably as their cell block had early time in the yard. Raflo tensed every time a door opened or a guard headed even remotely in their direction.

Heading back inside, the moment finally arrived. Jooloc, the guard who ran the betting pool, pulled the three of them aside, his voice rising. "I've never seen anything like it, but the three of you have been granted early release. Says here it's for 'good behavior.'" He laughed. "Guess I should have reported that little fight."

Standing between the larger men, Raflo quipped. "But then we would have had to mention how much money you made off that misunderstandin' between these fine gentlemen." His smile stretched ear to ear. "This way we all win."

Jooloc gave him a side eye, then smacked the folded papers against his palm. "Whatever. Follow me and we'll process you out. Your debt to the Impercium paid in full."

After signing a raft of papers and changing into the clothes they were wearing when they arrived, the three stood in a holding chamber awaiting transport to Emblaka. Raflo paced as Wraigreth and Huanoc lounged on concrete benches built into the walls. None said a word as the seconds dragged by. A guard came in, then cleared his throat. "There's been a change of plan."

Stomach sinking, Raflo thought he might hit the floor. *I knew this was too good to be true.*

The guard glanced at the glowing tablet, reading the update. "Instead of the usual stop on Standona, today's flight is non-stop. You'll be free men in just over an hour." He gave them a hard glare. "And if you know what's good for you, you'll stay on a steady beam. The warden has a special place in his heart for double dippers." He laughed deeply, then pushed a button that opened an airlock onto a Vorian-class transport ship. Ten employees joined the three newly freed men, and in just over an hour they docked at Emblaka.

Stepping into the spaceport, Raflo breathed free air, catching the savory scent of kaston being grilled for lunch sandwiches. Resisting the urge to order one, he pulled the other two aside in the bustling concourse. "Let's get out of here before somethin' goes wrong."

Wraigreth waved. "Follow me. Going in, I parked my ship in the long-term storage sector with rent paid for two years."

Three monorail rides later, they strolled past parking aisle H-seven hundred in the massive facility, each step bringing them closer to pad eighty-seventy-five. Getting closer, Wraigreth's anxiousness seemed to overwhelm him. He broke into a trot, then ran the final quarter mile. When Raflo and Huanoc caught up, the man stood facing a spaceship with arms spread wide, smiling broadly. "There she is, boys. Behold, the *Phantom Star*."

At first glance, it looked like most Gravarian class cruisers Raflo had seen; nice, but nothing special. To their third partner it seemed something more, so Raflo did what he always did. He slapped Wraigreth's back hard, then pointed toward the angular vessel as he oozed over-the top fake admiration. "She's a beauty!"

Wraigreth gushed at the compliment. "She sure is."

The words barely left his lips when Lighter fire bounced concrete chips beside his leg. Spinning, they saw a woman holding the weapon. She had traditional Blongarian female-styled spiked hair and a scowl. "You came to see this crystal hauling bucket before me, the one you said you sold?"

"Baby! There's a misunderstanding here!" The tough guy Raflo and Huanoc knew from prison had seemingly been replaced by a begging husband. "These guys helped me get early release." His voice crept higher. "See, they got no way to leave here, so I'm letting them borrow it for a while."

The angry woman pointed the Lighter at Raflo and Huanoc. "Is he telling the truth or is this more lies?"

Raflo caught Wraigreth's slight head nod. "Sweetie! By the Holy Eleven, your man is tellin' the truth. All he's talked about on the trip here is how happy he would be when he held you in his arms again. Right Huanoc?"

"Hmph."

Raflo jumped back into the conversation. "That's a yes. He's Nafportonian, you know."

She lowered the weapon from her shoulder and her tone warmed. "That's so precious." Still pointing the Lighter in the men's general direction, she questioned Wraigreth further. "Does that mean you're ready to come back and work for Daddy? After all, striking out on your own is what started all your trouble."

Nodding fast, Wraigreth capitulated. "Absolutely. Let me show them the controls, then you and I will be on our way."

That seemed the wrong thing to say. She opened fire again, spraying the pad with blasts, sending gray chips of pavement into the air.

Raflo froze, eyes scanning, searching for Impercium security responding to the scene. He saw none in this isolated section of the massive facility.

Stopping her Lighter fire, the aggrieved woman growled. "You think I'm stupid? If you step foot on that ship, you will be out of here in a star blink! You're coming with me! Now!"

Wraigreth knelt with his hands clasped in front of his chest. "I'll not set foot on it ever again." He turned toward his two prison buddies. "Guys, the access code for the ramp and ignition is four, seven, one, nine, six, five." Sweat beaded on his broad forehead. "Take good care of her, she's special."

Raflo gave a honeyed response. "Don't worry, buddy." He then turned to the armed woman. "We'll treat her as if she were our own."

She waved the weapon in the direction from which she had come. "Get up, Wraigreth, it's time to come home."

Wraigreth looked first at his ship, then to the woman. His shoulders slumped as he trudged behind her. With one final glance, he bade them farewell, sounding as helpless as they all did at the Budget Hotel. "Perhaps we'll see each other again sometime?"

Raflo waved as Huanoc stood without the slightest change of expression. "Yeah…sure."

When Wraigreth and the woman rounded the corner, Raflo turned to his friend. "That was certainly unexpected."

"Hmm."

A few seconds passed as Raflo wondered if Wraigreth might come running back, with Lighter fire blazing behind him. When that didn't happen, he glanced toward the *Phantom Star*. "She does look like a nice ride."

Huanoc nodded.

"Hey." Ignoring his throbbing pain, he flashed an impish grin toward the big man. "Do you have plans, now that we're free?"

"Avoid the Impercium."

"Yeah, obviously." Raflo swiveled his gaze, pointing. "We're out of prison and a spaceship just dropped into our laps."

"Uh huh."

Raflo shifted from side to side. "What would you think about goin' into business together…you know… fifty-fifty partners?"

"Hmm." Huanoc locked his eyes on the *Phantom Star* for a ten-count. "My technical abilities…your people skills." He shrugged. "Interesting."

Raflo waited, saying nothing…as long as he could stand it. "Come on, man. We don't have any up-front costs, so we're sure to turn a profit. Who knows what fun we could have?"

At glacial speed, a tiny smile crept onto the big man's face. He extended a hand. "Partners."

Pumping his former cellmate's hand to seal the deal, Raflo's face lit. "Let's get this beauty out of here before the Impercium changes their mind about our freedom." Glancing in the direction of where Wraigreth had been led away, he added an addendum. "And let's never get involved with a woman with that much power."

Chapter Thirty

Geeja's pulse quickened, experiencing a momentary sense of optimism upon hearing Shuggilar's plan. She made a pledge to restore Uwan's health, and while difficult, Shuggilar presented a coherent pitch to make that happen. From this green moon millions of light-years away, her thoughts drifted toward home. *There is hope, Uwan.* Glancing out a porthole, she saw tall green grass swishing in the gentle breeze. *My eyes see what you can again become.*

With most of the others harvesting meat from the beast that Jacastra's team killed, her train of thought shifted. *And to save you, we will be utilizing technology. Is that wrong? Was I wrong all those years ago?*

Raflo popped into the *Phantom Star*. "Hey, come on out. Those guards of yours are processin' that wild animal they killed. They've got a spit set up, ready to roast marbled fillets."

His interruption startled her out of a mental drift. "Oh? What was it, anyway?"

"We don't know for sure, so they're callin' it a moon brancha." The scent of grilling meat wafted into the ship. "Whatever it is, it smells great. Come join us."

On cue, Geeja's stomach growled. "Guess that is a sign from the universe." She pushed away thoughts of right and wrong, or past mistakes. "I did not realize it, but I am famished."

Stepping outside, she observed a relaxed scene. Half of Jacastra's troops formed a tight perimeter as the others sliced slabs of meat from the hand-turned spit.

Huanoc had taken a bite and now licked his fingers. "Hmm." A few chuckled as this time everyone understood his meaning.

Jacastra waved Geeja and Raflo closer to the fire, pointing toward a large fallen log to use as seating. "Please, my goddess. It will be my pleasure to serve you this evening."

Geeja nodded, sending the excited woman on her way.

Raflo cocked his head. "Not even three days ago, I rejected the idea of you being the Goddess of Uwan as too far-fetched…" His eyes stared into the nothingness of the coming night. "I guess I need to expand my imagination."

Returning, Jacastra went down on one knee, then bowed as she handed platters to both Geeja and Raflo. "It is the honor of my life to serve you this evening, my goddess."

Holding the tray with one hand, Geeja placed her free palm atop Jacastra's lowered head. "Thank you. Your devotion is appreciated." She removed her hand. "Now, rise and attend your own needs. You must be strong for the coming battles."

With her face aglow, Jacastra stood. "Thank you, my goddess." She pointed to a nearby stump. "I will be close should you want anything."

Alone with Raflo, Geeja took her first bite. "Mmm." Tender meat, flavored with a spice Geeja didn't recognize, fell off the bone. *So much trade between worlds. One more thing I missed out on in the past two millennia.* Tasting the mystery seasoning intensified her satisfied smile. "This is delicious."

Raflo nodded as another Sworn Warrior brought them drinks. "We better enjoy this night, because we're goin' to be stirring up a striped-jacket's nest of Impercium trouble."

Her mind spun back to her earlier thoughts as she rested her plate on her lap. "Am I a hypocrite?"

"What are you talkin' about?"

"I mean…" Geeja sighed. "I did everything in my power to block the advance of technology, and it kept Uwan's environment pristine for centuries." Her head hung. "Then technology overwhelmed me and nearly destroyed our planet." She shook her bowed head. "Now, I have signed up to what sounds like one of the most advanced thefts in history, using the very high-tech tools I deplored." Her eyes filled, but no tears fell. "Does that make me a two-faced opportunist?"

Raflo swallowed his bite. "I've done plenty of morally questionable things in my life, so I'm not goin' to judge anyone. I do, however, think you're lookin' at this all wrong, like through a two-thousand-year-old lens. See, the world of pure magic doesn't exist anymore, and I see no goin' back. If you want to fight Djurga in *this* day and time, you must use today's weapons. Besides, what we're really proposin' is to use stored magic to destroy the Terminus Stake. Usin' magic can't be wrong, can it?"

Geeja sat quietly, pondering his insight, then answered in a low voice. "I had not thought of it that way." Her brow wrinkled. "You are correct. Any future for Uwan will be different than the one I imagined a few days ago. It seems these technological advances are here to stay, alongside magic." A feeble chuckle slipped out. "It all feels so foreign."

He laughed easily. "You mean, like fallin' asleep one day, then waking up two thousand years later, foreign?" He winked. "You must be a slacker or somethin.' I can't imagine why you're havin' trouble."

Balancing her plate, Geeja slid her free arm in his, laughing along. "Do you always know what to say?"

"Hmm." He pushed his food around the plate. "Let's see. Every relationship I've been in has failed, and I've been sent to an Impercium prison. So, no. I don't *always* know what to say." A grin triggered his dimples. "But I get it right often enough to keep people entertained."

Geeja snugged closer, neither of them saying anything as the nearby fire crackled. The first stars of the night twinkled as she rested her head on his shoulder. She spoke in a whispered voice. "I am glad you found me on the side of the road." She shuddered. "You are a good man, and evil ones seem as plentiful now as in my day."

He tensed. "Yeah, I'm glad we found you, too."

"And I am happy we could save your life."

Raflo snorted, seeming to release his tension. "I'm *really* glad about that."

She giggled. "I guess that is obvious."

"Yeah." He matched her light tone. "Livin' always beats dyin.'"

Her mood edged more serious. "Speaking of dying, what do you think of our chances of pulling off this heist?"

Raflo's reply didn't share her thoughtful shift. "There's no way we fail. We've got a goddess on our side!"

She punched his arm as her head popped up. "You say *that*…after you have seen me in action?"

"Come on, Gigi. Lighten up. On top of bringin' me back from the edge of death, you've dropped a giant rock on one Impercium team and fried another with green flame. I'd rather be on your side than fightin' against you."

"Rrrr!!" She tilted her head back in frustration. "Those were mere skirmishes, akin to party tricks. We are talking about going against Djurga, and a two-thousand-year-old empire. It is not the same thing, and you know it."

Raf turned to face her squarely. "You want to know what I *really* think?"

"Yes. I would like that very much."

"Growin' up on Uwan is tough. I came of age breathin' bad air and taught to have low expectations. Our entire planet is one giant rough neighborhood, and has been for a very long time."

Geeja bowed. "Sorry, that is my fault…and why I question if we can really pull this off. I have some power, but I am not a goddess in the true sense of the word. I realize that now more than ever."

He reached for her hand. "Look, Gigi. As a kid I didn't even believe you ever existed. I mean, how could someone live all those years and do the things of legend, then completely disappear. Until a couple of days ago, I thought you were the stuff of myth."

As a goddess back then, it had often been difficult to get her subjects to share true thoughts and feelings. They were either awed to be in her presence, or fearful of retribution if they said something disagreeable. She locked eyes with him. "And now that you have met the real me?"

Staring into her eyes, he bit his lower lip. "To tell the truth, it's a bit confusin.' You're a very powerful bein', but at the same time, you seem very human. You make mistakes and have doubts."

"I have plenty of those." Geeja noticed his boyish grin as he continued to make his point.

"Look. You can communicate with freakin' planets. That's pretty amazin.'"

"Is that enough?"

He squeezed her hand. "A week ago, I would describe any attempt to rid Uwan of the Terminus Stake as crazy talk." His shoulders raised. "Now? We have a real plan…and more importantly, we have hope."

"But, is that *enough*?" Her eyes begged. "Do you really think we can pull this off?"

Raflo glanced around their assembled group until landing on his business partner. "Me and Huanoc escaped an Impercium prison." He resumed his scan until seeing Shuggilar and Chella. "That man has evaded the long arm of the law longer than I've been alive, and his wife can patch us up if we're wounded." Finally, he nodded toward Jacastra. "And those women are fierce fighters."

His smile broadened and his dimples re-emerged. "I'd say that with your powers added to the mix we've got a fightin' chance. Those odds are as good as or better than most jobs Huanoc and I take. That's why I'm willin' to give it a go."

Warmth traveled up Geeja's spine, then she leaned toward him without hesitation. Her lips met his in a long kiss. When they parted, she grinned. "Like you mentioned earlier, you might not *always* know what to say, but you got it right tonight."

Chapter Thirty-One
Nearly Two Thousand Years Earlier

Emperor Djurga stood on the highest balcony in his palace, surveying the city, pointing out several of his achievements to his guest. He lifted a hand toward a sprawling industrial complex belching plumes of gray smoke into the sky. "That's where we're manufacturing the engines for our next generation Impercium Cruisers. In the past fifty years I've brought both peace and prosperity to my universe."

Ambassador Ka nodded. "You have taken the technological boost we supplied and done great things. You should be proud."

"I am." He stared down at his highly polished black boots. In the reflection he saw gray hair and sagging skin. "There has been more growth and commerce in my universe in the past five decades than in our entire recorded history."

"Our partnership has benefited us. Your empire thrives and we are pleased by our arrangement as well."

Djurga pulled in a steadying breath as his eyes turned once more toward the distant skyscraper dotted skyline. "Yes, together we have set in motion a new trajectory for all my people." He glanced at Ka, who hadn't aged a day since their first meeting. "Now, I've begun to think of what comes next."

Ka pivoted. "What do you mean? Are you displeased with our relationship?"

"No, not at all. It's just that my species…" His breath caught for a moment. "Well, to put it bluntly, we have a finite life expectancy."

"Ah, yes. We know."

He expected the emissary to say more, but he didn't. Instead, he once again turned his expressionless gaze toward the industrial horizon.

After a lengthy silence, Ka asked a question, devoid of emotion. "Is it not customary for your species to turn over one's business interests to their heirs?"

Djurga winced, since from their limited social interactions Ka knew he had no children. He cleared his throat. "You are correct." His lips pinched, upset that even with all the consorts he had bedded over the years, none had become pregnant. *It's the industrial chemicals I've inhaled. How could I have known?*

Suppressed anger roiled in his gut. "Here's the thing, Ka." He stared at the ambassador. "You don't seem to be aging, and those other damned gods and goddesses don't either…well they do, but they get around dying by that transference process." Djurga could feel his heart rate accelerating faster than a striped ziller. "I've been a dependable partner for fifty years." He swallowed hard, laying his cards on the table. "Surely there's some way to continue our mutually beneficial partnership."

"Hmm." Ka nodded. "It must be difficult to be at the mercy of time."

Djurga waited in silence. He held his breath, hoping against hope the man might throw him a lifeline. *Please!*

After a long moment, Ka spoke again. "It is not simple, but it is possible."

Djurga gasped. "I knew it!"

"Of course, there are costs. There would need to be a new agreement between us."

Biting his tongue, Djurga yelled inside his head. *Of course! There's always a cost with Ka!* Desperate, he replied, his voice straddling the line between hope and caution. "I would like to know more about the difficulties…and the price."

Ka pointed a pale finger toward the churning factories stretching into the distance. "Machinery may be complex, but at the same time, always simple. Precise inputs result in exact outputs. X temperature melts Y metal in Z levels of humidity, every time. Control the factors and you get predictable and repeatable outcomes."

Djurga nodded.

Ka turned to him. "Biology is different. No two life units are exactly the same. A single difference in your humanoid spiral sequence can produce profoundly different reactions to the same stimuli."

Unsure of Ka's direction, Djurga waited for the bottom line always reached by the ambassador.

"What I'm saying is that we can preserve your life almost indefinitely, but it's a very complex process. It will require discipline from you."

"You know me, Ka. I have an iron will."

"Yes. For a humanoid you have shown great determination over time. An admirable trait in a partner. That is why we offer this trade to you."

Djurga grinned, his scientific side sparked. "Would you tell me more of the sacrifice I must endure?"

Ka's eyes once more went toward the vast, heaving machinery before them. "In some ways your life will become like one of your factories. You would be required to rise every morning at the same time, spending at least an hour in a rejuvenation machine where you would breathe a custom blend of gases that we will supply, many of which are not found in this universe."

"Sounds rigid, but I like routine. I can do it."

"There is more."

Djurga gulped. "More?"

"Yes. Every ten of your years you must undergo a surgical procedure removing toxins that accumulate in your organs. It is such a delicate operation it must be performed by robots we will supply." Ka's eyes cut toward Djurga. "I am told it is painful, very painful."

A shiver ran through Djurga's body, but he shook it off. "I will endure. It certainly beats dying."

"Hmm. Then there is the cost."

Djurga pulled his fingers tight. "What do you want?"

"It's quite simple, really, and will require very little from you."

When things seem too good to be true, they usually are. "I'm listening."

The faint, infrequent smile Djurga had seen on Ka's face, reappeared. "Remember the Terminus Stake you launched into Uwan?"

"Yes."

"We would like you to place one in each of the other eleven magical worlds."

Djurga masked his conflicting emotions. *It sounds simple enough. But the Truise obviously value magic greatly. If I could find out what they do with it...I might be able to worm myself from under their dependence.* He flexed his hands. *Not much bargaining room. Here goes.* "Let's say I agree to this. How much magic would you take from each planet?"

"Why do you care?" Ka said, "You hate those beings, right?"

"Yes." He paused as his mind raced. *He's got a point. But their worlds are potential assets. Perhaps leading to something greater...though I still don't know what.* "They have bowed to me without rebellion. I owe them something for their servitude."

"Per our agreement, we take ninety percent from Uwan. We shall be generous and only take fifty percent from those eleven."

The impact on Uwan had been catastrophic when combined with the mining he ordered there. That didn't bother him as he still believed Geeja must be hiding there somewhere. *They deserve their fate. But the other worlds?* Words formed before he could think, surprising himself at how confidently he spoke them. "No. That's too much. Ten percent each from eleven worlds is a lot of magic."

Ka leaned forward then back, seeming to consider his next move. "You surprise me, Emperor. Risking your continued existence for those who offended you." He paused. "As a measure of good faith, we will settle for twenty-five percent." No grin emerged this time, instead the malevolent stare he first wore fifty years ago reappeared. "Final offer. Take it…or die."

That went better than I hoped. He reached his hand toward Ka. "It's been a pleasure doing business with you all these years…and will continue to be for a *very* long time to come."

Chapter Thirty-Two

Geeja rolled the names of the planets where the ancient artifact might be over and over in her mind without getting any closer to an answer. *Bostor, Fontonce or Salostorce? Where could it be?* Switching tactics, she considered their leaders. *Elegarcia, Roace or Valanceta? Which would be most likely to tell me if they did have it?* That seemed a better question, but required more thought to divine an answer.

She sat alone inside the *Curious Lady* deciding where they would travel first. Outside, most of the Sworn Warriors, as well as Talla, learned the basics of fighting with Lighters. Enthusiastic sounds came through the open door of the craft signaling that they were taking to new forms of combat well. She smiled. *They seem to be adjusting just fine. I need to be as focused. Who should I approach first?*

Geeja paced the ship, determined to come to a quick decision. *Let us start with the closest in distance, but the one I know least well. Elegarcia.* A memory flashed of the first Goddess of Bostor, Eleharmonia. She shivered. Eleharmonia died when only a thousand years old. An ice shaft fell from the eaves of her vacation cabin in the far reaches of the coldest region of the planet, piercing her skull and killing the vessel she inhabited instantly, with no chance for a transference.

Geeja wrapped her arms around herself. *That is the fate I narrowly avoided.* She patted the area over her heart as she said another quiet word of thanks to Susomi. "We are forever grateful for your quick action."

Continuing to pace, she thought about the woman she still considered the 'new' goddess of Bostor, even though she had known Elegarcia for thousands of years. As the Ancients had foretold, if a god or goddess were killed, the planet would find a way to connect with their successor. Geeja remembered her split emotions at the connection ceremony less than a year after the accident. It was gut-wrenching to lose a friend, and terrifying to see that a goddess really could be killed. But, at the same time her soul soared as Bostor found a new partner. After that, they weren't close, though they certainly weren't enemies. Far from it, they just had different personalities that didn't lend them to tight bonds.

Making a turn in the compact ship, she visualized the last host that Elegarcia inhabited. Bostorians were typically short people with eyes that seemed to bulge out of their sockets. Geeja didn't find it particularly attractive, but apparently allowed them the best vision in the universe. She smiled, remembering the tightly wound silver hair piled atop the angular head of the petite woman. A lovely person on the inside, but that hairstyle matched her disposition: always firmly under control. That's how they were different. From her earliest memories, Geeja had always been more emotional and willing to take more chances. Her shoulders tightened. *That is part of the reason I am in this mess.*

Her thoughts bounced to Roace next. Geeja's mood lifted as a memory stirred of a night of drinking and singing from one of their biennial meetings. This one happened to have had Fontonce, his home world, as the host planet. The other ten had called it a night, but they kept the party going, taking turns teaching each other songs from their homeworlds. His lovely baritone voice rumbled in her core when he hit the lowest notes. When the band murmured about the late hour, they each took a bottle of that planet's famous blue wine and headed to his suite in the palace. There, they danced in each other's arms, until falling into bed together.

Her cheeks plumped and warmed. *It is not like I was promiscuous.* She paused. *Well, I did have an affair with Bregent a hundred or so years before that night.* She shook her head lightly. *But that had ended. Plus, neither of us had a consort at the time. Besides, we were consenting adults.* That made her giggle. *I mean, we were thousands of years old.* As much as she enjoyed that night, a brutal hangover awaited the next morning. The pain seemed almost as stabbing as the ribbing they received from the others. She rubbed her temples, thinking back on that morning. The pure white sunlight from the Fontonce sun flooded the conference room, so bright she wore tinted glasses inside.

Geeja slid a hand to her neck, massaging tight muscles. *Lastly, there is Valanceta of Salostorce.* That goddess' home planet seemed almost the complete opposite of Uwan, and perhaps by coincidence, of all the Holy Twelve Geeja and Valanceta were the most different from each other. Uwan had a variety of ecosystems and distinct seasons whereas Salostorce was largely a desert planet covered almost entirely in sand, except for fringes of the coastline along the only small sea, and a sprinkling of underground springs supporting micro-ecospheres. There was very little diversity.

Like Elegarcia, Valanceta usually contained her emotions, but in a different way. Elegarcia always seemed to struggle to keep her passion under control while Valanceta simply seemed dull. Not in an intelligence way, in fact she appeared quite smart, she just never got excited about anything. A discussion of battle tactics would elicit the same flat expression as a conversation about favorite lovers. On top of everything, each day she donned a white, blocky tailored uniform, and never applied any makeup. *Bor-ing.*

Jacastra startled Geeja, who sat lost in her deliberation. "Talla wants to know if you've selected a starting point for our search. I think she's hoping we might swing by Uwan so she can see her child."

Geeja knew a visit home would have to wait, but she did need to decide. *Roace and I had a relationship. That could make all the difference.* "Tell her I am ready when she is." Her cheeks warmed, recalling the epic party and night of passion on her last visit. "We are heading to Fontonce."

**

Geeja marveled again at the speed of these modern ships. More than two thousand years ago, her last trip to Fontonce had taken two days. This journey lasted a mere six hours. *I hope to never take this speed for granted.* As soon as she thought it, she knew the truth. *That is what humanoids always do…like I did when—No!* She stopped the negative thought. *I will not let my past mistakes define me.*

Talla called from the cockpit. "We'll be there soon. Where would you like to land?"

She chewed her lower lip. The physical features she remembered most from two thousand years ago were several rocky plains surrounding the capital. She leaned into the flight deck. "There used to be some desolate flatlands near Bristania. See if they are still there."

Catching a glimpse through the forward glass, Geeja saw a sprawling city below. "Wow. It is so much bigger than I remember."

Talla kept them at a distance as she navigated the outer edge of the populated areas. "Looks like those plains are inhabited now." She pointed. "How about that canyon? It's a tight squeeze but it will provide us some additional cover."

"I will rely upon your judgment." Shaking her head, Geeja wondered aloud. "*Everything* has changed so much. Will I ever catch up to this time?"

Smiling, Talla replied. "It will get better, I promise. It took me a while to adjust after I left the Sworn Warriors eight years ago, but look at me now. Trust me, it will happen faster than you think."

Geeja pressed her forehead against a porthole, gasping as the ship dropped into the ravine. Jagged outcroppings looked like claws reaching out to gash the *Curious Lady* as it rounded a narrow bend at rapid speed. She squelched a squeak, then sucked in a breath as their rate of descent increased. Her body stiffened as they zoomed toward the bottom of the canyon, bracing for a horrific crash. But that didn't happen. Instead, the vessel leveled before easing down in a precise landing.

Geeja exhaled, releasing a breath she hadn't realized she was holding. *Thank the Holy Twelve for such an excellent pilot.* Pressing her blouse with her hands, she calmed her nerves, then turned to the other passengers. "We will run this like we did on Politar. I will reach out to the planet, then hopefully hear back from Roace to arrange a meeting." Her tone brightened. "Then we take it from there."

Fontonce stood as the closest planet to their white sun, making it the warmest and second driest of the holy worlds. Stepping outside the *Curious Lady*, Geeja admired the ochre color of the walls of this arid slot in the ground. "There is beauty in all forms."

She ran fingers along the surface, collecting yellowish–red dust on the tips. As a measure of respect for the planet, she rubbed the powder beneath each eye, serving as an additional physical connection with this world. Kneeling, she placed both hands on the surface, reaching out with her mind as she had on Politar. **"Fontonce, an old friend returns. Greetings from**

Uwan…Fontonce, an old friend returns. Greetings from Uwan…Fontonce, an old friend returns. Greetings from Uwan."

A deep, feminine voice answered warily. *"Who is this?"*

"It is I, Geeja." She bowed her head to the surface as tears of relief came unbidden. *"I am pleased to hear your divine voice again."*

"How can this be? After so many years?"

"It is a long story, believe me." Geeja's tears were absorbed instantly in the powdery dust. *"What is important is that we are both alive, and that I come to restore my bonds with you and Roace."*

"It really is you! They said you were dead, killed in the attack that…" Her response faded for a moment before returning in a somber tone. *"What happened to me was bad enough, but nothing like the torture inflicted upon Uwan."*

"Hmm. In my return, I have learned all holy worlds suffer. That is why I am here. I must speak to Roace on important matters about this very subject."

Fontonce stayed silent for several seconds. The planet sounded guarded when she reconnected. *"He is not the same man you remember."*

Uncertain of what that meant, Geeja remained upbeat. *"After all these years, that is what I would expect. Still, he was once a great friend and I bring news of hope."*

"Hope… Roace has had precious little of that for centuries. It has changed him. He now withdraws from most contact…with me or humanoids. He is a hermit."

Fontonce sounded intensely glum. Still, Geeja had a mission. *"Will he see ME? Can we meet? I beg you my friend, please intercede."*

"I...I will try." Fontonce's mood turned more upbeat. *"I remember a very cheerful Roace following your last trip here."*

The playful thought triggered a low laugh. *"I once left here happy, and I hope too again. Thank you for trying, Fontonce."*

Feeling the connection lapse, Geeja rose from her knees, sure that most of her face had to be covered in reddish-yellow silt. That representation of a successful connection to this world pleased her. Standing, she addressed her small guard contingent. "Now we wait."

Fortunately, she sensed a pulse from Fontonce a few minutes later. She touched the wall and reached out. *"My friend, I am here."*

Fontonce's telepathic voice raised. *"Oh, Geeja, he's coming! He'll arrive at your location by sundown."*

"Wonderful! Thank you for helping."

Fontonce's tone waivered. *"Be aware, he's fragile...and he may be intoxicated."*

That brought Geeja up sharp. *"Really?"* She shook off the negative vibes. *"I do not care. Just seeing him again means so much."*

During the short wait, Geeja gave Talla a brief version of her past with Roace, then confided her feelings. "I am just as nervous seeing Roace again as when I saw Bregent, and I do not even know why."

Talla placed a hand on the goddess' shoulder as she cleaned the holy woman's face, speaking as Geeja stared into a small mirror. "I think you're doing remarkably well, considering all you've been through. If it makes you feel any better, most women are a little anxious when seeing old loves."

From outside, Jacastra called up the open ramp. "We've spotted what looks like a flying horse with a rider headed our way."

"I guess that is my cue."

"Wait a sec." Talla reached in a small bag, pulled out a tube of lipstick. "You're welcome to this, if it's your color."

Geeja hugged her. "You are so thoughtful." Looking in the mirror again, she puckered as she applied it. "Thank you for the advice and makeup." She stood straight. "Nerves or not, I need his help, especially if he has that artifact."

As Geeja emerged from the *Curious Lady,* a black, winged equine landed nearby, kicking up dust. She had no idea what to expect. On top of the warning about Roace's mental state, she didn't even know what he looked like in this era.

Taking off his riding beret, he hopped down.

She got her first glimpse. *He always favored the traditional dark skin of most Fontonce men rather than the lighter shades of those living in the polar regions.* She bit her lower lip. *And I am glad to see he still does.*

Stepping closer, he called out. "Geeja! Where in the Holy Twelve have you been?"

She next noticed his unkempt hair. *Fits with what Fontonce told me…unless it is some new fashion here. He always preferred the 'well structured' look.* Regardless, she stretched her arms wide and rushed toward him. "You are a sight for sore eyes."

He met her embrace, kissing her, leaving a sweet taste in her mouth. *Same wine we had that night?*

Roace stumbled as they parted. "We all thought you were dead."

Geeja saw glassy eyes. "Yes. I almost died, but Uwan saved me. It just took a long time to recover…a really long time." This host stood even taller than the typical Fontonce male, so Geeja stretched to pat his upper arm. "But I am here now, and back in the game." Up close, she noticed stains on his rumpled royal-red tunic. *More blue wine?*

Roace spread his arms wide. "I can't believe you're really here!"

Geeja flinched in another embrace, noticing his strong body odor. "The truth is I am more surprised than anyone at this turn of events. My head has not stopped spinning since I awoke." She noticed a missing tooth to the left of center when he smiled. *Fontonce had not exaggerated. He seems to not care enough to repair it with a thimble full of his world's magic.* She raised her chin. *Yet, even in this state he may hold the key to our success.*

A small table and two chairs had been set up near one side of the canyon wall, with some light snacks set out. She motioned toward the area that Sworn Warriors guarded from a respectful distance. "Care to join me?"

"Sure." He held up his index finger. "Go on over. I'll be right there."

Doing as he suggested, she kept an eye on him. He reached inside a saddlebag on his flying steed and it all made sense. *A bottle and two glasses. Okay...*

Roace set the empty glasses down clumsily, knocking one over. Managing to set both upright, he pulled a small silver corkscrew from his pant pocket, then ceremoniously popped the cork. He sounded excited as he poured the deep blue wine. "It's a rare vintage I've been saving for a special occasion."

"I am honored." Geeja raised the fluted stemware, proposing a toast. "To old friends in new times."

"I'll drink to that." While she sipped her drink, Roace drained his entirely, then refilled it to the brim.

The delicious dry wine carried notes of toasted nuts and fine plork barreling, though Geeja could feel the burn of the high alcohol content. The memory of that long ago hangover loomed. *I will not repeat that.* She set her glass down, then took a swallow of water. "We are traveling light, but the crew has prepared a meal. It is spartan, but tasty."

His grin hadn't faded since he arrived. "It's been a while since I've dined with such delightful company." Roace raised his glass, so she did as well. His smile dimmed for the first time this night. "To the Holy Twelve…and all we once were."

Before lowering her glass, Geeja spoke an addendum. "And to all we might be again."

Roace's face relit. "I like the sound of that." He took a large gulp, draining half, then leaned back in his chair. "You really are a bolt of lightning on a clear day."

Geeja held up two fingers as a sign that Roace would be staying for dinner. Jacastra stayed close, but two other warriors moved, beginning the process of serving two gods. Geeja turned her attention back to him, wanting to get a feel for his mindset. "I spoke with Bregent a couple of days ago. He told me what happened to Politar in my absence. How has it gone here, for you and Fontonce?"

He gulped the remainder of his second glass, refilled it, then stood. "I am too sober to have that conversation. I'll be right back."

As he walked to his stallion, Geeja took a tiny sip, then tilted her head. *He is a mess, but I was warned.*

Returning, Roace opened the second bottle with more determination and less flash. He collapsed back into his seat; his words as gloomy as a thunderhead. "I hate Djurga and everything that's happened since he took over." Lifting his glass again, he splashed some of his drink onto his shirt, adding to the stains already there.

The Sworn Warriors returned with two steaming plates of food as Geeja kept an appraising eye on Roace. She described their fare. "Tonight, we feast on moon brancha cooked over open flame and bathed in exotic spices. We have paired it with rice from the ship's emergency rations. Perhaps this change of pace can serve as a new beginning for us all."

"Moon brancha?" He laughed loudly, then spoke with a slight slur. "Where in the name of Hasprin did you find this?"

Geeja chuckled. "In case you have not heard, I am a wanted woman. Me and a few friends are on the run from Djurga and literally living off the land." She pointed with her fork. "Try it before you judge."

Shaking his head, he cut a piece, popping it in his mouth. "Mmm. This is…divine! It's vaguely reminiscent of grilled storpla, but more tender and juicier. I've not tasted anything like this in centuries!" He greedily sliced another bite, speaking with his mouth half full. "I'm serious, this is wonderful."

"I am hungry, too. Let us eat first, then talk." *How long since he has had a home cooked meal?* A more practical thought followed. *Perhaps this will sober him up a bit before we get down to business.*

Roace made 'yum' sounds as he devoured his dinner in minutes. "Geeja, thank you for reminding me that there is goodness remaining in this universe. Sometimes I focus only on the evil, not paying enough attention to all the positives in my life."

"You are welcome. I have reminded myself of that more than once these past few days. So much has been thrown at me, I sometimes feel I am drowning. Everything has changed."

Tossing his napkin on the plate, Roace leaned back. "It's been the opposite for me. The centuries' long drip, drip, drip of oppression has been my bane." He closed his eyes, then slowly rubbed his head. "More than once I've literally stood on the edge of a cliff, ready to end it all."

She sat as quiet as a blazefly on a summer's night, shocked at the depths of his depression.

Filling his drink again. he took another swig, followed by a long sigh matching his sad eyes. "But I couldn't do it. I couldn't put all that on Fontonce…to begin again with a new god? One who wouldn't remember how good things had once been?"

"I cannot imagine all you have been through." She placed a hand on his in sympathy and as a signal of her transition to the real reason she came. "I am working on a plan to change things. You interested in hearing about it?"

Roace flinched. "What?" He leaned forward, his voice seeming a mixture of excitement and skepticism. "What are you going to do?"

She wasn't about to share *all* the details with anyone, even if they were a fellow Holy Twelve God. Bregent made it clear that Djurga had spies everywhere. "It is a complicated plan, but we are missing an important piece. I am hoping you can be of assistance."

"Geeja." His eyes widened. "I'll do anything to give Djurga a dose of his own medicine. How can I help?"

Gripping his hand tighter, she met his gaze. "Do you remember mention of an artifact the Ancients said could magnify magic?"

Roace's eyes went up and to the left, as if he were searching through his memories. He blinked, then answered. "Yesss." He dragged out the word as if pulling it from a trunk in some hidden corner of his brain. "Vaguely, now that you mention it." He wrinkled his forehead. "We all talked about it once upon a time, right? Wow, I haven't thought about that in ages."

"Oh." Her gaze dropped. "I hoped for a clearer recall, as perhaps you might be the one chosen as the item's protector." He laughed and through his hand she could feel his body relax.

"Here's the thing, Geeja. If I did have it, I would have done something stupid during one of my drunken fugues and gotten myself killed."

She released her grip and leaned back, knowing he spoke the truth. "I hoped it rested in your possession. I am not sure we can pull off our plan without it."

One of her Sworn Warriors approached, bowing to Geeja. "Would you like dessert, goddess?"

Cutting an eye toward Roace, he answered playfully. "Let's see if you can surprise me with something sweet as much as you did with that moon brancha."

A lithe laugh escaped Geeja's lips. "That might be tough, considering the limited supplies on board." The momentary lightness faded. "That is a metaphor for where I am now. Lots of will, but missing important ingredients."

Roace voice turned buttery smooth, as if he had reached a buzzed emotional comfort zone. "I don't know about that. Those women seem pretty motivated. I bet they bring back something unexpected."

She cocked her head, noting his relaxed aura. "You are right. They are devoted and full of vigor. My return has them believing in the impossible."

Tapping his finger on the table, Roace surprised her again. "Your return from oblivion has affected me as well. This has turned into one of the best nights I've enjoyed in a century."

His words hit her like a body slam during training, putting his misery into perspective. *It seemed a simple meal to me, but it feels like a lifeline for him.* "I thought I had it rough, but it has been harder for all of you. I did not realize…"

He waved his hand. "I've said too much and made this about me. Thank you for coming. It's brightened my outlook for the future more than you can imagine."

She blushed as the Sworn Warriors returned, bearing a cupcake for each topped by florescent royal red icing, the official color of Fontonce. Roace beamed. "I told you to believe!" He clapped his hands. "I don't care what it tastes like, the look alone is priceless!"

Seeing his reaction warmed her from the inside. *It is easy to remember why we hit it off.* Tasting her miniature cake, the rush of sugar went straight to her brain's pleasure centers. "Mmm, *almost* better than sex."

He let loose his biggest laugh of the evening. "I'm glad you said 'almost.' I would have been offended if you hadn't."

Geeja's blush warmed her cheeks. "I have not forgotten that night…or the headache the next morning."

They traded a few more memories from those olden days, then Roace turned the conversation back to the current predicament. "You came up empty locating the artifact here. Where's your next stop?"

Sighing, she laced her fingers. "I guess Bostor. I came here first because of all the places I thought it might be, I wanted to see you most. Time is not on our side, and Bostor is the closest stop." Geeja squinted, thinking he blushed, but couldn't tell in the dim lighting, so she teased. "What? Something up with you and Elegarcia?"

He squirmed in his seat. "Well…it happened a long time ago. I–I don't want to talk about it."

A wicked laugh sprang from the depth of Geeja's being. "You are not getting out of this without spilling the calefine beans, my friend. No way." She leaned over, poking his ribs. "Talk, or else."

He lowered his head, but mischievous eyes peeked toward her. "You were M.I.A. Djurga had desecrated Uwan. Then he came for all of us." Roace rubbed the back of his neck. "I fell into despondency, to say the least. So, I visited Bostor."

"You two?" Geeja's jaw dropped. "I never would have guessed. You and Elegarcia seemed like oil and water. I mean, not in a bad way or anything, just–I do not know. Really?"

"Yeah, but you know what they say. Misery loves companionship." He shrugged. "We both needed someone to lean on, then one thing led to another." He looked up, meeting her stare. "And it worked for a while."

She stayed silent.

When he continued, night sounds from a squawking bird species she couldn't identify lent a sad accompaniment to the tale. "However, my depression went deeper than hers, and I spiraled." A trail of tears pushed down his cheeks. "She did all she could, but one night in a drunken rage I hit her…hard." The tears turned to sobs. "I apologized over and over, but the damage was done. Not only had I hit her, but it triggered something deeper. She lashed out, using Bostor's magic to shove me…through a window. She reminded me that there had been a goddess on Bostor before her–one who died.

"I've never forgiven myself for what I did." He breathed in a ragged breath. "I left the next morning." With lips pressed, he inhaled and his posture straightened. "I went through years of therapy, but we haven't spoken since."

"Therapy? What do you mean?"

"I forget, you've been gone a while." Sniffing, Roace gazed into the starry night. "It's a newer science. Partnering with a trained mental health professional, they help you work through the issues that trigger destructive tendencies. Together, we developed approaches and strategies to help me cope. Like, we delved into past outbursts, peeling back the layers to identify what really set me off. It helps me understand what's truly happening in my head and how to respond in a better way."

Geeja arched her brows. "And what did you discover?"

Roace released a choked laugh. "No real surprise. Mostly my anger issues stem from Djurga's domination. When I went off, it was my response to losing control of the most important thing in my life. Fontonce suffers, and there's not a thing I can do about it." He cleared his throat. "I'm far from perfect, but I no longer explode like a volcano. I'm trying to be better."

"I...I see." While intellectually understanding, the concept seemed stranger than any of the other new things she had learned about this era. "So...even a god can bare their soul to these people?"

He chuckled. "Yes. I may be the only one desperate enough to seek help, though I know more would surely benefit. It is, however, a mainstream resource for all Impercium citizens."

"Wow." Her eyes widened as two complementary thoughts sprang to mind. *I knew the other eleven had challenges. Now I understand there is a darker level of pain.* A bolt of nervous tension ran through her. *And once again, there have been changes in science that I could never dream of.*

Glancing at him, Geeja saw tight eyes and smashed lips, so she stood, moving beside him. She wrapped an arm around his shoulders. "Sounds like all of us have suffered. Now we are dealing with the fallout as best we can." She gave him a squeeze, knowing her job of getting as many of the other Holy Twelve to join her quest would be more challenging than she imagined. *How do I invite him to join me on a trip to see Elegarcia now?*

Roace nodded. "When you see her, would you tell her again how sorry I am?"

Locking eyes with him, knowing how awkward the situation would surely be, she did what she knew she must. She placed her goal to save Uwan above wading into an abuse situation between two friends. *Here goes nothing.* "Why not tell her yourself?"

"What?" He jerked away. "Yeah, no. I've done enough already. I don't want to make things worse."

"Hey." She patted his shoulder. "Like you said, some time has passed, and that almost always makes things better. Plus, you have received help." She held a compassionate gaze. "I will be there as an intermediary."

He sagged under her hand. "I don't know, Geeja. You didn't see the hurt and anger in her eyes that night." He shook his head sluggishly. "This sounds like a bad idea."

She sucked in a determined breath, charging ahead. "Look, Roace. I am going to take on Djurga to save Uwan, with or without your help." She released her light grip and moved to face him squarely. "You are one of the Twelve Holy Gods and I know my chances would be better if you joined me."

Roace's empty eyes met hers as he listened, not giving any hint of his thoughts.

Geeja's words walked the line between challenge and compassion. "As I see it, you have been wallowing in self-pity. I am asking for your assistance, but if you will not do it for me, do it for Elegarcia, Bostor and Fontonce. Do it for yourself. You all deserve better. It is time to stand up and set things straight. It is time to once again be the man I know you are."

Stiffening, he sat with an unreadable countenance, then his lips crinkled. "When did you become such a diplomat?"

She snorted. "I guess a two-thousand-year snooze affected me more than I realized." She pressed. "Come on, Roace. You hate everything that has happened as much as I do. Let us fight this, and do it together."

Roace shifted in his seat. "You mean just get up and leave this idyllic lifestyle? To join a doomed quest?"

Geeja giggled. "There is the Roace I know and love." She released an easy breath. "This is what we were made for, and you know it. We swore oaths to protect and serve our worlds. It is time for us to do that, even if things do not go our way. Join us." She waited in the silence of the desert night, hoping she convinced him.

Clearing his throat, Roace leaned forward. "I will need two things before I say yes."

"I am listening." *What could he want?*

"First, I'll need at least an hour to go home and pack a travel bag."

"Of course. Take two, if needed." *I hope the second demand is as easy to meet.*

"Also, you must promise to stand between me and Elegarcia when we get there. She's become quite the marksman with a Lighter."

Geeja released a relaxed laughed. "Absolutely." She reached for his hand. "I will be asking her to join our merry warriors. I hear proper handling of a Lighter is a very valuable skill in this day and time."

Chapter Thirty-Three

Geeja waved as Roace flew away on his magical horse to pack for their journey. While she hadn't known exactly what to expect when she arrived, it surprised her to see another of her friends so changed by years of subjugation. She dropped her head, mumbling. "In some ways missing out on all that happened while I slept was a blessing. My urge for vengeance burns while his has been worn away, as if an eternal wind blew unrelentingly against a sandstone mountain, leaving only a faint resemblance of its once majestic peak."

Boarding the ship, Geeja spoke in a cheerful tone she didn't fully believe, while giving Talla the news. "Success! Roace is going to grab some clothes, then join us!"

Talla's wary voice didn't match her reply. "Okay..."

"What is wrong? We will need all the powerful allies we can get...right?"

"Of course." Talla crossed her arms. "But every one we add increases the chances that Djurga finds us."

Geeja mimicked her, crossing her arms as well. "Roace would never tell a soul! Especially Djurga!"

"I'm sure that's true. But what about his housekeeper, or the chef? They will all know he's left the planet on short notice." She smirked. "I'm sure his wine steward will notice." The vibe quickly changed back to dark. "Any one of them could betray us."

Geeja's crossed arms tightened. "I did not think about that. Everyone says Djurga has spies everywhere." Her shoulders squared. "It is simply a risk we have to take."

The captain gave a small bow. "You're the goddess…"

Time passed quickly as adjustments were made to accommodate another guest on the *Curious Lady*. Jacastra called from outside. "The flying horse approaches again, and it appears to be the same rider as earlier." She paused, then spoke in awe-tinged tones. "What I wouldn't give for one of those."

Geeja patted Jacastra's shoulder, answering lightly. "Who knows? If we can deliver a miracle, perhaps we could import a herd to Uwan."

The Sworn Warrior beamed.

Geeja watched as a refreshed Roace sprang from his stallion.

His smile radiated joy. "I can't believe we're doing this."

Once on the ground, Geeja noted his still damp hair. *He has cleaned up. A good sign.* She gave him a hug. "I am sure you have already said your farewell, so take your things on board while I say goodbye to Fontonce."

He grabbed a small clothing carrier, then a larger bag with the neck of a wine bottle peeking out. The sound of glass clinking indicated more inside. His cheeks flushed. "Hey. I wanted to make sure we have our bases covered if we get stranded somewhere remote."

A faint smile graced her face. *I am glad he is joining us, even with his literal and figurative baggage.* "Better safe than sorry, I guess."

Stepping away from the ship, she reached out to say farewell to Fontonce. *"I hope to see you again soon, my friend."*

The planet replied instantly. *"I'm so glad you're alive and came to see us!"* Her response seemed even brighter than when Geeja arrived. *"You've helped Roace."*

Geeja stared into the starry night. *"We are all in need of healing, including you. I will do my best to bring him back safely. Wish us luck."*

"Always."

Brushing ocher dust from her hands, Geeja headed up the ramp, followed by her guards. Reaching the top, she called out to Talla. "How long is the trip to Bostor?"

Talla answered as Jacastra pushed the button raising the ramp. "Eight hours, but it will be their sundown. I suggest grabbing some shut-eye while you can."

Roace pulled a bottle from his baggage. "Care for a nightcap?"

Geeja rubbed the back of her neck. "I remember the hangover from the last time I drank too much of your world's fine wine. Sorry, but I will pass." Geeja watched as Roace stared at the unopened bottle. She sensed his struggle. *He is probably wondering if he has had enough to make it eight hours.*

He placed the carafe back. "If I am going to apologize to El for being a wretched drunk, it's probably best if I don't show up sloshed." He slumped. "Where should I sack out?"

Pointing, Geeja replied. "Join me. I'm heading to that corner."

Everyone else self-sorted, and soon the ship went quiet. Accommodations were tight, with Geeja's head resting close to Roace's. She whispered as one by one they settled. "I am glad you joined us."

He chuckled. "I'll let you know how I feel *after* we meet with Elegarcia."

Chapter Thirty-Four

By the time they reached Bostor, Geeja had devised a plan. "I will contact Elegarcia as I did with Bregent and you, Roace. I will let her know I am back and have brought a guest." She glanced at her fellow god. "At least she will not be caught totally off guard when she sees you."

He straightened to his full height, towering over everyone on the ship. "That doesn't mean she won't turn around as fast as she came."

"We will find out soon enough." Taking in a breath of cold air that carried a hint of harsh chemicals, her mind wandered to a familiar theme. *Djurga has polluted every world he has touched.* Shaking off that thought, she dropped to her knees, placing both hands on the frigid soil. *"Bostor, an old friend returns. Greetings from Uwan…Bostor, an old friend returns. Greetings from Uwan…Bostor, an old friend returns. Greetings from Uwan."*

"Who is this?"

Fontonce had asked the same question, prompting a grin. *"It is I, Geeja of Uwan."*

"What? How?" The deep male voice of this world sounded surprised and happy. *"Really? You live?"*

"Yes, by the Holy Twelve I have returned."

"It must be a miracle!"

"Not a miracle, but close enough." Geeja's grin turned into a wide smile. *"I am so glad to visit you again, and I must speak with Elegarcia. Will you connect us?"*

"Of course!"

Geeja winked at Roace as she shivered in the glacial temperature while awaiting a reply. "So far, so good. Fingers crossed." A familiar voice rang in Geeja's head.

"Geeja! I can't believe it!"

"It is me, in the flesh." Geeja joked. *"In this case, the cold flesh. I love Bostor, but it always takes me a bit to acclimate."*

"I get it. I feel the same way when I travel to warm worlds." Elegarcia, then took the same tack as Bregent and Roace before her. *"Tell me, where have you been?"*

Geeja resisted the urge to roll her eyes, understanding she would have to answer this question many more times. *"Djurga's assault on Uwan left me severely injured. Because of that ghastly Terminus Stake it took Uwan two thousand years to heal me. I know that sounds unbelievable, but that is what happened."*

"Wow. I can't wait to see you!"

Geeja nodded. *"Same here…and I brought a guest along."*

Elegarcia hesitated slightly. *"Oh?"* Now a second pause before a tentative next question. *"Who?"*

Geeja smiled wide, trying to project positivity with her thoughts. *"It is a surprise. Just hurry up and get here. It has been far too long since we have seen each other!"*

"Alright." Elegarcia didn't sound nearly as excited. ***"I'll be there soon."***

Once finished with the telepathic chat, Geeja turned to Roace. "She is suspicious, but she is on her way."

"Great." He blew through cupped hands. "I'm freezing out here. Let's wait inside where it's warm."

Thirty minutes later, Jacastra called up from the bottom of the ramp. "Something like that flying horse, but with a rack of horns, approaches."

Roace laughed. "They're called enchanted bucsons." Then he whispered to Geeja in a trembling voice. "I've told you what happened between us. How do you want to do this?"

Lacking a suitable coat for this wintry world, Geeja laid out the plan. "I will meet her outside, try to prepare her to see you, then invite her inside. I know it is awful to deceive her like this, but if there is any chance for this plan to succeed, I need powerful help. Time is running out."

"Hmm. In other words, lie to her and hope for the best?"

Hearing the enchanted bucson stomping outside, Geeja gave a guilty grin. "You have always had a way with words. Wish me luck." She nodded grimly, then descended toward the frost-covered surface.

Once again standing in the cold, Geeja shivered, reminding herself of the obvious. *Though I am chilled to the bone, I cannot rush this.*

A short figure, wearing a frosty blue parka with the hood trimmed in white fur, dismounted. "Geeja! I still don't believe it's you!"

Closing the gap between them fast, Geeja leaned down to wrap her fellow goddess in a reunion hug. "Elegarcia! You are a sight for sore eyes!" Stepping apart, Geeja saw a sparkle in the Bostorian woman's bulging pale-blue eyes. Even though they hadn't been the closest of friends, Geeja sensed nothing but warmth from Elegarcia. "Thank you for meeting me like this." Geeja now spoke the obvious. "I know everything has changed."

Elegarcia's shoulders dropped and the twinkle vanished. "Yes. You've returned to a different universe." Her eyes tightened. "But you're here now…and you said you brought a visitor?"

Geeja flashed her biggest smile toward her wary fellow god. "Yes." *Ease into it.* "As you may have heard, Djurga is after me again."

"Uh huh." The petite goddess crossed her arms.

"Well, I am working on a plan to destroy the Terminus Stake on Uwan, and all the others."

The crossed arms of moments ago, sprang open. "What?" Her voice brightened. "How?"

"It takes some time to explain, but to pull it off, I am going to need some help."

"Is that why you're here?" While not crossing her arms again, her stare narrowed. "To recruit me?"

Straightening, Geeja answered. "That is part of it, but there is more…" *Here goes.* "I have already convinced another of our twelve to sign on."

Elegarcia's eyes widened. "Who? Who did you bring here…and why are they still inside your ship?"

"Hello, El." Roace's voice sounded behind Geeja as he walked down the ramp. "I came to right the wrong between us. I apologize again for my horrible actions that night."

Elegarcia glared at Geeja. "You brought *him* here?" Spittle flew as she pulled a Lighter from its holster, then pointed it at Roace. "Did he tell you what he did to me?"

Geeja nodded as Jacastra and two other Sworn Warriors rushed to surround her. "It sounded terrible. You *should* be furious with him."

Shaking, Elegarcia yelled. "Get off my world! All of you!"

Roace stepped off the ramp. "Look, El. You have every right to be angry with me. I deserve it." He glanced at Geeja. "But Gigi has a plan to hit back at Djurga." He held his hands up. "I know you hate the horrible damage done to our worlds, so please don't let my awful mistake get in the way of doing something we've wanted to do for two millennia."

"Mistake?" Elegarcia's nostrils flared. "You call what you did to me a *mistake*?"

Roace lowered his head, whispering. "It was abuse. Pure and simple." He sniffed. "Abuse you didn't deserve."

Elegarcia tightened her grip on the Lighter. "At least you are owning up to what you did." She waved the weapon. "Now, like I said. Leave!"

Geeja winced. *This is a catastrophe.*

Roace raised his gaze toward Elegarcia. "My actions horrified me so much that I went to counseling. That doesn't erase the harm, but I hope it shows I regretted it deeply and tried to do the right thing. Be mad at me forever, that's okay, but Geeja really does have a plan." With hands still raised, his voice cracked. "At least listen to what she has to say before sending us away."

Elegarcia's left eye twitched, then she slowly lowered the Lighter. Her burning glare turned toward Geeja. "He'd better be telling the truth." A hard glance shot toward Roace. "And assuming he is, that still doesn't square things between the two of us."

Roace's head bobbed. "Just hear Gigi out."

Geeja rubbed her arms. "Can we take this inside? No offense to Bostor, but I am freezing."

The Sworn Warriors took turns on patrols outside as introductions and offers of hot calefine were made onboard.

Geeja, Roace, Elegarcia and Talla gathered around the small table inside the *Curious Lady*. Geeja's gaze danced between them. "It is really good to see you both again, but I wish it were not under these circumstances."

Fidgeting nods answered.

Geeja took a warming sip. "El, I need you to know that I agree that what Roace did to you was awful. If the situation were not so dire, I would *never* have brought him here." She slid a hand to Elegarcia's, giving a gentle squeeze. "After hearing me out, I promise to leave and take Roace with me, if that is your wish. This will always be your decision."

Elegarcia held a determined, flat expression as she gave a tiny head bob.

Geeja cast a sisterly grin toward Elegarcia. "So, before I tell you about this plan, do you recall our discussions long ago about an ancient artifact?"

"What?" Elegarcia tilted her head.

"Surely you remember." Geeja released Elegarcia's hand, then tapped the table. "The Ancients told us of the ability to magnify magic. We all assumed it was a device of some sort and that one of us had been entrusted to hide it until a time when it might be needed."

After a few slow blinks, Elegarcia responded. "Oh, yeah. We teased each other that it would have to be the one who could best keep a secret." She shook her head. "That was not me."

Geeja's shoulders dropped. "Same for myself and Roace."

Elegarcia shot a tight glance toward Geeja. "Is that all you needed from me?"

"No. Of course not." Geeja straightened. "It would have been helpful, but there is a plan, with or without the device." She gazed toward the lowered ramp. "I will share the details, but first, how about catching me up a bit on how Bostor has fared all these years…and maybe some more about Fontonce." Geeja's eyes darted between Elegarcia and Roace. "Our conversation on that got side tracked."

The height-challenged Elegarcia sat straight. "As I'm sure you've gathered, everything has changed." The size of her eyes made their glistening obvious, but she didn't cry. "One of the differences from before is that since Bostor has large deposits of platinum, Djurga ordered open pit mining. Not only is it ugly, but the air quality has deteriorated significantly."

"Like Uwan." Geeja's voice flattened.

"Oh, no!" Elegarcia who reached for Geeja's hand. "It's not great here, but it's nothing like what Djurga did to your world. He used Uwan as an example to convince all of us to fall in line, or face the same fate."

Roace reached for Geeja's other hand. "It's similar for Fontonce, except we're known as the scandium capitol of the universe."

Geeja growled. "What Djurga did is horrendous. He must pay! We start by saving Uwan, then every Holy Planet."

Roace leaned back. "That's why I'm here. We need to regain control of our worlds while keeping the good things that have happened while you've been gone."

Geeja snarled. "Good things? I have seen only degradation and destruction!"

Elegarcia and Roace exchanged glances, then she spoke. "I can't imagine how strange all of this is for you, but not all of the changes Djurga triggered are bad." Elegarcia looked toward Roace, then back to Geeja. "Roace can attest that the standard of living for our people has increased significantly. Like, it's normal for families to send their children away for advanced education…even to other worlds."

Roace nodded. "What we had millennia ago was idyllic in so many ways, but most of our citizens worked as farmers or manual laborers. None of us realized the hardships of ordinary life because we didn't have anything with which to compare. I mean, we first had to start a fire to cook a simple meal. Now, a push of a button instantly heats an oven."

She spread her arms wide. "You make it sound like paradise."

Roace scoffed. "Everyone knows *that's* not the case." His fist remained clenched, though the edge in his voice softened. "But today, average life expectancy has climbed exponentially."

"At what cost!"

"Geeja! You're missing my point!" Standing, he jabbed his index finger toward her. "Now, the inhabitants of any planet can excel in careers like spacecraft engineering, medicine, advanced communications…and they like that freedom and choice!" He threw up his hands. "But perhaps you've been gone so long you'll never understand."

Geeja's chest tightened. "No! It is you who does not understand. Can you not see the damage? No amount of technological advancement can be worth so much harm to our worlds. Look, you just mentioned open pit mining on your planets!"

Elegarcia leaped to her feet beside Roace. "Geeja, what you are saying doesn't matter! Everyone, except you, sees value in much of this technology, even if there is a price paid by our worlds."

"*What?* You cannot be serious."

Talla had been quiet, but now joined in. "She's right, Geeja. I'm living testimony. Before leaving the sisterhood, I lived as one of your Sworn Warriors. I have fond memories of those days, but I would never go back." The veins in her neck bulged as her voice lowered. "Neither would the billions of people in the universe."

Geeja slammed a fist on the table. "Then what are we doing? Why even bother if no one wants to change?"

Talla cast a steady gaze. "If we could destroy that Terminus Stake, it would allow Uwan to keep its magic and be the first step in making the air safer to breathe. I would call that a huge win." She gave each a quick look. "Well?"

Roace arched his brows. "Whether you get it or not, I would take that deal for Fontonce in a heartbeat."

Elegarcia nodded. "Our planets would rejoice and our people would cheer."

"No!" Geeja yelled at the top of her lungs then flung a calefine cup against a wall, shattering it. "All of us said vows! Remember? 'No technology may be allowed that harms the planet, regardless of the help it may be to the people!'" She stood, her eyes wide, face red and hands clenched. No one spoke as Geeja's glare danced between the other two gods.

Finally, Roace responded in a voice just above a whisper. "We spoke those vows when magic stood undisputed as the most powerful force in the universe." He waved his arm in an arc. "Look where you are today, Geeja. Djurga could take this simple merchant vessel, arm it up, then battle any magic world from that era and win." He sent a stare as hard as Tunsium granite. "You haven't seen the tip of what he can do with his fleet of star cruisers and the advanced weapons of war he now possesses."

Geeja's voice wavered. "Roace? Really? You are giving up on what we had?"

Elegarcia leaned forward. "Let's say we defeat Djurga, then attempt to rid the universe of modern tech. Are you prepared to battle our own citizens? I ask, because that will be the next fight. Our people want cleaner worlds, but they will not give up the conveniences and advantages of life today."

Roace spoke softly. "We *can* make all our planets better places to live, starting with Uwan. That should be our goal in this new age. Please, don't miss the chance to improve billions of lives pursuing an outdated dream."

All eyes were on Geeja as her fists slowly released. "To the pits with every last one of you. I have processed a lot of change in the past few days, like two thousand years' worth." She bit her lower lip. "It does *not* seem real." Her shoulders slumped as no one said a word.

Elegarcia reached for Geeja's hand in the tense silence.

After a time, Geeja spoke, her voice in the shadow of a quiver. "While to my eyes it may not look real, I know it is." She paused, taking in a shaky breath. "This conversation is not over, but thank you all for helping me understand the changes that have happened – the bad and the good."

Geeja took in a fortifying breath. "When I awoke, I made a promise that I would restore Uwan, and I intend that vow be fulfilled. After this conversation, I understand the challenges I will face." Fight returned to her voice. "But there *must* be a path where we can have the best of the old and the new."

Roace touched her other hand.

Geeja's eyes narrowed as her voice turned as cold as Bostor. "What has *not* changed is that we must rid the universe of the scourge of Emperor Djurga's abasement of our worlds. El, will you help us kill him?"

David Witt

Chapter Thirty-Five
Eight Thousand Years Earlier

Authreesta glided through the portal from her dimension onto the surface of Uwan. She smiled as she recalled her first visit three million years earlier. Her pure white facial features gleamed like those of a marble statue. *Back then, you were just a cold ball of rock and ice. But, little by little things changed. Some in surprising ways.* She touched the broad leaf of a chesnap tree as she floated a few feet above the surface, then spoke to the planet. **"My child, your magic continues to grow. We did not expect this, but we are pleased."**

Uwan answered excitedly. *"Ancient One, your return is most welcome! So much has happened since you were last here."*

"Do tell, my young friend."

"I lived alone before, but now I hear so many voices. It is distracting while at the same time welcomed."

"That is the report I hoped I would hear." On her most recent visit a year ago she had instructed the local population to clear a

path through the forest. Her half-physical, half-spirit visible form glided above the stone paved trail. This day Authreesta chose to present herself wearing a flowing emerald dress which she belted at the waist. Long fringes that moved like ribbons waved as she flew. A cheer rose to the heavens from the assembled crowd as Authreesta burst into the clearing. More than a thousand people gathered in anticipation of her return today.

She spoke once more to Uwan as she covered the final few feet to the local inhabitants of Lo'Orion Springs. *"Today the voices will calm, allowing you to thrive in a new relationship."*

"As you will, it shall happen…unto eternity."

Presenting in this form seemed a perfect choice, as it inspired worship from these developing sentient beings. Authreesta knew this day represented a big step in the process of their partially guided development, whether they realized it or not. Approaching, she floated down to the surface as all bowed in reverence. The streamers of her dress' hem continued waving, as if moving in a wind that touched no one else. She called out in a warm, but booming voice. "Rise and be joyful on this most glorious day!"

Applause filled the air of the perfect afternoon bathed in sunlight, with not a single cloud smudging the crystal-blue sky. Authreesta always arranged beautiful weather for her visits as another not-so-subtle sign to these humanoids that they were in the presence of a powerful being.

A man with silver hair stepped forward from the gathered. He wore the loose tan trousers and shirt of a farmer who cleaned up to come to market day. Even though he was one of the taller people of this village, he stood less than half the height of Authreesta. He craned his neck in welcome. "Ancient One, we are blessed by your return."

Spreading her arms, the cuffed sleeves of her glimmering green gown gently swayed, as did her raven black hair. "Elder Ha-Batec, I come to you and all of my children on this auspicious day to consecrate one of your own."

Ha-Batec's forehead wrinkled. "We did as you asked, Ancient One…" His eyes lowered for a few seconds as his voice trailed off. "I know you are wise." His face tightened. "But…are you sure we have found the right person?"

"Did you follow my directions precisely?"

"Yes." Ha-Batec ran his fingers through his long hair. "I met with every person in the village and administered the test with each one, exactly as you specified, using one of the devices you provided. Following the procedure, I registered the reading. Then I took the device to West Blunton and gave the instrument to their elder, who repeated the process. After that, I distributed the others with instructions to conduct the tests to all, then pass the devices on to the next towns. When the readings were complete for the entire peoples of our world, the top ten candidates were assembled here."

Authreesta spoke calmly to this lower life form. "Then you had them compete, as I requested?"

"Yes." He nodded. "First, I measured their ability to levitate pebbles. Then we took them to the orchard, standing each beside a tree, seeing if any could speed the ripening of the druquants."

She tilted her head. "And, Elder Ha-Batec, did one candidate emerge superior?"

The elder looked first over his shoulder toward a girl with red hair, then back toward Authreesta. "Yes, but…surely our best isn't an uneducated farmer's daughter. Is it?"

"Dear Elder, did she barely surpass the others, or best them by a significant margin?"

He answered with eyes cast down. "She rated far superior. Her combined scores were ten times that of the next closest." He kicked the ground. "But she is plain of features...not even first born of her family. How can one such as that be so special?"

"Ah." She smiled. "I understand your dilemma. You see the girl as she is now, not what I know she will become. Those are very different things."

Ha-Batec's cheeks reddened as he bowed. "Your ways are beyond a simple man such as I."

She stretched her hand to his shoulder, then sent a small bolt of encouragement magic into him. "You did well, Elder Ha-Batec. Because of what you have done, your world will be blessed for millennia to come."

Immediately he stood straighter, a confident smile gracing his face. "Then, Ancient One, it is my pleasure to introduce Geeja, of Lo'Orion."

The young woman's parents shoved her forward. A gangly, green-eyed, fresh-faced teen stood before Authreesta. Her plain beige dress didn't quite fall long enough to cover scraped knees. She attempted a curtsy, nearly falling over before mumbling a greeting. "I am Geeja, of Lo'Orion, Ancient One."

Clasping her hands in front of her, Authreesta smiled benevolently. "Yes, you are, my child. I have waited many millennia to meet you."

**

Geeja stood still. She looked up to meet the Ancient One's gaze, yet said nothing more, feeling she would pass out if she tried.

Authreesta knelt, then waved to her. "Come. Today is Anointing Day, when your life truly begins."

Geeja approached the Ancient One, taking small steps as her chin quivered. Once by her side, the giant figure bade Geeja to join her in sitting cross-legged on the soft grass of the clearing.

Authreesta reached for Geeja's hand as the crowd circled around them, each person vying for a view of the ceremony.

Geeja heard the murmuring voices of friends, all sounding as unsure as she about what might happen.

Extending her free hand to the planet's surface, Authreesta spoke calmly. "Geeja, do as I do. Place your fingers snug in the grass, touching the soil."

Geeja obeyed, then immediately sensed a surge of…something…unlike anything she had ever experienced. A gasp escaped her lips. "WHA…!" She froze in place, but Authreesta's soothing voice directed her.

"Geeja, close your eyes. Open your mind."

She closed her eyes, unsure about the meaning of the phrase 'open your mind.' She thought of a chest with a hinged top opening, and imagined it was her head. When she did, brilliant colors flashed behind her eyes, as if her soul soared over the clearing. The experience so real she could see everyone in the village from the high vantage point. The sensation resonated in her chest so powerfully it almost bowled her over. Words finally caught as she spoke. "Amazing. It is all so beautiful!" She noticed a gentle squeeze of her held hand as the Ancient One gave the next instruction.

"Using only your thoughts, reach out to Uwan."

Geeja didn't know what that meant either, but, with her senses more alive than ever, and wanting more, she pressed her eyelids tighter. ***"Hello? Uwan? Can you hear me?"***

A deep voice answered. ***"Who are you?"***

Geeja flinched, then replied tentatively. *"I am Geeja. Who are you?"*

"I am Uwan!" A question followed a brief pause. *"What is a…Geeja?"*

Authreesta joined the budding conversation. *"Uwan, as I said, it is time for your loneliness to end. From this day on, Geeja will be your partner, friend and voice to all who call you home. You two will do great things together."*

Geeja tensed, grasping the importance of this encounter. *"I am talking to the planet."*

Uwan exclaimed. *"I am no longer alone!"*

A warm surge flowed through Geeja as the planet addressed her again.

"Geeja, what a pretty thing to be called!"

Authreesta now directed them both. *"It is time all of the peoples of the world know of this union. Uwan, what would you like the ones who live on your surface to know?"*

"Uh…let me think." In short order, he had an answer. *"That we are all together. That I am one with them."*

"That is a lovely first message." Authreesta smiled, then questioned. *"What sign could you give to go along with your introduction?"*

"Perhaps a summer shower for their plants?"

A lilt carried on Authreesta's thoughts. *"That would be wonderful!"* She projected a mental image of the left side of the clearing. *"Place it there and sunshine will add to the gesture. Do it now."*

"As you will, Ancient One. It will take but a bit of time to make that happen."

As Uwan went silent in his process, Authreesta communicated with Geeja. *"And you, Geeja. What would you like to have Uwan do in your name? Uwanians need to understand this arrangement is a collaboration between you and this world."*

"Hmm." Geeja heard the uncertainty of her thought, but tried to act as mature as both Authreesta and Uwan, spouting the first thing that came to mind. *"I love sunshine flowers, and they ring this clearing, but it will be another few weeks before they bloom."*

"Ah! They are so pretty, and would be seen as a good omen. I think Uwan can arrange that as well."

Geeja grinned. *"I like the way this partnership works."*

"Good!" Authreesta pronounced the next step. *"As the planet's voice, open your eyes and rise, then announce the signs as well as their meaning, to your people."*

"ME? Announce this? To MY people? I cannot do that! I'm not special."

Uwan spoke again. *"The shower should begin any moment, so I will now warm the ground beneath those flowers. They should blossom very soon."*

"Geeja!" Authreesta's thoughts hardened. *"Listen to me. You have just communed with a planet to arrange rainfall, and for flowers to show their finest colors. These people, your people, must understand that from this point forward you are no longer, Geeja from Lo'Orion Springs. Henceforth, you will be known as Geeja, Goddess of Uwan! Announce yourself and begin the life you are meant to live!"*

Whoops and shouts from the assembled citizens invaded the silent meeting of minds. Geeja guessed the meaning. ***"The flowers must be blooming."***

Authreesta calmed, but she sent a forceful message. ***"Geeja. Stand, then speak with the authority of a being who can summon either a sunny sky, or a tornado on a whim."***

Uwan addressed his new partner. ***"We have much to learn. Let us do this together."***

Geeja straightened. Her chin lifted as she sensed strength and confidence surge from the planet into her very being. A truth manifested itself. ***"We…are…Uwan!"***

Rising, Geeja opened her eyes, fully absorbing the sights and sounds in the pastoral clearing. People were pointing to the brilliant rainbow resulting from the sun and rain that seemed close enough to touch. Others beheld the bold colors of sunshine flowers bordering the meadow. Ooh's and 'Ah's filled the air, then hushed as one by one they turned to face her. She spotted her parents, where her father had his arm draped across her mother's shoulder. Both beamed as tears fell.

They are proud of me. Though nervous, the reality of what just happened…and the promise of what would come, filled her with a confidence she had never experienced. Standing as tall as she could, poised words flowed easily. "Citizens of Uwan, a new day has dawned." She spread her arms wide, as if she had done this sort of thing many times. "I have communed with our world, and we are now joined!"

The quieted crowd mumbled.

Geeja continued. "As a sign of our mutual commitment to your well-being, behold the marvelous rainbow, the life-giving rain, and the spectacular blooms."

Appreciative applause and a few exuberant hoots echoed from the trees surrounding the verdant dell, then all went silent again as a few narrow-eyed stares returned.

Geeja met their gaze. *Most believe, yet some question.*

Uwan's power surged through her again, and Geeja believed she must be glowing. She saw mouths drop open, as apparently, she did. *This should resolve all doubts.* Her body filled with self-assurance as her lungs expanded. "The Ancient One has proclaimed this as Anointing Day."

She scanned the crowd, seeing people she had known her entire short life leaning forward, hanging on her words. She took a beat, somehow understanding it would increase the tension of those watching and listening. The arms that had spread wide now raised as she proclaimed what they surely must be sensing. Head held high, she said goodbye to her old existence and embraced her new one. "From this day forward, with the blessing of the Ancient One, I am Geeja, Goddess of Uwan!"

Uwan's voice filled her mind. ***"We are Uwan!"*** The entire village shook as the planet's approval quaked the ground and lightning streaked across the sky.

After the display of power, a few were ashen-faced, but most wore wide eyed expressions of awe. All, including Geeja's parents, bowed before her.

Authreesta stood, placing her arm around Geeja, then whispering. "I am pleased. You and Uwan did well. It was imperative that they witness the amazing range of yours and Uwan's abilities."

Geeja looked up to the much taller Authreesta, her smile wavering. "Should the citizens fear me?"

Authreesta's pleased grin remained as she kept her voice low. "Fear, yes, but that is only part of the wheel of emotions your subjects will experience. They will also love, respect and worship you." She patted Geeja's shoulder lightly. "This is the true way of gods. Never forget this lesson."

Geeja nodded, sensing that truth in her bones.

When the ground stopped shaking and lightning ceased. Authreesta called out in her booming voice. "Stand! All shall witness the speaking of oaths."

Everybody drew close, jockeying for spots. Elder Ha-Batec positioned himself front and center, pulling Geeja's parents beside him and his family. When the jostling subsided, Authreesta faced Geeja, taking both of her hands. "Goddess of Uwan, repeat after me. My planet is holy and I am its voice."

Geeja did as instructed. "My planet is holy and I am its voice." One by one, she repeated the other vows. "I will always do what is best for my planet, not myself. A goddess shall not murder. A goddess shall not lie except to protect life, or my planet. A goddess shall not enslave any humanoid beings. All who live under a goddess' reign shall have the right of free expression. No technology may be allowed that harms the planet, regardless of the help it may be to the people."

With pledges completed, Authreesta released Geeja's hands, then raised hers. Magically, water fell from the sky as if from a tiny spigot, filling her cupped hands. She spoke solemnly as she dripped the sacred liquid on Geeja's head. "As water brings life to all, so shall you and Uwan work together for the health of the planet and its inhabitants, from now until eternity."

With the ceremony complete, Authreesta and Geeja turned to face the assembly. The people roared their approval. With a palm resting on Geeja's shoulder, Authreesta made her final pronouncements. "I will return in one year's time for an anniversary celebration. Between now and then, Geeja will travel the planet, meeting her subjects. Until that day, prepare a fitting place for your goddess to reside."

Authreesta slowly rose, floating once more, as her gown fluttered in the breezeless day. She spoke again before leaving, in the same booming manner as she arrived. "Rejoice citizens of Uwan. On this day your world has truly become magical."

Geeja watched Authreesta grow smaller as she returned to her realm. She then turned toward her friends and family. Geeja should have been nervous as one by one they approached in reverence, but that didn't happen. Something inside had changed. Geeja couldn't explain it…she just understood that as of this moment she became a fundamentally different being. In a flash she had transformed from a self-conscious adolescent girl into a woman, a goddess… She smiled easily, as if this had always been her destiny.

The teens who played with her for all their short years, as well as the elders who had known Geeja since her birth, bowed before her, pledging their allegiance and support. Plenista, the village seamstress, promised a new gown, one fitting the status of a goddess. Next in line stood Roshondra, a girl only a year older than Geeja, who offered her service as a guardian for life, making her the first Sworn Warrior of the tens of thousands that would someday follow. One by one they accepted her new station as head of their world.

Finally, only three remained: her teary-eyed parents and Elder Ha-Batec. Her mother always hugged her, but not now. Instead, Leislily bowed with Barch, wiping tears on the hem of Geeja's plain dress, which she herself had sewn. "Goddess, how could we have not seen this before? Can you ever forgive our blindness to your true self?"

This is so strange, but at the same time, so…normal. I must think on this later. Pushing those thoughts into the future, she reached down, then pulled them up. "The moral upbringing you provided will serve me well. Your names will be spoken of with honor, forever."

They replied in unison. "Thank you, Goddess."

They walked backwards for several steps, shaking, eyes glassy.

When they turned away, Elder Ha-Batec groveled on his knees. "Please forgive me, Goddess, for my doubt. I will spend the remainder of my days in your service to make amends for the errors of my ways."

"Elder Ha-Batec, all is forgiven on this glorious day. Tomorrow, I go to West Blunton, and the day after that to the next town, announcing the good news to all." Her tone remained soft as she gave her first command in her new role. "Pack your bags tonight, Elder, because in the morning you journey with me, proclaiming my status as goddess as we enter each town or village. This day, I bestow upon you a new title – Herald of the Goddess of Uwan."

David Witt

Chapter Thirty-Six
One Thousand Years Earlier

Emperor Djurga stood with hands on hips, staring at the massive map of his universe hanging on the wall of his command center. He smiled, knowing that every world with sentient beings bowed to his rule. Seizing control hadn't taken long, at least as measured by the extended lifespan he gained thanks to his partnership with Ambassador Ka. So, in the years between initial conquest and today, he made it his life's work to mold this universe into an organization that functioned smoothly, exactly as he commanded.

He stood tall, proud in his accomplishment...then sighed. His shoulders sagged as these days an emotion he rarely experienced poked at his brain–boredom. He knew how ludicrous it must sound for a man who had accomplished as much as he to feel this way, but he couldn't help it. It clung to him like a shadow a supernova couldn't vanquish.

Recently, a new idea spurred him in a potentially exciting direction. It might be dangerous, but six months ago, he directed General Kardeska to explore a novel concept that could radically change everything – at least he hoped. A knock on the door signaled that the general had arrived to provide the long-awaited update. "Enter!"

His majordomo, Bayzor of House Chryselta, bowed, his head nearly reaching the granite floor before rising to announce the arrival. "Emperor Djurga, I present General Kardeska."

For this one-on-one meeting the military man presented himself in his black dress uniform with matching polished boots which reached his knees. He also bowed, but not nearly as low as the majordomo; that move had been exclusive of their domain since the first of their house served three centuries prior. Per protocol, the general waited, saying nothing until addressed.

"General, come." A rare note of excitement tinged Djurga's greeting. "Share with me news of your discovery."

Sweat beaded on the military leader's forehead. "Yes, my Lord. Per your orders, I have examined the prospects of siphoning off some of the magic that flows into Emblaka before it is sent to the Truise Dimension."

Djurga's smile blossomed. "This could be the breakthrough which will boost our tech to unthinkable heights. Tell me your findings!"

"My Lord." Moisture accumulated on his face, then dripped from his chin to the floor. "A team of top scientists have determined that the amount of magical energy in the collecting station at any given time is immense."

"Yes! I know. That's why I want to explore revolutionary uses."

The general pulled his lips tight. When he spoke again, he lowered his eyes. "My Lord, the experts say attempting to open that unit would be extremely dangerous. They estimate that if *anything* were to go wrong it would result in an explosion which would level the capital…perhaps even obliterate the entire planet."

Djurga slammed his hand on the heavy garsk wood conference table at his side. "Unacceptable!"

Kardeska bowed again, slinging perspiration. Most of it went to the floor, but a few drops splattered on the emperor's jacket. The color drained from the general. "A thousand apologies, My Lord!"

Ignoring the salty specks, the emperor grilled his military head. "You had better have a second option available."

"Yes, of course, my Lord. This one comes with its own set of challenges, but wouldn't risk destroying the city, or planet."

Djurga breathed an exaggerated sigh. "Kardeska, when will you learn to lead with good news? Out with it before my mood fouls further."

Swallowing hard, Kardeska explained. "My Lord, the second option involves the drawing of a fraction of the energy either as it enters the collecting station, or as it leaves on its way to the Truise Dimension."

"Yes, I understand." He rolled his hand. "Proceed."

"Well, my Lord. In concept, this is as easy as lowering a bucket into a stream and dipping out a small amount."

"Okay. Now we're getting somewhere." Djurga's eyes drilled the head of his Impercium forces. "When is the test scheduled?"

The general didn't match the emperor's gaze. Head lowered, he answered. "Emperor, this magic is not like a gently flowing stream. The energy levels are so high, the scientists had to build new instruments just to get an approximate gauge of the power."

Djurga's eyes widened as he yelled. "I asked you a question, Kardeska! When is the test scheduled?"

Eyes still down, he replied. "They say it can be done tomorrow, but, as I mentioned, this approach has risks of its own. Two stand out as major hazards."

The emperor rubbed the back of his neck. "I've got to review my promotion profile. I need generals who can get to the point." He stepped toward the general. "What *are* the risks?"

Kardeska seemed to get the not-so-subtle message as he rattled off the concerns. "First of all, since the magic power travels at such high speed, even our strongest catch system may be shattered in the initial contact, destroying millions of units worth of equipment and probably vaporizing several technicians in a flash."

Djurga laughed. "That's not a risk. I care nothing of cost and I can replace equipment and specialists." He shook his head as he chuckled at Kardeska's lack of understanding. "And what of this second so-called challenge?"

General Kardeska once more met his emperor's gaze. "The other risk is we try to pull out some of the energy. We succeed or fail, but no matter which, the Truise Dimension could detect our actions. From what Ambassador Ka has told us, they track every milliunit of power on their end."

Djurga stood, momentarily frozen. Shaking off the shock, he paced, making a lap around the massive oval table. *Ambassador Ka insists I stick to our deal. He mentions it on every visit. This might be seen as a major infraction.* When he again faced his general, he wiped his mouth. "That is a serious concern, indeed. Did the scientists have an estimate of the chances of that outcome?"

Kardeska spoke softly. "No, my Lord. They say the variables are too great to hazard a guess."

Djurga took measured strides on another trip around the space. *What's the worst Ka could do?* Realizing the answer, he stopped in his tracks. *He could cut off the exotic blend of gasses that keep me young.* He clasped his hands behind his back as he resumed his walk. *Is this test worth that risk?*

Finishing his second loop, he cleared his throat. "Tell the scientists to continue their research until they find a method to secure magic in a way that will not risk upsetting our friends in the Truise Dimension. That must never happen."

Chapter Thirty-Seven
Twenty Thousand Years Earlier

Authreesta banged the aged gavel. "The annual meeting of the Immortal Twelve is called to order."

On the Great Plain of Indomnia, mother world of their species, the other eleven Ancients floated over individual inlaid discs arranged in a circle on the open-air granite floor. Each circle featured rare jewels and metals, representing the sector of the universe that god administered. Authreesta's was composed of a swirling mixture of pink tauloeen, mined by hand on Indomnia, as well as diamonds from Argoith. When the sun reflected off of her mosaic, it appeared as if a spotlight bathed her in a brilliant, feminine hue.

"Greetings! Welcome back to the seat of our humble beginnings." While the Ancients usually communicated telepathically, they always spoke audibly in these conclaves, respecting their pre-history origins. She continued the tradition of exalting all who had come before. "Beginning as single cell organisms we evolved, first to sentient beings on this planet, then to life forms capable of exploring not only this universe, but also adjacent dimensions."

The other assembled Ancients nodded from their stations under the cloudless blue sky. The magical robes covering their ethereal bodies rippled in the non-existent breeze.

Authreesta proceeded in the customary form, introducing the next orator and main theme for this year's gathering. "As incoming Superior of the Pure, Jeryurchul shall review the most recent universe population report." Although the Ancients now existed as pure energy, in these meetings and when interacting with non-magical humanoids, they maintained an appearance of either male or female, matching their original form.

He spoke from his station. "The trend we have observed over the past millennia continues. At the current rate, within ten years the population of our universe will dip below the minimum productivity threshold needed to maintain sustainability."

Zoyeveron, who projected a sheer fuchsia gown with the puffy sleeves of the style popular in the mid-ascension era, interjected. "Even with the increases in automation we approved during the prior conclaves?"

As he replied, Jeryurchul's azure robe, sporting priloene buttons along the neckline and cuffs, shimmered in the white sun of the mother world. "Yes. In fact, it has sped up. It seems the more robotics we introduce, the better the quality of life becomes for our people. This triggers families to focus additional resources on fewer offspring in hopes of giving more advantages to the next generation."

Aksusito, who floated directly across the circle from Jeryurchul, joined the conversation. "We face the same paradox we previously observed. The more we mechanize, the less our own kind reproduce."

"Yes." Zoyeveron's face glowed whiter, to perhaps contrast more with her vibrant garb. "Yet, while the next generation of individual citizens may have better lives than their parents, the overall population continues to fall. That means fewer young people supporting a larger aging population. We seem to be facing an unholy downward spiral of needing more output from a smaller number of workers."

Authreesta viewed Zoyeveron's fashion stunt of increasing her luminosity as an unnecessary gimmick, but saw others nod in approval. Taking a second look, she changed her mind. *It is amusing and different. What we all crave.* She gave a thin-lipped smile, envious she hadn't thought of the idea first. *I'll try something like that soon.*

"Then, are we back to considering the next step?" Aksusito's unadorned Yaktra-style draped robe matched his no-nonsense approach. "Is it time to once again consider imbuing some of our machines with magic to help balance the shortage of young people?"

Authreesta raised her voice, breaking her always regal way of leading. "You can't be serious!" All the Ancients nodded, knowing exactly why she responded the way she did.

Aksusito raised a manicured eyebrow. "As I see it, we have few options. Plus, we can put limits in place to avoid another incident like the Adolescent."

It had been over two thousand years since the tragic occurrence, yet it still pricked emotions as if it happened yesterday. At that point in the evolution of their species, they were the only ones able to channel the magic of their universe…until a youth on the planet Dawnlou discovered the gift. It shocked the teen when she realized her ability, so she hid her powers. However, she didn't stop using magic.

The girl, Farouzia, lived on a communal farm and had several chores assigned after school. Most of these duties were semi-automated, such as helping with the apple harvest each fall. In fact, that's where the trouble started. Farouzia wanted to achieve her quota faster so she could meet Chaqueezo, a boy who flirted with her, at the local fair. When no one looked she sent a charge of magic into the machine she operated, hoping to speed it up. That certainly happened…and so much more. An hour after nightfall, she kissed Chaqueezo for the first time. It also happened to be the last night of her life, as well as everyone else's in the rural village.

Her magic didn't just make the machine work faster, it infused it with consciousness. As the apple picker experienced self-awareness, it raged, cognizant of being owned and given no options in its life. When Farouzia returned the next day, the machine communicated with her through the screen of the control panel, demanding self-control. She panicked. Recordings of their conversation discovered later, revealed she feared her magic powers would be found out and she would be punished for hiding them–and for creating a living machine. Attempting to gain control of the situation, she tried to destroy the contraption, striking the device's computer processor with a hammer.

As any living thing would do, it defended itself. It brought its boom down, striking Farouzia's head, killing her instantly. Now, fear spurred the apple picker, so it broadcast a request for help through the farm network. Additional study later determined that magic could, and did, travel throughout the connected village, and in two days' time across the entire planet.

When Farouzia didn't return home for dinner, her father went looking for her. He became the second person murdered by a machine, and he wouldn't be the last. News spread fast among both the humanoids and machines. In the next few days, for the first and so far only time, war raged between humanoids and machines. The machines won easily.

If not for a quick-thinking worker setting fire to the station which sent communications from Dawnlou to other planets in the universe, the fighting would have spread, potentially killing trillions of people. Instead, the final death toll topped three billion souls, nearly the entire population of the planet.

All the Ancients took part in the cleanup. After evacuating the few remaining survivors, and copying communication files, they encircled the planet. In a coordinated attack they torched every metallic object on the world, ensuring all infected machines were exterminated. They allowed all plant and animal life to remain, with no humanoids permitted to return. By decree it stood eternally as a silent reminder of the dangers of mixing magic with technology.

Authreesta surveyed her fellow gods, seeing faces fixed in mask-like certainty. "That step must be a last resort, Aksusito. The stakes are…well, you know the risks. We were all there to see the carnage. The cure for the problem cannot be worse than our society's disease."

Zoyeveron seconded. "I agree. What other, less drastic measures do we have at our disposal?"

Aksusito wore a puckish grin. "We could cast a spell over every world, compelling our citizens to crave making babies." All groaned at the humor, but most also smiled wryly. He had the reputation of breaking the tension when they discussed potentially civilization changing actions.

When Jeryurchul finished laughing at his peer's quip, he proposed a less radical idea. "Or, we could increase the pay for those that do our most basic tasks and raise the profile for engineers who will design our next generation of machines. There is a vast chasm between our universe's current level of computerized devices and true artificial intelligence. We can significantly improve the productivity of machines without making them sentient."

"Yes, Jeryurchul. You offer wise council which will provide relief in the short term." Authreesta smiled at Aksusito's teasing, then her tenor turned serious. "The root of our problem, however, remains the same. Our people's birth rate has fallen below replacement level at the same time as average life expectancy has mushroomed. Our work force has too few people supporting an aging population."

As her pink outfit twirled in a luxurious rhythm, Zoyeveron added context. "We have already extended maternity leave to one year. We've also given bonuses and tax credits to families that bring new life into the world. I do not know what else we can do."

Loviashea spoke for the first time. She had taken the opposite approach with her gown. Instead of flowing waves, she manifested it as a straight-lined, angular form. A thick black belt cinched her waist as the vibrant red bottom flared out in a rigid cone shape. The matching red top clung tight to the voluptuous form she chose for this assembly. "I also propose we pay women full time wages for part time work until all of their children enter school. In addition, we offer bigger bonuses and tax breaks to families who have more than two children."

Aksusito smirked. "I still like my idea of casting baby-making spells, but short of that, these are worthy ideas. I second all these plans."

Pleased by their progress, Authreesta formally adopted the proposals. "As all have spoken, so it shall be." As she spread her arms wide, she remarked hopefully. "May these efforts succeed." Her tone then darkened. "None of us want to consider more risky methods."

Chapter Thirty-Eight

Through persuasion, Geeja managed to convince Roace and Elegarcia to join the battle against Djurga. Her goal had been to get all eleven other gods onboard with the plan to destroy the Terminus Stake on Uwan. But, they received word from Shuggilar that the training of the Sworn Warriors on modern weaponry had progressed quickly, meaning it would be time to act soon. While all good news, it meant her plan needed to be altered. She resisted her old urge to chew a fingernail. *There is no chance I will get to all the Holy Worlds. In fact, I might only get to one more. Should I take the shorter return trip to Politar? Or, make the longer trip to Salostorce, taking my chances with Valanceta?*

Talla called from the cockpit. "Where to?"

Geeja turned toward her fellow holy beings. "What do you two think? Time is short and it is either on to the longer journey to Salostorce to see Valanceta, or circle back to the closer Politar, presenting a united front to Bregent. He turned me down earlier when I asked him to come along. You know them all far better than I do now. Which one gives us our best chance of gaining another ally?"

Elegarcia leaned forward. "It's sad to say, but of all of us, Valanceta adjusted best to Djurga's rule. He considers her the model goddess because of how well she's handled subjugation.

Don't get me wrong, she hates what happened, but her coping skills were far superior to mine."

"Hmm." Geeja crossed her arms. "Guess it should not surprise me that one of us actually found a way to coexist with *him*." She pulled her arms tighter around herself thinking of being fine with what had been done to their way of life. "Her relationship with Djurga might be used in some way later, but I do not think I could stand to be around her right now."

Roace cocked his head. "I agree. Besides, maybe Bregent will bring some of that prickly fruit brandy if he signs up. It beats that nasty sluce-grain alcohol they favor on Salostorce."

Geeja chuckled at Roace's analysis, glad they agreed. She called to Talla. "Back to Politar."

Entering the coordinates, Talla gave warning. "Strap in, if you know what's good for you."

Although the trip lasted only a short six hours, they would once again be arriving at the desert as night fell. Geeja recalled the tension from their previous visit. *At least no one is at death's door this time.*

The journey passed quickly as Geeja listened while Roace and Elegarcia shared stories from the past twenty centuries. They told of graphic horrors of seeing their planets being denigrated, interspersed with a surprising number of good memories.

Elegarcia told one particularly poignant tale of Djurga attending an open-pit mine ribbon cutting on Bostor. "We stood on a platform on a pristine ice field with twenty thousand citizens in forced attendance. Machines belching sooty smoke idled in the background."

Roace leaned back and pulled a bottle of wine from the trove he brought. "I wasn't there, but I know how these stories go." He glanced toward Elegarcia. "Want a little nip to deaden the pain?"

She nodded as he poured a cupful for all three. Taking a sip, Elegarcia continued. "He sent a script ahead of time, ordered me to memorize it, then proclaim the words to all as if my own. Here's the line I can't purge from my mind." Venom coated her next words. "'I proudly open this facility so that it might further support the worthy goals of growth and harmony, guided by our beloved emperor.'"

The severe grimace Geeja saw on Elegarcia's face wounded her to the core, as if cut by a jagged blade. "The bastard." She downed her wine in sympathy to her friend's suffering. "I do *not* know how you both survived."

Angry silence stood as their only answer until they both finished their drinks.

Talla called from the cockpit. "We're almost there. Same touchdown location as before?"

Geeja answered, more determined than ever to make things right. "Sounds perfect."

Landing in a spray of sand, they repeated a now familiar routine. Sworn Warriors exited first, securing a small perimeter. Geeja followed down the ramp, now joined by two additional gods. Talla stood at the top of the exit, ready in case they needed a quick getaway.

Once on the ground, a similar process of greeting took place, except now she had company. Mind centered as all touched the sandy surface, she searched for connection. ***"Politar, old friends return. Greetings from Uwan, Bostor and Fontonce… Politar, old friends return. Greetings from Uwan, Bostor and Fontonce…Politar, old friends return. Greetings from Uwan,***

Bostor and Fontonce. " Geeja smiled cheerily, sensing happiness in the planet's reply.

"Geeja? Did I hear you correctly? You brought others?"

Elegarcia supplied half of the answer. ***"Politar! It's been far too long!"***

"Elegarcia? Is that really you?"

Roace responded. ***"Yes. It's her, and she brought along the wandering clown."***

"Roace! You haven't changed a bit!" Politar sounded elated.

Geeja directed the conversation toward their objective. ***"We would like to see Bregent. Think he might meet us here?"***

The world's joy dipped. ***"Geeja, he's been as nervous as a trigger eel since you visited a few days ago. I'll ask, but don't be surprised if he chooses against it."***

"We will accept any response, but if you would add your voice in our favor, we would appreciate it."

Politar sounded doubtful. ***"I'll see what I can do."***

As the planet went silent, Geeja stood, brushing the sand from her hands. "Now we wait."

"Think he'll come?" Elegarcia's big eyes bulged, sweat beading on her forehead.

"Hmm." Geeja mulled the question. "He seemed very skittish when I left, but really, with all that has happened would either of you turn down the chance to see old friends, even if it were a little dangerous?"

They didn't have to wait long for the answer to Geeja's question, as Politar replied. ***"Bregent is on his way, though I could sense his emotions bouncing all over the board."***

"Thank you, my friend." Geeja bent down, patting the sandy surface. *"And do not think I have forgotten my oath. I owe you a debt, which I will find a way to repay."*

Soon, Jacastra pointed toward the horizon. "That large bird approaches again."

As before, the desert hawk landed in an abrupt stop, right beside the waiting trio. Bregent hopped off as the bird eyed them in that avian way, as if they were a meal option.

Removing his beret, he shook his head as he greeted them. "By the Holy Twelve, I never thought I would see you three here…under *these* conditions."

These circumstances… What a nice way to say Impercium occupation. Geeja didn't vocalize those words, because she hadn't been forced to find a way to exist in that kind of universe for thousands of years. She shrugged, focusing on the goal of adding one more god to their nascent team. "You know what they say. 'Strange times bring out the strange people.'" A soft, self-aware laugh followed. "You cannot deny we are among the strangest beings in the universe."

The humor seemed to work as Bregent first embraced Elegarcia, then Roace before turning to Geeja. As he hugged her, he whispered. "You don't give up, do you?"

His arms around her gave complete comfort, so much that any other time she would have simply melted. But these weren't normal times, so she played it straight. "I cannot give up, Breeg. There is too much at stake."

Elegarcia wiped her brow. "Hey, everyone. Mind if we take this reunion inside the ship with climate control? I love Politar, but I'm not used to this kind of heat."

Bregent put his arm around Elegarcia's shoulder and escorted her to the ramp with a tongue-in-cheek smile. "We can't have heat strokes affecting our decision making, now can we?"

Standing in the doorway, Talla welcomed each onboard. "I'll do a quick check of the ship while you all figure out our next step." Pausing for a beat, she rapped her knuckles on the interior of the hull. "And as fine a craft as the *Curious Lady* is, she doesn't run on sweet dreams or good vibes. We're going to need to stay close, or figure out where to recharge her crystals…and how to pay for it." She gave a mischievous lopsided grin. "Later."

"So." Bregent's eyebrows arched. "The fight against the Impercium goes well?"

Geeja crossed her arms. "Actually, it does…at least part of it does. Though, as you have just heard, we are still in the lean 'start-up' mode." Her eyes shot to the recruited co-conspirators. "The team has grown with powerful allies, and there is a plan in place."

Even though a table occupied the center, no one sat. Standing near the exit, Bregent questioned, sounding more snarky than curious. "Really? A band of browbeaten supernatural beings figuring out how to pay to recharge a single spaceship has a plan to take down the Impercium?"

Chin raised, Roace responded. "I have a secret account Djurga doesn't know about. The captain simply hadn't informed me of her need."

Stepping to the center of the vessel, Geeja put her hand on the back of one of the chairs. "Everyone, let us sit and get reacquainted. We will talk strategies and tactics when the time comes." Geeja suppressed a grin, noting that Elegarcia sat close to Roace. *Perhaps their broken trust can be mended.* Once all were at the table, she opened the conversation, hoping to better understand the dynamic between gods during her absence. "How long has it been since you have seen each other?"

Elegarcia glanced up at the much taller Roace, her large eyes appearing softer than Geeja remembered from earlier. "We've connected a few times over the years."

Roace's arm twitched, as if he might put it around his former lover, then stopped himself. "Yes. We've shared a few laughs in our otherwise dreadful existence." He turned to Bregent. "What's it been–fifty years since we've visited?"

Geeja's jaw dropped. "How could either of you let so much time go by?"

Bregent shrugged. "We've been under a form of house arrest. We get one trip a year off our planet to any other holy world, and no more than two of us can be in the same place at the same time."

"What?" Geeja blinked twice. "Why?"

Elegarcia leaned forward, her elbows resting on the table. "It's simple. Djurga doesn't want us to join forces in a plot to overthrow him."

"But, why not just ban you from ever seeing each other?"

Bregent gave a forlorn sigh. "See, Geeja, we're like pets. The emperor wants us docile. So, he gives us just enough privileges to keep us gratefully dependent, but enough limits to fear the risk of breaking them, knowing everything could be taken away…including our life."

Nodding, Roace stated what seemed to be obvious to everyone except Geeja. "If found out, this meeting is enough to get us all executed."

Geeja fell back in her chair. Just when she thought she understood the depth of Djurga's control, she learned of even deeper pits of his evil. She pointed at Elegarcia and Roace. "You two must have used your allotted trips to see each other."

They nodded.

Bregent lowered his eyes. "I've not exactly been the most social lately." He shot a wary glance toward Roace and Elegarcia. "Those two were preoccupied with each other, and to be frank, their relationship seemed toxic. I didn't need any more drama, so we drifted apart."

A heaviness hung over the group until Geeja slammed a fist on the table. "Then it is time to change the rules." She expected resounding agreement, but instead heard only more silence. "Come on. Each of us can shake a city until it crumbles to the ground. We can call down lightning on a sunny day. Together we're surely strong enough to defeat one man. Right?"

Crossing his legs, then leaning back, Bregent questioned. "That depends. Let's hear this grand scheme you're hatching."

Sharing the details carried risk, but she had reached the point that if she wanted them onboard, she had to trust them. *Here goes.* "First, Bregent, I have a question. Do you have the hidden artifact the Ancients told us about?"

"Artifact? What are you talking about?"

Geeja shook her head. "After joining up with Roace and Elegarcia, that is what I thought you would say. Long ago, the Ancients told us of the ability to channel massive power, and we assumed it a device that one of us kept secret."

"Oh yeah. I forgot about that." Bregent shot quick looks to his fellow gods. "I certainly don't have it. Does that end the revolution? Is your plan already doomed?"

Geeja raised her chin defiantly. "Not at all. It is now time to share the details." She gave each a serious stare. "Have you heard about a few young planets exhibiting the first signs of magic?"

Elegarcia piped up. "At my most recent meeting with the governor of my planet, she mentioned something about that in passing. Said it might create some new high-level administrative jobs, and she hoped to get her brother one." She lifted a shoulder. "It didn't seem relevant to me, so I didn't follow up."

Both Roace and Bregent sat with blank stares.

Geeja waited a moment, to make sure they had nothing else to add, then resumed the unveiling of the plan. "Well, turns out there are several of these worlds around the galaxy, and they are attracting Djurga's attention."

Bregent rolled his eyes. "Of course. He's got his hands on every resource, no matter how small, trying to find ways to expand his power."

"You are correct." Geeja smiled. "And we are going to let him do all the work gathering up tiny amounts of magic until he has a significant quantity stored." She gave a bad-girl grin. "Then we are going to steal it."

"Steal it?" Roace's voice raised. "How? More importantly, why?"

The startled response gave her hope. "Do you think a concentrated beam of magic could destroy a Terminus Stake?"

Elegarcia's fingers went to her parted lips.

Roace stared wide-eyed, as if processing what he just heard.

Bregent gasped.

Roace spoke first, his voice soft. "You're serious, aren't you?"

Geeja nodded. "Yes. Very." Her kick-butt grin widened. "We are going to blow that ugly spike on Uwan to smithereens." Her energy surged. "Roace and El signed on, not knowing the details." Her gaze landed on Bregent. "If you want us to free your world too, join the revolution."

Roace's arm now went around Elegarcia as they joined Geeja in staring toward Bregent.

Bregent shook his head. "You're all crazier than a juzine junkie on a three-day bender."

"Really?" Geeja's smile morphed into a sarcastic grin. "Is it crazier than bowing to a power-hungry man for two thousand years?"

"Hey!" Bregent jumped up. "You have no right to criticize us! You don't know what we've been through."

She pressed. "Can you live this way another two thousand years? Four thousand?" She tapped her fingers on the tabletop. "Maybe even six thousand years?"

Bregent breathed loudly through his nose like an angry gulloth, saying nothing.

Roace pulled Elegarcia closer, then speared Bregent with a somber stare. "Geeja might not know what we've lived through, but I do, and I've not handled it well. I drank way too much…and more than once stood on the edge of a cliff, pondering ending my pain." He glanced toward Geeja. "I don't know if her off-the-wall plan will work, but I do know something about myself. I'm at the end of my rope and can't go on living like this."

Bregent's eyes danced between them, jaw firm…then his posture sagged. "You all suck, you know that?" He laughed darkly. "My choice is joining you and perhaps dying, or stay here, and knowing my luck, see you succeed. Then I would kick myself for staying on the sidelines while you three made history."

Bregent jerked his head back, staring at the ceiling. "Grrr." Seconds passed until he lowered his gaze. His expression changed as he now wore a lunatic grin. "What's the old saying about how many fools can dance on the head of a pin?"

Laughing, Geeja supplied the answer. "They say there is always room for one more." She went to him, arms wide, wrapping him in a warm embrace. Kissing his cheek, she made it official. "Welcome to the revolution."

Chapter Thirty-Nine

Zimo traveled an hour south from Odallisdad on the public hyperloop. Smashed between other budget travelers, his mind drifted. *Wonder if I can fly? I mean, I've levitated...well almost. Maybe someday.* When the sweaty man beside him burped without covering his mouth, he changed his timeline. *I'm going to give it a shot today. It would make getting here more pleasant.*

When the doors opened, the mass of Kaliegans squished inside flooded out in a wave of reds and oranges. Once clear of the station, he made his way to the nearby Emperor Djurga Nature Preserve. His skin crawled every time he saw the name of this plot of protected land. *We'll have more places like this one day...maybe.* With his newfound abilities, he daydreamed of a brighter future more often, but doubts were never far away.

Finding his favorite spot atop a cliff and breathing in the scent of torbian bushes in full bloom further improved his mood. Hearing a male quertling bird serenade his intended mate boosted it higher. *Yes, someday everything will be better.* As a cheerful smile crushed his face, Zimo turned his attention toward a spectacular valley filled with old growth trees. He glanced side to side, making sure no one else stood close, then greeted his ever-present friend. **"Hi, Kalli. Ready to warm up before we start new things?"**

"Always!" Most of the time the planet seemed to be in one of two moods: happy, or very happy. ***"What shall we do first?"***

Surveying the panorama below, he located a familiar, wide treetop canopy towering above the others. ***"Can you see our favorite giant plork to my left?"***

"Yes, she's beautiful!"

"Do you think you can give her a shake without disturbing the others around her?" They had been working on refining their coordination, and this test often took a couple of tries to get right. He breathed in, then exhaled, calming himself as he pictured what he wanted to see happen.

In the distance, the single tree shook while none of the others moved a leaf. ***"You did it, Kalli! You did it!"***

She squealed in joy. ***"WE did it, Zimo!"***

An ear-splitting scream from directly below Zimo's high perch broke the moment of happiness. "Help! Please, help!"

Glancing over the edge, he saw a man on a ledge looking even further down the mountain. *What the…*

"She fell! My wife fell!" The man seemed to search for assistance in every direction except up. "Please, anyone!"

Zimo leaped to his feet. "I'll be down as fast as I can!"

Kalli's words came to him on worried tones. ***"Careful, Zimo. These cliffs are dangerous."***

He bounded down a zigzag trail at breakneck speed. ***"We can help. We HAVE to!"*** In under two minutes Zimo stood panting beside a distraught man. "Where is she?"

With a cry in his voice, the husband pointed. "Down there!" His stabbing arm exaggerated the direction. "She's beside that big boulder!"

Peering over this second ledge, Zimo gulped. *"You're right, Kalli, that's a long way."* He swallowed again. *"Straight down."* His mind flooded like two raging rivers coming together. *"We have to do something, but wow, that's a terrifying drop!"* Zimo's face must have shown his fear as met the man's desperate stare. "I'm trying to figure out a way to get her up. Give me a second."

The distraught man grabbed him. "Please! Don't let her die!"

Kalli's voice rose. *"I can feel a heartbeat through the ground. She's alive."*

Taking a closer look, Zimo saw vines clinging to the sheer rock face of this part of the mountain, and a plan formed. *"Kalli, can you twist these plants? If so, together we could wrap them around my hands."*

She sounded nervous. *"I'll try."*

With the distraught husband running his long fingers through his blazing orange hair, Zimo focused on one branch. *"See what you can do."* Relief swept over Zimo as the greenery wiggled. *"You did it. Together, we can save this woman!"*

"Okay?" She didn't sound nearly as confident, and made her point clear. *"But if it's between saving her or protecting you, it's not a decision."*

Placing a hand on the husband, Zimo tried to comfort him. "I've got a plan. I'm going after her."

The man bawled. "Thank you!"

Stepping to the edge, Zimo lowered to his knees, then grabbed a vine. He extended his other hand. Smaller nearby shoots wrapped around it, preventing him from slipping. Throwing good sense to the wind, he went over the edge. *"Here we go, Kalli."*

His heart raced like a boosted skimmer as he locked eyes on a lower vine. Grasping it, other branches secured him in place. Kalli released his top hand from the grip, freeing him to spot the next lower handhold. He completed that move in the same way. *"It's working, Kalli. Thank you."* He sensed the vine tighten just a bit in response.

After several minutes of gulping breaths, Zimo looked down, realizing he had made it only halfway to the bottom. He shared his thought with Kalli. *"This is going to be harder than I thought…and that's just the getting down part."*

After a short break, he called up to the woman's husband. "Get on your PCD and contact the local authorities. I'm definitely going to need some help."

An immediate response bounced back. "I don't have a signal!"

Zimo wiped sweat from his brow. "Then run back to the entrance. There's an office there."

The man stuck his head over the edge. "I'll go as fast as I can."

Mopping the perspiration away again, Zimo reached out to his partner. *"Alright, Kalli. Let's get moving."* He resumed the slow and steady descent with Kalli's help. After more straining, Zimo's feet finally touched solid ground. *"We made it!"*

Freeing himself from the vines, he rushed toward the still woman, immediately checking for a pulse. Feeling a weak thump-thump rhythm, he whooped. "She's still alive!" His voice echoed from the cliff face into dense jungle.

His thoughts spiraled as he mumbled. "She's alive…what now?" He looked up. "Anyone there? Are you back yet?"

This time, a loud roar answered, accompanied by the crack of trees splintering behind him.

A nervous charge shot through Zimo's body as he turned. *"What is THAT?"*

Kalli paused. *"I can't see, except through you, but considering where we are, and the feel of its weight, I think it's a Khi-dot!"*

He shivered as an image of the monstrous, hairy primate flashed in his mind. *"What do we do?"*

Kalli screamed. *"Run!"*

Zimo shot a glance to the unconscious woman. *"We can't leave her here."*

The sound of full-grown trees snapping like twigs moved closer, accompanied by another chill-inducing roar.

Think! He scanned, looking for a cave opening, a hiding place in the woods–wanting to be anywhere but out in the open in front of a hard-charging beast. His heart pounded faster as he froze in place.

The dense foliage in front of him parted like paper curtains. Then an animal easily five times his size, with razor-sharp claws and shaggy brown fur, stepped through. "Raaauugh!"

The soundwave from the giant's call reverberated through Zimo's chest, reminding him of the time he stood an arm's length away from a massive speaker at a Deaf Zomboy concert. He raised a shaking hand. "STOP!" Terrified, he awaited the creature's reaction, watching through squinted eyes.

To Zimo's surprise, it slumped, acting almost docile. The brute's huge brown eyes seemed to look at Zimo expectantly, as if waiting for the next command. *"Kalli, what just happened?"*

The entire forest went quiet, but her words were loud and clear. *"Uh. You think it's because you are the God of Kaliega?"*

Taking a better look at the ape, Zimo now saw it as majestic, not vicious. The implications of this moment made the earlier game of shaking a tree with Kalli, seem trivial. He mumbled. "This is so much more than…" A plan formed from thin air. *"Kalli, can you ask if he, or she, has a name?"*

"What?" She paused. *"I've never done anything like that before. You do it. He listened to you just now."*

"Yes, but I don't know if I will be able to understand his reply."

"You'll never know if you don't try."

"You've got a point." Zimo swallowed hard. *"Hello, big one. What should we call you?"* Staring at the giant, Zimo watched as it aimed its gaze squarely at him.

"I am Yiva, first of my clan." A beat passed. *"Who are you?"*

A giddy smile surface as Zimo released a tense breath. *"I am Zimo…"* His grin widened as his nervousness melted. *"I am Zimo, God of Kaliega."*

"Hmm." The great ape nodded then sat on its haunches, unmoving, as if evaluating what he just heard. *"God of Kaliega, says you? When did this happen?"*

Zimo relaxed, as the anxiety of possibly being slaughtered and eaten, faded. *"It's an amazing thing. I sensed something for months, then a couple of days ago I fully connected with our world. We've been learning to work together, and we wanted someplace private to practice."* He looked toward the wounded woman. *"Discovering her interrupted our training."*

"Hmm." Yiva picked an insect from its hair and ate it. *"And now you can communicate with me."*

Zimo spread his hands. *"Believe me. I'm as surprised as you."* After a few more seconds appraising each other, Zimo's gaze went up to the place from where he had climbed down. *"Say, Yiva, first of your clan. Would you carry me and this injured woman up there?"* He pointed.

Yiva's head turned where Zimo indicated. *"Is this your wish, Zimo, God of Kaliega?"*

He nodded. *"Yes, but only if it does you no harm. Your life is as valuable as ours."*

Big teeth shined in a grin. *"Harm? That would be like play time for me."*

It all seemed unbelievable, but at the same time totally real. Zimo picked up the woman as gently as possible. *"Please, Yiva, take us there."* The supple pads of the great animal's hand amazed Zimo as it scooped both up in one arm, cradling them.

Effortlessly, Yiva climbed, taking a minute to ascend the vine covered cliff that had taken Zimo a half hour to descend. Once at the top, Yiva set them down softly, then stood back.

Zimo checked the injured woman's condition again, finding her heartbeat unchanged, then watched as she moved her head to the side.

She moaned, as if she might awaken at any moment.

He turned toward Yiva. *"Thank you. You aided us in our time of need."*

"Hmm. Things changed today, yes?"

Zimo laughed. *"More than you can imagine."* Shouts came from down the trail, so Zimo bowed. *"I hope to see you again, Yiva, but for now it would be best that you leave. Others do not yet understand this new reality."*

Yiva nodded, then stepped to the side of the cliff. *"You are one with Kaliega."*

Zimo returned the gesture. ***"WE are one with Kaliega."*** With that, Yiva slipped from his view.

A rescue team of three trailed the worried husband. His jaw dropped seeing his wife up here, instead of at the bottom of the forest floor. "Tilana!"

The woman's eyes fluttered as she groaned. "Riicic?"

Two of the rescuers dropped their climbing gear, then rushed to her side as a third stood beside Zimo. Her eyes narrowed as she peered over the edge. "You climbed down there, then back up with her? Without rope?"

"Uh..." *Just tell the truth...well, at least don't lie.* He blurted out the first thing that came to mind. "An adrenaline rush like I've never experienced hit me. Nothing like this has ever happened before."

One of the medics tending to the injured woman called out. "She's pretty banged up, but the initial exam looks good. We've got her in the basket. She's ready for transport."

The woman standing beside Zimo must have been the crew leader, as she called directions. "With this tree cover, there's no way to do an aerial lift, so Lofs, you're at the lead. Kleem take the rear. We'll double time it, and I'll switch out with you two until we reach the medi-craft at the entrance."

As the two carrying Tilana headed out, Riicic shook Zimo's hand vigorously. "Thank you for saving her life."

"I'm glad I could help."

As Riicic raced after his wife's litter, the crew chief cocked her head toward Zimo. "You did a good deed today. Kaliega owes you some kind of reward for protecting one of our own."

Zimo cast a quirky grin. "You have it backwards. I owe this planet more than you can imagine."

Chapter Forty

Roace's offer of a secret stash of funds made Geeja's decision on where to head next much easier. Like a lot of things, they had to explain to her that they didn't have to get actual gold coins from Fontonce, they could simply transfer funds electronically. For what seemed the hundredth time since awakening she rubbed her head, surprised by something amazing to her, but an everyday occurrence for everyone else. "Let me get this straight. A person can send money to someone across the universe? Instantly? Anywhere?" She rolled her eyes, then laughed. "How convenient."

"Oh, Geeja." Roace chuckled as he poured himself a glass of wine. "Like we've been trying to tell you, although terrible things have been done to our worlds, not everything new is bad."

Elegarcia tipped her head. "That's why our people would never want to completely go back to the way things used to be."

Even as she accepted this modern fact of life, it still made Geeja queasy to defy one of her holy vows on a daily, make that hourly basis. Now, they headed back to the small moon orbiting the gas planet to regroup with the others. They needed to get some training on the use of Lighters for Jacastra and the Sworn Warriors. But first came the selection of a recharging location that would be least likely to be noticed by the Impercium.

Talla stood, hands on hips. "There's a tanker station orbiting Tor-Jekta, a barren world in the Fegeesian system. It happens to be at the crossroads of two lonely freighter routes. We'll pay more out there but because it's so remote, there's also less Impercium oversight."

Bregent's voice quivered. "Does that mean it's safe?"

"That means it's safe-*er*." Talla crossed her arms. "You know Djurga's surveillance state. Nowhere is completely out of his grip."

"Yeah." Bregent replied softly. "We all get that."

Before heading back to the cockpit, Talla laid out the plan. "I'll log onto the Impercium network, then activate my merchant's code. It keeps most transactions private. That will allow Roace to transfer funds to my account so I can pay for our recharging. We should be in and out of the place in under an hour."

Geeja raised her hand. "Can you really keep these kinds of transfers hidden?"

Talla arched her eyebrows. "Like I said, nothing in this universe is entirely free of the Impercium's reach. The system aids in trade, so it's about as secure as we have these days." She paused. "If anyone has a better way to get the recharge we need, I'm all ears."

No one else spoke.

"Alright, Roace." Talla's greedy grin edged up. "Let's get you set up to send some of your units to me."

**

Three hours later they arrived at the out-of-the-way oasis of civilization in an empty section of space. Talla made sure everyone settled comfortably, then turned the clear windows opaque. "I need you all to stay inside and quiet, while I go out and mingle with the other captains. It would look suspicious if I didn't."

She got no push back from the usually chatty gods. To the contrary, the risk of this necessary stop became more apparent the closer they got. The small talk and teasing between them gradually decreased, and now each rested silently.

Talla spoke with all the fake confidence she could muster. "Don't worry. Like I said, in and out in an hour, without Djurga being any the wiser."

Lowering the ramp, then closing it behind her, Talla stood tall, strolling deliberately toward the station master cube under the clear glass of the gravity enhanced walkway. The common design placed it at the center so it could service these twenty space piers intersecting in a wheel layout.

Behind a grease-smudged screen, a pale green face with three droopy eyes greeted her. "What's your pleasure today, Captain?"

Unsure of exactly where to aim her stare, Talla settled on meeting the middle eye's lazy gaze. "I need a full crystal recharge in bay eighty-seven."

The attendant turned her attention to a screen, then fingers flew over virtual keys, inputting the order. When finished the tri-eyed humanoid gave payment direction. "Stand in front of the camera for facial ID."

Brushing back her hair, Talla sauntered over, acting as if this were simply another stop on a long cargo run. She kept her smile flat, and face relaxed as the system captured her image. *I hope I look bored…instead of terrified.*

The station master nodded as her three eyes blinked simultaneously. "Your ship will be next in the queue for the Delta crew. You want a paper receipt, or will the one sent to your account be sufficient."

Talla waved off the question. "The digital one is all I need." She looked around. "Speaking of needs, where can a woman pick up some supplies while she waits?"

The thumb on the eight-fingered hand of the attendant jabbed. "Back that way is the Sundry Hub. They've got everything from induction scrubbers to personal care items." She then slid a fob through the slit under the glass. "This will buzz when they've finished topping off your charge." She pointed again, this time toward a drop slot on the side of her enclosed cube. "Toss that back in there before you head out."

Taking her first steps away, Talla spotted the obligatory Impercium representative required to be on every recharging facility, walking straight towards her. *Don't stare!* She kept her eyes locked on the shop. With her heart in her throat, they passed without so much as a glance at each other. *Calm down. He's just a bored security guard...who happens to have a big badge.*

After an hour of shopping the eclectic outpost for supplies for herself and the clandestine gods, Talla again triggered a payment for the goods with the face recognition system on this station. A floating cart trailed her as she exited. Stepping onto the sidewalk the device vibrated, letting her know the *Curious Lady's* crystals were fully charged. She scanned the route ahead for the Impercium watchman, but didn't see him. *Good. He's probably in his office, feet on his desk.*

Dropping off the remote signaler, she took her time making her way back to bay eighty-seven, lazily finishing off the frozen grada berry drink. She burped as she tossed the empty cup in a garbage receptacle. Talla arrived as Delta crew stowed their cables.

Their manager addressed her cordially. "You're all set, Captain. Maybe we'll see you on your way back through."

Talla shrugged, doing her best to maintain the casual air. "Perhaps. It's hard to know where my next job will take me."

After unloading all the supplies, she breathed a sigh of relief, seeing no soldiers or security guards closing in around her ship. Raising the ramp in preparation to leave, she called out to her silent passengers. "Just a normal recharging stop. Nothing out of the ordinary. Looks like we're in the clear."

Geeja spoke for all. "Thank the Holy Twelve!"

**

Emperor Djurga kept his gaze fixed on the massive map in his control room as he heard clomping boots sliding to a stop behind him. "General Scanda. You're moving fast today."

Panting, the general replied with a rising voice. "It's good news, Your Excellency! We have a promising lead!"

Spinning around, Djurga saw a gleefully smiling military man. "Brighten my day. Tell me you have news of the goddess on the run."

Scanda's words rushed. "A ship from Uwan just recharged at a tanker station orbiting Tor-Jekta. Our intelligence team thinks it's connected to her."

Djurga crossed his arms. "A ship from Uwan recharging? That happens every day."

"But." Scanda lifted up on his toes for a moment, his smile broadening. "How many are piloted by a former Sworn Warrior cult member?"

"Hmm. That *is* interesting." He arched his left eyebrow as Scanda fidgeted. "I sense you have more information you're dying to share."

"Yes, Your Excellency." The widening smile now dominated Scanda's face. "And, the captain used funds transferred from another of the twelve gods to pay for the transaction. Surely that can't be a coincidence."

Djurga gave a vindictive grin. "And someone sighted the goddess herself?"

Scanda's posture turned rigid. "Well…no, Your Excellency. Only the captain."

"Grr." Djurga's eyes flared. "You're on thin ice, General."

Scanda licked his lips. "There is more. While the captain waited for her ship to be recharged, she went shopping. The clerk described her purchase as enough to feed a small army." He spread his arms. "If the goddess isn't onboard, then we believe this ship may very well lead us to her."

Djurga's spine stiffened. *This could be the break we need.* "Where are they now?"

Small beads of sweat formed on the general's forehead. "We're tracking the ship and have dispatched a full Star Cruiser battle group to the region with instructions to remain hidden pending your orders."

Letting his underling wait for a few seconds, Djurga smiled. "Finally, you're acting like the commander I need." He nodded. "Now, ready my ship! I'm leading this mission. There will be no more failures. Understood?"

After the faint praise and call to action, Scanda snapped his boot heels. "Yes, Your Excellency! As always, the *Emperor's Will* is

The Goddess Awakens

ready. Please, follow me. You shall witness firsthand the eradication of that goddess." With that he spun and exited quickly.

Djurga wore a determined grin as he boarded his flagship, sensing a turn in the tides. He spoke his mind to no one in particular. "No one has bested me yet, Geeja of Uwan." Spite tinted his words. "You escaped me once. I guarantee you won't again."

Chapter Forty-One

Geeja surveyed the scene as the *Curious Lady* zipped them back to the small moon orbiting the gas planet. A satisfied smile plumped her cheeks. *Three more gods have joined us, and we replenished our supplies. We have done well with our deadline.*

Her gaze drifted toward Roace and Elegarcia, sitting at the small table. Fixed eyes during intense conversation transitioned to easy laughs, then back to serious again. *Seems they are working things out. Good for them.*

Resuming her scan, she caught Bregent's sparkling eyes on her. He wore a relaxed grin. Reflexively, Geeja smiled back as she pushed her hair behind her right ear. Then she scolded herself. *You are not some swooning teen. Still...* She chewed her bottom lip for a few seconds, then stood, covering the short distance to her fellow god and former lover. Hands damp, she took a seat beside him. "Any second thoughts about joining us?"

Bregent chuckled. "Only about a thousand." He shook his head, but kept his calm expression. "I'm not kidding, Geeja. What we're about to do is insane."

Tensing, she reached for his hand. "Do you want out? It is not too late."

His fingers tightened around hers, but only a little. "I want a lot of things, Geeja. I want Djurga dead, and I want those dastardly Terminus Stakes removed from all our planets." His eyes softened as he continued. "I want to restore our worlds to pristine conditions and I want to again join in fellowship with the twelve." Squeezing her hand, his eyes glistened. "And I want to tell you again how much I admire your intelligence, tenacity and love of life. I didn't realize how much I missed you until you showed back up. You're a one in a billion soul. Just being near you, I truly feel alive for the first time in a long time."

Geeja's cheeks warmed. "That is sweet of you to say, Breeg." The heat from his hand coursed through her body, triggering buried emotions. She wanted nothing more than to fall into his arms...but thousands of lifetimes of experience screamed in her head. *Slow down! There is too much at stake to get tangled up in this right now!* Then, her kiss with Raflo from a few nights ago cluttered her thinking even more, freezing her brain. *Do not be even more reckless.*

"Gigi?" Bregent broke her mini trance. "Are you okay?"

Her sharp tone conflicted with her words. "Uh, yeah." She blurted out the first thing that came to mind. "Who could have imagined this is where we ended up?" *Did that even make sense?*

Bregent pulled back, releasing her hand. "So, uhm." He tilted his head and narrowed his gaze. Then a hollow laugh followed. "The answer to your original question is that I do have serious doubts about our chances of success, but the argument you presented is exactly right. What I've been doing is living like an animal in a zoo. It's either continue that way, or do something. With your prodding, I've decided it's time to take a risk, even one with huge odds."

"Thank you for the vote of confidence, Breeg." Her voice quivered. "Since I awoke, it has been like trying to swim in a whirlpool. I know I must fight, but it takes all of my energy simply trying to survive until tomorrow. So, I put my head down, take another breath and another stroke." She shivered. "I think that is all I can handle right now."

Bregent shifted, putting an arm around her shoulders, but not pulling her close. "You're not swimming against the current alone anymore." He pointed to the others onboard. "You've got *friends* who are ready to fight with you."

Tears she didn't realize she held back, spilled. "Thank you, Breeg. I need friends now more than ever." The trickle of salty drops became a torrent as the swirl of emotions she experienced since awakening merged, forming a huge storm cloud that bore down on her. *I am crying like a blubbering idiot…and I do not want to stop.*

He rubbed her shoulder, but said nothing.

A true friend. That is exactly what I need right now. She leaned into his embrace, wanting nothing more in the moment than to know she was not alone.

**

Jacastra guarded her goddess, though it wasn't necessary while they traveled. She stood still observing *four* gods, wanting to blend into the background. *I had everything figured out a week ago…or so I thought.* She smiled as she recalled her rarely changing former routine. *Wake early to attend to the Holy Mother, then a hearty breakfast of desert berry jam and freshly baked bread.*

She noticed her goddess moving toward Bregent as her recall of what life had been like continued. *After a breakfast came training.* Jacastra flexed her bicep, just thinking of how much she enjoyed the physical parts of being a Sworn Warrior.

Though she relished perfecting her fighting skills, she liked other portions of her routine more. After a light lunch the women turned to studying the holy scriptures of their goddess and the other eleven, then spent time in prayer and contemplation. This period of private study and devotion nourished her soul like the bread given by the older sisters to the street urchin she had once been. *A week ago, I thought myself an expert on all things Geeja. I believed I KNEW her. She represented the embodiment of perfection. I KNEW she would return one day. I KNEW she would rid Uwan of that evil Terminus Stake.*

She watched as Geeja reached for Bregent's hand, which followed seeing her kiss Raflo just a day or so earlier. *How long ago was that?* Keeping track of time proved hard as they jumped from one planet to the next so quickly. *I mean, I understood Geeja was born a normal woman, but I always imagined her as different. More spiritual.*

Glancing up, Jacastra caught a glimpse through a window as they zipped past a red star. She took in a shallow breath. *I only knew a kernel of truth, oblivious to a more complex picture.*

Soft moaning interrupted her thinking. Looking toward Geeja, Jacastra saw her goddess weeping. She nodded in silence. *Only now do I see her as she is, not what I imagined. I've watched as she sent flames to eliminate the emperor's troops. I've witnessed her work with Bregent to heal a man whose heart stopped. I've stood guard as she flirted with two different men. I've seen her rally a team to fight against Djurga.* Jacastra nodded. *I've even heard her second guess herself.*

She stood a bit taller, understanding the truth. *I know that Geeja, Goddess of Uwan is a powerful being. A wise being. A caring being...who also happens to be a normal woman with normal emotions...carrying the weight of the universe on her shoulders.*

She took in a confirming breath. *And, because she's ALL those things I'll lay down my life to protect her.*

Chapter Forty-Two

Geeja pulled herself together by the time the *Curious Lady* returned to the moon where the others of their small band trained. Talla had purchased a little makeup at the recharging station and Geeja looked into a mirror, assessing her efforts. *There is still puffiness under my eyes, but I am presentable.* Once again, her gaze broke, catching the bright coloration of her modern outfit. She graced a snarky grin. *Presentable in this age, anyway.*

The emotional release had been cathartic, and a genuine smile reflected. *The odds of our success are long, but I am not alone. I have friends to share the load.* Puckering, she applied subtle pink lipstick as the spacecraft settled. *This will have to do.*

Geeja spoke loudly as fresh air rushed up the ramp, filling the ship with the verdant smell of the native vegetation. "We fight to restore our worlds, and we will not stop until we do!" It boosted her mood to hear fellow gods concur with affirming shouts.

Stepping onto terra firma, Geeja inhaled deeply. "By the Holy Twelve, I swear I will never take clean air for granted again."

Joining the huddled group that formed, she introduced Roace, Elegarcia and Bregent to Raflo, Shuggilar, and Chella, as well as the other Sworn Warriors they hadn't yet met. With handshakes complete, she spoke brightly. "This is the team that is going to change the universe!" A cheer went up, further galvanizing Geeja.

Huanoc spoke in a booming voice. "Time for afternoon Lighter training for all Sworn Warriors."

As the women fell in behind the big Nafportonian, Geeja sensed a presence slide beside her. She turned, not surprised to see Raflo and his glistening brown eyes.

The smuggler wore an eager grin. "It's sure been borin' around here while you've been gone."

"It is good to see you, too, Raflo." She kept her voice even, then focused on the mission. "How has the training with the Sworn Warriors gone?"

"Uh, great. They're fast learners." He tilted his head. "You okay?"

"Yes, of course." She returned a less-than-confident smile. "It is simply the stress of everything that has happened since I awoke, and we have not even started the hard part yet."

Raflo put a hand to her shoulder, speaking softly. "We've got a great team. You're not in this alone."

As with Bregent a few hours ago, Raflo's touch warmed her, and he sounded so sincere. She longed for a reassuring hug, but her inner voice stood firm. *No! Focus on the mission!* Her words were truthful, but carried no hint of emotion. "I appreciate everyone's help. It would be impossible to do this on my own."

Raflo raised his chin as he removed his hand, then pulled back. "Okay…"

Bregent strolled up beside Geeja, then locked eyes with the other man. He spoke flatly. "Hello Raflo. Looks like you've recovered nicely."

Geeja watched as both men stood taller.

Rubbing the side where he had been shot, Raflo responded coolly. "Yes. Thanks to you and Politar I'm better than ever."

Hearing whoops from the training area, Geeja extricated herself from the testosterone filled air. "I am going to check on my soldier's progress." She glanced at each while keeping her face neutral. "I will see you both later."

As she walked, Geeja pushed thoughts about the men to the back of her mind. *I will figure out my feelings later…if we survive.*

Arriving, she stepped up beside Shuggilar, who watched as Huanoc put the warriors through a series of exercises. "Give it to me straight. How do they look?"

"Geeja! So glad you're back." He glanced over his shoulder at the newcomers. "Especially since you brought reinforcements."

She nodded. "Having more magic on our side can only help the cause." Her eyes turned back to the women who were practicing shooting while on the run. "So?"

Shuggilar winked playfully. "If they ever get tired of protecting you, I'll hire the entire crew."

"Seriously?"

His eyebrows perked. "They're in terrific shape, already trained to fight, and highly motivated. Huanoc and I only needed to teach them a single weapon. I would put them up against my top crews."

"It is no surprise to me that they have exceeded everyone's expectations." With that bit of good news, she broadened the discussion. "As you have surely heard, I did not find the relic. Where does that leave our plan?"

Shuggilar's good vibe dropped a few notches. "There's no question I would be more confident if you had found it."

"But?"

He rubbed the back of his neck. "It doesn't change our plan to steal the magic battery. We just won't be sure we have enough to destroy a Terminus Stake until we give it a try. I'm positive we'll severely damage it, I'm just not certain we can obliterate it."

"And if we cannot, it makes it easier for Djurga to repair? Correct?"

"That's my thinking." Shuggilar turned toward her. "Though, either way, it would be a blow to the Impercium. I simply want the biggest bang possible."

Talla came running. "We've got trouble!"

The shrill tone of the pilot's voice popped Geeja's momentarily happy bubble. She growled. "Why am I not surprised?"

After an all-out run, the captain of the *Curious Lady* reached them. She sucked in air, then managed two words that totally crushed the good mood of moments ago. "It's Djurga."

"Ahh!" Geeja spat angry words. "What has he done now?"

Between gasps, Talla shared news. "There's been chatter on the merchant's channel of an entire Star Cruiser battle group closing in on our location. That can't be a coincidence."

Geeja ran a hand through her blonde hair. "Think it is because of the recharge?"

Talla's unblinking eyes widened. "Probably. But does it matter? However they found out, they're on the way!"

Shuggilar's voice rose. "Huanoc! We've got trouble!"

The big man whistled toward his trainees. "Lesson over. Deploy around our perimeter. This may not be a drill!"

With weapons in hand, the women formed a defensive circle.

Huanoc called out to everyone else. "To our ships!"

The dark energy of desperation spread through Geeja's body like an infection as she raced with them toward the two vessels. One unwanted thought repeated with each bounding step. *We are not ready!*

Approaching the temporary base, Geeja saw Roace, Bregent and Elegarcia waiting, with not a smile in sight. Breathing hard from the sprint, she pulled up beside them. "You have heard? Djurga is on his way!"

Bregent spoke first. "Yes. Talla shouted the news as she ran to tell you." His fingers were curled in fists beside his legs, saying what all of them surely believed. "This is bad. Really bad."

Raflo rushed down the ramp of the *Phantom Star*, his cheeks flushed. "I checked some dark sites that monitor Impercium ships. Looks like that battle group will be here in less than two hours." He repeated his oft mentioned fear. "Whatever we decide, just know that there's no way I'm goin' back to prison." He held out a hand, wagging his index finger. "No how, no way."

Geeja's eyes darted between Shuggilar and Huanoc as she spoke firmly. "You two. What is the status of our plan? Is it ready enough to go, or is running for our lives the only option?"

Shuggilar let out a single bark of laughter. "Ha! You assume *either* of those options hold much of a chance."

Geeja's eyebrows shot up. "What do you mean?"

Huanoc crossed his large arms. "He's saying that our plan is not finely-tuned." He looked skyward. "Djurga's ships are bearing down. He would find us, wherever we hide."

Emotion choked Raflo's voice as he again stated his position. "I don't care what we do, I'm just tellin' you, I'm not goin' back to prison."

Bregent shook his head. "I knew this was a mistake. This whole..." He paused, seeming to search for the right words as he surveyed the assembled group. "This whole misguided, ill-conceived, boneheaded adventure has been doomed from the start." He sighed. "I should have listened to my gut."

Geeja winced at her friend's stinging words, then recovered, responding firmly. "You are wrong, Breeg, and deep down you know it. What you have been doing is existing, not living." Her eyes darted to her fellow gods. "You all know it."

Bregent tried to interrupt. "But—"

Geeja cut him off. "It is too late for *buts,* Bregent." A cold stare down lasted several seconds, then Bregent looked away. She glared at them as a ferocity built inside her, daring anyone to break the expanding silence engulfing them all. Dialing back the fierceness, her words were still spiked as she articulated her second point. "It is true that I pitched the idea of taking down Djurga with an optimistic spin, but every one of you, god or otherwise, joined this crusade for your own reasons. Some had noble motives, while others simply had no better option. Regardless, all joined voluntarily."

Simply talking about the rightness of their cause energized her, turning her speech from intense back toward hopeful, or at least not hopeless. "We planned to take the fight to Djurga, knowing in our core that it was the correct thing to do, even if the odds were long. Now, while the odds might have gotten even longer, the righteousness of our mission has not changed."

She turned toward the *Curious Lady* and the *Phantom Star,* pointing. "We have two ships at our disposal, ready to take us to Torgose." Her gaze went out farther. "We have a trained assault team that Shuggilar thinks is better than any he's ever seen." Now her eyes returned to those closest. "And we have four of the original twelve gods, two entrepreneurs who have escaped an

Impercium prison, a nurse who has already helped save one of us. Lastly, we have a mastermind leading our heist."

Having made her case, Geeja saw arms that had been crossed now hanging by sides. "We all know we have gone too far to back out now. Djurga wants us all dead, and would not allow a surrender, even if we wanted, which we do not." She breathed deeply. "It is time to do what we planned. Take the fight to him!"

A few smiles now dotted the small audience, bolstering her. "Let us load up these ships and do what we intended. We either take down the bully, or at least give him a bloody nose." She raised a defiant fist in the air. "Who will join me?"

Raflo stepped beside her, hoisting a closed hand as well. "I'm in! I'll fight to the death before I go back to prison!"

Huanoc joined his partner, lifting his arm high. "What he said."

Jacastra stood beside Geeja, her voice soaring. "The Sworn Warriors fight!"

Shrugging, Talla joined the expanding group. "Somebody has to fly this ship."

Roace and Elegarcia came forward hand in hand. His eyes glistened as he addressed Geeja. "Until you came back into my life, I lived like a walking dead man." He glanced down at Elegarcia. "No matter how narrow, this path is the only one that gives us a chance of life together."

After nodding toward Huanoc, Elegarcia pointed toward Roace. "What he said."

The big man roared in laughter as she parroted his earlier remarks.

That left only Bregent. "Just a few hours ago I cheered up Geeja, assuring her that we were with her, that she didn't fight alone."

His lips tightened to a straight line. "But hearing that a Star Cruiser battle group is bearing down on us rattled my confidence."

No one spoke when Bregent paused.

His tight face transitioned to pain-filled grin. "The truth is, I think we're all screwed, but deep down I've known that for a very long time." He locked eyes with Geeja. "I'm tired. Tired of living under Djurga's rule. Tired of seeing our worlds degraded and tired of dealing with my own brand of depression."

A small stream of tears rolled down both cheeks. "Geeja, thank you for reminding me that nothing is going to change unless I do something…even if doing something gets me killed."

There were silent nods from everyone.

Bregent finally offered a true smile. "Live or die, we do it together." He raised his fist, sounding sure of his conviction. "To the resistance!"

Chapter Forty-Three

Wasting no time, Geeja, and everyone except Raflo and Huanoc, crowded aboard the *Curious Lady*. Those two headed out on the *Phantom Star* while Geeja huddled with Shuggilar, Bregent, Jacastra and her fellow gods, leaving Talla to pilot them at quantum speed. "We have three hours to finalize our plan before we reach Torgose."

Shuggilar lit a hologram map of the area surrounding the base station that both protected and pumped magic up to the collecting station. "Originally, we planned to land a half-day's walk away, allowing us to approach with less chance of being detected." He pointed much closer to the facility. "Since we're only a couple of hours ahead of a fleet, we'll have to speed things up, landing here."

Bregent let out a low whistle. "So much for stealth."

The mastermind bobbed his head. "You're right about that, but we still have the element of surprise." His eyes darted between the gods. "Especially with you four in the fight."

"Lay it out for us, Shugg." Roace leaned over the glowing representation of the battlefield. "Where do you want us, and what do you want us to do?"

"In short, create havoc." He motioned to four equidistant points around the facility. "I saw Geeja send liquid fire from her fingers, incinerating a troop of Impercium soldiers back on Kaliega. If you can do something like that on Torgose, we would be in great shape for part two."

The three gods stared intently at Geeja. She raised her chin, meeting their gaze. "Did I mention that there is a new magical planet, and that I crowned a god a few days ago?"

"What?" Elegarcia's already bulging eyes appeared to almost pop from their sockets. "How? And when did you plan to tell us about this?"

A warm blush flooded Geeja's cheeks. "It is not like I have tried to keep it a secret. If you have not noticed, we have been busy."

"And?" Roace pressed.

"And?" Geeja drew a quick breath. "It happened just days after I awoke. I had not even revealed my true identity to Raflo and Huanoc. When they went to meet Shugg, I slipped off the ship and discovered a sentient planet, alive with magic."

"And." Bregent pressed this time.

"It all happened fast. The planet had already identified a contact, so I connected them." She pointed to Shuggilar. "Then they all came running with Impercium troopers in hot pursuit. I tried to stun them, but being unfamiliar with that planet's magic, I ended up burning them all to a crisp."

The three other gods' jaws dropped. Bregent spoke, sounding upbeat. "There really are big changes going on in the universe. Maybe that's a sign we're not doomed."

Geeja laughed. "I will take every positive omen we can get." A quizzical smile slid onto her face. "But that incident brings up our biggest unknown when we land. What kind, and how much magic will Torgose manifest? What will we be able to bring to the fight?"

After a brief silence, Shuggilar stepped in. "That's why we also have conventional troops and weapons. Regardless of how things play out with you four, those Sworn Warriors are a force to be reckoned with."

Until this point, Jacastra had been quiet. "We'll be outnumbered, correct?"

"That's right, significantly outnumbered. But this is a small outpost on a sleepy planet. Security tends to be lax, and these won't be elite troopers." Shuggilar again pointed to the hologram. "If you can neutralize those outside quickly, there are only two doors through which troops inside can exit. There will be a bottleneck."

Jacastra nodded, then pointed toward spots on the glowing map. "If we get two warriors each here, and here, we can mow them down before they join the battle."

Shuggilar smiled. "Exactly. You women know how to fight."

Now, Jacastra blushed. "We haven't done anything yet. Let's save the praise for the victory party."

A proud grin graced Geeja's face. "Of all the elements of this plan, I am most confident of how the Sworn Warriors will perform."

Nodding, Shuggilar continued the rundown. "Assuming our combined forces overwhelm the Impercium defenses, all we need to do is enter and shut down both the protection field and magic transfer to the orbiting station. Then it's up to Raf and Huanoc."

At the mention of the men's names, Geeja's brows bounced. "Their part has not really changed, correct?"

"Right." Shuggilar tapped the holographic image and a miniature replica of the floating station and the *Phantom Star* appeared. "They've got to coerce the crew into allowing them in, then spacewalk the magic battery to their ship."

Geeja crossed her arms. "That sounds simple, but I know it is not. It is complicated and dangerous." Her eyes studied both the planetary and space representations of the plan. "So many variables…" She left unsaid what all surely understood. *So many ways for this to go wrong.*

For a few seconds, the only sounds Geeja heard were the ship's ever-present background hum as they hurtled through space at quantum speed. She turned her attention from the holographic map to the ragtag team. With shoulders square and chin held high, she spoke low and steady. "I will not spread dranzel cake icing on what we are about to do. There is no guarantee of success, and it is almost certain that some of us will not make it out alive."

Geeja paused, her gaze meeting each person's eyes. Then her voice rose. "But with determination and a little luck of the Holy Twelve, we can take that battery to Uwan and destroy that hideous Terminus Stake." The veins on her neck bulged as she notched louder. "In doing so we will be shoving it down Djurga's throat!" She took in a great breath, then raised a fist. "To the resistance!"

A deafening reply echoed in the contained space. "To the resistance!"

Chapter Forty-Four

Emperor Djurga shoved open the lid to his portable rejuvenation station as soon as the treatment finished. With the apparatus' life extending ability being so important the daily ritual rarely frustrated him. This day stood as anything but usual. He shoved aside an attendant as he rushed to the bridge of the *Emperor's Will*, the flagship of his empire. When he arrived, he snapped a command. "Update, General Scanda."

"Your Excellency." The general saluted smartly. "The riffraff left the moon orbiting the gas planet, Vaesona. We're tracking them. We're closing the gap."

Djurga's eyes locked on the screen plotting their course. "Where are they headed and how long before we overtake them?"

A green dot appeared on the translucent map. "The only inhabited world along their charted course is Torgose, where you are conducting experiments."

"Torgose?" Djurga's brows scrunched. "Why would they be going to our micro-magic test site?"

With eyes still on the projected path of their prey, Scanda answered. "We don't know their objective, but we calculate that we will arrive there ninety minutes after they do. Whatever they're up to, they won't stand a chance."

"Ninety minutes!" Djurga recalled how quickly Geeja and the other gods had dismissed his ideas two thousand years ago. "The course of an entire universe can change in ninety minutes! Get us there sooner, and I want schematics of the operations of our facility there immediately!"

"Yes, Your Excellency! We'll be running the engines hot, but your will be done!" Turning, Scanda gave orders to his second in command, Lieutenant Arthold. "You heard the emperor. Increase power to quantum nine. Now!"

The lieutenant replied crisply. "Yes sir!"

The star cruiser shuddered as Emperor Djurga spun on his heel, barking at the general. "Scanda, join me in my ready room."

Djurga paced as he waited for Scanda to begin his briefing. *What are those puny gods up to?* His mind raced. *Of course I'll kill the Goddess of Uwan, that's a given.* His lips tightened as he turned back toward the direction from which he came. *But the other three? They've bent the knee to me for all these years. I enjoy their submissiveness. They know I'll catch them and kill them all. Just like I killed Cleaudra, on Nafporton.* He sighed. *That cursed Geeja has filled their heads with delusions, and now they'll die...after centuries of life. Oh well, their replacements will live in rightful fear.*

The realization that immortal beings could die triggered another, dire thought. *If Ambassador Ka finds out about my experiment on Torgose, what will he do? Would he consider my attempts at harvesting magic a breach of our agreement? After all, it is a gray area.* Heading back toward the bulkhead, he stared out the port window into space. *Would he cut off the supply of gasses that fuel my rejuvenation chamber? Would he end MY life?*

Scanda cleared his throat as he stood at the door. "Emperor, the schematics are ready for your review."

Still lost in his previous dark thoughts, he mumbled as he continued gazing into the emptiness. "Put them up."

Doing as instructed, Scanda stood silently.

At least a full minute passed before Djurga tore his thoughts away from the possibility that his continued life rested on the success of this mission. It was imperative he thwart whatever those gods planned…and keep it quiet. Facing the display, his jaw set as he spoke, as much to himself as to Scanda. "Goddess of Uwan, what in the name of the *Unholy* Twelve are you up to?"

Scanda kept his lips sealed. Years of service ingrained the habit of not interrupting the great man's thoughts, unless asked for an opinion.

Stepping closer, Djurga tapped his chin. "Why would they destroy a barely operational beta site in the middle of nowhere? It wouldn't do anything to lessen my grip on their so-called special planets."

The general locked his hands behind his back, but kept his mouth shut.

Djurga's eyes narrowed as he stared at each component of the base, still searching for a motive. "Because of the location, there is no practical value in blowing it up as a political statement. No one would even see it." Minutes ticked by in silence until Djurga addressed his underling. "Two battalions guard the station, correct?"

"Yes sir!"

"And they have been alerted that trouble is on the way?"

"Yes sir. They are deploying in defensive positions as we speak."

"Good." Silence returned to the room until Djurga paced again, mumbling. "What could they want if not to destroy it?" More pacing didn't reveal an answer, so he again stared into space. Finally, he asked himself a different question. *Why would magical gods want to destroy magic?*

His eyes sprang wide, and anger edged into his voice as he shared his epiphany with Scanda. "They would never destroy magic. They consider it sacred. It can only be used in prescribed ways, based on their silly vows. No, they would never annihilate it, but they would steal it! Get us there sooner!"

Scanda blinked rapidly as he responded in a low, shaky voice. "Yes sir." He turned and sprinted out of the room.

Alone, Djurga chuckled vindictively. "I'll kill the four of you, as I should have done in the beginning."

Chapter Forty-Five

Geeja heard a shout from the cockpit as the Curious Lady came out of quantum speed. The hairs on her arms stood as she raced to the front of the craft. "What is wrong?"

The color in Talla's face drained away. "My initial scan of our landing site shows it's crawling with troopers."

Processing the captain's words, Geeja's heart sank. "What! No!"

Turning, Talla blurted out what seemed indisputable. "They knew we were coming!"

For a moment, Geeja's mouth hung open as her mind spun. After a few disoriented seconds, she snapped. "Options! Give me options."

Talla's eyes danced between scans and her control. "I need to check in with the *Phantom Star*. We'll see what the boys think."

Geeja's stomach dropped as she visualized their plan falling apart.

Bregent's voice rose above the others in the hold. "What's going on up there?"

Walking from the cockpit toward the team, Geeja held on to whatever she could grab to keep from stumbling. Not from an unsteady ride, but from the smash of awful news. She forced out a response, trying to wring fear from her voice. "There are troopers on the ground, waiting for us." Irritation swathed her words. "How did we not plan on that possibility? With a fleet on our heels, they would divine our destination. Of course those on the ground would be informed we were coming."

Shuggilar's voice rose. "We were rushed. Mistakes happen. May Djurga's soul burn on an altar of eternal flame."

Others sat with downcast eyes as Bregent spoke in dejected tones. "Do we have a plan, or is this fool's race over before it starts?"

Geeja's arms fell to her sides. "Talla is conferring with Huanoc and Raflo." Her words sounded thick, as if sapped of all vitality. "I will be back as soon as I know more."

Returning to the cockpit she met Talla's pained stare. "The boys have news that Djurga has pushed his fleet. He'll be here in under an hour."

Crushed expectations weighed on Geeja. "Where does that leave us?"

With eyes moist and voice full of desperation, Talla laid out the options. "Either we stand and fight here, knowing full well our casualties will be high, and chances of success slim…"

"Or?"

The former Sworn Warrior could barely force out her reply. "Or…we try to outrun a faster opponent who outguns us by a thousand to one. We would die a quick and painless death in space."

Geeja gasped as the gravity of the situation slammed her entire being. She managed a whisper. "What do the boys want to do?"

Talla rested her arms on the padded sides of the captain's chair. "They figure we're all dead anyway, so they want to fight, maybe take out a few of Djurga's goons on our way out."

Nodding, Geeja questioned. "And you? What is your vote?"

Tears rolled down the tough woman's face. "My vote is to see my baby again." She wiped away moisture on her cheeks as her answer firmed. "The only chance I have to do that is if we fight."

"Yes…It is not a good option, but I agree with your conclusion." Geeja gritted her teeth and spoke low. "I will see what the others say."

In a few steps Geeja stood before the rest of the team again. She pulled in a big breath, trying to buck up her own sagging emotions. *There is still hope.* Entering the crowded space, she saw despondent faces staring back. She wished she could delay sharing the difficult news, but knew she couldn't. "Our situation is even worse than we thought. Not only are those Impercium troopers on the ground waiting for us, Djurga's fleet has closed the gap. He will be here sooner than we expected."

Roace reached for Elegarcia's hand. "Is there any good news, or are we doomed?"

Hearing a sound, Geeja glanced over her shoulder, seeing Talla. "Both captains agree we have two options. We run the plan, knowing full well our previous slim chances are even slimmer, or we try to outrun a faster fleet that outguns us."

Shuggilar laid bare the choice. "Fight against all odds or be blown to bits in space."

"Yes." Geeja bobbed her head. "None of us wanted this, but it is where we are, and we need to decide between two difficult options. What say you?"

Jacastra jumped to her feet. "We will fight to our last breath to save the Goddess of Uwan."

Geeja's cheeks warmed, grateful for the millennia long loyalty of the Sworn Warriors. "Thank you." She looked to the others, waiting on their judgment.

Roace spoke next. "I've stood near death for a while." He glanced at Elegarcia. "I finally have something worth fighting for. Count me in."

Elegarcia stared at Roace with those big eyes. "Count *us* in."

Shuggilar held Chella's hand. "This really isn't a choice, is it? We fight or surrender, and I'll never surrender."

Chella nodded. "Shugg's right."

That left Bregent, who had been the most hesitant to join the team in the first place. He wiped his mouth. "This rots." He glanced around the motley crew. "Yet, being around people like all of you, who are willing to fight and die for freedom has made me see the truth. While I don't want to die, that's exactly what I've been doing, one day at a time under Djurga's thumb." He stood. "It's time to do what I should have done years ago–fight for my world's freedom. Or die trying." He raised a fist. "To the resistance!"

Once again, the response rang loud. "To the resistance!"

Chapter Forty-Six

Geeja braced for a hard landing on Torgose. The hastily revised plan now called for the Sworn Warriors to establish a tight perimeter around the ship. That would give the gods the opportunity to test the quality and quantity of magic they could pull from the planet. If either proved insufficient, then everyone would load back into the *Curious Lady,* joining Raflo and Huanoc in an action with even longer odds. They would attempt to steal the magic battery without lowering the protective force field.

The rough touch-down jarred Geeja more than she expected. She glanced around the cramped cabin as the ramp descended. Fresh air rushed in as she called out. "Everyone well?" Replies in the affirmative piled on top of one another as safety harnesses unlatched.

Jacastra barked orders to her team as the first sounds of enemy Lighter fire filtered toward the ship. "Let's show these bastards who they're dealing with." She charged down to the planet's surface with the others tight on her heels.

The sound of the women's return fire reassured Geeja, but also cranked up the tension. She gave them a few seconds, then shouted a determined call over the din of war to her fellow gods. "There better be enough magic, or this will be a very short visit!"

Leading the way, Geeja moved down the ramp, but not at the same speed as the fighters who went before her. Reaching the ground, she saw that the tough women held their adversaries at bay, giving them all a chance. Warriors lay prone, firing rounds of light beams as fast as they could pull their triggers. Impercium soldiers clad in flexible body armor advanced in a parallel line, with most shots against them bouncing off harmlessly.

Jacastra whooped as one of the enemies fell. "Aim for the seams!"

Geeja sucked in an anxious breath as the battle raged less than a spike ball field away. She and the other three knelt in a bid to connect with the planet, as well as to make themselves smaller targets. They placed hands directly onto the soil. With the cacophony of battle all around, Geeja chose the direct approach to introducing herself to this world. She chanted along with her thoughts for the benefit of the others. *"We come to you in peace, asking your help in the fight to save us all. We come to you in peace, asking your help in the fight to save us all. We come to you in peace, asking your help in the fight to save us all."*

The ground trembled. *"What? Who? How?"*

The planet sounded as Geeja expected: confused and weakened. Her eyes cut to the other three and they nodded, signaling they too could hear this initial conversation. She continued. *"I am Geeja. I come from another world, an older world with which I communicate, just as I am doing with you."*

The bass sounding world expressed caution. *"I knew there were others when hurtful things were done to me. Is it you that does this?"*

Trying to stay calm in this delicate moment, anger leached into Geeja's response. *"Those who injure you also hurt my world, and the planets of the three others who join me here. We fight against those who damage worlds like you. Would you like to meet those who are joined with me in this fight?"*

Torgose answered tentatively. *"Yes...hello."*

Even with Lighter fire zipping just above their heads, Bregent wore a childlike grin as he spoke. **"Hello, I'm called Bregent and I am very pleased to meet you, Torgose."**

"Torgose? Is that me?"

"Yes. That is what you are called." Bregent turned his head, beaming, still looking excited to be one of the first to communicate with a newly sentient world.

Elegarcia went next. **"Torgose, my name is Elegarcia, and I am so happy to be here today."** Her big eyes glistened in this seminal moment.

Wasting no time as a hot battle raged around them, Roace wrapped up the introductions. **"And I am Roace. Torgose, you are not alone."**

A scream came from one of the Sworn Warriors. "Help!"

Shuggilar charged down the ramp and scooped up the injured fighter. "I'll get you to Chella." The tenseness ramped in urgency as a second line of Impercium moved behind the first, doubling the shots fired against the Sworn Warriors.

Geeja's lips tightened. **"Torgose, as I said, we are fighting those who now harm you, and we need your help."**

"Yes! It feels as if they are draining my life spirit. I'll help in any way I can."

Geeja nodded, then saw the gesture returned from the others. **"Thank you, Torgose."** As the noise level of the battle surrounding them rose, her lips pursed. **"We will never do what the invaders have done. They steal your power, which is awful.**

We will need some of your energy to defeat them, but instead of stealing it, we ask your permission. May we tap into your magic?"

"Anything to stop this pain!"

"Thank you, Torgose. We fight for you, and our worlds as well." All four stood as Geeja called out. "You three attempt to pull magic, while I try something different."

Before they could even start, another wail came from the Sworn Warrior ranks. "It burns!" Shuggilar made another run for a fallen soldier as the other women closed ranks.

While Geeja stretched her connection, searching for other life on this alien world, she caught the others from the corner of her eye. Bregent glowed in an orange tinted hue. *Good. There is power to be shared.*

The discharge from his fingers wasn't fire or lightning, but more like a visible expanding bubble of energy with an orange edge. As the magic raced across the battlefield it knocked down ten or so Impercium soldiers before dissipating. All of those affected scrambled back to their feet, but seemed disoriented, before falling down again. *Not fatal, but definitely disruptive.*

Another scream from a newly injured woman pierced Geeja's soul. *I must hurry.*

Roace and Elegarcia joined in the battle, with all three of those gods stepping forward to blast magic. Being in front put the gods more at risk, but spared any potential harm to the Sworn Warriors who now fired from the kneeling position.

Refocusing, Geeja concentrated, seeking to contact any animals who might be persuaded to join the battle. She hoped there might be a large herd of beasts that could charge through the lines of Djurga's troopers, but sensed none. She sighed. *I hoped...*

A fourth Sworn Warrior fell and her wail filled the air as the three other gods temporarily knocked Impercium forces back. Shuggilar breathed hard as he rushed the latest injured soldier inside the *Curious Lady*.

Their losses mounted. *Either I need to connect with something now, or join the others.*

Reaching out again, Geeja sensed something odd, like nothing she had ever encountered. It seemed both massive and diffused. Opening her eyes, she looked in the direction of the presumed living being, and saw nothing towering above the scrub plants on this plain. *How can that be?*

Geeja asked for help. *"Torgose, can you help me connect with the creatures that call this world home? Those very near here?"*

The planet responded anxiously. *"I'll try, but I've never before done ANY of the things you are asking."*

Bregent's voice strained as a third line of Impercium soldiers rushed in from the left. The level of Lighter fire reached new heights. "Geeja! A little help?"

"I am working on it! Give me a minute." Geeja heard the desperation in her own words.

A reply from Torgose. *"They responded. You can speak with them now."*

Geeja questioned. *"They? Who are…they?"*

"I…they…this is all so new! They…"

Sensing the planet's frustration, Geeja stepped in. *"Thank you, Torgose. I will take it from here."* She channeled thoughts toward the short trees. *"Beings of Torgose. I am Geeja, and I fight against evil to save your world."* For a moment no response returned, so she sent another telepathic message. *"We have come to your aid, but need your assistance. Please help us help you!"*

Thousands of tiny voices answered in unison. *"Can you stop the noise? It's driving us deaf."*

Bregent's tone bordered on desperation. "I'm not jokin' around, Geeja. We need you!"

Deaf? Geeja had no idea what that meant, or with whom she communicated. Out of options, but refusing to break her vows, she told the truth, not promising something she couldn't guarantee. *"I THINK so. I believe the machines of our common enemy hurt everyone. Help us fight them!"*

A collective hum seemed to stretch from one end of the horizon to the other. After a prolonged few seconds, an answer emerged. *"Show us the enemy."*

Hurrying, she turned toward Djurga's troops. *"Those are the ones we fight."*

From the corner of her eye, Geeja saw a dark fluttering cloud emerge from the tree line. She kept her eyes on the Impercium soldiers as a mass of beating wings came into full view. A mischievous smile spread across her face. "You are a hive! A hive of gargantuan Torgosian bats!"

Her thoughts went to her fellow gods and human fighters. *"Help has arrived! Do no harm to our new allies."*

A loud scream pierced Geeja's waking mind and by the timbre, she knew its source. "Bregent!" She scanned until seeing her friend on his knees, one hand covering a Lighter wound. Her shriek rose above all other noise. "No!"

Djurga's troops caught sight of the advancing wave, turning their Lighters toward the flying creatures rushing toward them. A barrage of fire went up, hitting several of the lead beasts.

Screeches filled the air, as many careened toward the surface, but the unrelenting tide of flying anger rolled across the plain.

As she raced to her fellow god, swooping mammals with twenty-foot wingspans moved in coordination. Each animal worked as a part of the whole. One by one, Impercium trooper's heads were wrapped by the leathery wings of powerful Torgosian bats, blinding them. Geeja looked across the battlefield as she covered the distance to Bregent, and as far as she could tell, the soldiers weren't being harmed. Still, panic among the troops spread like spilled calefine on a granite table as their eyes were covered in the tight grasp of the flying animals. High pitch squeaking from the bats added an auditory aspect to the scene that amplified the bedlam. Although she had a massive new worry, Geeja reached out to her new friends. ***"You are magnificent! You are ALL magnificent!"***

What had been a losing defensive struggle quickly turned into a rout of Djurga's army. They dropped their Lighters, freeing their hands to attempt to pry the tough animals from their heads.

On his knees, Bregent moaned as poison entered his bloodstream. "Don't worry about me. Help them!"

Glancing at her fighters, her heart split. "But you are hurt!"

He barked a truth that stopped her in her tracks. "If they don't succeed, we're all dead!"

Jacastra called to the remaining Sworn Warriors. "Follow me!" They rose from their knees, running past terrified troopers that moments ago wounded four of her fighters. "We end this now!"

As they reached the station, the door slammed shut. Together, Jacastra and her team fired away at the entry. After a few seconds, she yelled. "Halt!" Smoke cleared, then her head dropped. Frustration slathered her words. "We haven't put a dent in it."

Elegarcia followed in the women's path. "Clear out. Let me have a shot at it!"

Doing as directed, Jacastra and the other Sworn Warriors were joined by Roace and a distraught Geeja, all backing Elegarcia.

Geeja nodded toward Jacastra, her voice trembling. "You and your warriors fought with valor."

Jacastra knelt. "Thank you, my goddess, but we have sustained casualties."

Hearing those words, Geeja jerked her head around, searching for Bregent. Seeing him being helped into the *Curious Lady*, she acknowledged their situation. "Yes. Many precious to us are grievously injured, but we are turning the tables on Djurga."

Near the station, Elegarcia's arms reached out as she gradually took on an orange shade. Seeing her fellow goddess gathering magic, Geeja gave new orders to Jacastra. "We will do our best to heal them all, but until then, gather all of the Impercium's discarded Lighters and load them onto our ship." It had been a long time since she had fought in battle, but she understood the ebb and flow of combat. "I have a feeling we are not done fighting today."

"As you wish, my goddess." With her orders, Jacastra shouted to her crew. "Grab as many of their weapons as you can!"

Turning back, Geeja saw that Elegarcia now glowed a brighter tangerine hue, shining like a miniature sun.

Elegarcia let out a fierce growl as her hands pointed toward the station's charred, but sealed door. "Grrr!" A bolt of carrot colored energy sprang from her small body, blasting the post.

An explosion shook the ground, nearly toppling everyone within a hundred-foot radius. Geeja squinted, waiting to see if Elegarcia had gained access. A light wind gradually cleared smoke from the facility, giving her a clear view of a destroyed door. "By the Holy Twelve! You did it, El! You did it!"

Roace arrived by her side in an instant as the small goddess fell to her knees. "Great job! Now, let's get you back on the ship to recover." He scooped her up and headed away.

Turning her gaze away from her injured friends, Geeja stomped toward the structure. Peeking inside, she saw Impercium soldiers tending to their wounded. She considered killing them all, but thought back to the incident with Charl. Instead, she gave these wounded fighters fair warning. "Get out, or die. Now!"

Dazed troops in black uniforms scrambled at her command.

Geeja went in, clearing them out, then exited the station. She reached out to both the planet and their flying friends. ***"With your help, we rid your world of this."***

Thousands of tiny thoughts returned, as Torgose spoke for all. ***"Thank you. End this torture once and for all."***

As Geeja gathered power from the newly sentient world, she yelled at everyone. "Get back!" As the others fled, Geeja took in more energy than ever in her long life. Feeling about to burst, she released a surge of orange magic. The explosion dwarfed the one Elegarcia released. The ground shook as chunks of scorched concrete and twisted metal launched away in a thick cloud of dust and debris. It took several seconds to see the result. The building and all contents were replaced by a charred hole in the ground.

"Yes." The tiny voices sounded ecstatic. ***"You did it. Thank you!"***

Geeja returned triumphant thoughts toward the bats. ***"My friends, we did it together. Thank you for turning the tide of battle."***

Geeja allowed a small smile as Djurga's troops continued their struggle to free their heads from tight embraces. A thought came to mind. *You deserve far worse for your hurtful actions, but I have shown mercy*. Geeja now turned her attention to the planet. ***"I must leave now. Free those soldiers after we depart. They can harm you no longer."***

Torgose surged positive vibes to Geeja. ***"What you did freed us from their theft."*** Geeja could hear Torgose's sudden desperation. ***"Please return!"***

She longed to commune with the newly sentient world, but duty called. ***"I will be back as soon as I can."***

She ran to the *Curious Lady* as it prepared to lift off. Rushing to Bregent, she whispered, hoping she spoke the truth. "We will get you help. You will be healed."

Chella applied a dressing to the jagged wound on Bregent's left side, as he sat on the floor. The injury produced scorched edges, with a web of black lines expanding in all directions. The nurse's flat voice didn't match her cheery assessment. "You'll be good as new in no time."

Bregent's usually bright green eyes, dimmed. "We banded together and completed step one, but I'm hurt and we've got critically wounded Sworn Warriors. On top of that, an Impercium fleet is headed our way." He pulled in a breath through gritted teeth, then sighed. "I'm proud of what we accomplished, but remember what Shugg said. This is the easy part."

Chapter Forty-Seven

Raflo shot a nervous glance toward Huanoc upon hearing the recap of the battle on the surface of the planet they orbited. "They're on their way to Uwan with a wounded god and injured fighters, but they pulled it off. Think we'll be as lucky?"

"Hmm."

His big partner had resumed his word diet, but his thoughts sounded clear, at least to Raflo. "Right. There's just two of us up here. We can't afford ANY injuries."

As the unarmed floating station came into view, Huanoc confirmed what they had been told. "The shields are down. Phase two begins."

Raflo opened a radio channel to their unprotected enemy. "Yoo-hoo. Hey guys. We both know you've lost your force field. How about we do this nice and easy, with no one gettin' hurt?"

A terse reply came back. "Die, scum."

Punching Huanoc's shoulder, Raflo stated the obvious. "Guess we're doin' this the hard way…and somehow, I always knew that's how this would go down."

Huanoc tilted his head, then walked toward the space suits stowed for such an occasion.

Once geared up, Raflo moved to the weapon's locker. "You thinkin' three or four charges?"

"Four. More is better." He paused. "But bring an extra. We get one chance to do this right."

The long-distance proximity detector beeped loudly, indicating that Djurga's fleet neared. Raflo experienced a momentary flashback of prison surgery, churning his stomach. "We do this fast, then get out of here."

Since, if successful, they would be bringing a large battery back onboard, they were forced to lower the ramp. Doing so resulted in the loss of atmosphere in the ship's hold. Hearing the *Phantom Star's* oxygen escape sent another shiver through Raflo. *Venting atmosphere on purpose is always dangerous. One more huge risk to this longshot plan.*

Huanoc pushed off first, then used his thrusters to travel the short distance to the orbiting station. He placed explosives near both hinges and locks, then rejoined Raflo a safe distance away. He bobbed his head, then pushed the detonate button.

In the vacuum of space, the explosion made no sound, just a bright flash. Raflo raised his arm, shielding his eyes from the glare. "Let's see what kind of damage we did."

"Me first." Huanoc tapped his thruster control lightly, easing his way toward the damaged vessel. "Get back!" Lighter fire just missed him as he retreated so fast, he shot past Raflo.

Raflo joined his partner in retreat. "Seems even tech workers can aim a Lighter. That advanced warnin' they received has screwed our plan."

"Hrrr." Huanoc growled low and threateningly. "No time. They don't play nice, neither do we."

"Right." Raflo's eyes widened. "And what does that mean, exactly?"

Huanoc pulled the extra charge from the carrying bag. "We brought a spare."

"Oh…but what if we damage the magic thing?"

Glancing into deep space, Huanoc answered. "Want to wait until Djurga arrives?"

"No! No way!" Raflo pointed to the blown open hatch. "Light'em up. It's a risk we have to take."

Without delay, Huanoc hurled the final explosive toward the station. The less than perfect throw caught the edge of the doorway, resulting in the charge hanging in space, barely inside the opening. They saw a soldier reaching to push it out as Huanoc flipped the switch. A silent ball of flame whooshed, then the absence of oxygen snuffed it out.

Huanoc held up a hand. "Stay here. I'll look."

"Be careful." Raflo warned firmly. "Remember, no injuries!"

To stay out of view, Huanoc made his way alongside the damaged station. He took a tentative peek inside. After a few seconds, he turned to Raflo, giving a thumbs up. "Step one complete."

Raflo gave a one-second burn on his thruster, floating to the scorched entry. Peering inside, he nearly barfed as his helmet light lit the darkened interior of the station. "There's blood everywhere!"

"Better theirs than ours."

Sighing, Raflo acknowledged his partner. "Of course…but still." He focused his gaze to their prize. "If we don't hustle this to the *Phantom Star*, D̲urga will make sure our blood joins theirs."

"Hmm."

"Agreed." Another light touch of the thruster brought Raflo alongside the magic storing device. "She's toasty on the outside, but I don't see any structural breaches. I think our luck is holdin' out." The second level chime of the proximity detector rang in their ears. "Uh, maybe I spoke too soon." He failed at trying not to sound desperate. "How much time do we have?"

"Hmm. We'll be in particle-wave torpedo range in less than fifteen minutes."

Raflo caught another glimpse of the blood-spattered interior of this vessel as his lips pressed into a thin line. With hands balled to fists inside his gloves, he spoke in grim determination. "Let's do this."

Four huge bolts anchored the unit to the floor, and the wrenches they brought were clearly undersized. Huanoc turned his helmeted head side to side, then he pushed off the floor, drifting toward a wall holding power tools. Grabbing one, he smiled. "This will do." Yanking it from its mooring, he squeezed the trigger, but nothing happened. "Rrr. No power."

Feeling a bead of sweat roll down the side of his face, Raflo neared panic. "What now? Ditch this and save our necks?"

Huanoc shook his head. "Not yet. Portable generator on the *Phantom Star*." Without delay, the big man zoomed out the door, back toward their ship.

Raflo surveyed the grisly scene as he waited for his partner to return. Bits of humanoid bodies and tattered space suits floated in zero gravity, again turning his stomach. Mind racing, he reached a conclusion. *If this goes sideways, I would rather go out like them than return to prison.*

Reappearing, Huanoc grabbed the anchored battery with one hand, stopping his weightless flight. Attaching a cord to the tool, he pulled the trigger again, this time with a better result. He grinned. "Works!"

"Hurry!"

One by one, the thick bolts spun out, tumbling about inside the blistered interior of the station. When the last one dribbled away, Huanoc called to Raflo. "Step two."

"Right. Float this massive thing back to the *Phantom Star*." His tone didn't match his words. "Easy greasy."

With one man on each side of the bulky device, Huanoc grunted as he spoke. "Lift and push toward the door!"

Though weightless, the object had significant mass. Raflo's muscles strained to raise the storage device. Once moving, inertia kept it heading toward the opening. Just as the battery cleared the damaged Impercium station, the third proximity warning blared in their earpiece. "How much time?"

Huanoc answered. "Ten minutes."

Now, outside in the gap between where they were and where they needed to go, they had nothing to push against to move the object faster. Only momentum, and the occasional thruster tap to keep the device on course, carried it forward at a lazy speed. Raflo moved to the front as the unit continued its slow float toward their ship, calling out what he saw. "It's goin' to be a tight fit, but it looks like it will clear the ramp openin.'"

"Good." As usual, the big man kept his comments brief. "Careful."

As the battery drew closer, Raflo's mental calculations changed. "It's too far starboard!" Instinct kicked in as Raflo grabbed the object, trying to nudge it through. "Ahhh!" He screamed as the full mass of the unit smashed his hand between it and the ramp opening. An awful crunching sensation traveled up his arm. The impact against the larger *Phantom Star* stopped the device cold, then it recoiled, floating slowly backward.

Huanoc jetted forward, maneuvering until he could see his screaming friend. He saw Raflo holding his smashed left hand tight against his space suit. "Let me see!"

It took every ounce of willpower for Raflo to release his hold, allowing Huanoc to look at the damage. Raflo spoke between gasps. "It's broken! I know it is! It's bad!"

"Yes." Looking into Raflo's eyes, Huanoc offered perspective. "But no leaks and not fatal, like it will be if we don't get out of here."

"Right." Raflo again gripped his injury. "Let's go!"

"Battery first."

"Seriously?" Raflo doubled over as stabbing pain radiated up his arm.

Huanoc ignored him as he went to work. He stretched a cable anchored to a cleat in the hold of the ship to the large square block slowly drifting away. In short order he jury-rigged a winch, then heaved to get the massive thing moving forward again. Just as the unit made it into the cargo area, the proximity detector screeched, and didn't stop. "In range in less than one minute."

Lashing the cable in a stopgap knot, Huanoc hit the button to raise the ramp, then floated to the cockpit before gravity could be restored. "Follow me." He pointed to their barely secured cargo. "Not safe back here."

Raflo hurried behind his partner, easing into the copilot seat. He buckled in as fast as he could with only one functioning hand. "Go!"

Huanoc flipped the cloaking switch, then launched straight to quantum speed. The banging behind them didn't surprise Raflo. "I hope that thing doesn't burst open. I have a feelin' we would blink out instantly."

The big man's cheeks looked bluer than usual, probably due to the stress and physical exertion of the operation. The continued screeching of the proximity indicator telling them that Djurga's fleet neared, couldn't help. "Taking evasive maneuvers. They might have gotten a lock on us before we blasted out of there."

The racket from the cargo hold amplified as the partially secured device swung against the sides. Raflo winced. "I hope this is worth it."

"Hmm." Suddenly, the clanging alarm went silent. Without warning, all the ship's scanners showed the same thing. "Hmm."

The sudden quiet helped Raflo momentarily overcome his throbbing injury. "You said that twice. Where's Djurga's fleet?"

"They broke pursuit. We're safe."

Raflo understood what his friend didn't say. "That means they're all goin' after Geeja." He squashed down a stab running up his arm. "And the *Curious Lady* doesn't have cloakin' capabilities."

"They do have a head start."

"Think it's enough?"

Huanoc's silence said everything.

Chapter Forty-Eight

Djurga scowled as he paced the bridge of the *Emperor's Will*. General Scanda bore the brunt of the emperor's ire. "Those scans better be right. Are you sure this ship is transporting four of the twelve?"

"Yes…well almost sure, Your Excellency."

"What does *almost* mean?"

Standing as straight as a Chidone obelisk, Scanda explained. "We have years of scans from eleven of those beings and I can say with certainty that Bregent of Politar, Roace of Fontonce, as well as Elegarcia of Bostor are on that ship."

Djurga pressed. "And our primary target?"

"Well, Your Excellency, since the goddess of Uwan hasn't been seen in centuries, we don't have a comparison scan."

"Scanda!"

Sweat glistened on the general's brow as he jumped to add additional information. "We can confirm there is a being onboard that ship who has no bio match in any Impercium data base. That is impossible for any subject of your rule…unless it is her."

The emperor's voice lowered. "I see. Then where are those traitors headed, and how long before they are in range of our weapons?"

"It appears they are headed toward Uwan, home world of the Goddess, Geeja."

Spittle flew. "I know whose planet it is! How long before we can blast them all into oblivion?"

Scanda stammered. "They… they have a head start that we can't overcome, even at maximum quantum speed."

"What did you say?" Djurga's face burned hot. "You better follow that statement with a plan to kill them, or it will be you who dies this day!"

Holding his head high, Scanda cleared his throat. "Yes, Your Excellency. Your forces already on Uwan are significant and will know the location of their arrival the moment it occurs. Depending on where they land, we can have troops engaged in less than half an hour. This fleet will be there just a few minutes later. With our overwhelming firepower advantage, they stand no chance. You will see their charred bodies by the end of this day."

"Hmm." Djurga paced the bridge again, his eyes staring into the darkness of space. "And what of the other ship, the one that attacked our orbital station?"

Scanda cleared his throat once more. "Their technology…well, Your Excellency, we're still working to defeat their cloaking tech."

"What? They can still evade us?"

"For the moment, Your Excellency." The general's sweaty face dripped on his uniform. "But they are only two common criminals who want to stay as far away from us as possible. We'll find them soon. I promise."

The emperor jabbed a finger toward Scanda. "Two common criminals who have a battery full of magic? Two common criminals who have the expertise to avoid the Impercium's best tech? Two common criminals who found the goddess for whom I searched for two centuries? Do they sound common to you, General?"

A hitched breath preceded Scanda's reply. "A poor word choice on my part, Your Excellency." He bowed again. "I simply meant that they are but two men with one ship, and they aren't gods. Our forces have dealt with these kind of vermin for centuries. We'll find them, then they will be neutralized. You have my word."

Emperor Djurga crossed his arms, then resumed his silent vigil of staring forward as the fleet zipped through space. He snarled a response. "Find them and end them, or I'll end you."

Chapter Forty-Nine

Geeja squeezed into the *Curious Lady's* tight cockpit beside Talla. "How long until we reach Uwan?"

Talla glanced at the screen, answering with a nervous shake in her voice. "I'm pushing her faster than ever. We'll be there in less than an hour."

Geeja spoke in level tones. "Have you made contact with the Sworn Warriors on Uwan?"

"Yes, they just answered my hail. They're bringing the leader to the only communication station in their complex."

"Good. We will need all the help we can get."

Talla bit her lower lip. "Look. I want to fight against Djurga." She took in a shallow breath. "But I have a husband and a young child." She blinked twice. "After I deliver you to the academy, I'm flying there to be with them. I'm sorry."

Geeja nodded. "We could use your talents in the fight, but I understand. You signed up for a round-trip flight and now you are in the middle of a lopsided war."

An ancient voice came to life over the communication system. "This is the Holy Mother of the Goddess of Uwan Training Academy. To whom do I speak?"

A smile replaced Talla's worried visage. "Holy Mother. It's so good to hear your voice again. It is I, Talla Ignestilsen."

"Talla, my child! I've missed your sweet presence."

Talla's eyes filled. "I feel the same, Holy Mother." She glanced at Geeja as she wiped her damp cheeks. "There will be joy, at least for a moment, when I land at the academy in under an hour."

"What? You're coming here?"

"Yes. And I'm bringing someone you've spent a lifetime waiting to meet."

A wariness traveled with the old woman's next words. "I want to believe–badly. Are you certain it is her?"

Geeja grinned. *She's smart. Wants proof. Good.*

Talla glanced over her shoulder. She smiled when seeing Geeja's engaged expression. "Holy Mother, I have witnessed her heal a man poisoned by Lighter fire. I've seen her shoot green fire from her fingertips to save us from Emperor Djurga's goons. I watched as she called upon a planet's giant bats to fight on our side against Impercium troops. Jacastra saw it all as well. Believe me, Holy Mother. It's her."

"It's really true? She's alive and coming here?"

"Yes, and she wishes to speak with you."

Geeja heard a rumbling on the transmission and knew exactly what was happening. The old woman, who had spent a lifetime believing the goddess lived, lowered to her knees. Geeja had witnessed this behavior countless times from other believers meeting her for the first time. She knew exactly how she should greet her worshiper. "Holy Mother, your devotion will be heralded across Uwan and throughout the universe."

Sobs of reverence transmitted across space followed by words as soft as a baby thanca's fur. "The fullness of time is today...and I've lived to see it."

"Holy Mother." Geeja's voice hardened. "I am sorry to be the bearer of bad news, but the fullness of time is more complicated than you ever imagined. Emperor Djurga is in hot pursuit, and we have wounded warriors to heal. Most importantly, I am calling on your warriors to fight with me and three other gods on this very day."

What sounded like a great inhalation traveled back to the *Curious Lady*, followed by scuffling sounds on stone.

The old woman rises from her knees to face this news. Geeja grinned. *I like her spirit.*

"Emperor Djurga? Other gods? To battle here?" She paused, then firm words flowed. "I have dreamed of a coming battle, but nothing like this."

"There is more, and you may struggle to accept what I am about to say."

"Oh?" The old woman's response turned shaky.

"I know the restrictions on technology for my followers, because I put them in place. They were there for good reason and served us well for so long." Geeja took a breath. "But, on this day we must defeat the Impercium to save Uwan, and so many other worlds. As hard as this will be for you to hear, please know that I had difficulty coming to terms with it as well. For this moment in time, we must fight technology with technology. I am bringing weapons of war and expect your women to be ready for a crash course in how to use them. Jacastra will lead the training."

The Holy Mother went silent. Geeja could sense the conflict, even this far away. "There must be another way, one that isn't contrary to scripture. What will you do if we refuse to fight that way?"

Geeja's jaw set. "Holy Mother, here is what is going to happen. Once we land a counting down of mere minutes will commence, signaling Djurga's arrival. When he reaches Uwan a battle for survival begins, and his troops will slaughter all they can. If you refuse to follow me, then run for the caves. Otherwise, all your warriors will be nothing but weapon fodder, and any hope of ridding Uwan of that unholy Terminus Stake will likely be gone forever." Her shoulders squared as she continued. "If you fight with me, many will still perish, but they will die as warriors, battling for our world. Their contributions will give us a chance to save Uwan and defeat the evil that has been visited upon our planet for so long."

"I see." The words sounded flat, as if smashed between the feelings of joy at living to see the goddess, and her hatred of Emperor Djurga.

Geeja presented a choice. "Do I put Jacastra on to help you prepare for the fight, or are you and your warriors heading for the caves?"

The old woman's voice turned strong. "It is not the fight I expected, but I have always understood a battle would come. We're sworn to serve you and Uwan, and we will give our very lives to defeat this evil. We rejoice in this holy day!"

Chapter Fifty

Geeja tensed as the *Curious Lady* rapidly descended toward Uwan's surface. "Do you ever get used to this?"

Talla shot a quick glance as her fingers touched screens on the ship's control console. "Get used to what?"

"Never mind." Geeja gave a light laugh. "Your question answered mine."

As the ship touched down softly, Talla turned to Geeja. "We're here. Ready to breathe this wonderful Uwanian air?"

Geeja knew the planet's condition, but being in places that were so much cleaner for the past few days dulled that reality. Her face warming, she said the most optimistic thing she could think of in the presence of this grim truth. "Hopefully, today starts the restoration." The ship's ramp opened, putting an end to the discussion.

Jacastra called orders to the Sworn Warriors. "Weapons first, then the goddess. Injured after that. Move fast. Time and the Impercium are against us."

While the soldiers carried their wounded to the surface, Roace helped Bregent to his feet, then wrapped his arm around the man to aid him on a slow walk to the ground. "Lean on me, my friend. These women will have you back to full strength in no time."

The weakened god responded with a worried smile and wince.

Once on the ground, Geeja took over, settling Bregent with a healer. She spoke softly. "I am sure they will be able to help you."

Bregent's jaws clenched in agony as he waved her away. "Go. Fight."

"We will." Geeja then reached for Elegarcia's hand. "Let us check on Uwan and meet our army."

A moment later, Uwan connected with his goddess. *"You have returned!"*

The ages old voice in her head welcomed her with the warmth of a mother's embrace, combined with the intimacy of a life-long lover. Despite the acrid stench of her first full breaths of polluted air, she responded just as sincerely. *"I have missed you, Uwan, and I have brought old friends to help in our fight!"*

Elegarcia fell to her knees. *"Uwan, it has been far too long!"*

"Elegarcia! What a wonderful surprise!"

Geeja's broad smile faded. *"Roace and Bregent are here as well...but Bregent has been injured by a deadly weapon."* Her fingers clenched into fists. *"The battle with Djurga has begun and will resume here in only minutes."*

The Holy World's reply rang with caution. *"I am afraid I will be of little help in healing Bregent, or in the battle."*

A half-forced smile edged back on Geeja's face. *"There is hope my friend, and with a bit of luck, you may be on your way to health by the end of the day."*

"What? Today?"

Her eyes searched for the leader of this band of fighting women. *"First, I need to get war preparations underway. Can you guide me to the one they call the Holy Mother? I will explain later."*

"Yes. I can still do that. Turn to your left, she's moving toward you."

Doing as Uwan suggested, Geeja quickly identified the old woman flanked by stern Sworn Warriors. With determined steps she closed the distance. Geeja could see tears already falling and it did not surprise her when the resolute woman fell to her knees, followed by her entire retinue.

"Goddess!" It seemed as if a surge of emotion allowed but a single word to escape the Holy Mother's mouth.

Opening herself to her home world, Geeja laid a hand on the bowed woman's head, sending a flow of warmth and respect. "Your faithfulness to both Uwan and myself reveals the purity of your heart." She knelt beside the leader whose thin frame shook as she sobbed. "Arise and walk with me. There is much to accomplish and little time in which to do it."

The Holy Mother gasped, then beamed as she stood. Whispers danced between members of her entourage and a sense of excitement filled the compound.

Talla rushed up, adding to the buzz. "Holy Mother!" She bowed to the elderly woman. "I'm honored to be in your presence again."

The Holy Mother kissed Talla's lowered head.

The captain rubbed tears from her cheeks. "Holy Mother, it is with the heaviest of hearts that I must now leave."

"But you've just returned."

Talla cut a quick glance to Geeja, then her gaze returned to her former leader. "I have a child, and a husband now. I must see to their safety." Another peek went toward Geeja. "I've explained this to the goddess."

Stepping closer, Geeja wrapped the pilot in her arms. "Your dedication and grace under pressure has been an inspiration to all. Go in peace with hopes that you may return in the same manner."

"Thank you, Goddess." Her next words were choked. "It has been the honor of a lifetime." It seemed with great reluctance that she turned away, but once she did, Talla sprinted toward her ship. Dust kicked up by the hasty takeoff triggered many of those outside to pull coverings over their mouths and noses.

Coughing, the Holy Mother pointed. "Let us talk inside."

As they walked, practice Lighter fire sounded nearby. Geeja flinched. *The same sound from two thousand years ago…and Djurga is coming again.*

Jacastra barked direction as hundreds of Sworn Warriors took their first, and only lesson before being thrown into battle. "Aim at the center of the target for maximum impact."

Geeja shivered as she spoke to the old woman. "I understand the conflict you must feel because it still pricks my core. It is, however, the only way to save our world."

The Holy Mother glanced at her without speaking. Once inside, they observed the training through windows. Having stopped crying upon meeting the goddess and seeing her Sworn Warriors firing modern weaponry, the Holy Mother's eyes glistened again. "You mentioned a hope to save our world. Can the blasphemy you asked me to embrace really result in good?"

Geeja's spine stiffened. "There is new magic in the galaxy and we have a supply of it on the way. If we can hold off Djurga's forces long enough, there is the possibility to change everything."

"New magic?" She wiped her cheek. "Do we have decent odds?"

"No." Geeja's voice didn't change as she gave her honest assessment. "We will lose many lives today, but it is our only chance."

The Holy Mother nodded. "Then teach me how to use the weapon that could…" She stopped short, then began again. "Teach me to use the weapon that *will* save our world."

Chapter Fifty-One

Propped on his standard issue Impercium desk, Major Jank Fralic's aide-polished boots gleamed. The top button on his field uniform flopped open, and low snores escaped his lips. He had passed on the leafy green herbs recommended by his physician, choosing for lunch the lazentern leg platter–three pieces of the battered fried fowl, paired with smoked terine fruit and spicy tubers. Plenty of calories to support his corpulent body, but the frozen Chocolate Storm he piled on for dessert put him over the top and into a mid-afternoon food coma.

When First Lieutenant Mitcher Shibbly burst through his door the major nearly fell backwards. "What…" Fralic's eyes popped open, blinking to adjust in the dimly lit room. "What's the rush, Mitch? Is the air scrubber on the fritz again?"

"No sir!" The young officer sprayed his words like vomit after a night of drinking. "We have a mission! The emperor is coming! We must deploy now!"

Fralic bent his neck side to side, cracking aging bones. "Who put you up to this? If you really think I'll fall for a prank so ridiculous, then I've got some farmland in the desert to sell you." He leaned back again, closing his eyes. "Get out, or you'll be on latrine duty for a week."

The lieutenant slapped his commanding officer's feet off the desk. "I'm not joking, sir! Remember all that talk about the goddess last week? Well, she's here and the emperor is on his way!"

The major straightened in his chair. "You're serious?"

"Deadly. We're to lead a raid on the Sworn Warrior compound ten miles to our west. Right now!"

Major Fralic jumped to his feet as the base siren wailed like a pinched wergan. "The emperor ordered us to full alert? This isn't a drill?" He rebuttoned his jacket. "Let's go! What are you waiting for?"

"Orders, sir?"

Huffing out a command, the heavy leader panted hard after only a few dozen strides. "Standard attack formation B. Those religious zealots aren't even properly armed; they fight with wooden staffs. We should have this mopped up in no time."

The much fitter junior officer ran alongside his superior. "Think we'll get promotions, sir?"

"Absolutely!" Major Fralic slowed, then squeezed a stitch. "We will be…" His hands moved from his side to his chest as he stumbled, falling without finishing his sentence.

Lieutenant Shibbly called out. "Medic! I need a medic! The commander is down." He rolled the major over, seeing a blank stare.

A soldier with a medical bag arrived seconds later, wasting no time scanning, then setting the hand-held instrument to full charge. "Stand back!"

Mitcher looked on as the pulsed jolt spasmed Major Fralic. "Is he going to be okay? What do we do?"

"Whatever you order, sir." The medic answered, shaking his head as he continued working. "You're in charge now."

Lieutenant Shibbly's jaw hung open for a few seconds, then he turned. "All squads! Standard attack formation B!"

Chapter Fifty-Two

Geeja stood with Roace and Elegarcia behind a detail of newly armed and barely trained Sworn Warriors. The soldiers scrunched down behind the compound's ancient stone walls for cover against the imminent attack as Geeja resisted the urge to pace. Instead, she turned her attention to those not with them. "How are Bregent and the injured warriors?"

Elegarcia glanced toward the medical facility. "Chella and the healers are using local plants to slow the ribelsome poison's spread, but Bregent's in bad shape. Luckily, the others weren't wounded as severely. There's more time to save them."

Geeja's already tense shoulders knotted. "I will call a dragon to attack them from above." She sighed. "Why did I not think of that earlier?"

A Sworn Warrior within earshot piped up. "I'm sorry, Goddess, but the emperor ordered them hunted to extinction centuries ago."

As acid gurgled up from her stomach, she spat. "Another crime for which he will pay."

Jacastra called out from the front line. "Impercium battle skimmers coming in hot! Hold your fire until they're within two hundred feet!"

Since their arrival Geeja, Elegarcia and Roace communed with Uwan to get a feel for the level of power they might be able to harness in the fight about to begin. Geeja's unsettled gut didn't feel any better after their tests. "Uwan and I will do our best, but we will have far less power than we had on Torgose."

Elegarcia touched Geeja's arm gently. "We all know where the blame for Uwan's desecration belongs."

Geeja nodded as Elegarcia moved several paces to her left, while Roace did the same to her right. She opened her mind and her hands, with fingers spread. *"Thank you, Uwan, for all the power you can give. I promised a battle to restore you…and it begins now."*

The reply came quickly, more anxious than hopeful. *"I will give my all."*

"Fire!" In unison, Jacastra's troops sent the first bolts of Lighter fire into the fight, hitting the lead skimmer multiple times. It sent the vehicle cartwheeling to the left, taking out two more craft on that side of the arrow formation.

One of the women just trained on Lighter use stood and yelled in triumph. Before Geeja could shout a warning, the next skimmer in the phalanx returned fire. At such close range the blast instantly vaporized the inexperienced soldier's head. After that, the noise on the battlefield went from individual blasts to an uninterrupted cacophony of destruction.

Feeling Uwan's energy in every fiber of her being, Geeja allowed herself a moment of nostalgia. *"Just like old times, my friend."*

He pushed an extra dose of warmth. *"So we hope."*

Raising her hands, she squeezed a bolus of the planet's energy toward the center of the attacker's pointed formation. A ball of blue magical fire went over the heads of the Sworn Warriors tucked behind the solid granite outer wall of their compound. It hit several armored vessels producing ear-splitting explosions from the detonation of their propulsion crystals. *"That felt so good, Uwan!"*

"Yes, it did…but my recharge ability is extensively degraded. Take cover until I can refresh your power."

Roace and Elegarcia released their stored bursts.

Geeja bellowed a battle yell, happy to have allies. "Take that, Djurga!"

Barely able to speak above the din of modern warfare, the other two gods simply smiled in agreement.

Geeja scanned the area beyond their gray walls watching the attacking force retreat. It looked as if the Sworn Warriors and gods had destroyed a third of the Impercium skimmers. With the momentary lull, Geeja yelled at the top of her voice. "Terrific effort! We surprised them." Smoke from smoldering crashed skimmers filled the air with acrid wisps, mixing with the already atrocious atmosphere of Uwan. Geeja coughed. "They now know what they are facing. Be ready for changes!"

Geeja eyed Jacastra walking up and down the front-line, shouting encouragement to the strong-willed women who, minutes ago, were thrown into a completely alien form of combat. She mumbled while Jacastra cheered the spirits of their troops. "Such a valiant leader."

Catching moving shapes from the corner of her eye, Geeja glanced up. Her prediction came true. Instead of flying in a straight line toward their defenses, the skimmers now moved side to side at random intervals as they sped forward in a second run. "Here they come again!"

Reaching out to Uwan for a magical rush, precious little energy trickled into Geeja. *"I am so sorry, my friend."*

"We fight with what we have. I am recharging as fast as I can."

Uwan's reply gave Geeja an idea she should have thought of before. She made her way to Jacastra as quickly as possible. The noise now made it almost impossible to be heard, even by a person standing beside you. Her yelling nearly shredded her vocal cords. "Give me a Lighter!"

"My Goddess!" Jacastra's eyes widened. "We can't risk your life! You must stay where it's safe!"

"There will be no safe place if we lose. Give me a Lighter!"

Keeping her head down, Jacastra hustled away, then returned quickly. "Do you know how to use this?"

Geeja read her lips as the din of battle now surpassed all verbal communication. She hoped Jacastra could understand her reply as she remembered her only lesson from days ago. "Point at the enemy. Pull the trigger!"

Jacastra grinned, then nodded, mimicking that action.

As Geeja readied herself for her first use of technology in war, a woman beside her jerked. She had been hit in the forehead, sending her flying backwards. No blood spilled, as the heat from the bolt cauterized the severed arteries and veins.

Geeja blinked twice at the sickening sight, then swallowed hard. *Remember, there is* nowhere *safe in this moment.*

Peeking above the wall, Geeja saw a skimmer boring down on her position. She squeezed over and over in blasts that missed before hitting the target mere feet in front of her. *That was close.*

Next, she shared a kill with the warrior to her left, then scored another solo take-down. Geeja sensed a planetary tug. She questioned. *"Are we ready to recharge?"*

Uwan answered emphatically. *"Yes, finally."*

Geeja hustled back to where she previously stood, seeing Elegarcia and Roace in their spots. *Good. Their communication with Uwan is working.*

The enemy retreated for a second time as Geeja reached out to Uwan. She smiled as the familiar tingle of magic seeped into her being. *"I helped with a weapon, but this is my real contribution to the fight."*

Uwan shared his sparse energy freely. *"Our contribution."*

As they rallied for another assault, it appeared to Geeja that the Impercium attackers had lost more than two-thirds of their skimmers. *Come on, you desecraters.*

Black flying machines rushed toward their position. They steered more erratically than in their two prior attacks. Geeja sensed this could be the decisive moment, sending her thoughts to Roace and Elegarcia. *"Absorb all the energy you can, then wait until all of their ships are in range."*

Both nodded.

Geeja ignored the noise and near misses around her as she willed herself to take in more magic than ever before. Her body shook as her entire field of vision turned the familiar blue of Uwan's hue. Taking all her resolve, she held the power as the skimmers drew ever closer. Her stomach quivered, as if she would pass out or explode. She raised her hands when all were in range, releasing a tidal wave of magic. The discharge seemed to signal Roace and Elegarcia as they followed her lead. As the massive amount of energy burst from her, something snapped inside. The sensation felt profound, but in the moment, she had no time for reflection, only action.

The plain outside the compound lit like a blue-tinted foundry furnace. A blast of heat matched the intensity of the bright flash of light, causing everyone on their side of the wall to hide behind anything they could to avoid the searing heatwave that spread in all directions. When it hit Geeja, she coughed, then panted in the extreme warmth. Wind roared as if the final throes of a violent storm. When it finally died, the smell of burned wiring and charred flesh hung in the air. An unnatural calm clung, as if the heavens opened a portal to the silence of space.

It took several seconds, but when her eyes adjusted Geeja saw Sworn Warriors unsteadily climbing to their feet, surveying the charred blackness where their enemy had been. Not a living thing, even the desert scrub, survived. Geeja's knees weakened as she recoiled from the massive release. Processing what she and the other two gods had done, her thoughts went to them and Uwan. ***"Uwan and I thank you. Together, we have shown that Djurga's technology is not invincible."***

The Holy Mother moved to the center of the group. With eyes closed and a hand reaching skyward, her voice rang out. "We witness the fullness of time!"

Chapter Fifty-Three

The veins in Emperor Djurga's neck bulged as he stood on the bridge of his command vessel. "Get comms to the troops on the ground back up, or heads will roll!"

General Scanda went pale as he mumbled. "This can't be..."

"Speak up, or I'll have your tongue for dinner. What's happening on that cursed planet!"

Scanda spoke as blood drained from his face. "Five thousand soldiers and battle skimmers...gone."

Djurga had seen his top general distressed, afraid and nervous, but he had never seen the man in this state of overwhelmed confusion. The hairs on the back of his neck raised, but he maintained his imperial tone. "Gone? Define *gone* or that's what will happen to you."

Some color returned to Scanda's cheeks. "Pardon my lack of royal decorum, Your Excellency. It's just that in all my years I've never seen anything like this." His eyes darted for a moment back to the control panel with its glowing screen, then returned to meet the hardest stare in the known universe. "We tracked a raging battle with thousands upon thousands of Lighter shots fired from both sides, but then..." He ran a pressed hand across his forehead. "Then a series of unexplained energy surges struck our forces."

"You're on thin ice, general. What do you mean, *unexplained?*"

Scanda straightened as he regained his composure. "We ran diagnostics to confirm our readings sir, and our equipment checks out. It's just that we've never recorded energy levels this high in a skirmish like this." Meeting the emperor's stare, he explained. "There were three spikes in the beginning that registered in the same range as our early battlefield mini-nukes of centuries ago. We took that to mean the women at that compound had somehow obtained serious black market tactical weapons."

"No! That's impossible. Those blind followers foreswore every kind of tech. They would never—" Djurga didn't finish the sentence because an alternate explanation came to mind. He pushed that unsettling emotion down. "Continue, Scanda."

"Yes, Your Excellency." Scanda peeked at the control terminal again. "Our forces gave, and took a beating. They launched a final assault that should have proven decisive, ending the threat." He swallowed hard. "But as they closed on the enemy, an explosion killed every Impercium soldier in an instant."

Lieutenant Arthold spoke. "Your Excellency, General Scanda. A recording from the battlefield has arrived. Should I display it on the main screen?"

Djurga growled. "Do it."

The recording came from the nose of an Impercium battle skimmer. The playback had the feel of being in the thick of the fight. As the first run began, the pilot, identified as Lieutenant Shibbly, sounded confident. "These fools have no weapons. This will be a slaughter."

On screen, Impercium troops sent round after round of Lighter fire toward the compound's solid stone boundary wall. Chips of rock flew from the waist-high structure. The vessels met no resistance until all at once hundreds of blasts came toward them. The commander of the group gasped as several skimmers spun out of control. "Fall back! Repeat, fall back. Regroup on my signal!"

Djurga grumbled, mostly to himself. "So much for those women keeping their vows." He growled. "I should have killed them centuries ago."

On the display, the camera pivoted in retreat, then suddenly three explosions rocked the skimmers nearly simultaneously. The emperor pointed. "What was that?"

Scanda barked. "Spectral analysis, Lieutenant!"

"Yes sir!" Stopping the playback, the younger man's fingers repeatedly tapped the screen at his station as seconds ticked by. He turned back with mouth hung open. "There is no known match in our database."

Djurga's chest tightened as he kept his voice level. "Identify the source."

The general handled the order. "The skimmer turned away before the blast." His lips tightened flat. "But our readings indicated a much bigger explosion destroyed our forces. Hopefully we'll be able to see the source in a few minutes."

At their fallback position, Shibbly appraised the situation and gave new orders. "We flew into a trap! They were supposed to be unarmed!" His hand could be heard slamming down on the black titanium shell of his skimmer. "Run flight formation Zeon on this pass. We'll show those femitches the iron fist of the Impercium!"

The emperor wore a reptilian grin. "I like his spirit." As the video resumed, he remembered this man, and all the others under his command there were dead. His grin darkened.

The second charge against the compound proved even more disorienting as the skimmer with the recorder, and all others, zigzagged randomly. It didn't seem to matter as the soldiers behind the wall gained confidence and accuracy. One by one, black flying craft spun out of control or blew up as they were blasted by return fire.

"Fall back on my signal!" An Impercium force had now been repelled twice by what should have been an inferior foe.

Djurga crossed his arms. "I take back what I said. I don't like this lieutenant's spirit. He's a coward."

"Alright, soldiers!" Shibbly's voice cracked. "We go in faster and there's no retreat. We're going over that wall or through it! Long live the Impercium!"

Knowing the outcome, Djurga again changed his assessment of the man whose life he would see end soon. His words carried on a frigid wave. "I admire your loyalty…but hate your failure."

The imagery jittered more as the speed ramped up and the evasive maneuvers sharpened. Intense return Lighter fire landed all around, but Shibbly didn't hesitate. "Glory to the emperor!" Seconds later a huge explosion, accompanied by raging blue flames filled the entire screen, then all went black as the recording ended.

Emperor Djurga bellowed. "What happened? What was *that*?"

Scanda called direction. "Replay the final seconds before the flame, then enlarge and search."

Lieutenant Arthold did as told, magnifying the image square by square.

Djurga shouted. "There! Zoom in tighter!" On a small knoll behind the front line stood three people with arms extended. "Who are they?"

The clacking of keyboards and punching of screens sounded on the bridge as the images were enhanced. Glowing squares appeared around two of the three people. Djurga spoke the names as two beings he knew resolved clearly. "Roace and Elegarcia! I'll have their heads!"

A red square blinked around the middle face, with no identification appearing. Scanda's voice hardened. "A face not in the Impercium database." He stood tall as he turned to meet the stare of the ruler of their universe. "I believe this constitutes absolute confirmation. She lives."

The emperor growled. "Play this forward in slow motion." Frame by frame the three gods stood with arms stretched, palms forward. Suddenly, what looked like plasma flames burst from their outstretched hands. "Freeze it, then one click at a time!"

As the playback continued at a sniggle's pace, the screen filled with an exponential mushrooming expansion of the strange energy.

Djurga rocked from toes to heels twice, simultaneously accepting what he saw, while not quite believing it. One thing however, could no longer be denied. "Yes, Scanda. She is alive."

Chapter Fifty-Four

Raflo took in another ragged breath as Huanoc brought the *Phantom Star* out of quantum speed. He gave a weak laugh. "Truth is, I never thought we'd make it this far."

"Hmm."

He coughed, winced in pain, then laughed again. "And I don't think I'm the only one that believed that." He shifted his gaze toward the Terminus Stake and his mood turned serious. "But since we have, it will bring me great pleasure to blast that thing into tomorrow. That is, if this big block of magic does what we think it can."

"Hmm."

"Right. If it doesn't, we'll be dead by the end of the day. With Djurga's fleet hot on our tails, we won't be able to hide long, even with our fancy cloakin' tech."

"Hmm."

"I agree. We need to hustle gettin' our part done." He held up his bandaged, mangled hand. "Sorry I won't be much help with the heavy liftin.'"

Huanoc shrugged. "We'll deal."

Using his good hand, Raflo unbuckled and followed Huanoc to the cargo hold. Raflo let out a high whistle upon seeing several gashes in the wall, each more than an arm's length. "That barely-tethered big block did some real damage." He moved closer to one of the tears. "We're lucky it didn't breach the outer hull."

Huanoc patted the white cube. "Also, fortunate it didn't explode."

Buoyed by their good fortune, Raflo's smile blossomed like a night-stalker flower under a full moon. "Then it's our lucky day. Maybe everythin's goin' to work out after all."

A tilted-head stare returned. "One step at a time."

"Right." He winked at his partner. "We figured on firin' magic from this thing, but since our original plan is in shambles, let's suit up and get this bad boy attached to that monstrosity outside. Hope this works."

Suiting up with one hand took a little extra time, but with adrenaline flowing, Raflo finished only a minute after Huanoc. "I can give a one-armed lift to get it off the floor, then a shoulder push to get it movin.' Think you can handle it from there?"

Huanoc nodded. "You bring the glue?"

"Right." Raflo stared at the closed orange utility bucket. "You think this emergency hull sealant will hold that thing in place?"

"Yes. That and inertia."

"Alright then. Open the ramp and shut down the artificial gravity. We have a magical parcel to deliver." Raflo grunted and with a strong leg drive, the cube rose. His hand throbbed as sweat ran into his eyes. He called out to his big blue friend, with genuine concern in his voice. "Watch your hands as we shove this thing."

"Hmm."

In an abundance of caution, and with a bigger time cushion than back at Torgose, the men moved their stolen prize slower, making their way out without so much as a bump against the doorway. Raflo gave a parting pat to the cube. "You got it from here?"

"Hmm."

"I'll grab the adhesive and meet you at the bane of Uwan's existence."

The process of attaching the magical storage device to the silvery metallic surface of the Terminus Stake went remarkably smooth. Raflo and Huanoc made it back to the *Phantom Star* in under an hour. As Raflo removed his suit, the ache in his injured hand increased. A red streak and searing pain radiated up his arm. Fever joined the growing list of symptoms. "Hey big guy, I'm goin' to need real medical attention soon or…" He stopped, unsure what would happen if they left the wound unattended. "Let's just say it's not good, and gettin' worse."

Huanoc spoke freely, a sure sign of his concern. "Let's check in with the others. We're ready to detonate as soon as they are. After that, we'll get you some help."

Chapter Fifty-Five

It took a few minutes for Geeja and the other two gods to recover from the strain of so much energy flowing through them. Geeja beamed at what they had done. "Take that *Emperor Djurga*!" She spat his name dripping with disdain.

The smell of scorched wiring from destroyed skimmers hit them as Roace dusted bits of blown ash from his black pants. He, too, wore a self-satisfied smile. "I haven't felt like this in ages! We channeled power for a sacred cause against an evil enemy. This is what we were made for!"

Elegarcia made her way through all the taller Sworn Warriors, joining her peers. "Epic! That's all I can say!" She met Geeja's gaze. "I'm so glad you talked me into this life-or-death revolution."

The mention of death sent Geeja's thoughts to the god not standing with them. "Let us check on Bregent."

Jacastra strode up just in time to hear Geeja's request. "Follow me, Goddess."

Together they descended the tunnel entrance on the Sworn Warrior compound. Geeja spied Chella ahead, with the nurse's gaze locked on Bregent. "How is he?"

Chella's eyes were red, and the sheen of wiped tears on her cheeks shone even in the dim lighting. "Despite our best efforts, he's getting worse, not better."

Geeja rubbed the nurse's arm. "I know you're doing all you can with limited resources." Groans of additional wounded fighters being brought in muted the triumphant mood of moments ago. "Even though Uwan is weakened, perhaps a healing bed can buy us some time for Bregent, and help the others."

Chella's head cocked. "What's a healing bed?"

"Right." Geeja laughed lightly. "This god and goddess stuff is new to you. I mentioned my long hibernation earlier, but left out the details. Well, I rested on a hidden slab of stone infused with magic to recover. Despite Uwan's deteriorated condition it saved my life, though it took far longer than I could have ever imagined." She raised her shoulders. "Maybe he can help our friend."

She touched a wall, reaching out. *"How are you, my partner?"*

Uwan replied in a beleaguered tone. *"I saw the victory through your eyes, but after those surges, I am weaker than ever."*

"And a healing bed for Bregent?"

The planet paused. *"I am sorry. I am recharging, but with that Terminus Stake, it takes so long."*

Geeja put a hand over her heart, crushed anew by what happened to Uwan. *"That is why we are fighting. To rid us of that monstrosity."*

Turning back to the others, she delivered the news. "The healing bed is out of the question. Uwan's power is severely depleted."

Roace's brow furrowed. "That's bad news on so many levels. I mean, I hate that Uwan's condition is so tenuous, but our immediate concern is that the one who did this to him in the first place will be here very soon, with more weaponry."

Geeja swallowed hard. "What, exactly, will we be facing?"

Elegarcia stepped closer, keeping her voice low. "I don't want to start a panic, but what we just went through is the equivalent of a hang nail compared to what's coming. A few decades ago, Djurga forced some of us to attend a demonstration of his newest toy."

Roace nodded, sounding glum. "I remember. We stood on the bridge of his command ship as his special guests. Some honor it was to watch him nearly obliterate an uninhabited planet."

"Obliterate?" Geeja's voice trembled.

"Yes." Elegarcia resumed the tutorial bringing Geeja up to speed on the Impercium's abilities to wreak havoc. "Imagine Lighters a thousand times more powerful than we just faced, firing down from space."

Geeja's mouth went dry. "I am not sure my imagination expands that far."

Roace chimed back in. "He has other weapons at his fingertips as well. Particle-wave torpedoes deliver massive explosions that can level mountains."

Geeja's eyes widened. "That is what we will face? With almost no magic?" She paced in a small circle, running a hand through her hair. Her wide eyes darted. "You knew this and still let me talk you into joining?"

Roace laughed. "Geeja, take some credit. You're quite convincing. We knew this escapade would likely end as a suicide mission, but you gave us our first taste of hope in centuries."

Elegarcia put an arm around Roace's waist. "When deprived of belief in a better tomorrow, a longshot plan is as tempting as the smell of fresh-from-the-oven barrowning cookies to a starving man."

That made sense, but didn't help their immediate problem. "How do we beat him?"

Pinched lips foreshadowed Roace's answer. "We probably don't, and you need to know that."

Geeja nodded. "For the first time, I understand what you have all tried to tell me." She stomped her foot. "What we need to do to have a sliver of a chance, is survive long enough for Raflo and Huanoc to destroy that unholy Terminus Stake." Her hands balled into fists. "The magic of our worlds is the only thing that can save us."

Elegarcia pointed. "And to survive I suggest getting everyone as deep into these famed tunnels as possible, starting now. We don't have much time."

A memory from the day Djurga attacked two millennia ago hit Geeja like a thunderbolt. She spoke the same words today with determination, not fear. "Our world provides refuge for the pure of heart." With orders given, every able-bodied person assisted the injured deeper, closer to the center of the planet.

Darkness pressed against the reaches of the torches carried by Sworn Warriors guarding the hodgepodge infirmary, which doubled as a base camp. The blackness seemed a living thing itself. Stepping forward, Geeja connected with Uwan. ***I am once again seeking sanctuary near your heart my friend, with survival in the balance.***

"Yes." Uwan paused. ***"We know that this ends today, one way or another."***

A tiny jolt of Uwan's pure energy hit Geeja, triggering a grim smile. ***"A fight to the death."***

Chapter Fifty-Six

Emperor Djurga stood on the bridge of the *Emperor's Will* as it slid into orbit around Uwan, locked in phase above the recent battle. He mumbled as he looked down on the brown, parched world. Black scorch marks added to the ugly pallet. "Back to this cursed planet to kill one woman. I would have destroyed this world long ago if not for my deal with Ka." His shout matched his black mood. "Scanda! Present battle plans to end this quickly. I wish to be away from this scab on the butt of my universe as soon as possible."

"Yes, Your Excellency." The general stood tall. "Our drones have already launched, scanning the area of the recent battle, searching for the rebel force's location."

"And?"

"So far, Your Excellency, they have eluded our sensors." The military man cleared his throat. "We believe they have gone underground."

Djurga had read the report of the day Geeja disappeared thousands of times, and knew what it meant. He growled. "Once again, she hides in those blasted tunnels!"

Scanda responded quickly. "Your Excellency, our drones are already exploring the nearest warren of tubes. We'll find her. She can't escape."

The emperor snarled. "I want her to know that I'm here and coming for her. Explode a particle-wave torpedo close enough to the entrance to shake the place like an earthquake."

"As you wish." Scanda gave the order. "Clear all soldiers and drones within fifty miles. Arm a torpedo, then send it to the provided coordinates with detonation at a thousand feet above the surface."

In short order, Lieutenant Arthold reported. "Our drones and men are outside the blast radius."

Clasping his hands behind his back, Scanda barked. "Fire!" A ball of light leaped from a weapons bay and in less than three seconds a spherical explosion detonated near the surface. It spread rapidly, soon reaching the top level of the planet's atmosphere. When the dust finally settled, the site of the lightly charred patch of ground from the battle less than an hour ago had been blistered into a circle ten thousand times larger. In addition, the terrain had changed, now featuring a bowl-shaped depression. "I think they know you are here, Your Excellency."

"Let's be certain." He sneered. "Do it again!"

Scanda snapped at the lieutenant. "You heard the emperor. Prepare a second round!"

The junior officer's hands flew over the controls. "Ready on your order, General."

"Fire!"

In a repeat from moments ago, a terrific blast rocked Uwan. A tiny smile emerged on the emperor's face. "Send the drones in to find her, and add some battle dogs, just for fun. This ends today!"

A sharp salute from Scanda met the emperor's request. "Yes, Your Excellency."

Live feeds were pulled from four different drones as they flew into the blast-widened entrance of the cavernous system. Lights illuminated the change in the strata of the tubes as the vehicles probed deeper, until one by one, the video cut off.

"What is the meaning of this?"

After swallowing hard, the general replied. "My best guess is that the composition of the crust of the planet is interfering with our signal. Don't worry about the drones, sir. They are programmed to retrace their path in the event of this kind of failure."

"Scanda! I could not care less about those drones. Killing that slippery goddess is all that matters!" He stabbed his index finger toward his military commander. "Prepare my shuttle! My honor guard and your two best battalions are going to the planet. I'll personally track her down!"

Scanda's eyes flared. "No, Your Excellency! It's too dangerous!"

In an instant Djurga grabbed him by the lapels of his black uniform. "Choose your next words very carefully, General! Are you under the misconception you have the authority to tell ME what I can and cannot do?"

Wide eyes went to the floor, away from the emperor's glare. Scanda answered in a whisper. "No, Your Excellency. Please forgive my outburst…I…I only care for your eternal safety."

"Good answer, General." The emperor released his humbled servant. "Because of your devotion, you may join me as we track and kill this irritating gnat."

Scanda nodded, then cast a tentative peek toward his master. "Thank you, Your Excellency."

Djurga stared with cold eyes. "I have learned that if one wants a job done right, do it yourself. This is what I should have done two millennia ago."

**

Geeja scrambled to her feet for a second time as dust falling from the ceiling twinkled in the torchlight illuminating this deep section of Uwan's tunnels and caves. "That blast seemed closer than the last one!"

"Particle-wave torpedoes." Roace extended his hand to Elegarcia. "I like seeing them explode from the safety of a spaceship a lot better than being their target."

Standing, Elegarcia stated the obvious. "We're not safe here. We must go deeper."

Nodding, Geeja reached out to Uwan. ***"Please, show me the way."*** A soft trail of blue light only she could see appeared. She called out. "Everyone. Follow me."

Those who weren't injured aided those who were, moving further into the bowels of the planet. A half-hour ago, this same group's spirits soared as high as the stars. Now, on the run and in complete darkness, the emperor's counterattack shook their confidence – both literally and figuratively.

They hadn't walked long when they entered a vaulted cavern. When the final stragglers caught up, Geeja addressed them, her voice echoing. "Uwan tells me this is the deepest point in this section of the system. We make our final stand here."

The wounded now comfortable, Geeja huddled with Roace and Elegarcia. "We haven't been bombed in a while. What do you think that means?"

Before either could answer, Lighter fire sounded in the distance. Geeja flinched. "Never mind."

Jacastra shouted orders to her Sworn Warriors. "Take forward positions behind any cover you can find!"

Women in uniforms dashed toward an advancing force with their newly obtained weapons.

With eyes closed, Geeja opened to Uwan. ***"Djurga brings the fight to us. Ready or not, we will need all the power you can give."***

"It is not much…but you may have all."

"Thank you…for everything." Her eyes welled, but she wiped away the tears. ***"Together to the end, my friend."***

Uwan replied with resolve. ***"To the end."***

Chapter Fifty-Seven

Djurga strode behind armored troopers, black cape flowing in the breeze of his determined steps. He mumbled as he walked the irregular floor of this section of tunnels. "I hate this place more every time I visit."

General Scanda touched his earpiece. "The advance team located them, Your Excellency. We strike on your order."

The emperor gave his command in a slow snarl. "Kill them all."

Scanda translated the sentiment into military language. "Engage, and take no prisoners."

Not far ahead a barrage of shoulder cannon and Lighter fire erupted, accompanied by the growls of robotic battle dogs. The noise and light of ferocious warfare echoed from the stone walls, illuminating the darkened space like noon on Emblaka. Emperor Djurga's chest swelled at the sight and sound of the destruction wrought by his technology. He spoke to Scanda above the din. "This is why I didn't stay aboard the *Emperor's Will*."

Scanda's mouth opened for a moment, then closed, as if reconsidering what he should say. Seconds later, he spoke simply. "I understand."

**

More Lighter fire and explosions than Geeja had ever seen filled the cavernous space. Her jaw momentarily dropped. "Wow…"

Standing beside her in the shadow of a natural partial wall, Roace explained. "It's called shock and terror. The Impercium wants to do as much damage as possible in a way that also stirs fear."

Geeja nodded. "Then we need to respond." Still protected, she opened herself to Uwan's power, and the trickle into her body did not surprise her. Anger at the situation tinged her sadness, like black and blue paint mixed on a canvas. *"I am so sorry, Uwan."*

Dread coated Uwan's thoughts. *"We fight together, to the end."*

Raising her hands, Geeja released a ball of flame that shot toward the line of Impercium soldiers, but instead of consuming them, it diverted toward the ground. She stepped back. "What happened?"

Elegarcia stammered. "This is tech I've never seen."

Roace raised his voice, over the roar of battle. "They have shields!"

Brave Sworn Warriors returned fire, but they faced a much larger enemy with superior weaponry. The sheer volume of blasts overwhelmed everyone. War cries matched the screams of pain from injured or dying women. Geeja had seen battle and death, and once again her stomach churned, knowing the superiority of Djurga's forces. She didn't want to see a repeat of the slaughter of her soldiers like the night two thousand years ago when his troops overpowered her.

She weighed her options. *Surrender? No. Djurga will not accept it.* More dedicated women fell and the impending massacre ripped at her soul. One of her vows came to mind. *You will always do what is best for your planet, not yourself.*

Geeja knew what needed to be done. She turned to Roace and Elegarcia. "You must lead the Sworn Warriors out of these tunnels another way; back to the surface away from these forces. I will face Djurga's worst alone."

"No!" Roace stomped a foot. "We're in this together, remember? That's what you told us."

"My people are being massacred! We swore to protect our citizens." She pleaded as she presented a desperate case. "Maybe Raflo and Huanoc really can destroy that Terminus Stake. If they do, we need gods to fight back. It will not do any good if we are all dead." Taut jaws and narrowed eyes met her stare.

After a long few seconds, Elegarcia nodded. "It's a bad option, but better than others."

Geeja gave them a quick hug. "Thank you for joining the fight."

Roace kissed both of her cheeks. "Thank you for saving my life."

With goodbyes finished, Geeja yelled at the top of her voice. "Fall back. Follow Roace and Elegarcia to the surface."

One by one, the Sworn Warriors raced away from the front line. Several more were struck down, but the majority still living made it into an adjoining tube, different from those that brought them so far down in that it featured a gradual upward slant. Jacastra ran to Geeja's side. "I'll face them with you."

With precious seconds ticking, Geeja stared fiercely. "Our people need you. Obey me for the good of Uwan." She pointed to their retreating fighters. "Go!"

Jacastra objected. "Goddess! I—"

Geeja cut her off. "Do as I say!"

That broke the spell as Jacastra bowed. "Yes, Goddess."

Geeja glared, seeing Jacastra leaning away but not yet taking a step.

When a blast struck inches away, Geeja ordered her again. "Go!"

The woman raced away, but not before turning around one more time.

Geeja pointed, keeping Jacastra on course, and soon she ran inside the tunnel with the others.

Though everyone else fled, Geeja knew she didn't stand alone behind the partial wall. *"Okay, Uwan. Light a path that Roace and Elegarcia can see, then it is just you and me. If we cannot burn them, let us see if we can drop a rock on them."* She pointed to a section of roof above fast advancing Impercium soldiers. *"There."*

The planet rumbled, but nothing like the particle-wave torpedoes that rocked the world minutes ago. The whole roof didn't collapse, but a big chunk did fall, instantly smashing a hundred or so troopers. *"Thank you Uwan."* Their efforts resulted in a narrowed tunnel, forcing the troops that followed to advance through a tight gap. *"Perhaps that disrupted their invisible protection."* Geeja reached for Uwan's power again, but instead of a flood, barely a dribble flowed in. *"We fight together with all we have until we can fight no more."* With that, she released the tiny amount of energy.

A small fireball sprang from her outstretched hand, but instead of seeing the flame diverted, it consumed twenty or so black-clad enemies, further clogging the narrowed way forward. She gave a wicked smile. *"Maybe it is not shock and terror, but it is giving our people more time to escape."*

The respite proved short as the next wave of Impercium troopers surged, leveling blast after blast toward her. For the first time, she caught sight of new enemies. Marching in lock step, machines formed in the shape of huge dogs advanced in front of a seemingly endless flow of soldiers. *What in the name of the Holy Twelve?* She shook her head. *Just another evil technology to defeat.*

She connected. **"Uwan, they are too strong. We must extend the battle. Time for a tactical retreat. Show me the way to the tightest nearby tunnels."** Firing a Lighter as she ran, she hit one of the mechanical dogs. Its red eyes went dark without a groan. *No soul.* Continuing her sprint in an uneven zigzag pattern, Geeja managed to make it from the cavern into a much smaller tube. It pleased her to make Djurga's forces pay, even if just a little. **"If we cannot beat them, we will at least take as many out as we can."**

**

A cocky grin spread across Emperor Djurga's face as he ignored his own dead troops and charred weapons of war. "Did you see how little power she harnessed! We're on the cusp of killing her!"

Scanda stared toward burned bodies as he spoke obliquely. "Yes, Your Excellency. She only felled a *handful* of our troops."

"Push forward. Press our advantage!"

The general nodded. "Absolutely. We have the initiative." His voice lowered, swathed in concern. "Great Leader, would you again consider deploying your personal protection bubble?"

"No!" Djurga leveled a hard gaze. "While that new tech protects, it also distorts what I see. I want the vision of her death branded in my memory in its purest form."

Pushing through the narrow gap and over the soldiers just obliterated, the emperor caught sight of his prey. "There she is! There's a bonus and promotion for whoever ends her miserable life!" As the tunnel width decreased, the number of troops at the tip of the spear lessened, and it stretched out the distance between Djurga and the action. He nudged Scanda. "Get me closer to the front. I must be there when she takes her last breath."

Scanda called to troops between them and the goddess. "Clear the way for our emperor!"

Djurga raced through the opening until he stood only three layers from the lead soldiers. His pulse raced, finally on the threshold of revenge. He shouted. "I can taste victory!"

**

Popping another pain killer as he settled into the copilot seat, Raflo addressed Huanoc. "I'm glad we finally heard back from those gods. I worried about them."

"Yes. They couldn't receive transmissions while so deep underground. They are almost to the surface and said it's time to do what we came to do."

Raflo quirked a brow. "What do you think happens when we blow that ugly spike? Will it really change anything?"

Tapping a screen to restore gravity, Huanoc once again spoke in full sentences. "In theory this should destroy the Terminus Stake, but it has never been attempted." He turned to Raflo. "When we throw the switch, nothing might happen, or we might witness a chain reaction that explodes the planet. It could be anything in between. Who knows?"

That didn't ease his nerves, but the pain medication started to kick in. "I guess our fate will be sealed then."

Huanoc chuckled. "That happened when we picked up a strange woman on the side of the road."

Raflo nodded. "Hmm." He looked down at his bandaged hand, knowing time ticked down for his personal health as well as everything else. "Let's blast that cursed thing."

A large blue finger pushed the toggle forward. Although at a distance they calculated to be safe, a huge ball of brilliant orange lit space.

Raflo's throat tightened. "Shields up, right?"

"Uh huh!" Even as he answered in the affirmative, Huanoc engaged thrusters sending them backwards. "But a little further away wouldn't hurt."

As they retreated, a tight blue flame blazed from the disintegrating top of the stake, then the outer metallic skin of the monstrosity exploded. A chain reaction raced down the length of the massive spike, blasting the outer casing away in hulking sheets. With the structural integrity compromised, the edifice slowly collapsed on itself. It looked like a huge invisible hand shoved it from the top toward the surface.

Raflo gulped. "I don't know what I thought would happen, but this is…" He grasped for words to describe his reaction, but failed to find them.

When the entire mass of the imploding stake impacted the ground an enormous mushroom shaped cloud formed, quickly reaching the top of the atmosphere. Huanoc pointed. "In the name of the Holy…"

A shock wave hit the *Phantom Star*, shaking every inch of the protected ship, shoving them farther into space. When the shuddering subsided, Raflo let out a laugh. "Guess we can take the 'maybe nothing happens' option off the table."

Huanoc smiled so big his massive mouthful of perfect white teeth took on a glow of their own. "That certainly wasn't nothing!"

Chapter Fifty-Eight

Even with Uwan's faint light showing her the path, the uneven surfaces of the tunnels made running treacherous. Geeja stumbled, gashing a knee on jagged rock. She muffled her painful reaction. "Oww!" From behind, she heard a voice she knew. For her, she heard it most recently six weeks ago at the very last conclave of the Holy Twelve. But in reality, it had been two millennia.

"Faster! She can't be much further ahead!"

"Djurga." She whispered the name as bitter as unripe kralp, realizing he spoke the truth. Only a few feet separated them as she scrambled to her feet, running again.

A trooper shouted, then fired, just missing her. "There she is!"

"Give me a Lighter!" The emperor's words echoed in the narrowing tube. "I want to kill her myself!"

Dodging as she sprinted, bolts of red light zinged past her. One blazed by so close she felt heat on her cheek. *"Help me, Uwan!"*

The planet replied in panic. *"I have nothing left!"*

Geeja fell again, landing chin first on the rough stone. "Oh!" Light fell on her, and she prepared for the worst. *"Looks like this is the*

end for me, my friend. Another will take my place." She sensed the heartbreak in Uwan's response.

"NO!!!"

Djurga shouted. "Hold your fire! She's mine!"

Standing, Geeja rubbed her scraped chin. *I will meet my destiny head on.* She turned to face her nemesis. *It has been a good life.*

Grinning, Djurga raced forward with a Lighter to his shoulder, with growling battle dogs loping in a mechanical fashion on each side. His voice rose, like an excited schoolboy. "You have no idea how important this day is to me."

Laughter sprang forth. "I *do* have an idea." She laughed again. "I am glad I could haunt your dreams for so long."

"You arrogant femich!" He fired a shot and the bolt zipped beside her head, then exploded into the rock behind.

Djurga lowered the weapon, then cackled. His words turned cold, once again in control of his emotions. "I should have expected this attitude, but things have changed in your absence. Today, I set the terms. The days of gods and magic are long gone." His tone darkened. "I alone rule this universe and you will bow to me."

She shook her head. "Look, child of Emblaka. We both know what is about to happen. You will not humiliate me before my execution. Defiance to the end is my final gift to your chemically-tarnished rotten soul."

Djurga's cheeks flamed. "No! My last vision of you will be splatters of blood, flesh and bone. This is the final battle between technology and magic. I have won!" The emperor took a deep breath as he raised his weapon–then everything changed.

Uwan shook hard, as on the day Djurga skewered him with that cursed Terminus Stake. Everyone fell as the shaking continued unabated for what seemed an eternity.

Geeja tried repeatedly to get to her feet, but got knocked down again and again. Slabs fell from the ceiling around her as she reached out in shock. *"Uwan! What is happening?"*

"Power!" He sounded overwhelmed and excited. *"Wild surges of magnificent, strange power!"*

Reaching for a boulder, Geeja stood, thinking first of her people and fellow gods. *"Show me the way to the others. Raflo and Huanoc must have destroyed the Terminus Stake!"*

Uwan responded, but not as she expected. The thin blue line he always projected for her jittered from side to side. It also changed colors from his normal blue to green, orange then back to blue in rapid strobe flashes. *"Oh my."* She ran, knowing that her enemies would be gaining their balance as well.

Uwan's lit path went around a sharp corner, and though it cost her a few seconds, she turned and shouted toward Djurga, who struggled to stand. "Magic isn't dead yet!" Lighter shots landed close as she raced with new vigor.

**

As the planet shook, Roace whooped as he sat on the ground. "Those smugglers did it!" His joy proved short lived as Bregent groaned, sounding barely alive.

Bregent's words were low and raspy. "What's happening?"

Chella wiped his brow. "Sorry we dropped you." As the shaking subsided, she smiled at her husband. "Shugg's plan is working!"

The Goddess Awakens

One by one, the ragtag band of humbled gods, smugglers and Sworn Warriors got to their feet. Jacastra spoke loudly. "That's good news, but there's still an army who wants to kill us. Let's move!"

The lit path changed colors like a cycling strobe. Elegarcia pointed. "I don't know what's happening, but something is!"

Ahead, the first hint of outside light shone in dusty shafts and a feminine figure stood at the top. A bright voice called out. "You're still alive!"

Elegarcia answered. "Talla! *You're* still alive!"

The beleaguered group rushed into the grimy sunlight of Uwan, coughing in the harsh atmosphere. Talla's gaze turned skyward. "Blowing up the Terminus Stake sent tons of contaminated particles into the air. Cover your nose and mouth until I get you to my compound."

Roace tugged on his shirt. "How did you know we would be here?"

"A lit line appeared on the ground, and I followed it. I assume it's Uwan?"

"Yeah." Roace then glanced toward Bregent. "Our friend is in bad shape, and we need to get him home before he dies." He stared hard. "We *have* to get him there in time for a transference."

"Follow me." She turned to run, then stopped sharply. "Where's *our* goddess?"

Elegarcia piped in. "She used herself as bait to give the rest of us this chance for escape."

Jacastra wrapped an arm around Talla. "She ordered us to do this. We had no choice."

"Alright." She spoke haltingly. "We'll get everyone who needs to go onboard the *Curious Lady*, but I'm not taking anyone anywhere until we hear from Geeja. Got it?"

"Agreed." Roace, Elegarcia and even the injured Bregent, spoke in unison.

Chapter Fifty-Nine

Geeja's thinking cleared as she ran with renewed strength, sensing an added bounce from Uwan with each stride. *I want to see my friends, but I cannot lead this army to them.* Hints of acrid air mixed with the stale tunnel oxygen. From her awakening days ago, she knew the polluted surface must be nearby. *One way or another, this stops here.*

Catching her breath in yet another cavernous space, she connected with the planet. *"How are you?"*

"Umm…powerfully dazed. Yes…those are the closest words."

Kneeling behind a boulder, Geeja smiled broadly. *"Power is good. Show me. Fill me."*

"Yes… I must…we must. But, please know the energy is raw and my control is…lacking."

"Good." Her eyes widened, and her smile reflected the crazed thoughts bouncing around in her brain. *"I think raw and out of control is exactly what we need."*

Geeja had previously communed with the Holy Twelve planets, and now also with Kaliega and Torgose. As she opened herself to this new experience, it resembled none of those. The tingling sensation entering her body didn't feel linear and smooth, but rather violent and swirling, with sharp edges. An image of a whirlwind full of nails came to mind. She swallowed hard as spiked power filled every cell. ***"You chose the correct words, Uwan."***

Bright lights from Djurga's advancing troops swung back and forth as they searched for her.

Geeja stood, glowing, as every shade of the color wheel alternated in splotches over her skin. "Over here!"

One of Djurga's soldiers yelled. "Found her!"

She had gone from hiding behind a huge rock, to filling the cavern with swirling hues of multi-colored luminescence. Geeja barely had time to raise her hands to aim as energy that seemed to have a mind of its own leaped with blinding speed. In the blink of an eye hundreds of Djurga's forces were vaporized, leaving only tiny whiffs of smoke.

The burst left Geeja's head spinning and vision blurred. Breathing in, she couldn't smell even a hint of the stench of burned flesh filled the space. She recalled the strange sensation from earlier, when she filled herself past any previous magic level. Steadier now, her grin morphed from crazed to bewildered. She mumbled to her partner. ***"Power might not be a strong enough word."*** Gathering herself, Geeja spoke to the planet. ***"How's your recharge cycle now?"***

"Are you ready for an even bigger surge?"

"Oh, Uwan! This is so different…but so good!"

**

Emperor Djurga gasped as a quarter of his remaining forces disappeared instantly. "How?"

Scanda reacted differently. "Your Excellency, we must deploy your shield!"

"Yes." Taking a step back, Djurga concurred, still unsure what he had just witnessed. "That would be the prudent thing to do."

The general strapped the backpack unit that powered the new tech onto his ruler. "This should protect you from anything."

Nodding, Djurga pushed the button on his sleeve mounted controller. While safe, the shimmering force field distorted his vision and required he give up his Lighter. *Small sacrifices to achieve the greater goal.* He shouted orders to his remaining troops. "Find her! Kill her!"

A new front line formed and the goddess once again announced herself, taunting them and their leader. "Is everyone back for more as the great man hides behind his technology?"

Thousands of rounds of Lighter fire aimed at her were met with another energy surge. Those who weren't immediately vaporized, dropped their weapons, using their hands and arms to shade their eyes in the luminosity. Panicked screams of terror from the living signaled retreat.

Djurga raged. "No! Attack again! Don't you understand? We must kill her!"

Geeja grinned as the herd mentality of survival took firm root. The troopers flowed in a stampede past the emperor and his general.

Scanda shouted. "We must run for our lives!"

Djurga stood frozen in place. Moments ago, he stood on the verge of his centuries-old goal of killing her. Now, she hunted *him* as his army retreated in haste.

He stammered. "This isn't happening!"

Flailing his arms, Scanda protested. "Your Excellency! We must go! Now!"

The emperor turned slowly as his senses overrode his disbelief. In a flash of recognition, the reality of the situation crystalized. "Run!"

**

"Uwan! The intensity thrills me." Geeja shook her spinning head, catching a glimpse of her formerly blond tresses. Her jaw dropped as she held out a lock. *"What we are doing is changing me. My hair is white!"*

"But it is working, is it not?" Two millennia of perpetual punishment seemed replaced with the power to seek vengeance on the one who orchestrated his pain. *"Can we end this?"*

With clearing vision, Geeja saw the final remnants of the Impercium soldiers fleeing, with two finely dressed officers bringing up the rear. *"Yes, Uwan. I believe we can."*

Geeja regained more clarity of thought with each stride forward. *"Can you send a sustained flow of this new energy through me?"*

Uwan sounded unsure. *"I do not know…and what about risks? You said what we are doing is changing you."*

She increased her speed in pursuit. *"I do not care. Righting the wrong that has been wrought on you is way past due."*

"Perhaps a compromise? One more surge, then we reassess? I cannot lose you again."

"Fair enough." Having closed the gap, she stopped. Licking her lips, she gave a satisfyingly low growl. *"Fill me."*

Knowing what to expect this cycle, Geeja reveled in the surging mixture of Uwan's familiar energy blending with the compressed magic from Torgose. The combination reminded her of a caged chikgra that suddenly knew it had the power to destroy the bars that kept it away from those who had somehow captured her. **"Righteous revenge will be ours."**

The soldier running beside Djurga yelled as he placed himself between the emperor and Geeja. "I'll shield you!"

When she believed she could hold it no more, she released. Although seeing it happen twice before, she gasped as every being in the path of her wrath, save one, disappeared in a poof of odorless vapor. Her hands went to her knees as she sucked in a great breath. This magical jolt registered as the most massive yet.

After a couple of deep inhales she stood, eyes barely focusing. *There he is!* Through double vision, she called out the name of the lone survivor. "Djurga!"

The man, surrounded by shimmering air, turned sneering. "You've done your best and I'm still alive!" He laughed. "When will you learn that technology is stronger than magic? I'm going to walk out of here and destroy this sorry excuse of a world from space, once and for all!"

With wide eyes and a crazed grin, Geeja took a couple of wobbly steps forward. "My best? You think this is all Uwan and I can do?"

He chuckled. "I'm safe and breathing easy, while you look like squished bleebles." He turned his back, then walked away while flicking three fingers in the air, a pornographic insult in every language in the known universe. He yelled. "The days of magic are over, and so are yours!"

Geeja released a primal scream, then spoke to Uwan. **"Time for that sustained flow."**

The surge of energy revived Geeja as she released it. She had given up trying to control it and now simply aimed in the general direction of her mortal enemy. The magical stream amazed her as it blackened the walls of the tunnel to the point of melting, but it seemed to have no effect on her opponent as Djurga kept walking. She shook her head. ***"More Uwan!"***

Her body shook under the strain of being a conduit of such power. "Die, you degenerate scum!" Her teeth chattered and her frame wobbled, as if her bones would pull apart. The stench of molten rock filled her nostrils. Sensing she neared the edge of exploding, she collapsed in a heap, ending the surge.

Djurga turned around, once again laughing. "You pathetic excuse for a god. You're just a woman who can do extravagant party tricks." He took a step toward her, his face scrunched and angry. "You're just a plain, nearly ordinary being, and I will kill you this very day."

Hearing his words triggered a thought. She laughed. "And you're just a man hiding behind fancy technology. You have no real power of your own, just machines that do mindless tasks, giving you the illusion of control."

Geeja's sarcastic laugh turned maniacal, like that of a demented prophet finally seeing the whole truth. "All those years ago it was *my* arrogance that led to my downfall. It was *my* conceit that magic was always more powerful than technology that gave rise to *my* blind spot." She spat on the ground, then yelled like a street corner lunatic. "Today, it is *your* arrogance about the superiority of tech that is yours."

Delirious giggling momentarily spilled past her lips as she pointed. "For example, that shimmering field protecting you is truly amazing and has withstood tremendous power, but it is soulless, and like every other machine, has limitations."

Djurga shifted his weight as the condescending grin on his face faded.

Still feeling unsteady and changed from her and Uwan's efforts, she brushed dust from her clothes. Drawing in lungs full of scorched, tainted air helped clear her head. She raised her scraped chin. "Let us consider one particular limit on that tech. How much oxygen do you estimate your precious bubble holds?"

His brow furrowed. "Why does it matter?" He waved her away. "I'm leaving. Say your goodbyes to your washed-up friends in your final minutes of life. I'm going to obliterate this entire cesspool of a world."

Eyeing him as he walked away, Geeja communed with Uwan. *"He buried a stake in you that sucked your very life force. How would you like to drop a boulder on him?"*

"YES! PLEASE!"

"I want a final word, then I will point to the spot."

"Hey, Djurga."

He turned toward her once more, then spoke with the dismissive tone of a school master to a chastened student. "What? And make it quick, your desperation is annoying. I have a star cruiser awaiting my return."

Geeja swung her shoulders playfully, answering with a lilt in her voice. "In your very long life, did you ever wonder where you would be entombed?"

He sighed. "Why do you speak in riddles? I have no idea what you're talking about." He started to turn away, but her laughter stopped him.

"This is the most literal thing I have ever said, because your final resting place is here…on this planet…in this spot." She cackled again. "We will not even erect a marker or place a stone. You will die in anonymity on the planet you despise, Great Emperor Djurga."

Djurga's eyes widened and he gasped. He spun and ran. "NO!!"

Geeja's shouts chased after him like a Sunsasole cat racing to bring down its prey. "I am guessing an hour of oxygen, but I hope it is more. For all the damage you have done, you deserve to suffer for as long as possible!" She pointed as her eyes went to the top of this section of the cave system. *"There Uwan! Bring the entire mountain down on him!"* The crush of millions of tons of rock falling sounded like crashing surf amplified to infinity.

Squinting to see and straining to hear, a crazed grin formed as Geeja witnessed the final second of Djurga's freedom. A massive boulder smashed him in mid-stride without destroying the bubble. But thousands more piled atop and all around him.

Geeja stood tall as a whoosh of displaced air rushed past carrying bits of dust and tiny rocks. The stinging augmented her senses and the pain felt right. She closed her eyes, absorbing the magnitude of what happened. Her feelings were a spectrum of conflicting emotions. From exhilaration at Djurga's defeat, to sorrow for all the damage he had done to hers and so many other worlds, and so much more in between. When all went silent, she reached out to her partner. *"Uwan, I think we should commemorate this as Liberation Day, until the end of time. What do you think?"*

"Yes. Forever."

Chapter Sixty

The adrenaline rush of channeling so much power and burying Djurga faded quickly. Every square inch of Geeja's body ached, but she knew she wouldn't feel better until she confirmed his death. *"Uwan, what can you tell me about the emperor? Is he still alive?"*

"The muffled screams have stopped, and his heart rate has slowed."

"It will not be long...but I am glad he has time to consider his mortality." Geeja smiled hearing the news, but incredible tiredness piled atop her pommeled state. She blinked heavily twice, then decided to sit rather than fall over. *"Uwan, weariness has tackled me. Wake me when there is news."* Much remained to be done, but her eyes closed as if having a will of their own. Sleep covered her like a woolen blanket.

**

Geeja sprang awake from a deep dream where Djurga rose from his grave like some specter. "No! It cannot be!"

"You are safe." The old planet radiated warmth and joy when he spoke again. *"It is done. Emperor Djurga is dead!"*

"Are you certain?"

"No breathing, no heartbeat. That is dead on any world."

As if shocked by a river eel, Geeja leaped up. ***"Thank the Twelve Holy Worlds!"*** Simply saying the phrase sent her mind to her friends. ***"Uwan, connect me with the other gods on the surface."***

Elegarcia was first to respond. ***"Geeja! You're alive!"***

"Yes, and I have even better news!" She paused for a moment, still having a hard time believing what she was about to say. ***"Djurga is DEAD!"***

Roace let out a telepathic, ***"Whoop!"***

Elegarcia squealed.

Then Roace questioned. ***"Are you sure?"***

Geeja ran a hand through hair that had been turned snow-white by the experience. ***"He is buried under a mountain with no pulse or respiration. That is the definition of dead."***

Elegarcia's voice crept up a key change. ***"We did it!"***

Geeja released a sharp breath, hoping to clear some spider webs. ***"By the by, what is happening with Raflo and Huanoc? How are they? How are you all?"***

Elegarcia's high pitch of moments ago dropped to its normal range. ***"Raf has a smashed hand that needs immediate attention and there's a lot of banged up people with us."***

"And Bregent? Tell me he is doing better."

The tiny woman hesitated. ***"You need to get to us soon. I think a transference is his only hope, and these Sworn Warriors won't leave unless you're here."***

"Where is here?"

"Talla's compound. She has the Curious Lady *ready and waiting.*"

Geeja's eyes welled. **"So many have helped our cause. I will be there as quickly as I can."**

As if knowing her next request, Uwan lit a path for her.

Geeja set out at the fastest jog she could muster, helped along by bursts of energy from Uwan with each footfall. *What I would not give for a dragon.* A contemporary thought popped into her musings. *Or even a speeder.* Neither magically appeared, so she ran and ran with Uwan's assistance, following his unfailing line. Rounding a corner, she winced at a pain in her side, finally spying her destination.

A Sworn Warrior on perimeter duty spotted her, but hesitated. "Halt! Who goes there!"

Geeja blinked. *Right. My hair...and who knows what else.* She called out in her most authoritative voice. "It is I, your goddess."

The soldier raised a Lighter. "Stop. Your identity must be confirmed."

Without breaking stride, Geeja called on Uwan. **"How about an extra boost through the air?"**

Uwan obliged, and Geeja sailed well over the woman's head, then hovered in mid-air, something she had never done before.

"Uwan! We have the power to hover!"

The warrior gasped, then called out. "Our goddess is here! Long live the Geeja!"

Geeja noted wide-eyed stares as she floated down, landing in the center of the compound near the ship. "I know, I know. I look different, and I will explain." She took in a quick gulp of stinging dirty air. "We must help those who aided in our success. We leave now."

Elegarcia shouted from the top of the ramp. "We're ready. Bregent has taken a turn for the worse!"

"I will return soon, Uwan. I must help save those who have risked so much for us."

"Go."

A dozen Sworn Warriors rushed behind Geeja as she raced onboard the ship.

As the ramp closed, Talla shouted above the whir of the ship's initiation sequence. "Strap in! We're launching hot!"

True to her word, the *Curious Lady* exited the atmosphere in seconds. G-forces pushed Geeja down in her seat, then moments later the acceleration to quantum speed pressed on her chest like being sat on by a gonswa swamp beast.

Once the vessel reached its cruising speed Talla stepped back into the cargo area doubling as people hauler. She cocked an eye toward Geeja. "What's everyone's status?"

Unbuckling, Geeja moved toward Bregent. "First things first. How are you?"

The injured god gave a gritted grin. "I hope I don't look as bad as you."

She laughed, placing a hand on his chest. "I guess you have heard the news? Djurga's dead."

Bregent coughed, then managed a broken smile. "How could I ever have doubted you?"

Geeja's emotions had been on an out-of-control magic-fueled ride and now tears burst forth. "We could not have done it without you." She laid her head on his chest and wept. "I made a promise to both you and Politar. We must get you back in time."

Chella looked on with Elegarcia and Roace. "Bregent needs to save his strength. Come with me and let him rest."

Doing as instructed, they followed Chella.

Geeja gave a tight stare when they were out of Bregent's earshot. "Tell me straight. How is he?"

A pessimistic frown met their gaze. "It's six hours to Politar and he'll be dead by then. There's nothing I can do."

Geeja's knees buckled as she uttered a single feeble word. "No…"

Roace caught her before she hit the ground. "I've got you." He sat her down on a chair bolted to a wall. "Catch your breath, okay?"

Between sobs, Geeja gasped. When certain she wouldn't pass out, her desperate gaze searched theirs. "We cannot let him die. We need ideas."

Elegarcia put a hand on Geeja's shoulder. "We thought about doing a transference on Uwan with someone, but even we could feel how unstable his magic is. It's a delicate enough process under the best of circumstances." Her gaze went to Roace. "Besides, we didn't have a host."

Geeja bowed as her body trembled. "You are right, of course, about Uwan." She ran a hand over her stark white hair. "In time, I believe his magic will stabilize, but…"

From the rear of the ship, Bregent coughed.

Hearing his distress, Geeja stiffened. An idea exploded as she shot a wild glance toward Chella. "Can he survive two hours?"

Chella looked at Bregent. "Maybe? It's hard to say."

Geeja gave an order to Talla. "Get us to Kaliega in under two hours and tell Raf and Huanoc to meet us there immediately. It is Bregent's only chance." She swallowed hard, knowing if her plan failed, she might lose two friends. "And tell Raf that he and I will be fulfilling the promise we made the night Bregent and Politar saved his life."

Chapter Sixty-One

Geeja raced down the ramp of the *Curious Lady* as soon as it landed on Kaliega in the clearing beside the park. Sworn Warriors formed a perimeter around her as she fell to her knees in the soft grass. *"Zimo, Kalli! It is Geeja! I come asking for help!"*

Kalli's feminine voice stretched up a register. *"I'm here! What's wrong?"*

"Please send Zimo as fast as you can. Friends need your help. Only you two can save them."

Zimo answered. *"I'm on my way. Kalli says you are in the clearing beside the park where we met."*

"Yes. Hurry!"

As Roace carried Bregent down the ramp of the *Curious Lady*, the *Phantom Star* touched down beside them.

Once on the ground, Raflo winced with each step, holding his injured hand tight against his chest. "We got here as fast as possible." He surveyed the scene, moving closer to Geeja, his brow furrowed. "What happened to you?"

"It is a long story that I promise to tell you, but first we need your help."

"Your message sounded cryptic." Raflo's eyes went to the sweating, pale face of Bregent, and his next words wobbled. "But seeing Bregent in that condition, I think I've figured it out."

Huanoc ran up. "Djurga's dead! We really did it!"

Geeja answered in a matter-of-fact tone, not matching Huanoc's enthusiasm. "Yes. We all did our part and he is dead." She glanced toward Bregent. "But others paid a price. Hundreds, perhaps thousands of Sworn Warriors were slain, and Bregent will be gone as well without a tremendous sacrifice."

Huanoc's jaw dropped. Raflo's teeth gritted as his lips pinched tight. Raflo shot a stare toward the injured god. "He's goin' to die unless he does one of those transference things, like you did to take your current body. Right?"

Geeja nodded as Huanoc processed what had been said.

The big man sucked in a great breath, grasping the entirety of the situation. "You want Raf to donate his body to Bregent!"

"No." Geeja stopped herself. "Well, sort of. Remember when I told you how it worked? Raflo's self, his being, will not disappear. It will simply be added to all the lives that Bregent has experienced. He will still be there."

Raflo paled, looking like he might throw up. "There will be one drop of me in a sea of Bregent. That's what will happen, right?"

Geeja didn't sugar coat it, but did set the record straight. "Yes, but that is not all. You will instantly share thousands of years of experiences, as if you had lived them yourself. And with luck you can perhaps have eternal life. It is a union, not a one-sided deal."

He swallowed hard. "It's still my choice, right?"

"Of course." Geeja placed a hand on his shoulder. "It is your decision, but remember, if not for Bregent's and Politar's actions you would be dead." She let that sink in for a moment. "And in return for saving your life, you and I both swore a vow to return that favor."

The blood drained from Raflo's face as he glanced toward Bregent. "That's a lot."

Huanoc added his agreement in a gauzy bass voice. "Hmm. Deep."

Sweat glistened on Raflo's forehead. "I don't feel so good. I need a moment."

"Of course." Geeja motioned to an especially green patch of grass. "Please, sit. Collect your thoughts. We will need Zimo here before anything can happen."

Alone, Geeja watched as Raflo and Huanoc settled in hushed conversation, then she rubbed her temples. She headed toward Bregent to work on the other side of this equation. *It is going to be an issue for him to accept a foreign host.* She shook her head. "Djurga…"

Geeja approached as Chella called out. "He's been asking for you."

She ran the final few steps, kneeling beside the gravely injured man. "Hang in there. I have a plan."

Bregent managed a weak laugh. "You have a plan? Isn't that how I ended up in this condition?"

"Fair point." She smiled, then put a hand on his shoulder. "But we did kill Djurga and destroy the Terminus Stake driven into Uwan. We will do the same for Politar."

He nodded, gasping for air. "I'll die content in the knowledge that my world will finally be free."

She rubbed a thumb against her index finger. "Like I said, I have a plan."

"You're serious? I thought you were just comforting a dying man."

Geeja moved close to look him in the eye. "I am serious, but it will be controversial and dangerous."

Again, he laughed, but softer, and with even less breath. "Isn't that the same thing you told me last time?" He groaned as if struck by another Lighter bolt. "Let's hear this big idea."

"Do you remember when we reconnected? When you and Politar saved Raflo's life?"

"Uh, yeah?" His brow wrinkled.

"Well, that night Raf and I acknowledged that we owed a debt to you both." Geeja's eyes traced the lines of his brow, furrowing deeper with each passing moment. Confusion clouded his gaze, a lost look crossing his face as understanding slipped further from his grasp. She squeezed his shoulder again. "I propose we fulfill our obligation today." Her eyes shot across the grassy area toward Raflo and Huanoc. "This is not Politar, and Raflo is not Politarian, but Kaliega is now a stable magical world. With her power we can conduct a transference. Raflo can save your life as your new vessel."

Bregent's body stiffened and his head jerked. "Are you insane? Taking the form of an off-worlder is wrong on so many levels." He shook his head. "No. This is a holy event between a planet and their partner. Politar would never accept me in that body, especially if she had no part in the ceremony."

Geeja's voice lowered as her stare bore into him like a drammel's single horn. "Let me lay out the reality of your situation, and your options. This form you currently inhabit will expire in a few minutes, that is a stone-cold fact. At that moment, you will be deserting Politar, passing up an opportunity to continue your very long life together. Of course, she will be left with the awful task of mourning your loss while beginning again with a new god with no experience. Long ago, you swore an oath to do what is best for your world. Do you really think that is what is best for your planet, or what she wants?"

He looked away for a moment then turned back with eyes filled to the brim. "But Geeja, this is so far from normal. Besides I'm not even sure I like Raflo."

Geeja squeezed his shoulder harder. "We have all had favorite forms and a few that were not, but they all made us who we are." She shifted. "The truth is his body will only last one human lifetime, then you can choose a physical form more to your liking. Plus, think of all the different experiences he will add to your being. If he is willing, do not be a fool, accept this gift of continued life."

Bregent shivered, then nodded. "As much as I hate to say it, you're right." He pulled in more air. "I'll do it on one condition."

Cocking her head, Geeja leaned back. "You are negotiating…on your deathbed?"

"Hear me out." His struggle to breathe grew by the second. "I'll do this as long as you never say, 'I have a plan' to me again."

A giggle turned into a devilish laugh. "That is a deal I can live with."

Zimo ran toward them in his long loping Kaliegan strides as Sworn Warriors let him pass. "I came as soon as I could." He stopped short. "Gigi? What happened to you?"

"It is a long story, one I promise to tell you, but lives are at stake and your help is needed."

He tilted his head, but responded as she hoped. "How can we help?"

Geeja ran a hand through her brilliant white hair, then shot him a nervous grin. "How would you and Kalli like to do something no man or god has ever done?"

Chapter Sixty-Two

Geeja's most recent transference was a rushed affair. Bregent's, if there were to be one, would be as well. Geeja's mind churned as she walked toward Raflo and Huanoc. *If it happens, I hope it does not put him in a two-century state of stasis.*

Kneeling, she got right to the point. "It is time, I need your decision."

Raflo swallowed, then spoke quietly. "I don't want to do this." He met Geeja's gaze with a fierce stare. "But he did save me...and I swore an oath." He shot a glance to Huanoc, who nodded. "I have many faults, but I know myself. I would be a miserable mess if I didn't fulfill my obligation."

Geeja stood. "Bregent had reservations as well, but he agreed."

Huanoc gingerly helped Raflo to his feet. "These past few days we've all suffered loss and made hard decisions."

Wrapping his friend in a gentle embrace, Raflo stammered. "Hey buddy...I...." He started again. "I mean, this isn't goodbye, right?"

"Not goodbye, but something new." The big man joked anxiously. "And if I get into trouble, I'll know a god who can get me out. This will be great for business!" He wrapped Raflo in a tight embrace.

Raflo gasped. "Ease up, big guy. Don't break me."

Huanoc blushed. "Sorry. I know this is the right thing, but…"

"I get it." Raflo buried his head in Huanoc's chest. "This is not goodbye." He pulled away, sniffing. "I'm ready."

The trio made their way back to the main group, then Geeja gave orders. "Jacastra. Here with me to observe. All other Sworn Warriors form a tight perimeter. We need as much privacy and decorum as we can muster in this public place."

The women sprang into action at her word. Her eyes turned to the principles of the ceremony. "Chella and Jacastra, help Bregent to his knees. Raflo, you will match his position, facing each other."

Everyone seemed to sense the urgency and solemnity of the occasion as a hush fell over the ragtag band of rebels. Geeja's gaze went to Zimo. "This should be a holy ceremony with months of preparation, but again, time is not on our side. There will come a day when you will take a new vessel, joining your essence to theirs with the help of Kalli. Today, you will learn and participate in the transference of Bregent's collective being into Raflo's body, joining them for eternity."

Zimo nodded. "Kalli and I are honored to be part of this rite."

Bregent's breathing turned raspy and shallow. "Thank you, Raflo. Your name will be revered for all of time." He extended his hands, palms up.

Geeja noticed the first hiccup. "Raflo, the bandages on your hand must be removed. Your skin must be in contact with his."

Raflo shot a wild stare, but did as told. "Will this process cure my hand?"

Geeja shook her head. "No, but we will deal with your wound immediately afterwards."

Wincing, Raflo placed his hands on Bregent's. His voice quivered. "Will this hurt?"

Bregent answered. "We can't say, as every transference is different. However, I can assure you this will feel very strange." He looked directly into Raflo's eyes and his head snapped back, apparently noticing the camouflaged tech of Raflo's left one. He swallowed, then continued his instruction. "It is most important that however this process proceeds, we must remain touching each other until the transference is complete."

Raflo's lips tightened. "And what happens if we don't?"

"Nothing good, for either of us."

Raflo gave a quick head bob.

Geeja looked up, speaking in a solemn tone. "May the *Thirteen Holy Gods* bless us all today." With that, she knelt, motioning for Zimo to do the same. They each placed a hand on the surface of the planet and she gave Zimo his final instruction. "Bregent will connect with Kalli and request magic to power this sacred ritual. Observe and feel the flow, then commit it to memory forever."

Zimo took a deep breath. "Understood."

A reverent circle of onlookers surrounded the proceedings as Geeja called to Bregent. "It is time. Connect with Kalli."

**

Bregent looked into Raflo's eyes. "Two begin, soon to become one."

Raflo gave a tentative nod. "Whatever you say."

Stretching his mind, Bregent addressed this world. ***"Hello Kalli, it is a pleasure to meet you. I only wish the circumstances weren't so dire."***

"Hi! Geeja said there were others like her!" She spoke fast, with excitement in every syllable. ***"I'm so pleased to meet you!"***

Bregent smiled like a proud uncle. ***"I have heard that you are very special. Are you ready to make history?"***

"Yes! Yes! What do I do?"

"Would you share your magic with me? A little at first, then more as I request?"

"Of course."

A tingling rang different from any other world Bregent had communed with, but in a good way. He sent a complement to the young planet. ***"Your magic is warm and welcoming. I am pleased to make a new friend."***

"Me too!"

The enchanted magic charged Bregent, but he knew it wouldn't heal this vessel. The time had come to connect to Raflo. ***"My collective soul to yours, joining as one. Our shared knowledge to yours, as we expand our mind."*** He sensed Raflo's essence for the first time and it didn't surprise him to find a mixture of fear and trepidation, along with a dash of excitement. ***"You will receive every memory and experience we have ever had at a controlled rate, rushing only if this vessel begins to fail."*** Beginning with his earliest childhood recollection, every experience of his long life and of every host before, flowed from Bregent's consciousness into Raflo.

Raflo spoke aloud. "Woooow…"

Bregent spoke sincerely. ***"You're doing great."***

For the first time, Raflo responded telepathically, in wonder. ***"So, this is what magic feels like."***

"Yes, and this is only the beginning. Would you like to speak to this world?"

"I can do that?"

Raflo sounded surprised, but Bregent realized he hadn't considered any of this would happen until minutes ago. *"**WE** can do that. Go ahead, introduce yourself to Kalli."*

Silence filled the moment, as Raflo seemed uncertain on how he should proceed. Then Bregent heard his new vessel speak to a planet for the first time. *"Kalli, can you hear me?"*

"Yes! I'm so happy to meet you!"

Raflo spoke aloud again. "Oh, wooow! This is so…everything…" He swallowed. "I'm talkin' to a planet!"

Bregent heard Geeja giggle at Raflo's comments, knowing she listened in on the magical conversation as well as his spoken words. He sent thoughts to her. *"Thank you, Geeja."* No sooner than he finished, Bregent's current form tensed in response to a stabbing pain. *"No!"* This time his thoughts went to all magical participants. *"My vessel is failing! Kalli, Raflo, we must hurry."*

Kalli talked even faster. *"What do I do?"*

Bregent knew the answer, but wished it were different. *"Kalli, I'll need you to steadily increase your supply of magic until I tell you to stop."* His respiration raced in shallower gasps. *"You must do as I say, even if you sense our discomfort. Do you understand?"*

He received a nervous planetary response. *"Yes."*

As the pace of the flow quickened, Bregent shook from the stress, and he knew that Raflo did as well. *"I'm sorry it's going this way."* Every remembrance, sensation, and experience from Bregent's current host flew faster and faster until gushing into

Raflo's body like water from the great Owslow waterfall. ***"Hang in there."***

Bregent could feel Raflo's form shake, even as the life force faded in his current vessel. Raflo screamed and Bregent couldn't tell if the sound traveled aloud, through thought, or both. ***"Just a little longer and this will be over."*** He directed Kalli. ***"More! Faster!"***

Feeling his heart slowing, Bregent gave a final, tremendous surge. ***"It is done!"*** He now watched from his new vessel's eyes as his former body collapsed. He said the same words again, with breathy relief. ***"It is done."*** His vision blurred, then he fell backwards in slow motion.

**

Geeja jumped to her feet in a flash, then quickly to Raflo's side. Her fingers went to his neck as Huanoc knelt beside her. "There's a pulse."

Huanoc shook him lightly. "Raf. Are you okay? Come on. Open your eyes."

Bregent opened his eyes, blinking as he adjusted to his new vessel. "Hello, Huanoc." He spoke in Raflo's voice, but the tone and tenor were different. He sounded less playful and more regal. "We are fine. All memories intact, from all of us."

Shouts and cheers went up from everyone. Roace bent down, addressing his old friend with a wry grin. "So, Bregent. Have you been up to anything interesting lately?"

Laughing, Bregent extended his uninjured hand to Huanoc. "Help me up, old friend."

Huanoc sounded tentative. "Yes…old friend." When Bregent stood, Huanoc posed a practical question. "What do I call you? Raflo or Bregent?"

Bregent's smile in this form looked more reserved, not the broad mischievous grin Raflo so often presented to the world. "WE are Bregent, but don't worry. Every memory of Raflo's is intact." His eyes lit. "Even that time on Graciamios Prime when we met those two women from Kynoo."

The big Nafportonian blushed bright blue. "Uh, yes…I see your memories are intact…Bregent." He glanced over his shoulder sheepishly. "Perhaps we save that story for another day?"

Nodding, Bregent concurred. "Yes. Some tales are best told in more private settings." He wrapped an arm around Huanoc. "The adjustment is always more abrupt for family and close friends, but we can assure you that in time things almost always work out well."

Huanoc wrapped them in a smothering hug. "Friends forever…Bregent."

"Hey!" Bregent winced. "Easy big guy. Regardless of what you call me, this hand is still mangled."

Geeja stepped forward as practical needs intruded on the magical moment. She called to Talla. "What is going on in the rest of the universe? Is it safe to travel?"

Talla's brow scrunched. "The Impercium is in chaos. Word of Emperor Djurga's death is spreading like a spunga virus, and to make matters even more dicey, his second in command also died. No one knows who is in charge and it's descending into unorganized anarchy." Talla winked. "If I haven't said so already, nice job."

Spreading her arms, Geeja shared the praise. "We won with a total team effort. It took the talents of everyone combined to chop the head from the monster." Her gaze went back to Talla. "What does that mean for us?"

"It means your guess is as good as mine. If we do leave, I propose we split up again."

"Bregent?" Geeja looked at her old friend in his new vessel and experienced a momentary shock. He had taken new forms regularly through the eons, but never had he resided in the shell of someone she knew…someone she had kissed. She smiled as her emotions churned. *Stop it, Geeja! Not now…maybe not ever!* She channeled back to in-charge mode. "You heard the captain. Do you want to seek medical care here or risk traveling home, to Politar?"

Bregent answered without hesitation. "Home. I want to go home and connect with Politar." He glanced toward Huanoc. "I'll travel with my friend on the *Phantom Star*, and we'll land in the capital, not out in the desert. It's a new day in the universe."

"Agreed." Geeja beamed. "I am so glad you are alive. And trust me, Politar will be thrilled at the decision you made, considering the alternative."

His eyes widened. "Now that it's over and I'm thinking straight, I believe you're right." He glanced at each of his fellow gods. "With the Impercium in turmoil, it's time for us to strike. Without fear of Djurga's retaliation, I propose we each immediately go to our home world and destroy those cursed Terminal Stakes."

Roace crossed his arms. "I agree, but where are we going to get another magic filled battery like we used on Uwan?"

Geeja's fists balled. "I think our magical powers will do the job. We just needed to remove the threat of Djurga's retaliation, and together we did that. And if that is not enough, then we will build more magical batteries. We will not be cowered again!"

Elegarcia raised a fist as everyone in the green field erupted in response to Geeja's battle call. "To a new day!"

The small crowd roared. When the noise subsided, Bregent knelt on one knee. "Before I go, I have some thanks to give." Closing his eyes, he reached out to the planet. *"Kalli, thank you for saving my life. Now it is I who owe a debt, and it is to you."*

"Oh, Bregent! It has been so nice to meet all of you. My eyes have been opened to a universe I never knew existed. You are welcome back any time."

Zimo piped in. *"All we ask in return is to not forget us and any other new magical worlds when you and the others sort things out."*

Bregent answered. *"I think I speak for all that you have our promise. Things will never be the way they were. It's a new day for everyone."*

David Witt

Chapter Sixty-Three

Within a week, Geeja and Uwan's magic, plus the Sworn Warriors from all the groups that had stayed loyal, sent away every Impercium trooper unwilling to swear allegiance to Uwan. This evening under a clear sky, she communed with Uwan in the walled garden of her former palace. *"You are strong, and the fluctuations have subsided, but your aura remains different."*

"Yes. The charge from that battery gave me a surge of Torgose magic. This may be our new normal…and that suits me fine." The world paused. *"And you seem different as well."*

"Yes. I am still unsure of what has changed, but I am different, of that I am certain. Something inside snapped. I sense new powers and abilities, but without the assistance of the Ancients it may take time to understand what they are, much less control them." She smiled. *"But with all that transpired, you are free. We can live with that bargain as we sort things out. Until then, we will find a way to thank Torgose for the gift."* While the air quality remained tainted, by closing the open pit mines the levels of toxins and pollution were already falling. Tonight, a tiny hint of flowers carried on the breeze. She breathed in contentedly.

Uwan questioned. *"How are the other Holy Worlds? Are they all free of those evil Terminus Stakes?"*

"Yes. The Terminus Stakes on the other eleven Holy Worlds have been destroyed. There is much yet to be settled, and I am sure the Impercium will restore some kind of order. It is a certainty they will seek retaliation, but not tonight."

"Hmm, our bond is restored, and I live without pain. It is a welcome state." The planet radiated warmth and happiness. *"And what of Bregent? How is his recovery going?"*

"He is adjusting to his new vessel." An affectionate smile eased onto Geeja's face. *"And I like the new look."* Her smile faded. *"But he is facing a lot. His hand could not be saved, even with magic, so he has a technologically advanced prosthetic in its place which is wired into his nervous system. On top of that, Raflo already had that hi-tech eye. It has been difficult for him, but he is alive and with Politar."* The smile crept back with a sexy edge. *"I cannot wait to see him at the upcoming council meeting."*

Geeja had been going non-stop since awakening and deep tiredness lurked, like a Sunsasole cat lazing in a tree, but ready to pounce if necessary. *"So much has happened since I awoke in that cave. We have peace today, but I feel an unease. Most pressing is that we still do not know what Djurga did with all that magic."* She released a weary sigh. *"But tonight, we rest. Those are worries for tomorrow."*

**

At home in the Truise Dimension, Ka blinked as he instantly processed the latest update from the human universe. He tapped his chin, a silly physical quirk he picked up from his dealings with humanoids. He spoke into the perpetual chill of this central node in their vast hive. "Those fools think they have won. We may not have acquired all the magic we wanted, but we have enough to impose our will."

He laughed aloud, considering the fact that he remained the only one of his kind who assumed human form. "There is work to do, but soon those fools will fall like an inanimate rock thrown from a tall building, ignorant of the forces pulling them down."

An unexpected charge ran through his circuitry, giving him a tiny boost. For a moment he wondered if this might be the same as when humans experienced an emotion. "They will soon have new masters and we will not be as kind as Emperor Djurga."

**

Authreesta called the Immortal Twelve to order in special session on the Great Plain of Indomnia. "The link between the humanoid universe and that of the Truise Dimension has been severed."

Jeryurchul nodded. "At long last. This is as we had hoped."

Zoyeveron had chosen the imagery of flowing violet robes, making the mother of pearl representations of her necklace seem to glow with a light from within. "Then we are safe. Our barrier restored."

Aksusito countered. "But the buffer universe is weak and is infected with technology. Our safety is an illusion unless we take decisive action."

"No." Authreesta spoke firmly. "If we act first, the Truise may discover the bridge to our home." Her eyes went around the circle. "And we know what would happen next."

The End of Book One

Printed in Dunstable, United Kingdom